"WAIT!"

"Lady, I been waitin'. I think mebbe all my life. Miss Annie Mapes, I am compelled by the violence of my feelings to marry you as soon as possible."

His powerful hands held her head for an openmouthed kiss that was deep and long and unlike any she had ever known before.

A kiss was not supposed to be like this! A kiss had always meant two pairs of closed lips pressed lightly together. It had not meant a questing tongue and a hard body tightly pressed to hers.

"Annie!" Jack said. His lips moved over her face then returned to her mouth.

When he kissed her a second time, it was a gentler but no less thrilling kiss. There was an insistent banging under her ribs and she seemed incapable of movement. Her knees were jelly. She had not known such feelings existed!

Jack pressed his lips to the milky softness of her neck and his heart hammered in his chest. It was like she was the first woman he had ever touched! His desire was a raging thing, emptying his mind of everything but the way she felt in his arms. He kissed her mouth lightly and tasted its soft wetness and then he looked at her. Her eyes were closed and her chin was lifted. She seemed to have stopped breathing.

"Funny," he whispered, "Not a week ago I thought I wanted to see the world, and now here I am . . . staring it in the face."

<u>BOOK YOUR PLACE ON OUR WEBSITE</u> <u>AND MAKE THE</u> <u>READING CONNECTION!</u>

We've created a customized website just for our very special readers, where you can get the inside scoop on everything that's going on with Zebra, Pinnacle and Kensington books.

When you come online, you'll have the exciting opportunity to:

- View covers of upcoming books
- Read sample chapters
- Learn about our future publishing schedule (listed by publication month *and author*)
- Find out when your favorite authors will be visiting a city near you
- Search for and order backlist books from our online catalog
- Check out author bios and background information
- Send e-mail to your favorite authors
- Meet the Kensington staff online
- Join us in weekly chats with authors, readers and other guests
- Get writing guidelines
- AND MUCH MORE!

Visit our website at
http://www.pinnaclebooks.com

DARE TO LOVE:

Black Jack Dare

Wynema McGowan

The story of a man, his family,
and the woman he loves.

Pinnacle Books
Kensington Publishing Corp.
http://www.pinnaclebooks.com

To my sister, Elaine

PINNACLE BOOKS are published by

Kensington Publishing Corp.
850 Third Avenue
New York, NY 10022

First Printing: June, 1998
10 9 8 7 6 5 4 3 2 1

Printed in the United States of America

Chapter 1

Spring, 1828
Estado de Tejas, Mexico

"Dare!"

"Nuh?"

Jack Dare's response was a reflex. Awake but still fusty from sleep, he did not lower his chair, which was tilted back on two legs, nor did he move his hands, which were lightly curled in his lap. But he did lift his hat brim enough to see a man standing in the road, swaying like a massive oak in a twister wind. A bottle dangled from one hand and a pistol from the other.

The setting sun looked like it was perched on the man's left shoulder but Jack knew who it was, all right. Wully Small. Drunk again. Or more likely, drunk still. Wully had dropped twenty-four dollars in a poker game the night before and most of it had ended up in Jack's pocket. Twenty-four dollars might not seem like much to some but when it took a month to earn twenty . . .

"Git up outa there, Dare!"

"You worked up about somethin'?"

"Damn straight!"

"What?" Horse teeth stuck out of drawn-back lips; Wully's idea of a smile.

"Let's jus' say yore sittin' in my chair! That'll do."

"You're runnin' your mouth pretty reckless, Wully!"

"I know 'xactly what I'm doin', Dare."

All pretense was gone now. So was Jack's smile. He lifted his considerable chin and laid a hard eye on his antagonist. "Wully, you couldn't find your ass in a muleyard. G'on home now. 'Fore you do somethin' you won't live to regret."

As he spoke Jack glanced beyond Wully to the far side of the road. Sitting in a halted wagon were a gray-haired woman and a boy. Standing beside it was another woman—a young woman—and two children. Pilgrims to the promised land, looking around, pointing at this and that, completely unaware that they stood smack in his line of fire.

"I ain't kiddin' now!"

Wully had used his gun to motion and about fell over. As he righted himself, there had been a brief moment when his pistol was squarely centered on the gray-haired woman's forehead.

"C'mon outa there."

Jack tried once more. "Damnit, Wully, I'm tryin' to have a nap here!"

"Then I'll shoot yuh where yuh sit."

"Awhell."

"I mean it, Dare . . . !"

Jack stood slowly. "Well, all right."

When he stepped off the boardwalk, he held his hands ear-high and his fingers slightly curled. He advanced about ten paces and then he stood waiting, his gun in his belt but death in his eye, tall and ten men tough.

The town looked drowsy in the last of the day's sunlight. A small spiral of dust spun itself out on the road and a sign creaked in the wind. Somewhere a goat blatted and two jays chattered angrily at each other, but beneath those sounds a sort of silence had fallen.

Both men looked at each other for a long minute and both knew that the time for talk had passed. Wully closed one eye and stiff-armed his pistol. Jack reached between his shoulders and drew his knife and threw it. Wully's shot made water geyser out of a nearby wood trough, then he dropped to his knees and put his forehead on the ground.

Out of the corner of his eye Jack Dare saw Billy Yates and his brother Blue come up. Their carbines were primed and their eyes moved everywhere as they scanned for sign of Wully's compadres. Jack knelt to check Wully and found him dead.

"Oh, the poor unfortunate!" said a cultivated voice that was thick with concern.

"Drunk?" asked another.

"It appears so."

Jack looked up. The young woman was holding the two children pressed to each flank with her hands wrapped around their eyes. He looked away. He looked back. Under a small flowered hat was the sort of face that people write songs about. He straightened and stood staring. He had seen a lot of females in his life, but he had never seen the likes of this before.

Annie Mapes stood transfixed by the angry accusation in the frontiersman's eyes. What had they done to cause such ire?

She waited for him to tell her but nobody said anything. Actually, nobody even moved. They might have been statues if not for a languid breeze that lifted a strand of ebony hair off the man's shoulder. Suddenly he pointed at her, grim-lipped and apparently mad enough to spit . . . because he did!

"Cripes Amighty! Don't y'all have enough sense not to stand smack in the middle of it?"

It? she thought. "Sorry. Where should we have stopped?"

"Goodgawdamighty! You still don't understand, do you?"

It wasn't until he saw her flinch that he realized he had hurled his words like a club. His anger departed as suddenly as it had arrived. He hauled his eyes to the dozen or so townspeople who were lined up on the boardwalk like crows on a fence. Damn busybodies! "What're y'all lookin' at?" He waved at them. "G'on about your business now. G'on."

Blue and Billy Yates had each taken one of Wully's arms and were dragging him toward the livery stable and its owner— who built coffins as a sideline. Dare picked up Wully's hat and slapped it against his leg. The girl shrugged and said, ''Sorry.''

The frontiersman gave her a last scalding look before he followed the others and she thought: What are we looking at? How could we not look at a mountain of grease-blackened buckskins with shaggy, black hair and a slab-rock face and pistols sticking out of everywhere?

And if all that weren't enough, one could hardly ignore a voice that could be heard a mile up wind!

Little Nona pointed to the man whose vee'ed boots were making lines in the dirt. ''What happened to that man, Annie?''

''He'll be all right, sweetie. He's just had too much to drink.''

Her two charges Nona and Mittie Williford nodded knowingly. They had no trouble accepting that; they had been orphaned by a drunken spree that had ended in a fatal wagon accident.

Having reached a black maw below a faded sign that read: LIVERY, the two skin-clad men dumped the drunkard facedown in the dirt and disappeared inside the building. A few seconds later the big frontiersman stepped over the body and did likewise.

''See? They have laid him to rest right . . . right over there.'' Curious, she thought, letting the man lay out in the hot sun like that.

On second thought, at least here in Tejas they have the decency to remove their drunks from harm's way. Men froze to death every winter in Philadelphia. Some right in the middle of the street!

A flurry of movement drew her eye to the livery roof. Someone was up there! As she watched, two snarled heads popped over the roof's ledge. Bare, dirty feet quickly followed, as with youthful agility the boys settled themselves above the livery sign.

They were nut brown from dirt and had stick bodies, paddle-sized feet and tufted heads, but she thought them a most handsome pair. She could see their means of ascendancy—two warped barrels stacked one on top the other and then canted against the side of the building.

Maybe—provided they survived their descent—this daring duo would be students of hers.

"Mrs. Fuller?" An elderly man was hurrying toward them, one who was notable for his brown frock coat and brushed high hat.

"I'm Emma Fuller."

Annie turned to help Emma alight from the wagon.

"I'm Lloyd Cooper and this is . . ." He turned then waved impatiently at a woman who was cautiously picking her way across the two rut road. "That lady over there is my wife, Alma."

"Welcome to Sweet Home!" the woman cried and then returned to watching her feet.

A wise woman, thought Annie. In addition to clumps of cow pies and trailings of horse apples, Sweet Home appeared to have at least ten dogs for each of its 208 human beings.

"Sweet Home," Emma breathed and turned to Annie. "We finally made it!"

We did indeed, thought Annie. With all the excitement she had hardly had a minute to look around. She did so now, and reminded herself not to allow charm and quaintness to color her opinion.

She soon found that to be an unnecessary concern.

They had come in on the single puttied road that halved the town before making a Y at the edge of the settlement. One branch peeled off into the piney woods while the other copied the curves of a creek called the Crow. At that confluence there was the vine-entangled, weed-choked remains of a hundred-year-old mission called St. Vincente.

The mission had been built by Franciscan friars in the early 1700s. The small settlement that grew up around it was populated largely by mestizos—the progeny of Spanish Conquistadors and Indian mothers, a hardy and industrious race, but often the prey of Comanche and Kiowa raiders. Between 1740 and

1780 the village was twice burned and was subsequently abandoned until Stephen Austin obtained permission from Mexico
City to colonize an Anglo community on the site.

These things they had learned before they left Philadelphia
through correspondence with Mr. Cooper who was Sweet
Home's mayor, and through subsequent conversations with Mr.
Austin's agent who had assured them that they had no reason
to be concerned about Indians in 1828; Sweet Home had been
established for almost ten years now.

At first glance, it looked more like ten months.

They stood about square in the center of town which was
comprised of some twenty buildings loosely built around an
old rock-curbed well. A few were clapboard and a few were
adobe but the majority of the buildings were made of peeling
logs. The business establishments included a barbershop/bath
house combination and a saloon called Dirty Dave's. Sharing
a common wall with an apothecary shop was a general store
and a small bank which was, if she remembered correctly,
owned by the mayor.

Directly across the road was a tinsmith's shed and next to
it, the land and assayer's office. Beyond, on the edge of town,
was a blacksmith's shop and a freighter's depot with an attached
corral inhabited by a dozen rabbit-eared mules.

Set off by itself was a low-slung adobe building with four
horses tied in front. Its sign said "Dulce's" but did not indicate
the nature of its business.

Finally there was the livery and she had come full circle.

Apparently those men at last remembered the drunkard
because one of them came out and grasped the man by the
back of his collar and hauled him inside.

As she was watching this unconventional exit, she happened
to see a flare of light inside the livery. She stared there and
within a short time, she saw it again. Someone was standing
in the dark, smoking and staring back at her!

Of course, as soon as she realized that, she immediately did
an about face and presented the ill-bred clod with a very stiff
back. She righted her hat and shook out her skirts.

It is a shame that manners do not grow on trees because, unfortunately, that is probably the only way some people will ever acquire any! After allowing considerable time to pass she pretended to be looking at the two boys on the roof and took another quick look into the livery.

Still staring! Mannerless uncouth lout!

"This is my wife, Alma," the mayor said.

Good! Mrs. Cooper had joined them at last.

"Alma, here's Mrs. Fuller and her family. All the way from Philadelphia!"

"And I'll bet you are our new schoolteacher, Miss Mapes."

"Yes," Annie said and offered the woman her hand. Alma Cooper was in her fifties and looked enough like her husband to be his kin. Both were portly, gray-haired, round-faced and toothy. "Please call me Annie."

"Delighted, my dear. And you shall call me Alma. Oh, I can't tell you how glad we are to have you here!"

"We certainly are! But I feel terrible about all the commotion just now," said the mayor.

"It never fails, Lloyd," Mrs. Cooper complained. "Just when you hope to appear the most civilized."

Mrs. Cooper rolled her eyes as she spoke. They were large and lively but they did not point in the same direction. Annie gave up on trying to determine which one the woman saw with and focused on the bridge of her nose.

With a nod, Emma indicated the livery. "Who is that poor man?"

"Wully Smith," said Mrs. Cooper. "A terrible bully and brawler and a member of that awful Crow's Nest gang." Then she added. "They are such a blight on our community!"

Annie saw the mayor nudge his wife, concerned, she imagined, about the impression she was giving their newest settlers. "And the big man with the fiery . . ." She had been about ready to say "eyes" when she sensed that the others were looking at her curiously. She hastily amended her question to: ". . . disposition?"

The mayor shot a look over his shoulder where the three

men now lounged outside the livery, talking and smoking. "Captain Dare is the one leaning against the wall. The fella who looks a lot like him is his younger brother and the other one is Billy Yates. They are all Austin's men."

"Stephen Austin?"

"Yes."

"I didn't know he lived here."

"He doesn't. His headquarters are down at San Felipe but it was his idea to hire some men to keep the, um, riffraff in check. Soon as he got approval, they were on the job. A man of action, our Mr. Austin."

"Approval?"

"From Mexico City."

"Ah."

Lloyd Cooper purposely did not relate Austin's instructions to him on the day the money was allocated. "Cooper, I want you to hire some men who will put the wholesome fear of God into the hearts of every thief and murderer in the territory. I don't care if they are red, white or purple. Nor do I care how it's done. Just . . . do it."

"Are they like our constables in Philadelphia?" asked Emma.

"In a manner of speaking, only they do most of their law enforcing from horseback."

"What are they called then?"

"All manner of things. Citizen soldiers. Home guard volunteers. Peace troopers. But we've been calling them rangers because they cover so much land, much of which is open range . . ."

When Cooper paused to wait for a wagon load of logs to rattle by, his wife said, "Lloyd, please! Can't we at least get out of the middle of the road?"

"You are entirely right, Alma. Come right this way please! Everyone will come to our place first for a relaxing supper then I'll take you to your new home."

Across the rough road they went, the Coopers with Emma Fuller in between, then Annie holding Nona and Mittie by the hand and finally Charley Walters who was driving the wagon which contained all their earthly belongings. Along the way they had to skirt a rooting pig, a couple of indifferent dogs and several foraging chickens.

Over her shoulder Mrs. Fuller said, "Isn't this exciting, Annie?"

"Yes. Very." Emma Fuller had more color to her face than Annie had seen in weeks. It was a sight that did her heart good.

They were passing the three men who stood in front of the livery. Annie looked over and looked away, just that fast. Those black eyes were hidden by his hat but she felt them study her for a long time before they looked away.

Funny how she knew the precise moment when he had finished.

"I hope you won't be disappointed," said the mayor. "Your new home is sturdy and spacious but quite simple."

To that Emma replied that anything would suit them as long as it did not roll, pitch, rock or bump.

"Shug'll be plenty pissed about Wully."

Jack was watching the Coopers and those pilgrims walk off and almost didn't hear his brother's comment. "I doubt Shug Clarke much cares what happens to Wully Small."

"He might," said Billy. "I think he was his cousin."

"I didn't know that."

"I ain't surprised to hear it," said Blue. "Those fellas all look pretty close bred to me."

There was no love lost between the Crow's Nest boys and the younger rangers. They would get into a leg-biter once a week, regular.

The pilgrims had paused on the Cooper's porch. The girl bent to say something to the little girls and they went inside with Alma Cooper, which left the *alcalde* and the two pilgrim women standing on the porch. Cooper said something and all three faces turned their way. Jack propped the sole of one moccasin back against the wall.

"Blue, why don't you go out to Shug's place an' tell 'im

that his poor cousin Wully got drunker'n hell an' fell on my knife. Ask him if he wants to send someone in for the body."

Blue clapped Billy on the back. He loved to bedevil those fellas. "What d'you say, Billy? Wanna ride along?"

Billy grinned back. "I don't mind if I do, Blue." With that they mounted up and rode out.

When Jack'd finished cleaning his knife, he tested its edge on his arm hair before he sheathed it. Those women and Lloyd Cooper still had their heads together and he thought, just what Sweet Home needs. More helpless pilgrims.

Lloyd Cooper detained Annie and Emma on the porch, saying that he wanted to apologize to them out of the children's hearing.

"What knife fight?" Annie cleared her throat which she hoped would modulate her voice. "I didn't see any knife."

"I did," said Charley whom they had forgotten entirely. He stood on the path looking up at them. "It went . . . zing!" He had put most of his body into splitting the air with the flat of his hand. "Just like an arrow!"

"Good Lord!" said Emma and held her throat. "Do you mean that drunk is . . . dead?"

"As a door," said Charley and grinned gleefully.

Emma and Annie looked at each other in shock. A man had just been killed! It seemed impossible and yet apparently it had happened. And so fast that they had missed it entirely!

Annie looked over her shoulder, revulsion and disbelief plain upon her face. As if he'd been waiting to have her attention, the man who had wielded the knife pushed off the wall, unwrapped his horse's reins from the hitching post and slung himself into the saddle. Then, looking neither left nor right, he started to ride slowly out of town.

"Dare!" called the mayor. "Hey, Dare! Come on over here a minute, will you?"

Emma was gripping Annie's arm so tight she was close to

cutting off the circulation to her shoulder, but since Annie was glaring at the killer she said nothing.

This man was the one who had been staring at her from inside the livery! She didn't know how she knew it, but she did.

The man turned and walked his horse up to the gate. He crossed his hands on his pommel, nodded to the Coopers and then looked square at Annie and grinned. He had a wide mouth and a multitude of teeth. A hundred at least.

Now she was furious. Who does he think he is? First hollering at her like he did then staring at her as if she had newly arrived from the moon? She would love to stare right back at him but she would not allow herself be so rude. She would make do with a quick withering look . . .

Which turned into a swallowed snicker. Good grief! He should never have removed his hat! The way his hair spiked made him look like he was exploding!

It was difficult but she schooled her face and concentrated on the mayor.

"Sorry to hold you up, Dare, but I didn't want these newcomers to miss meeting one of our most important settlers." Cooper actually sounded proud of him! Amazing! "They've just arrived from Philadelphia!"

"That so?"

"This is Mrs. Fuller."

"Ma'am," he said and returned to scrutinizing Annie. She purposefully stared off down the street then flicked some lint off her sleeve and then tucked a strand of hair behind her ear. She looked at him and then looked away. One corner of his mouth was curled into a knowing little smile! He acted like he knew exactly what she thought of him and found it mildly humorous!

She would not look his way again unless she had to.

"And this is Miss Mapes who is going to be our new school-teacher."

She had to.

"Ma'am."

She nodded coldly and immediately dropped her eyes to his horse. A magnificent animal. Deep brown with white socks and a frayed tail that plumed in the breeze. As if it knew it was being admired, it tossed its head and stamped at a buzzing fly. Muscles rippled and flexed under its sleek shiny skin.

"Too bad about that trouble earlier."

"Yeah. Well."

His voice was deep and resonate but his accent and manner of speaking was that of an uneducated and ill-refined man. Which was precisely as she expected.

But being uneducated does not necessarily mean that a person has to be completely insensitive!

Quite suddenly she experienced a flash of insight: He was about to apologize for hollering at her. It was a useful bit of information because knowing in advance allowed her time to decide exactly how she would react, and she was the sort who liked to be prepared for every eventuality.

She thought a minute then . . . All right. She knew precisely what she would do. She would lower her head the least little bit. Acknowledgement? Yes. Forgiveness? Never! There were no acceptable excuses for subhuman actions.

The mayor was speaking again.

"Well, you take care of yourself, Dare."

"Sure. See yuh, Cooper. Ladies."

He flopped his hat back on and turned his horse and Annie thought: it may have more effect if I totally ignore him when next we meet.

She would not think about the fact that he had not given her a choice in the matter.

Drily Emma said, "Good thing that man's not a politician."

"It's true that he's not much for small talk, but he's the man you want when there's trouble."

"Does he like that kind of work?" Annie was acting off-handed but her expression showed both confusion and a bit of humiliation. She really had expected him to apologize.

"I . . . I never asked him if he did, but I imagine that he does. He must. I can't see him doing anything he didn't like."

Emma shuddered. "I cannot fathom why a person would want that job. Fighting wild Indians for a living. Imagine!"

"I think there are some men who actually enjoy testing the limits of their courage. God must know why. Frankly, I don't."

Cooper's eyes were following Dare's retreating figure. It was only natural that Annie's did too.

He had reached the fork in the road and as he directed his horse to the left, he stood in his saddle and lifted his hat to them, as if there were some way he could have known they were watching. It simply infuriated her. Folding her arms she turned and smiled at Mr. Cooper. "You were saying . . ."

"Well, only that sooner or later his luck's bound to run out. The law of averages and all. Why, just since we moved here he's been shot four times and cut twice!"

"Where?"

Cooper looked at Annie and his cheeks pinked. "I, um, don't think it would be appropriate for me to say where . . ."

"No, no!" How exasperating! Of course she had not meant where on his body. "I meant where did the . . . altercations occur?" She pointed at her feet. "Here in town?"

"Oh, heavens no! Out there." With that Cooper made such a sweeping motion with his arm that Emma had to grab her hat. "That sort of thing almost never happens in town. Really."

He looked sincere but Annie was skeptical.

"Well, ladies, shall we go inside? I'm sure Alma's all ready for us. I'll lead the way, if I may."

Halfway inside he stopped. Annie and Emma bumped bodies. "You know," he said. "Now that I think about it there have been a few times . . . why once was right across from Garlock's. Cowardly act that . . . firing at Dare from an alley . . ."

Cooper's voice and person faded off into the interior of the house while back on the porch Emma Fuller and Annie Mapes were exchanging a look that said: Great Scott! What have we let ourselves in for?

Chapter 2

Evie Dare sat in a stretched cowhide chair on her splintery porch, fanning herself with a bird-wing fan and taking the evening's ease while she contemplated the moon and listened to the soft sounds of the night. From the woods she could hear the frogs down on the creek and the whir of a night bird's wings. Crickets chirred in the bushes by the steps and through the open door she heard her girls talking softly among themselves as they straightened up the cabin.

She smiled contentedly. This simple thing had always put her at ease, sitting on her porch in the twilight.

Dark shadows blotched the land but she could see the cotton-woods that lined the creek and beyond the reflection of the stars and moon in the water. To her left she could see the winding path that led off to the east and the settlement of Sweet Home, but to her right her view was limited to the live oak she'd kept her sons from cutting down when they first cleared the land over seven years ago.

It pleased her to remind them that she had been right about that old tree. Even if an Indian could sneak up and hide in it, none'd had the gall to try it. Not that it could not shelter a dozen of those red devils. It was eighty feet high and forty feet wide and so old that its lower limbs slanted downward to form a leafy dome around its trunk. On those days when her chores allowed she liked to take a few minutes and stand in its shadow. Most often the birds would be going at it and the squirrels would be scampering from limb to limb. But there were times when it was as silent as an empty church. There was something magical about it then. The way the layered leaves allowed the dusty streaks of sunlight to fall onto the ground below. Almost as if the leaves had been especially grown to form just such a pattern.

Its magic was not limited to the day. On a clear night like this the stars would flicker through the leaves as if there were a hundred tiny candles tied to its limbs and she would imagine that she was not alone, that the others who had once stood there were present too.

Sometimes the feeling was so strong she would have a hard time convincing herself that it was her imagination!

While it is true that many mountain people like herself tended to be superstitious about such things, she didn't know if she believed in spirits or not. All she knew was this: if spirits really existed, they were under that old tree.

A muttered curse immediately drew her attention to its source, which was Goldie's little three-sided shed. She stared there a minute and then her frown faded. Looked like it was nothing serious. Except to Goldie. It appeared that a piece of wood had slipped in his hand. Now it probably had a mark on it that only he could see.

He was always working on something, her son Goldie. This time he told her that he was making a chest for fine things. When she told him that she didn't have any fine things, he had replied that she would some day.

Evie snorted softly. She stood more of a chance of getting the fine things than she had of getting that chest he was making. Why, she had ten dollars that said it would never even see the inside of their cabin!

Practically every time Goldie got a piece finished that little fella from town would come out and offer him hard cash for it. For a while Goldie would say no, but in time he would end up selling or trading the thing for something he thought they needed more. An axe blade or a bullet mold. Maybe some new shoes for the girls.

It always amazed Goldie that people were willing to pay good money for his things. He'd say: "Hell, why don't they jus' make their own stuff? All they got t'do is go cut a tree an' work with it."

As if anyone could make things like he could. When it came to working with wood, Goldie had the hands of a master craftsman and the patience of a saint.

She amended that last to: sometimes he had the patience of a saint. None of her children were known for their tolerant natures.

Goldie bent to blow some dust off the wood and when he straightened he came within an inch of braining himself on the roof, and that made Evie smile again.

Jack and Goldie were both big men, broad across the shoulders and thick through the neck, but Blue was her tallest and she wasn't even sure that he was done growing yet!

Standing beside her strapping sons, a stranger might have trouble believing that she was their mother. She was a mere five feet in height and weighed less than a sack of corn. Though she was only fifty-seven she looked twenty years older. But she would look the same age when she died, a fact that would cause people to say that she must have done all her aging during her childbearing years, and they would be right. Except for suffering from wet weather "cricks in her jints" she was remarkably healthy.

Evie Ellis Dare had never been pretty but she was not unpleasant to look at. She had a wide peg-toothed smile, bead-bright black eyes and a rounded nose not unlike a peachpit. She wore her hair center-parted and knotted at the back of her neck, which accentuated her small, well-shaped head—which she had passed on to her girls, and her large jug ears—which she had passed on to her boys.

She had a fine wit, a contagious laugh and a flash temper and these things she had also passed on . . . but without regard to gender.

She never once struck her girls but her boys learned not to stand too near to her and misbehave because whatever she had in her hand was likely to be laid upside their heads. She once coldcocked Blue with a hoe handle—whacked him across the back and put him down like a poleaxed steer. And her children were proud of everything about her—even that.

While it was true that she was uneducated, she possessed a meticulous memory, a calculating mind and the sort of imagination that would never run in the rut. The Dare aphorism—if they'd had one—might have been "Be fruitful and multiply!" She married at fifteen and had the first of her twelve children nine months and two days after her wedding day. She had six boys in a row and named them all Jack . . . because it was her favorite name. She would have been satisfied to leave it at that but someone suggested that it might be hard for outsiders to keep them all straight. Finding merit in that argument, she decided to lead "Jack" with her favorite colors. Black for her eldest then Red, Golden, Brown, Silver and finally, after a three-year breather Blue, who would be her last son.

She turned to females then and had six girls in a row. Asked how she managed not to have any more boys, she replied that she had simply told The Almighty that the next boy He gave her would be named Yellow, and that she thought Yellow Jack would be an awful name to give the poor kid. Apparently the Lord agreed.

Having found this unusual name-calling to her liking, she named her six girls after places, or what she thought were places. Her eldest girl was Swede, then came Asia and China and then the twins, Irish and Britain and finally Denmark, who was called Markie and who had been born sightless.

Markie was her last child, not because she didn't want any more but because her husband died.

If a person threw out the twins (something she had seriously considered on more than one occasion) then the oldest and youngest of her children looked the most alike, but all the Dares bore a marked family resemblance with the same square, strong-boned faces, high foreheads and determined jaws. They had long upper lips and full lower ones and bright, black eyes beneath thick, straight brows. They also had what is known in the hills as Indian hair—that stiff shiny kind that is without a hint of curl.

As far as temperament went, they all inherited their mother's fiery nature and their father's stubborn streak, but as for their other qualities, they had either been born with them or had acquired them on their own because after the first couple of children, Evie Dare'd had neither the time nor the inclination to do more than teach them the bare essentials.

In spite of their being shorted on direction, somewhere along the way they had each picked up a strong sense of right and wrong and had never had to wallow around worrying about what they believed in. She would proudly say that there are some people who'll agree that five is an even number—if somebody bigger and louder says it is. "But not none of my kids!"

However, if she thought on it—and she had—she'd have to say that if there was any one thing a person could point to and say *now that right there* is what sets those Dares apart, it would have to be their grit. As children or as adults, it had always been their most conspicuous characteristic. The sort of hardheaded courage that made them refuse to lie down under any circumstance. She thought it was probably what gave them their best chance of surviving in this land, provided they stayed close to each other and stayed strong.

Then again sometimes nothing was enough because they would still have to contend with fate and rotten luck.

Tejas was a place where the weak, the few and the hesitant got killed. Animals or humans. It made no difference. It might not always be so, but that's how it was in '28.

As often happened at that time of night, she started thinking about all her dead children and soon had to lift her hem and wipe her eyes.

Three of her daughters, Swede, Asia and China had died before they walked and were buried south of Knoxville, Tennessee, alongside a road that would later become known as the Natchez Trace. That same farm also held the remains of their father, who had passed on to glory only months after their youngest child was born.

Two years later a fire raged through their home and destroyed all of their worldly possessions and Evie decided it was time for a change. She'd move the entire clan to the northern most province of Mexico: Tejas. She'd heard it was the land of opportunity, a place where her children would have a decent chance to better themselves.

It would not take much. Their neighbors gave them a few things: seeds and some clothes, but other than two muckle-dun mules and their weapons, they left Tennessee with little more than their wits, their uncommon skills of survival and their courage.

They sought land—a lot of it—and they found it on the east side of Crow Creek, which was, as the crow flies, only a few miles from the then tiny settlement of Sweet Home.

They soon discovered that what they had heard about Tejas was true. There was plenty of wild game everywhere. Duck, goose, prairie chickens and turkey abounded in the woods, deer and antelope flourished on the prairies, and the creeks and rivers were alive with fish.

There were also panthers and musk hogs but, poor as they were, no Dare had ever been hungry enough to eat them.

They lived in a stick-and-mud wattle until they could clear some land and build a cabin and somehow they survived that first winter, packed into that little cabin like peas in a pod. Early the following spring they built another cabin and connected the two with a roof.

The next few years they trapped and hunted and sold skins and meat until they had enough to buy chickens and shoats and whatever tools they could not make. Every so often the boys would round up some wild cows which they found to be plentiful and not awfully smart. They sold most of them and kept only a few beeves for their own use, but over the years those hearty few had grown into a sizeable herd.

Being a backwoods family, the Dares were used to living off the land. Evie and her girls planted only enough to feed the stock, to provide fresh vegetables for the table and to fill the 'tater hole with preserves.

Then just when she thought her brood was safe, calamity struck and half her sons were killed. Three within the same year and two on the same day!

Oh, Lord, it takes a strong person to live on after something like that. Yea, it does!

Brown was felling a tree when it took a twist on him and struck him such a blow under his jaw that it snapped his neck like a twig. Evie had scarcely gathered herself after his death when her second- and fifth-born were massacred by a band of Kiowa Indians. God had made her live through a lot of heartache in her life but she had almost not survived that day.

It wasn't only that they died. It was that she had been caught unprepared. Once her kids were raised, she had quit readying herself for their loss.

With each birth she had held herself back from the child in the beginning. It was that or go crazy. She knew a woman who had fourteen kids and saw only two live long enough to get out of three-cornered pants. But as her children aged she began to relax. Five years . . . ten years . . . fifteen . . . twenty until finally the day came when she quit listening for the sound of a certain cough and stopped watching for the red speckled cheeks and glassy eyes of a killing fever. After the family made the move to Tejas she had even started dreaming about wedding days and wives and about gran'kids that people would look at and say: Why, look at that, Evie, that boy's gonna have your chin!

Three grown sons. Killed within a year of each other. Red and Silver . . . Visshus and Sunny . . . probably within minutes. One look at their poor mutilated bodies and a part of her joined them in death.

She called her fifth child "Sunny" because of his good-

natured temperament and for the same reason, she had nick-
named her second child "Visshus."

There were times when she thought she might've done Red
a disservice. A kid called Visshus probably felt like he had to
live up to his name.

In both cases, their names were a fit. As a result, Visshus
spent his early years looking like he'd been chewed on . . . her
eldest and closest to Visshus in age had been the one most
responsible for that . . . but Visshus managed to escape serious
damage until he was a grown man. Then during a supply buying
trip to Opelousas, Louisiana he got into a brawl with three
fellas and got his knee shot off. He claimed he stayed on his
feet long enough to win the fight but besting three men with
one leg would turn out to be the easy part. Leery of reprisal—
those three had been home-town boys—he locked the door to
his room for two weeks and doctored his knee himself. Using
a thin stick he would push a whiskey-soaked rag through the
two bullet holes in his knee and pass out. Run the rag, pass
out. Run the rag, pass out.

Didn't take long for that to wear thin, he'd say and laugh
big. Lord, that boy had a big laugh.

When he thought he could ride he tied two boards to his leg
to keep it stiff and then tied a rope around his ankle and ran
it across his horse's chest. He then tied the tag end of a rope
around his pommel which left his hands free for his reins and
his weapons. There was a lot of rough country between him
and Sweet Home.

It ought to have worked but it didn't. One unexpected leap
of his horse and he was out again only this time on the back
of his horse's rump. He ended up holding the end of the rope
in one hand, his pistol in the other and the reins in his teeth.
And that's how he rode. Clear across Tejas.

When Evie first heard the story she thought: well, that's a
Dare for you. Tenacious as a turtle.

Unfortunately, that durn knee never worked right again. Visshus was sensible about it; hell yes, he walked stiff-legged but
at least he walked.

In the end that knee would cost him his life, and that of his younger brother as well.

Blue, Jack and Goldie took off after the Kiowa raiders who had murdered their brothers and were gone for over two weeks. Evie did not ask them what happened when they returned; she knew they wouldn't be back if they had not punished the wrongdoers. As it turned out, they had retrieved their brothers' scalps and weapons and had nineteen Indian ponies which they had taken as bounty.

So now it stood at six. Three and three. Jack, Goldie and Blue. Irish, Brit and Markie.

Far as one thing went, they were all smart as a two-bit whip. Then they went off every which way. Goldie was the most even-tempered of the lot and Blue was the least. Irish was the tomboy and Brit fancied herself high-toned. Standing in a row by herself—with the face of an earnest angel and the mouth of a guttersnipe—was her youngest, little blind Markie. She was sure to be a beauty someday but their only hope was that no one ever told her so! She was already spoiled silly. Evie's face softened. Poor Markie. That those beautiful eyes could shine with such mischief and intelligence and yet never shine with sight.

Evie was proud of all of her children and loved them all fiercely but if she were pressed, she would have to admit that she had a special place in her heart for Jack. Maybe it was simply because he was her first and she had not thought it was possible for her to produce such a wonder. (And then had set about producing eleven more!) Or maybe it was because she'd had to turn to him so often back in the bad days and because he had always been there when she had.

He'd had to grow up way before his time, what with his father dying and then with the fire and all. But he had been up to those challenges and all others since.

She liked to think of Jack as the child who was most like her. Wily and crafty as a fox. Diligent and thorough. Fair to a friend. Fatal to all foes. Unacquainted with the meaning of fear.

Time and again she had seen him pit himself against something or someone, and she could have been a rich woman if she had bet on Jack Dare to quit last. Someday, someone might come along who'd take him down a peg or two, but Evie doubted that she would ever live to see it.

By leaning left in her chair and dislocating her neck, she could just make out the dark glow of his pipe. She looked and scratched and then settled back.

Something's up. He had been mostly silent at supper. First he didn't hear Markie's question about the Mexican word for spook and then Blue'd had to ask him twice to toss him a hunk of bread. No doubt about it, there was something gnawing on him tonight. Oh, yeah. There was something, all right.

Chapter 3

Jack had bathed in the creek. Stuck his head under the water and stayed there until his breath gave out then floated for a long time with only his bony kneecaps and nose breaking water. Like it was the only thing he had to do.

Now he was lying on the flat rock beside the creek, listening to frogs croak and an old hoot owl that never tired of asking the same question.

Occasionally, indistinct conversation floated down from the house. Once a wolf bayed and started the dogs up and he heard Goldie holler, "Damn-you-dogs-shut-up!"

If there had been a dog barking in Sweet Home it would have quit too. Without even stretching their tonsils, any of the Dares could knock little limbs off a tree a hundred paces away.

When he was dry he pulled on his buckskin pants and settled on his heels for a smoke. He packed the bowl of his pipe from a mixture of willow bark and rough-cut tobacco, worked the flint fire starter until he got a spark and then he drew deeply.

It was a quiet night—warm but not sultry—with a white-gold half moon and a scattering of stars that shone small and bright against a pitch black sky. It looked clear now, but he thought the faint northeast breeze held a hint of rain.

Suddenly something—his mood, the night or the impending rain—took him back to a night much like this one. A long ago night, for he'd been only six or maybe seven and green as a gourd. Thinking of it now made him chuckle and shake his head.

They were still living at the old place, of course, a two-room farmhouse made of raw timber taken from an abandoned building at a ferry crossing. The boards had been so warped he could stick his hand between them.

By that time he was already sharing a bed with three brothers and thought it two too many—Visshus hogged the covers and Brown ground his teeth. He generally slept in spite of them, but not that night. For whatever reason he had lain wide-eyed for hours.

It had started raining about dusk, one of those hot summer storms that would always begin with jagged lightning slashes and a driving rain before it would settle into a soft steady soaker. He had gone out onto the porch and was leaning against the wall, drawing in the clean coolness and listening to the tune played by an overturned bucket. By a faint light that came from a crack in the wall he was checking out a place where he had dug out a splinter when suddenly he heard sounds that did not go with the storm. The rustle of a shredded corn-shuck tick and the creak of rawhide ties. Pleading whispers and raspy breathing. Soft cries that sounded like pain. Only they weren't.

The sounds were coming from the little lean-to where his parents slept and about that fast it came to him that his parents were mating!

At first it sickened him. That they would do such a thing! Then he started to respond in ways he did not understand and it didn't sicken him at all. Strange emotions came over him and things began to happen, things that were unrecognized by him because they had never been experienced before. Stiff as a tree he stood there with a blazing face that felt hot as fire in

the damp night air. Was what was happening to him happening
to his parents too?

Pretty soon he didn't give a rat's ass about anything but
himself. Holymanaliveboywow! The things he felt! Why hadn't
anybody ever told him about this?

It would be some years before he experienced a man's feelings when mating, but it was less than a minute before he found
out what happened to a boy who was holding onto himself like
a drowning rat on a rope!

He smiled now, not because he had recalled the moment so
clearly—there probably wasn't a man alive who didn't remember the first time he discovered the pleasures of sex—but
because it seemed odd that he should think of that night now,
on this night.

And then with sudden insight he understood that too. That
night was the first time he had wished for someone who was
his alone. And this was the second. "Huh!" He added another
pinch of tobacco to his pipe then leaned back against a tree
and stretched out his legs.

Something had made him think about having a woman, not
a woman like the one he'd had the night before but one who
was his own, and he couldn't recall ever feeling that way as a
man. He must not have, because if he had, he'd've gone and
got himself one.

Apparently this was also the sort of night that made a man
stop and take stock because that's what he'd found himself
doing earlier. And he had come to a couple of interesting
conclusions. First that he had no complaints about his life thus
far. Tejas was a damn hard land but the Dares had prospered
until they had both money and land. And it would take a war
to separate a Dare from either.

In effect, everything he had set out to get for his family was
theirs. He ought to be satisfied, but he wasn't. Something was
eating at him and destroying his satisfaction. At strange times
a growing restlessness interrupted his thoughts and left him
feeling out of whack, like he was walking with one foot on a
log and the other in a bog.

He didn't like it. Somehow somewhere something important had changed. He had no idea when. Hell, he hadn't even realized it had happened!

Lately he had felt the need for something more—only he didn't know what more it was that he had to have and he used to think that he had always known that. Had ever since the summer he turned seventeen. The same summer his Uncle Gib had come home from the mountains. The old man came now into his memory, a tall, gaunt-boned man with thin untended hair and pale watery eyes.

Everybody had been glad to see him come and everybody had been sorry to see him go—especially Maw since he was her only living brother—but only Jack had been so taken with what he'd had to say while he was there.

He couldn't understand why the others didn't feel as he did. What his Uncle Gib talked about was all Jack could think about. Rivers called the Yellowstone, Powder and Tongue; places like Little Goose Pass and South Pass, mountains named the Bitterroots and the Absaroka Summit, men named Bridger and Kit Carson and John Colter; strange Indian tribes called Crow, Kaw, Cree and Blackfoot.

That's when he decided that his life lay to the north and west. In the big mountain country.

After Gib left, Maw observed that her brother had not lost his way with words. "Why, I once saw him tell a man that the mule he was lookin' at was actually a small, large-eared horse an' before I knew it, the man was stoppin' people in the road to show 'em the especially fine piece of horseflesh he'd jus' bought.

"Oh yeah, Gib's always been able to do that. If a person'll let 'im."

Well, Jack must have let him, because after Gib left what he'd described kept flashing through Jack's mind like cards riffed by a sharper. Cool moonlit nights. Tall, sweet-smelling pines. Snows that lay like a thick winter blanket over timbered mountains and peaceful valleys. Rivers as yet unseen by any white man. Bears that walked on their hind legs like a man, and moose the size of a cabin. Strange Indians in strange getups, and fur-clad white men who looked stranger still.

And it was all right there. Just waiting for the likes of Black Jack Dare.

It didn't take long for Jack to tell his uncle that he would like to go back with him when he went. Instead of the enthusiasm Jack had hoped for, Gib urged caution. He said that old men like Bridger, Carson—and himself—were few and far between. That the average age of the mountain man was twenty-two and that most of them never live to get a whiff of thirty. Why? Jack had asked and got about a hundred answers in return.

'' 'Cause they get kilt! The Indins burn 'em or the grizzlies eat 'em. Snakes bite 'em or mad animals do. Trees fall on 'em or they get buried by loose snow or they step in their own traps. Some get rolled on by their horse. Or dragged to death. Or trampled thin. Then the weather'll set in and they'll starve to death or freeze to death or drown in the rivers. But if they make it through the hunting season, then they'll go to meet the other survivors an' half of 'em'll ever leave. The rest of 'em'll get poisoned by bad whiskey or cut for their shoes or shot for their woman.''

Sounded good to Jack! Hell, who wants to live to be thirty anyway!

''Tell you what,'' his uncle finally said. ''If you still feel the same way next spring, meet me at a place called Three Forks at the junction of the Gallatin, Madison an' Jefferson Rivers. You show there, we'll give it a go for one winter an' we'll see how frisky you are come spring.''

Jack had every intention of doing just that but within weeks of his planned departure, his paw died. They had hardly gotten over that when the farm burned.

Well, that did it for Maw. All of a sudden she got land-fever and kept insisting that they had to move to Tejas. Well, he had to at least go along and see them settled.

Once there, they'd had to find the land and buy it. Then they'd had to build the cabins and plant the feed crops. And then they'd heard about a fancy doctor up in St. Louis who fixed up people who were blind and they needed every dollar they could lay their hands on for that.

There had been one thing after another and now here he was, rubbing on thirty himself! Goodgawdamighty! He was probably too long in the tooth to survive the trip!

Lately he had decided that if he was ever going to go he ought to just do it. There was no reason why he had to stay in Tejas any longer. If the number of men who were hanging around the farm was any indication, both Brit and Irish would be married before the year was out. (Though it was Goldie who ought to marry first, being the best father material of the lot.) Markie and Maw would be fine with Goldie and Blue . . . ! Blue Jack Dare, better known as Hell-Without-The-Fire.

Damn kid was bound get shot, way he threw himself at every dangerous situation. He was about the most incautious . . .

Jack stopped himself right there. Best clean up his own house first. Getting boxed earlier by Wully Small had not exactly been a stunning example of vigilance on his part!

No doubt about it, he had been careless, playing cards half the night and diddling Dulce the other half, especially after coming off a hard three days of looking for the cowards who had killed Hap Pettijohn's freighter.

An ugly business, that. Whoever did the job took everything of value and left eight yoked mules thirsty in their traces. Mules being mules, they had waited until they figured they had waited long enough and then they headed for home . . . and brought the ravaged wagon and the dead driver right into Hap's feedlot.

The most valuable thing the robbers took was a crate of rifles made by two brothers named Hawken. To say that the owner of the mercantile, Bowie Garlock, was upset was putting it mildly. He had ordered the arms all the way from St. Louis and had paid for them in advance.

Bowie offered Jack's troop a reward for the return of the arms but they all declined. A good price on a rifle would be reward enough for them.

Unfortunately, less than an hour after they set off, it rained.

They not only lost the trail but they spent the next three days all wet.

The thing was, he figured he knew who the guilty men were. One of them was probably laid out over at the livery right now. Which was why he had played cards with Wully Small to begin with, hoping Wully would say something that would give him an excuse to ride out to the Crow's Nest and look things over. That was what Wully's friends called it. The Crow's Nest. The locals had more aptly named it the Rattlers' Den.

In Jack's opinion, Sweet Home had two problems; Indians who killed the settlers at will and white men who killed the settlers at will, and Wully Small had been one of the latter.

An abundance of those men had drifted down to Tejas because they had heard there was no law and until recently, they had heard right. Mexico City was far away and the feder-ales were few and often as fraudulent as the criminals.

Of course, men like Wully had to contend with the Indians too, but they recognized each other and would band together, like they had out at the Crow's Nest.

There might be twelve men there at any given time, tending no crops and running no stock. Killer-faced men like Shug Clarke and his brother Bittercreek, or the Elliotts and the Dag-gerts, men who'd made names for themselves up north and were beginning to make names in Tejas too. On instinct alone Jack was willing to bet on their guilt, but that wasn't quite enough. Plenty of men had been hung on a hunch before but not by Jack Dare. The ones he'd hung had either been caught in the act or caught with the goods.

Which was why he'd sat across from Wully Small and Riley Mott the night previous, and felt like a coyote, continuously circling, waiting for one sheep to drop out of the pack and stand alone.

As far as he was concerned both Small and Mott might as well have had ''murderer'' written across their hairy faces but neither had said anything useful and now one of them never would.

He could go out to the Crow's Nest and demand to see all

their belongings but it would be a declaration of war and guilty or not, the Crow's Nest men would have the right to open fire.

It also went against his own beliefs.

Like all the others, the Dares had not come to Tejas to get a social conscience. They came to be independent of society's rules and regulations and to live as they pleased without anyone bothering them. When they arrived they were ten strong, six men and four women who were prepared to defend what little they had to the death. Unfortunately they would soon be tested only not by those who would take their belongings or their land, by those who would take their lives. Indians.

The Comanche and Kiowa had always ranged from where Sweet Home stood to the headwaters of the rivers that the Spanish had named the Colorado and the Brazos. Sweet Home was not the nearest settlement, but for some reason it was hit more often. Indian raids were the main reason the town organized the ranger troop. To avenge and revenge. That was their job.

There'd been no rangers to call upon back when the Dare brothers were killed but the Dares wouldn't have called on them anyway. Where they came from a man who did not revenge a grievance against himself or his family was considered less than a man. That sort of thing was part and parcel of a man's measure and no Dare had ever come up short there.

Within two hours of finding their brothers' bodies, they were on the raiders' trail.

Word of the Kiowa raid against them had traveled fast. Though they hardly knew anyone in Sweet Home, when Goldie, Blue and Jack rode in to buy powder and supplies, there were several men there who were ready to ride out with them. They declined all offers but the willingness of the people gave them food for thought.

By midday they were at the spot where Goldie had found the bodies. To anyone who could read sign it was easy to see what had happened.

Visshus and Sunny had been looking for some stock that

had wandered off. They found the trail of the missing horses and followed it for more than three miles. Watching sign, maybe talking softly amongst themselves, they rode over a little hillock and down into a bushy slew and that's where the Kiowas were waiting for them. A curtain of arrows must've rained down on them because both of their mounts were found dead there.

Afoot the brothers somehow fought their way clear and made a run for cover some four hundred feet away. Only Visshus couldn't run.

Knowing their brother Sunny as they did, they knew he'd have told his brother to head for the woods . . . that he would hold them off until he could get there safely. But they also knew Visshus and knew that he would never leave Sunny to face the enemy alone.

They had probably cursed each other roundly and had both been madder than two badgers in a barrel, but in the end they met the enemy together. And they died together.

The Dare brothers had not sold their lives cheap. The Indians had carried off their dead and wounded, but the tracks clearly showed that there had been over twenty Indians in the beginning and less than a dozen in the end.

For eight days the three brothers rode, eating nothing but jerked meat and stopping only long enough to rest the horses. Nobody'd had much to say which is probably why it took so long to notice that Blue had held an unnatural silence ever since they'd left the farm.

Jack knew Blue was hurting—he had turned fifteen that summer and had been closer to Visshus than anyone. He searched for healing words, but he found none. None for Blue. None for himself.

On the ninth day they caught up with the Kiowas, who were camped beside a shallow stream. There were eleven of them. Their ponies—including the horses that their brothers had been tracking that fateful day—were picketed twenty feet away.

The brothers lay up on top of the little ridge and watched them, eating off an antelope spitted on green sticks over a low fire, wiping their greasy hands on their hair, talking and laughing among themselves. Two injured Indians lay a little apart from the rest. One had a bloody rag tied around his head. The other's right arm was in a sling. Neither man moved much.

Then one of the Indians finished eating and dug in a pouch that hung at his waist and used a burning stick to light a pipe that had belonged to Visshus.

Jack knew the minute Blue recognized the pipe. He could follow the anger as it hummed through him, swelling his shoulders and turning his face into a turnip with white dots. He was halfway over the hill before Jack could grab his pants leg and haul him back. Grappling silently they tumbled downhill. Gaining the upper hand, Jack threatened Blue with the butt end of his pistol but he turned blank eyes on him. He was clicking his teeth like a mad dog and staring at him like he'd never seen him before! Jack thought he was going to have to take his brother home tied head down on his horse. There was a long minute then Blue nodded once and they rolled apart, snarl-headed and red-faced. Blue leathered his knife and Jack gave Goldie a half-worried, half-mad look.

When they moved off a ways to collect their mounts and check their weapons, Blue acted as calm as ever, but Jack knew that either his brother or that Indian would die on that day.

When they returned to Sweet Home they were driving the Kiowa pony herd in front of them and Blue had eleven scalps draped over his horse's neck like a wreath.

It was not long afterwards that the *alcalde,* Lloyd Cooper, acting on behalf of Stephen Austin in San Felipe, offered them all a job as ranging peacekeepers. The money was good. They talked it over and decided that they would take the mayor up on his offer but not all three of them.

Since Goldie was the best shot of the lot and therefore the best hunter, Jack and Blue informed him that he ought to be the one to remain at home to keep the larder stocked, protect the women and continue to make the things they sorely needed to sleep and sit on. Goldie refused and nominated Blue. In the end they drew straws and Goldie lost, which resulted in the exchange of hard words and an accusation of cheating. Goldie settled down some but he still grumbled a lot and claimed that he'd gotten the raw end of the deal. "I'd sooner fight a horde of savages'n I would stay at home with the women."

That had been over six years ago. Fast, hard years for Jack and Blue because the horse tribes like the Kiowa or the Comanche were always stealing the settlers' stock—if not the settlers themselves—and chasing them down and exacting retribution soon occupied the majority of the rangers' time.

They had the complete support of the populace and Stephen Austin because there was nothing like a massacre to put a damper on immigration. About two years ago, when it had seemed that the depredations were subsiding, the new settlers had poured in practically every day. Now lately the attacks had been on the rise again and the only new immigrants had been hard, horny-handed males. Some stayed but most moved on. Unfortunately the ones who stayed were often not settlers who hoped to have a wife and family but troublemakers like the men at the Crow's Nest.

A rustling drew Jack's attention to some nearby bushes where yellowy eyes caught the moonlight and flared redly. Probably a possum, he thought, and returned to the immigrant problem. In particular, the wagonload that had arrived that afternoon.

Imagine that! Two women, a shave-tail boy and two little girls coming all that way without a man! And who would figure a girl like that for a schoolteacher? Hell she looked no more than sixteen herself and about as tough as a ball of cotton.

Jack sucked a final draft of smoke into his lungs and then knocked the dottle out of his pipe. Wait till the men of Sweet Home get a gander at her! There'll be a stampede they'll hear clear down in Coahuila. Hell, he had fifty bucks that said she'd be married within the month. Only he'd never get a taker.

The fact was that in Sweet Home even a homely female—and she was anything but—could marry within days simply because she was a product in high demand. Very high demand. It was spinster heaven.

"Spinster," he said and chuckled out loud as he remembered how she had curled her lip at him and tried to skewer him with her eyes. He must've ruffled her feathers somehow, the way she was jerking herself around and beating her legs with her skirts. Made a man want to give her something she could really get mad about!

Jack's thoughts were interrupted by soft footfalls that he recognized as Goldie's. The two men grunted at each other and Goldie started shucking his clothes. Jack stretched for the crock of soap and handed it to his brother and without speaking, pointed to the rough sacking cloth towel that was draped across a tree limb.

Goldie eased his big body into the water and sat there silent for a time. On a branch overhead a night bird joined the frogs and crickets in song and on the opposite bank the possum crouched in the bushes and waited patiently for the humans to leave.

"A soft night."

"Yeah."

"Could rain, though."

"Yeah."

Goldie glanced over at his brother. "Anythin' goin' on in town?"

"Not much." Both men looked downstream when a fish jumped with a splash.

"Say, Goldie . . ."

"Yeah?"

"You recall the first time you noticed your pecker?"

Goldie had started to scrub. Now he stopped. "Huh?"

"I said, do you recall . . . aw hell, never mind."

Jack stood and hitched his pants. "Well, Goldie, I want you to be the first to know. I'm fixin' to leave for the mountains."

"What?" Goldie sat stunned, one hand raised like an oath taker and the other clapped over one hairy armpit.

Like most, Evie Dare made her soap from wood ash lye and coarse lard, but she liked to add a healthy dose of horse liniment for "backbone." As a consequence, it behooved a person who'd started washing to keep going. Left on too long, Evie's soap would remove a layer of hide right along with the dirt.

The smell of singed hair finally brought Goldie around. "What mountains?" he called, but by then his brother had already disappeared into the shadows.

Chapter 4

The two Dare cabins had been built on a slight rise so that from the porch a person looked out over the creek and beyond, to the rolling acres of woodland. The prevailing breeze, if there was one, would cross the creek and cool the cabins then carry the critter smells out into the fields behind them.

Both cabins had steeply pitched shagbark roofs and were connected by a covered passage. The walls were made of unsawed logs that were the devil to keep chinked, but knowing about the Indians' fondness for creeping up on sleeping settlers and firing arrows in on them, it was the twins' job to re-chink with mud and grass at least every other month.

Two smoke-scarred and slightly canted chimneys anchored the end of each cabin. Every wall had large square windows covered with heavy wooden shutters. When closed, all the windows and the two doors had rifle slits cut in at eye height. To defend against anyone who would lank-down and belly crawl in, slits had also been cut into the walls about a foot above the floor.

One cabin was a big room where the living and eating was

done, but much of the cooking was done outside, in a stone oven that had been built between the cabins.

The three girls slept in a crook-back loft reached by a wood and rawhide-tied ladder anchored to the puncheon floor in the main cabin. Evie Dare slept in a little walled corner off the front room. The three brothers bunked together in the other, smaller cabin.

As Jack neared the porch their newest dog ran to meet him, barking excitedly and leaping at his legs. Son of Sally. When he stopped to pet it, it fell over on its side and parted its hind legs. "Sorriest damn dog I've ever owned."

"That's what you used to say about Sally."

Markie had come out onto the porch.

"An' now I can say it about her son. Thanks to who?"

She sat on her hands and grinned in his direction. "Me!"

The puppy was the direct result of Markie letting the bitch out of the pen where Goldie had put her when she went into season. Markie had no excuse—other than that she hated to hear Sally whine—because she knew before anyone else when an animal was ready to breed. She claimed that the animals started to smell different.

She could have said that they turned a purple color that only she could see and nobody would have argued with her; she had been right that many times.

If there was one thing the Dares did not need it was more hound dogs, they already had six: Sally and Fanny for coons, Nip and Tuck for bear and ol' Yew and Whistler for whatever they could tree these days, which wasn't a lot, they were that old now.

"I cleaned your guns, Jack."

"Thanks, Irish."

Since they had finished their nightly chores, Brit and Irish had come outside too. Jack felt an argument brewing between them, but there was nothing unusual about that.

The twins looked more alike than a halved apple but in temperament they couldn't have been more different. Irish, for example, would rather bite a boy than kiss one while Brit had been observed practicing kissing on her own hand. (This Irish told Markie and Markie told the entire family. And anyone else within shouting range.)

Irish pointed at her sister. "Maw, Brit has got goose lard all over her face again!"

"Brit, I swan!"

"Stinks up the whole bed."

"Oh, Irish!"

"It's true," exclaimed Markie. "It does!"

"I don't see if it's anybody's business if I smear cow hooey on my face."

"It's our business if we have to sleep with you."

"That's what it smells like, too!" said Markie. "Cow hooey."

"Why do you do that, girl?" Evie seriously wanted to know.

" 'Cause I don't want to get old and wrinkly before my time . . ." For once Brit thought before she spoke. She had almost said "like you."

Evie looked at her daughter whose face was not only seamless but prettier than a summer sunrise. "I think we better get you girls interested in something other'n fightin' amongst your-selves." To her eldest, she said, "There's gonna be a school in town. Six days a week every month but September, October and December. I was thinkin' it wouldn't hurt the girls to go."

She parleyed with Jack as she would have done with a husband, and had done so even before her husband died because Jack had always been a quick, level thinker and, unfortunately, his father had not been.

Otis Dare had been what the hill people call light-minded. Evie had not noticed it right off 'cause she had been looking at his shiny black hair and fine manly figure. It was only after they were married and he bought a horse known throughout the county as Sorefoot that she knew she was smarter than him.

Not that she had not loved him. He was kind, good, hardwork-ing and honest and she missed him to this day. Probably always would. She rested her head against the back of the chair and watched a miller circle the lantern. My, but he'd been a handsome devil, that Otis Dare.

"Maw!" exclaimed Irish. "Us girls can go to school?"

"Can we really?" asked Brit.

"For a spell. I figure it can't hurt you none. Lord knows, it might help."

"Oh, Maw!"

"I can scarcely wait!"

Jack waited for the hubbub to die before he asked. "How much?"

"One dollar a month."

"For all?"

"Each."

Jack blew though his lips in pretended distress.

"Well, now jus' hold your horses," said Evie. "I think we can do a trade. I asked Lloyd Cooper if he'd like Goldie to make the furniture for the school, and he said he sure would! Jus' send Goldie over, he says, so the new teacher can tell him jus' how she wants things done."

Goldie had finished with his bath in time to hear that last. He pulled the towel off his head and said, "Damn it, Maw, I wish you would quit lookin' for work for me. I can find plenty by myself."

Irish said, "Maw, did you say the new schoolteacher's a she?"

Evie nodded. "Jus' arrived from Pennsylvania. Cooper said jus' y'all wait 'till you get a look at her! I tole Cooper to tell her that I've got three good-lookin' sons . . ."

"I met her," said Jack and without even trying he saw again her high, red-streaked cheeks and full dark-lipped mouth and large grey-blue eyes, and it was only then that he realized that she'd been in the back of his mind all this time. Through the ride from town. Through his ruminating bath. Right up to now.

From Markie, "Can I go too?"

Irish proclaimed: "I don't want to go if Goober can't!"

Brit folded her arms. "Me neither."

"God, I suppose you'll all have to go. Jack?"

"All right with me," he said.

Something in his tone made his mother look at him but he was staring off somewhere with a strange gleam in his eye.

"Good!" said Markie and lifted her arms to her brother.

Jack grunted and groaned in play-like pain as he drew her onto his lap. "Ahh Goober you're about t'bust my leg! Sittin' on laps!"

He kept that up a while but the truth was, he secretly hoped she never grew too big for him to hold. This little one had always held a special place in his heart. From the moment he first laid eyes on her squinched and wrinkled face.

He buried his lips in the little well between her braids to inhale her sweet smell and she started squirming like a hooked worm.

"Ow, Jack! You're scratchy!"

"Am I?" He must be. Dulce'd complained about his beard last night.

He rubbed the hard black stubbled growth on his chin. He probably looked rough as a cob. Probably scared the beejesus outa little miss priss today! He smiled.

He couldn't say why that pleased him. He didn't make a habit of scaring little girls out of their wits. Actually he was generally real careful about his person. He always got his hair cut every six months . . . whether it needed it or not . . . and hell, he just didn't feel right if he didn't shave at least every ten or twenty days. Excluding, of course, the lustrous horseshoe of hair on his upper lip.

"Jack, do you think I can learn to read?" asked Markie.

"I suppose." He said it though he didn't know how she would. Her eyes looked normal and stared straight but she had been born blind as a potato. They had always held the hope that something could be done for her, but last year they'd found out for sure . . . blind was how she would end her life as well.

All of them had gone upriver to St. Louis so Markie could

see a famous doctor about her eyes. Hell, it took them three days just to find the man! There were more people in that town than they'd ever thought possible.

They had never had the doctor's name but they'd had a good description of him, so they fanned out and started asking everyone they saw. That was an experience in itself. Like Maw said: "There's some mighty strange people live in this world. And most of them live in St. Louie."

They found him all right and the entire family had crowded into the tiny examining room to watch the frizzy-headed doctor peer into Markie's eyes and then bathe them with a clarifying lotion, and then move a light here and there in front of her face and then feel all the bones in her head. Somewhere along in there he got real peeved with them and told them to step back so he could draw in some unused air.

But they all had to get close enough to pet her when he told them that there was not a thing he could do for her. She would be blind forever.

Of course, everyone took the news harder than Markie. "Oh, for pity's sake. I don't care one way or the other."

With the money that was to have been given to the doctor for a cure, each girl got a store-bought dress and a pair of shoes, and all of the brothers got a new pistol. Goldie picked out a set of wood tools and Maw got herself a new hat with purply paper flowers on the brim which she came to value so much she would only wear it inside and only on special occasions. Pretty soon it got so Christmas wasn't Christmas unless she served dinner with her special hat on.

Three more days in smelly, crowded St. Louis, they couldn't wait to go back home. They were standing on the dock waiting to board the boat when they discovered that Markie was missing. After a frantic ten minutes, they found her standing beside a fiddler who was playing "Yankee Doodle Dandy" for coins.

Somehow she had picked the single sound of that fiddle out of a hundred others and had been drawn to it like a calf to its mother's bawl.

She announced that she had decided to stay on in St. Louis and learn how to play the fiddle. She just couldn't get over the sound it made.

Blue carried her on board but seeing her tear-streaked face was too much for Jack. Minutes before the gangplank was to be removed, he raced down and bought the fiddle for her.

Well, a person would think he had handed her the moon. She was never without it and played it night and day. So much, in fact, that they were afraid it would take root under her chin.

Her playing left a lot to be desired in the beginning. Blue said that for pure listening enjoyment he had heard cat howls that were more musical. Jack, on the other hand, said he was reminded of an ungreased wagon wheel.

But by the time the boat docked in Natchez, she had taught herself to play well enough to have a lady tell her that she sounded just like an angel. They told Markie the lady carried two goat-horn trumpets. Angel, my butt!

But now that he thought about it, he supposed that incident was why he had not told her that she couldn't learn to read. Anybody who could teach themselves to play a fiddle ought to be able to do just about anything they set their mind to!

Jack was thinking all these things when he heard a horse splash across the creek. He gave a groan and said damn! He'd sure been looking forward to sleeping in his own bed for a change. To which his mother said, "You coulda slept in it last night, if you'da seen fit t'come home."

Jack kept his eye on the approaching rider and did not respond to his mother's comment. There are some things a man does not discuss with his mother and in Jack's book his whore was one of them.

Clyde Maxey stepped off his lathered horse and touched his hat to the women. "Ladies. Jack. Goldie."

"Clyde."

Goldie filled a bucket with water from the rock cistern and set it in front of Clyde's horse while with perfect precision Markie walked to the well, took the gourd dipper off the hook and filled it for Clyde.

"Thank you!"

Clyde Maxey was a lean, loose-limbed man with a ginger beard that made him look older than his age, which was twenty-six. Like most men in Sweet Home he was unmarried, but he had high hopes that he would not always be. And since the Dare twins were on the top of every bachelor's list, he had his hat in his hand and a smile on his face and was attempting to look serious, sincere, stalwart, fun, clean, courageous, God-fearing, hearty, handsome and hardworking. . . . all at once.

Having no preference as to which one he married, he was spreading his smile equally between the two girls, however only Brit was smiling back and she quit as soon as she saw the frown Jack shot her.

"What's up?" Jack was still giving Brit a hairy eye.

Clyde spat before he spoke. "Indians hit a place twenty miles west of the Olsons. Farmer, wife and two little ones." He glanced at the women then figured they had probably heard worse. "Killed all but the wife."

Jack went inside and returned with his rifle, shot pouch and powder horn. "Where's Blue?"

"Still in town," Markie said.

Clyde whistled softly and shook his head. "After that skull-breaker last night!"

The conversation interested Irish now. "He got his ear re-sized last week. Looked like he'd grown a pine knob on his head."

To which Goldie added, "It looked like a fit to me. Damned kid's got a wood head!"

Evie mumbled, " 'Minds me of that ol' tomcat we used t'have. One night he'd come in actin' like he was on his ninth life. His ear'd be tore an' there'd be big snatches outa his fur, but the next night, there he'd be . . . right back at it."

Fighting was not her youngest son's only failing but Evie no longer concerned herself about Blue and his women. Wasn't a bit of use. He had been the same since he was two. If there was a female around, that female could count on Blue Dare's total regard. Till the next one came along.

After surveying the sky Evie told Irish to run and get her brothers' ponchos. To Clyde she said, "I believe you're gonna get some rain."

Belatedly realizing somebody had said something, Clyde stopped sparking Brit and looked at Evie, "Ma'am?"

"Never mind."

Jack led his horse up. He wore leather leggings and a long buckskin hunting shirt that was cinched at the waist by a wide belt. Threaded on it was a wide cowhide scabbard that contained one of the two knives he always carried. Stuck in his belt were three pistols and crisscrossing his chest were two rawhide twangs, one with a shot pouch and the other with a powder horn. He carried his long rifle. Rolled up behind his cantle he had extra pants, a blanket, powder and lead, a tin cup, a wooden bowl, an extra horseshoe and finally, a couple of *cabestros* or braided hair hobbles. Coiled around his pommel was ten yards of lariat.

Clyde said, "I saw Luke in town. He said he'd get He-Coon and meet us at the Y. You want me to, uh, swing by the cantina?"

"No, I'll go." Jack grunted and accepted the two ponchos from Irish. The girls had fashioned them out of squares of canvas for him and Blue. What the two men never told their sisters was that they had to take them off as soon as they got anywhere near a hostile encampment. In a drumming rain they could be heard for fifty miles.

Goldie asked Jack if he wanted him to come along. "Naw, you go ahead an' go huntin' tomorrow as planned." Jack mounted. "But wait for me on that other thing."

"What other thing?" Goldie asked but Jack had wheeled his horse and was gone. Close behind him was Clyde . . . who had to either quit shining Brit or quit his job.

"What other thing?" Goldie asked everyone who was left.

Evie was watching Jack's horse splash across the stream. "I think he meant that you should wait about goin' over to the school."

"The school?"

"To talk to the teacher about the furniture."

"Oh." Goldie had forgotten all about that. He looked away. He looked back. "Why?"

Evie shrugged. "Who knows what he's got on his mind."

"Well, I sure don't. He jus' told me he was goin' to the mountains."

"What mountains?"

"Hell, I don't know." Goldie flung the towel on the porch step. "He's got me goin' six ways from Sunday."

"Mm," said Evie but now it was she who had the strange gleam in her eye.

Amber light spilled out of the two tall narrow openings that served as windows at Dulce's cantina. From within came the sound of a strumming guitar and the click of castanets, filling the night with a sad recollection of a long-lost love. Unfortunately a fractious voice rose above the music and spoiled everything.

"Ain't you got no bigger cup'n this? Hell, I can spit more'n this holds!"

Jack dismounted and led his horse around the side of the building to the single back window. Through the thin cowhide cover he heard a thick hoarse moan that he recognized as his brother. "Blue!" Nothing. "Blue, I know you're in there!"

"Go away, dammit!"

"Blue!"

After a minute, "Whut!"

"C'mon. We got to ride."

"Awshit! Not now!"

Jack grinned. "Yeah, now. C'mon."

"Can't it wait till mornin'?"

"No, it can't." Jack knew exactly what he was interrupting since he had been in exactly the same position on the night previous. "Let's go."

"Damn!" There was the rustling of a corn-shuck mattress, then, "Well, darlin', I hate like hell t'have . . . OW! Darlin'! That was my wound . . . OW! Damn!"

There was a string of Spanish curses and the sound of something hard hitting the wall then his brother was outside, his boots in one hand and his hat brim in his teeth, trying to sling on a hickory shirt.

"What's up?" Blue asked when he could.

"Not much now, I'll wager."

"Damn you, Jack!" Blue took a roundhouse swipe which Jack easily dodged. After all it had been Jack who had taught— no, *shown* would be a better word—his little brother how to fight in the first place. Might be time for a few more lessons.

"You better not have called me outa there for nothin'."

"Let's hope it won't be for nothin'. You up for a long ride?"

"Hell, yes, I'm up for a long ride. I was just havin' myself one."

"The other kinda long ride."

"Do I have any choice?" Blue slammed his hat on the back of his head and leaned against the wall to tug on his boots. The unbroken stream of Spanish profanity continued inside.

Jack hid a grin. "You sure you won't play out?"

"Hell, you're the ol' man! You'll play out long 'fore I do."

Jack couldn't rebut that; he was probably right. As he prepared to mount, he took as close a look at his brother's face as the moon would allow. Obviously Blue'd been wearing his chip again but then, he generally did.

Nobody knew why Blue had grown to be so cantankerous, but nobody could remember a time when he hadn't been set on doing what nobody wanted him to.

Sometimes Jack wondered if Blue would ever cross the line from wild to bad. Not out of meanness but solely for something to do at the time. Jack had seen it happen before. Something held in check was given its head and a man went along for the ride. One step taken down a strange path led to another and then another and before the man knew it, he'd passed the point of no return.

Not that Blue had done anything to warrant his brother's worry. So far he had been as straight as string. So far.

"You get another eye like that one an' the dogs'll try to tree you."

"Har, har." Mounted now too, Blue rocked his hat into position and wheeled his horse. "Well? You comin' or not?"

Jack threw Blue's poncho hard enough to make him wallow in the saddle and while his brother was fighting his way free, he kicked his horse out in front.

About the only thing Blue hated to eat was dirt.

They met up with the others on the opposite side of town. A few nodded and one or two lifted their hands but a clap of thunder obliterated any greeting that they made. As one, they turned their horses and rode.

There were nine men and one Tonkawa scout. Billy Yates and Luke Bryant were twenty-two like Blue. Jesse McIninch, Ed Cox and Clyde Maxey were in their late twenties and their oldest member at thirty-eight was also the lone Tejano, Hector Salazar. Clyde was the troop's second in command.

Some of them, like the Dares, were backwoods men who hailed from Kentucky, Tennessee, Georgia or Missouri—but all had lived in the area long enough to know it well. Most worked at other trades in addition to rangering. Luke was a surveyor and Clyde was a tinsmith. Ed was the town assayer and Hector Salazar its best shoemaker. Jesse was a well digger, and Long Bob was a daytime farrier and nighttime dealer at the saloon. Billy Yates farmed.

Whatever else they did, it wasn't enough. All had been pressed into this hard duty because they needed the hard cash.

Nobody knew much about the tall rangy man who called himself Long Bob Benning. Some said that his name wasn't Benning at all and that he was wanted for murder back in Virginia.

He had never said where he was from, but then, none of the rangers had ever asked either. He could ride and he could handle himself and that was all they cared about.

The men had voted for their captain when the company was formed, and they'd selected Jack who, besides command decisions had the dubious honor of arranging burials for downed men and sending any valuables—if there were any—home to the man's family or loved ones—if there were any. For that he received two dollars more a month in pay.

They had lost five men since the beginning. Not bad, considering the amount of action they had seen.

Taken as a whole there was little to distinguish them. All were well-horsed and well-armed. Most wore wide-brim slouch hats and long brush coats or ponchos over buckskin leggins and moccasins. One exception was Blue, who wore a pair of hand-tooled boots he had purchased in Brasoria for an outrageous amount of money and another was Hector Salazar who wore a steeple-style sombrero and slashed pants. He also had leather *tapaderos* on his stirrups that were almost long enough to touch the ground.

All possessed the basic skills and traits that made them perfect for their work but as far as tracking went, none compared to their Tonkawa scout. Old He-Coon could keen an enemy's scent like a hound on bloodied game, and every other Tejas tribe was an enemy of the Tonkawa.

They rode out of town to the east which took them by a cabin that had been unoccupied for nearly a year. Several of the men—including Jack Dare—noted the thin spiral of smoke that curled out of the chimney.

A girl stepped out onto the porch as they rode by, merely a black form with the light behind her but Jack recognized her from the way she held herself. It was that schoolteacher girl from up north. She was slender-waisted and big-breasted and she made a nice line against the light from within.

She half lifted one hand, as if she had been about to wave and then thought better of it and fiddled with her hair instead.

Yeah, Jack grinned, that was her all right.

"Hey!" Blue yelled to the others. "Wait'll y'all see the new schoolteacher. Ooowee! Is she somethin' or what . . . !"

Suddenly Blue slewed around in his saddle. "Hey!" he hollered after his brother's retreating figure. "Where t'hell're you goin'?"

"Y'all keep movin'. I'll catch up."

Chapter 5

Annie Mapes heard the riders and stepped outside but all she saw were dark shadows moving down the road. Soon they were gone and the sound of drumming hooves was replaced with the soft rush of the creek moving behind her and the cottonwoods rustling in the gathering wind.

Suddenly a rider burst out of nowhere and raced down the lane and reined up a few feet from the porch. Annie stood stock-still while the man surveyed her from head to toe. She felt her face heat and her heart begin to race. His hat was pulled low over his face but she knew who he was even before he spoke. He pointed a gloved finger at her.

"Don't do nothin' 'till I get back."

"What?"

"Be four, mebbe five days. A week at the most."

His horse danced and then raced away. First she glanced behind her and then she stared after the rider, utterly puzzled. For a moment she'd thought he meant her harm, but obviously she was wrong. His intent was something else entirely. But what? she wondered. Was that supposed to be a message?

Ah, yes. She relaxed. The furniture maker.

Good Lord! She stiffened. Was the knife killer also the furniture maker? This afternoon Mayor Cooper had said that a man would be getting in touch with her about making things for the school. He must be the one!

Amazing. That man was the farthest thing from her idea of a furniture maker!

On second thought, that was extremely prejudicial on her part. A man probably had to wear several hats to make a go of it in Tejas. No doubt he worked a farm as well. Alongside his plump wife and ten children.

Well, it was all so simple once she put a rational eye on it. He'd had to leave town for a bit and was asking that she wait until his return to arrange for the furniture for the school. He must be concerned that she would buy elsewhere before he had an opportunity to make a bid.

Well, she had no intention of selecting any other furniture maker. First of all, Mr. Cooper had said that the man he had selected was the best craftsman in the province and since Mr. Cooper had the power to let her go if she did not suit, she intended to please him by following his suggestions to the letter.

However, that certainly did not stop her from picturing the knife wielder again and thinking: Amazing!

Still a bit befuddled, she sat at the table she had pulled up in front of the low-banked fire, and composed herself. A minute later she was softly chuckling.

If she had a major character flaw (to which she would admit) it was an overly imaginative mind. Unfortunately it had just manifested itself in the most ridiculous way. For instance, there had been a brief moment when—again she chuckled to herself—the thought had raced through her mind that the man was going to toss her onto his horse and ride off with her!

Really! How preposterous!

She shook her head. Clearly she'd need to take herself firmly in hand! Such flights of fancy were not at all appropriate for a small-town schoolmarm. Not at all! Even if the small-town schoolmarm was only nineteen. Well, almost nineteen.

She rested her elbow on the table and her chin on her fist. Funny how often the thought of that man had popped into her mind today and how easily she could visualize his face. It was unnatural, almost as if she had known him long ago and their meeting today had sparked sudden recognition on her part.

Of course, that was pure poppycock. In the first place she had never been anyplace where she could meet a man of his sort. In the second place, she certainly would have remembered meeting someone who looked like that!

Well, enough woolgathering. She picked up her half-finished letter and read what she had written so far.

Dearest Abel—Our first night in Sweet Home! It is late and I am very tired, but I am much too excited to sleep. So much has happened! We were not in town five minutes when a man was killed ... right in front of our eyes! ... dispatched by some sort of a peace officer named Dare. Mr. Cooper, the mayor (or alcalde as they say here) told us that such things almost never happen but if his wife's expression was any indication, I believe that he was not being entirely truthful.

She unstoppered the jar of ink, dipped her goose-quill pen and continued to write.

Actually we saw little of the fight because the deceased man (called a bloody brawler and a bully by our mayor's wife) had been standing directly in front of us and therefore blocked what was happening with his body. When it was over two men strode out and took hold of each of the downed man's arms—apparently they had been pointing their long rifles at the man (and us) all along!—and summarily removed him from the street.

As far as I could see the event did not even merit curious conversation. Some townspeople had gathered but when told by the knife wielder to disperse, they willingly did so, after which business continued as usual.

So there you have our first encounter with a Tejas ranging trooper. Let us hope it is our last! The mayor described the man as an uncompromising individualist and the absolute epitome of valor and courage but frankly I was reminded of one of those criminally insane footpads who prey on the streets of Philadelphia after dark!

In any case, dear Abel, I now know what you must wear in order to fit in here: first, you need long boots and deerskin leggings, a buckskin shirt with a beaded belt into which you must stick three (yes! three!) pistols and then a thrummed scabbard to sheathe a huge knife that is three inches wide and nine inches long.

Annie paused and thought: There I go again! The man's entire being had leapt into her mind's eye just that easily.

She stared into the low fire, remembering the way his slow gaze had gone from her hair to her eyes and then dropped to her chest and then rose again to her lips, and how he'd left every place he touched burning like a hot coal. She touched her cheeks and found them warm even now!

This had never happened before.

Of course it hadn't. The men she knew were refined and civilized and gentlemen to the core.

Really, she had never imagined that anyone could be that rude! Why, he had looked at her so intently it was almost as if he didn't believe she was real! Like he wanted to bare her to make sure. Rude, crude man.

With horror she realized she had written "rude" on her letter. She hastily scratched it out and dropped extra ink on it so it looked like a blob.

For the tenth time that day she wished Abel had been able to come along with them. Abel O'Neal was not only her fiancé but he was her best friend, and she missed him terribly! From the time she was eight she had talked to him about everything important that ever happened to her. Now here she was living through the greatest adventure of her life and she was being forced to do so without him!

Besides, she did not like to have to deal with people like that man. She wanted Abel to do things like that.

With that thought she almost started to write Abel about the knife-wielder, especially about how still and intent he had been when he had looked at her and the way she felt like she had known him from some previous time or place. That feeling had been so unusual Abel was certain to find it interesting.

But then, as she was formulating her first sentence, she thought better of it. It's too hard to describe all that in a letter. She'd just have to tell Abel when he arrived.

Actually she should probably start a list. This strange land and its peculiar people were so different from those they were accustomed to in Philadelphia, she suspected that in six months' time she could have quite a lengthy registry of interesting items to tell him.

She sighed. She had been unprepared for Tejas. She had known it would be a change but she did not know it would be such a drastic one. For all the similarities between Pennsylvania and Tejas they might as well be in another world. Sighing she dipped her pen and began again.

We next had the pleasure of joining the mayor and his gracious wife for supper at their home. The food served was excellent—venison loin with wild onions, fresh stewed tomatoes and browned biscuits with wild bee honey. For dessert we had a delicious peach pie. Everything was really quite good!

One negative thing: It was somewhat of a shock to me to see the flag of the Mexican republic flying in the alcalde's yard. There are so many Americans here it is easy to forget that we are in a foreign country. I must admit . . . not seeing Old Glory will definitely take some getting used to.

After our lunch we proceeded straight to our new home. The alcalde's house might be the most substantial in Sweet Home, but I much prefer ours which is on the east end of town and which was formerly owned by the Augustus Katy family. (Although Mr. Cooper did not so state, I suspect that the family must have fallen prey to some disease else why did they leave their furniture and utensils . . . indeed even some of their clothes!)

Our cabin is made of logs and consists of three rooms, one large one with two smaller ones off either end. In the center is a fireplace made of river rocks and it is there where much of the cooking is done. Primitive but really quite practical. Two old sycamores shelter the house from the sun and wind, and peach, plum and pecan trees are growing within a few feet of the back door.

It had started to rain, bringing a cold wind and a much lower temperature. She rose and added another log to the fire then pushed the heavy door closed. Sitting again, she reread her last lines.

Everyone else has retired early. Poor Nona and Mittie were asleep on their feet and, though I know he would never admit it, so was our young teamster.

Poor Charley Walters. Still so distrustful of them. Or perhaps anyone, and probably with good reason. One could only imagine what he had been through. Emma and Annie longed to ask him about his life but neither could bring themselves to do so. Taciturn as he was proving to be, they would probably never know more than they knew now.

Young Charley has been a little less silent since we departed Philadelphia and he was a godsend with the team and heavy work, but I fear he still carries resentments about the life he was forced to lead since his parents died and left him alone and homeless. I have great hopes that he will open up once he starts to attend school and begins to lead a more ordinary life.

Once again she set down her pen; this time to reflect on the weeks just preceding their departure.

They had found their teamster, young Charley Walters, simply by telling the hansom driver to stop beside a ragtag band of young men standing on the corner of Fourth and Chestnut, one of the most disreputable parts of Philadelphia. Emma—who had the voice of a stentor—called out that she needed a teamster to help drive her party to Tejas. Once there, she said that she would guarantee the teamster employment either by hiring him herself or by seeing that he secured a position elsewhere. They would, she said, travel by boat to New Orleans then follow the path of Jean Lafitte and his pirates from New Orleans to Matagorda Bay. From there they would proceed by wagon to the town of Sweet Home, and it was for that leg of their journey that they required a teamster's services.

Any candidate for the job, she added, must be strong, able and at least fifteen years of age. Naturally, he must be capable of handling a team of oxen or mules.

Nobody moved for a long minute and Annie could quite imagine what was running through those young minds. Who are these two women and what is their diabolical scheme?

"Well," cried Emma. "Step up!"

Finally, a tall thin boy with a ravaged face came forward. "Who are you?" Emma asked. After the boy replied that his name was Charley Walters, Emma asked him where his parents were and he replied, "In the Valley Forge Cemetery."

"Oh," said Emma, uncharacteristically chastened. She paused momentarily and glanced at Annie, but then she stiffened her spine and continued. "Have you any other kin, Charley Walters?" When the boy shook his head, she asked him if he could handle a team and before he could reply she cautioned him against lying . . . "It's not the sort of thing that a person can fake, you know." Still nothing. "Well, can you or can you not handle a team?"

Then, as Emma would later recount on many occasions and for many people, there was a nod of the boy's head and . . . "another poor soul was lifted out of poverty and into gainful employment in a new land." (Emma read Shakespeare on a regular basis and her speech could be quite dramatic . . . should the occasion warrant.)

Abel had been fit to be tied and had rattled off a litany of impediments against their hiring "some unknown urchin off the streets of Philadelphia." What if he killed them all in their sleep? "But," Emma replied, "anyone they hired in St. Louis might do the same." To that Abel said that at least the St. Louis teamster would come recommended. "By whom?" his stepmother countered. "We know no one in St. Louis. Perhaps the person we would hire there would be even worse, a complete incompetent. This way at least we get to see if young Charley will suit us before we leave."

"And if he does not, then what?"

"Why, I will fire him forthwith, of course."

"Oh, mother," Abel's voice rang with exasperation. "You haven't fired anything other than your curl maker in your entire life!"

Even Annie and Abel had had heated words over it, but of course in the end the two females "ganged up" on him and Abel was forced to relent.

Emma and Annie often congratulated themselves during the trip. Charley had performed every duty they had asked of him, in a most exemplary fashion.

But in spite of five weeks of constant companionship they now knew exactly as much about Charley Walters as they did on the day they first met.

Annie looked over at the little alcove where he slept like a flung rag. Sticking out of the blanket were size-twelve feet, clad in the white yarn socks that Emma had made during her shipboard confinement. Aside from his attitude, Charley's only other defect was blocked nasal passages. His snore could rattle closed shutters like a hard wind. And did.

Emma had become quite fond of him, but Annie wasn't surprised about that. Emma Fuller adopted people for an occupation. Abel, her stepson, then Annie, then the orphaned sisters Nona and Mittie Williford and now finally, young Charley Walters.

Physically the three youngsters had made the trip in fine shape, but their surrogate mother had not. About two weeks out of Philadelphia Emma began to tire easily and could not gather enough energy to leave her cabin. Annie had hoped that her lethargy was due to sea sickness and would pass once she set her feet on terra firma, but she still did not seem to be herself. Emma was in her fifties but until lately she had always been quite robust.

Annie stepped into the other room to check on her and found everyone sleeping soundly. The two sisters, Nona and Mittie, lay mere inches apart which was as they preferred to be when awake as well. Annie then checked Emma and found that she was not doing such a bad job of snoring herself.

Emma Fuller was her mother's cousin. When Annie was

three, her mother and older brother both died of influenza and when she was eight her father died of a heart ailment. That was when Emma brought Annie to live with her in south Philadelphia. At that time the only other inhabitant of the old brownstone was Emma's stepson, Abel O'Neal who was two years older than Annie.

It was only natural that Annie and Abel should become friends, and as they passed out of childhood, they became even more than that. Annie thought Abel was the most admirable person in the world and Abel thought the same about Annie. What one could not do, the other one could. What one felt, so did the other. It was inevitable that they should want to remain together as adults; hence, they decided to marry.

She adjusted Emma's bedcovers. Soon Emma and she would be even more closely related and frankly, Annie couldn't wish for a finer mother-in-law. Generous to a fault and the kindest person she knew, Emma Fuller had been canonized in Annie's young mind long ago. If ever she would question her opinion, she had only to look at Nona and Mittie to justify her veneration.

One day while attending First Presbyterian Church their minister had asked if anyone would be willing to share their home with two children of recently deceased parishioners. The church sponsored an orphanage but, like most religious institutions, it preferred to place such unfortunates in a Christian home if possible.

The minister had barely finished his sentence when Emma stood. Abel and Annie did not realize what she had done until they noticed all the parishioners who were turned in their seats, smiling and nodding encouragement at them.

Just that fast their family had grown to encompass Nona and Mittie too. Actually, the little orphaned sisters were the reason why they had come to Tejas to begin with.

For no reason that any physician could see, Nona was frail. Various nostrums and remedies were tried but she still sickened easily. Their family physician suggested a drier climate and one night the idea came to one of them (though they never could precisely remember who had it first): Why not go West?

Plastered all over the city were placards and bulletins extolling the territory west of the Sabine and though they had never considered it before, they decided they should at least look into it. Accordingly Emma, Abel and Annie went to Carpenter's Hall to hear a cartographer's lecture on Tejas. Annie and Emma thought it sounded too good to be true, the proverbial land of milk and honey, but Abel was intrigued. The idea had taken root and he soon became convinced that their future and fortune lay in Tejas.

He argued that every other person in Philadelphia was a lawyer but down there lawyers were certain to be as scarce as hen's teeth.

Not only was Nona's health bound to improve, but they would all prosper and thrive.

Further, they would be a part of a grand new adventure: the settling of one of the last frontiers.

No one could be more persuasive than Abel when he set his mind to something and before they knew it, they had agreed to everything. Through the Normal school she was attending, Annie responded to an inquiry about a teaching position and subsequently corresponded with the mayor of Sweet Home, one Lloyd Cooper. Unbelievably he responded favorably to her application!

She knew that she was fortunate to even be considered for the job. Most towns hesitate to hire women teachers because they don't think a woman is capable of punishing the larger children properly. (She preferred forms of punishment other than corporal anyway but did not see the need to tell Mr. Cooper that.)

Mr. Cooper wrote that . . . *two years of good service will merit a twenty-five cent raise in pay. You must, however, have excellent moral character and should you marry, you will be required to resign your post at once . . .*

While it was true that she and Abel intended to be married as soon as he got to Tejas she harbored the secret hope that by the time he arrived, she would have proved herself so indispensable to the school that they would insist on bending the rules on her behalf. Of course she knew that as soon as she found herself with child it would mean immediate dismissal whether she was indispensable or not. But to her thinking, a baby would more than compensate her for losing her job.

Originally they had planned to relocate en masse but when Nona sickened again, Emma and Annie decided to take the girls and leave as soon as the child was well enough to travel. Abel would follow in six months, when he finished his preceptorship and could arrive in the new land ready to become a practicing lawyer.

Six months without Abel. To Annie, it would seem like six years. She paused to picture him, a tall, straight-standing man with sandy, ever windblown hair and wise blue eyes.

She loved his eyes. She told him they were what made him look like a lawyer.

"Is it the crinkles?"

"Perhaps," she had replied.

"Good, it's working then."

"What is?"

"Taping my eyelids at night. I've been at it for years, striving for just that right legal look."

She smiled now, recalling his sunny good humor. Sometimes she thought that was what she liked best about him but, in actuality, he possessed every trait she esteemed in a man, or in a mate. He was kind and thoughtful, well read and a stimulating conversationalist, hardworking and very diligent.

And he was also terribly smart! He had graduated first in his class both from the William Penn Charter School and the City College of Philadelphia, which some were already calling the University of Pennsylvania. Add to all that his easygoing nature and his true love of children and he was, in a word, perfect!

And oh, how dear he was to her! With a rush of emotion, she returned to her letter.

Dear Abel, you were so right about Tejas! It is truly beautiful here, and I know you will love it. But you must see it for yourself, for I simply cannot do it justice in a letter. All I can

say is that so far all that they told us about it has been true:
indeed, sky is higher and the woods denser and more fragrant
and the animals more plentiful and the men much larger!

Immediately she scratched out the last five words. Then she
stared at the paper in shock, only she did not see inkblots or
scratched-out words or entire sentences covered with curly
waves. She saw the fluid line of a man's lanky body and the
way it had blended with his horse so that the two had seemed
one. *Don't do nothin' 'till I get back.* She heard the words
again as clearly as she had heard them from his own lips.

She shook her head and knuckled her eyes. She must be
more tired than she thought. She kept drifting into a sort of
dazed state, somewhere between awake and asleep. Somewhere
full of vivid visions.

Opening her eyes brought her letter into sight. It was a
mess! Worse than a child would do. She rubbed her head in a
subconscious effort to clear it. Why did that man continue
to plague her? Was it merely that most common—and most
dangerous human failing—fascination with the unusual?

Certainly he was unusual, but frankly she was beginning to
worry about herself, that she would find someone of that ilk
so interesting. Whether the man had been within his legal rights
or not, he was still a calm killer of men. She *would* get a grip
on herself and think no more about either the incident or the
man. Really!

Hastily, she began to write again: *I must close if I hope to*
get this letter posted tomorrow—I have been told that the mail
rider only comes twice a week. Sorry about this sloppy writing.
I must be more tired than I thought!

She chewed on the end of the quill and stared at the paper,
hoping for an inspirational closing. She would like to write
something stirring and impassioned, maybe even something
daring! But after some moments of frustration, she gave up.
She was, unfortunately, an extremely self-possessed person.
Even as a child she had been dispassionate and reserved. She
doubted if she could change that part of her now. Actually, she
wasn't sure that she wanted to try.

Rather laconically she signed off with *Dear Abel, I pray for your well being and I am counting the days until your arrival, As always, Annie.*

The patter of rain drew her. She rose to stand in the doorway and look outside. Drawing a deep breath she smelled grass and wet earth. She folded her arms and leaned against the jamb. Might as well stay up now. It's almost easier to function with no sleep than it is after an hour or two.

Shortly before daybreak the rain moved off to the north and in the east a mother-of-pearl dawn broke, lighting some hills in the distance so that they looked like spiny backbones against the sky.

Suddenly the woods were full of life. Thrushes called, a woodpecker tapped and a mockingbird mocked a jay. Then in one of the sycamores a bluebird commenced singing a song so solemn that it almost sounded holy.

It was all so moving. The vivid dawn. The painted hills and the rousing birdsong. It probably would have brought her great peace . . . if not for one niggling thought: Where on earth had he been going at such an ungodly hour?

The rain followed the rangers all that day and all the next, but they rode on, wet to the bone, grim-faced and—aside from the sucking sound hooves make in mud—mostly silent.

Any visible sign of the raiders had been washed away long ago but He-Coon said he knew where they were headed. Since the Tonkawa had come through for them before, Jack decided to give it one more day.

No one, least of all Jack Dare, had forgotten about the farmer's wife. To call off the pursuit now would condemn her either to death or to the life of a slave. Those that they had liberated from that life had told them that death was preferable.

So the troop rode on, tired and soaked to the bone, peering owlishly into a world that was like a black blanket over their heads.

On the third day the rain quit and sure enough, He-Coon cut

the Indians' sign. At dusk that night the Tonkawa said he estimated that raiders were camped within three miles of them and Jack sent him ahead to scout it out.

Jack and the rest of the men stepped off their horses to adjust their vitals. Some of the men had goatskins of water or wooden canteens which were shared with those who had jugs of whiskey. Fearing that they might signal their presence, they refrained from smoking tobacco, but most chewed and all spent a considerable amount of time going over their weapons.

When He-Coon returned, Jack sat on his heels, as did the Indian, to talk things over. Familiar with this routine, the rest of the men stood around and patiently awaited their instructions.

Jack offered He-Coon a twist of tobacco which he accepted and tucked into his cheek. Then Jack waited until he had it worked into the shape he wanted.

The Tonkawa was the deep brown of old saddle leather with flat black eyes and a deadpan expression. He wore three earrings in his right ear and hanging on his hairless chest were two necklaces, one that was made of beads and claws and another that was made of shells, bones and feathers. A ribbon of tattooed dots banded his forehead, a pattern that was repeated on his bare chest just above his heart.

Unless it was bitterly cold, he never wore more than bison-hide moccasins and a long breech cloth.

Nobody knew much about him. In the beginning some of the men had asked him a few questions about himself—more to make conversation than to pry—but the Indian had responded with a shrug and a grunt. Afraid he would take offense and wander away, nobody had pressed him further. Against any Indian tribe, He-Coon was the most impersonal and efficient tracker any of them had ever seen. But if their quarry was the Comanche then he really put his heart into his work. At times more heart than the rangers wanted.

They once came on a remote spot and saw a body tucked into the crotch of a tree, which was a favorite form of burial for the Comanche. Scattered at the base of the tree were the bones of two horses that had been killed when their owner died. Another Comanche custom. With an eerie light in his eyes, He-Coon immediately poked the body down with a long stick and unwrapped the blanket. The corpse was that of a fairly young brave, tied with his legs drawn up and his head down on his knees. With a glee that no white man could understand the Tonkawa set about dismembering the corpse until there was nothing recognizable left.

It was a strange feeling, riding away from that desecration. Nobody had wanted him to do it but nobody had wanted to stop him either.

"Are the raiders Kiowa?" asked Jack.

"Comanche," replied He-Coon, and came as close as he ever did to smiling.

"Too bad," muttered Blue who since his brothers' death had preferred killing Kiowas over any other tribe.

As Jack stood he was thinking, He-Coon and Blue. Now there's a pair to draw to. "All right, boys. As usual, there'll be a guaranteed pay raise to any man killed."

Most of the men snickered. He always said that. They always snickered.

Then he added, "Don't forget the woman."

Though he reminded them about the captive he knew full well that a stray bullet from one of their guns would be the least of the woman's worries. Nine times out of ten the Indians would kill a captive as soon as they realized that the camp was coming under attack.

"White woman not alive," He-Coon said.

"You saw her body?"

"No."

"Then how do you know?"

He-Coon shrugged. "Know. White woman not alive."

Unfortunately, he was right. But then, neither were her killers when that night was over.

Chapter 6

The following Monday dawned hot and muggy, and by nine o'clock the sun was already a searing orb in the cloudless sky. Anxious to get the trip to town out of the way before it got worse, Goldie Dare hitched the team early and then started loading the wagon. From his work shed he collected a flat piece of hard walnut, a piece of sugar maple and some hickory samples. He added a few tools and a notched stick for measuring. Then, almost as an afterthought, he brought out one of the two benches that he had made for the house and roped it down on the wagon's flatbed. It was a halved log—split lengthwise—with six hand-hewed legs.

The last thing he did was get two twisted garlands from the tack room and toss them over the mules' heads. Markie had made them from indigo weed, which helped to keep the flies away.

He was about ready to pull out when his elder brother came around the side of the cabin leading his horse. Goldie watched him tie the horse on back and climb up on the leaf sprung seat and then fold his arms and brace one boot on the horizontal crossbar. All without saying a word.

Goldie climbed on the wagon seat too, which protested their combined weight with a mighty squeak. He thumbed up his hat and took a hard look at his brother, but Jack had found something especially interesting about the off mule's ass. So Goldie tugged his hat back into position and unwrapped the reins from the whipstock and with a flick of his wrist, they were on their way, rattling down the road that led to Sweet Home.

A half mile from the house Jack's soft tuneless whistle joined the jingle of bit chains and the clop of the mules' hooves, and still neither man said a word.

The two-rut lane threaded through tough little scrub oaks then came out into the open where the sun was a hot blinding yellow and well settled on the treetops by then. Here they would follow the creek a ways, straddling a tufted row of scraggly but determined grass.

Goldie liked the ride into town. Seemed there was always something new to see, especially after a good rain. This time there were the little yellowy wildflowers that he had always thought were too frail-looking to fit the land. Flitting among them were small white butterflies, flying low to the ground as if they were trying to get out of the glare.

Aside from his brother's mindless whistle there were few sounds to disturb the quiet: a flock of quail that had whistled and taken flight as the wagon rattled under a ragged elm; an angry prairie dog that'd popped out of its hole to chatter at them.

As they neared town there were more farms but they were still few and far between. They passed a woman wearing a man's hat and working a field with a scythe and then further on, a man with a sack of seeds following a boy who was making holes in the dirt with a stick. They were newcomers named Green who had a half finished cabin down the road. Both Dares lifted their hats when the man turned toward them and waved.

The dusty stale heat had gathered force by the time they passed through town. It was obvious that the townspeople were saving themselves, for there were very few of them on the streets. Earl Durrell waved at them as he carried water to a trough in the livery corral and Bowie Garlock stopped sweeping the walk in front of his store in order to do the same. Then they were beyond the town and heading up the schoolhouse road.

Jack's whistle petered out as soon as the schoolhouse hove into sight. One look at him told Goldie why. It's near impossible to whistle through your bottom teeth when you are grinning like a 'gator. Jack then said the first words of the day, a muttered, "There it is!"

"I recognized it."

Goldie spoke tartly and with damn good reason! He sure knew the damn school when he saw it. Hadn't he spent over a week working on that damn roof? Boiling like coffee on a too-hot fire while Jack and Blue were out gallivanting around the countryside?

As he looked at it, he had to admit, it did sit on an awfully pretty spot and it was a damn fine-looking building—even if he did say so himself.

The raw sawn schoolhouse had been positioned on a freshly cleared hillock that faced the town, so that its people could look up and see it there and think of their kids inside. In back there was a long creekside meadow that dipped and rolled between wooded land until it reached the water and in front there was a ring of old oak trees that had been left for shade. It was there, in the stubbled yard, that the schoolteacher and the mayor of Sweet Home stood.

"Goodgod, Goldie! Look at that girl!"

Goldie looked, but at this distance all he could see was a shapely female with her hands clasped in front of her.

Well, he could see a bit more than that, namely that she had an abundance of black hair coiled on the back of her head and great tits.

Unfortunately, he said so and the next thing he knew he was on his hind end, looking up at Jack who was glaring down at him from the wagon seat. From where it ached Goldie could tell that Jack had hit him with his left. Caught him just under his ear and rolled him right out of the wagon.

"What t'hell was that for?"

"You! Lookin' at her chest like that. Damn you, get up from there an' I'll give you another!"

"Hell, you ain't never looked at a woman's face first in your en-tire life."

"That ain't the point."

"What is then?"

"I . . . ain't sure."

Goldie stood there, fists clenched and lips in a mad-dog roll, but Jack's anger was gone, replaced by an expression that Goldie had never seen before. Warily, Goldie climbed back into the wagon and then leaned in to take a closer look. "Well, you're either thinkin' for the first time in your life or you got the piles. Which is it?"

"I ain't sure."

"What the hell's wrong with you lately?"

"I ain't sure about that neither."

"Well, somethin' has afflicted you."

Dolefully. "I know." He finally looked at his brother. "Here . . . let me . . ." He made an attempt to brush off the back of Goldie's shirt but got his hand slapped away. "Goldie, honest! Before I knew what hit me, I'd hit you. Goldie!" Now he'd grabbed his arm which Goldie shook off. He edged over on the seat.

"Goldie, you wanna know somethin' strange?"

"I know all the strange I need."

"I mean it, Goldie. This is something really strange."

"Whut, damnit?" Goldie kept one eye on his brother while he worked his jaw with his hand. It didn't feel busted.

"I looked at her face first." Jack hadn't realized that before, but it was true.

It was true! Hell, that ought to mean something!

"An' then you looked at her chest."

"Well, course I did. What d'you think?"

They both laughed. Goldie punched Jack and Jack punched

him back. Goldie tried to kick Jack in the nuts, but Jack blocked it and grabbed Goldie's leg and tried to lever him out of the wagon onto his head. He was failing in that, so Goldie grabbed Jack's head in a hammerlock and tried to rip off his nose but Jack bit Goldie under the arm 'till he yelped and let go at which time Jack grabbed Goldie's ear and would've succeeded in twisting it off if Goldie hadn't stomped his toes hard and gave Jack a chopping blow to the back of the neck. Goldie moved in for the kill but Jack head butted Goldie and said things so incredibly foul that Goldie started laughing.

Some of the Dares were big laughers. They'd throw back their heads and squinch their eyes closed. Markie was one. Visshus had been one. Goldie was one. It had been Jack's intention to really lay Goidie out but then he got started laughing too and neither could quit.

They kept it up for a while then still chuckling, they retrieved their hats and settled back, thoroughly woolragged. Their hair was off in all directions but hell, it never would do right anyway. Their faces were blotchy under their tans. Jack had a mouse on his cheekbone. Goldie had a loose tooth on the right. But they grinned at each other, happy as two boardinghouse puppies. Hell, it'd been a long time since they'd had such a satisfying little tussle. As Goldie punched a dent out of his crown, Jack brushed a boot heel off his brim and said, "Hey, we better go. They're standing yonder looking at us like we're a couple crazies."

Goldie looked with the eye that was not puffed and saw that it was true. The little schoolmarm and Cooper stood staring at them with slack jaws and shocked eyes.

"All right. Try not to act like a damn idjet."

"Me? If there's an idjet in this wagon it ain't named Goldie."

Jack thought about popping him another one and decided against it. Instead he tried to slick down his hair . . . which stuck straight out under his hat . . . and practiced holding his arm so the ripped-out sleeve didn't show.

Annie was trying not to look stunned, but she was. The one man had flown out of the wagon and landed square on his

head! He did a somersault and ended up like an overturned
turtle! But instead of being gravely injured—which he certainly
had every right to be—he shook himself like a big bear and
climbed back on board. What followed appeared to be a death
fight confined to the seat of the wagon. Then, it suddenly ended
and now in they rode, two big grins that looked like white
gashes across their faces.

Which gave her another reason to be shocked. She had hardly
recognized the knife wielder, not only because he had shaved
and cut his hair to a nearly respectable length but because of
what that grin was doing to his face, softening the harsh planes
and lightening his eyes and smoothing his brow. Why, in overall
appearance that simple smile had made him look . . . almost
presentable!

"Hello, boys," called the mayor as they drove up. When
they stepped down and came forward, Cooper asked Goldie if
he was all right.

"Yeah. Why?"

"We saw you fall outa the wagon back there."

"A bump . . ."

"A bee . . ."

Both men had spoken at once. They looked at each other
and the one said, "He had a bee on him and I, uh, tried to, uh,
you know, knock it off."

My God! thought Annie and sent her eyes on a nervous
circle around her head.

"Huh!" said Cooper. "Well . . . Miss Mapes, meet Mr. Dare.
Mr. Dare, this our new teacher, Miss Annie Mapes."

He lifted his hat which looked like it'd had a previous life
as a pancake. "Call me, Goldie, ma'am." Then he indicated the
knife wielder. "An' this here's my helper, Abner Apazootus. He
carries my wood samples for me but he ain't to be trusted with
sharp things hisself. Poor fella!" Goldie shook his head sadly.
"I musta tole him a hunnerd times not to run with that axe!
Caught him square betwixt the eyes. Now he just grins like
that. All the time. Looks like a harebrained idjet, don't he?"

She looked slant-eyed at Goldie. "Abner . . . ?"

"Apazootus."

"No."

"No?"

"I don't think so. You see, I have already had the . . . pleasure of meeting this . . . gentleman and I already know that he is Mr. Jack Dare."

"No, ma'am." Goldie shook his head and tapped his barrel chest. "I'm Jack Dare. "

"What?" She looked from one to the other. They both nodded.

"Oh, no!" said Cooper with a hand in the air. "Don't let them get started with that!"

"Get started with what? What do you mean?"

"They love to get strangers going with that name business."

"I'm afraid I don't understand."

"They're all Jack Dare."

"All who? . . . whom, um, whomst?"

"All the Dares."

She looked from one brother to the other. "You are all named Jack?"

"Well, all the males. Right, boys?"

"That's right," said Goldie. "Our maw's idea of a little joke."

"I see," said Annie, which was the farthest thing from the truth. She wrestled with that for awhile . . . they were all named Jack? A local custom? Lack of imagination? Monogramming made easy?

She decided to deal with it later. What matters, she thought smugly, is that I had the man correctly pegged. I *knew* he was no cabinetmaker!

Goldie looked at his brother. He'd quit grinning only now he was looking at the girl with the sort of heat Goldie'd only seen in a whorehouse.

"Well" Lloyd Cooper consulted his stemwinder. "Perhaps we better get started. "

"Good idea," said Annie and as if herded, everyone headed toward the school.

Obviously the structure had been built by oversized men because entry could only be gained by a thigh-stretching leap onto a sawed hickory log that served as a step. She noticed, however, that she and Mr. Cooper were the only ones who had any problem with mounting the step.

Inside the two Dares clumped around, looking at one thing or another and making her little schoolhouse into a shrunken and hollow thing. She looked around and tried to see it with their eyes but that wasn't easy because . . . well, she loved it.

It was a plain, one-room building with four windows and one door. There were wooden pegs on its rough-sawed walls, a puncheon floor, and exposed beams overhead. Although presently unpainted, the place, as Lloyd Cooper had told Annie, would be calcimined as soon as the materials arrived to do so. At the time she had made an appreciative reply, but she was really quite happy with it as it was—woodsy and quaint-looking.

The only piece of furniture acquired so far sat in a corner, a three-legged chest on which there was a washbasin and upturned pitcher. No door covered the opening cut for that purpose nor were there any window coverings yet.

Earlier Annie had looked at the windows and thought cheese-cloth would be nice to keep out the bugs. The Dare brothers were looking at the same openings and thinking wood, thick and slotted, to keep the Indians out.

Lloyd Cooper deferred to her, so Annie began. "As far as furniture goes Mr. Cooper and I have come to an agreement about what I think we need and what Mr. Cooper says we can afford."

She waited, smiling and Goldie looked at Jack with eyes that asked: Was that supposed to be a joke?

She gave a little shrug and pulled a slip of paper from her pocket. Her eyes flitted from Goldie to Jack then back to her paper.

The cabinetmaker's eyes were like melted chocolate on a white cake. The knife wielder's were coal black, squinted by sun and distance and unsettling . . . very unsettling.

"We only want to order the bare minimum to get started."

"Uh-huh." Goldie folded his arms. "Well, that's understandable. What were you thinkin'?"

"Well, most schools nail narrow tables to the walls and put the students on benches that face them. Which means that the students have their backs to the teacher. Originally it was thought they would be less distracted that way but . . ." She glanced up and stopped. Both Dares had wrinkled foreheads and blank looks and she realized that she was wasting her time. Neither man had ever set foot in a schoolhouse before. ". . . I see the benches nailed to these three walls and . . ."

As she walked across the room, Jack went walleyed trying to keep one eye on the schoolmarm and one on Goldie. He supposed she had to lift her arm to point, but did she have to hold her breasts like that when she did it?

". . . and the tables placed in front of them. My desk would be here, in the center. That way, I can see all the students and all the students can see me."

Lucky kids, thought Jack.

"Lucky kids," said Goldie and gave her an I-meant-nothing-disrespectful smile. She blushed and gave him a small smile back.

"Thank you."

Jack fumed and Goldie knew it. In fact, it made his day.

"So . . . we will need three tables as long as these walls, as well as three benches of corresponding length. Then we'll also need two straight chairs and a desk for me that is nice and wide." She looked at Goldie. "Would you like a piece of paper?"

"What for?"

"To make . . . for making notes?"

"Nuh-uh. I got every precious word right here." He tapped his temple and Jack made a disgusting noise with his nose.

"One question, ma'am."

"Yes?"

"You think you're gonna want those benches with backs? Or without?"

"Without, I think. With the tables turned that way the children can rest their backs against the wall."

"Sharp as mustard," Goldie said. "No wonder you're a teacher!"

"Why, thank you!"

Jack was really haired up now and Goldie had to lay a finger across his grin. "Did you see that bench out there on the flatbed?"

"Yes, I did. Three more exactly like that one would be perfect."

"Good!"

"Fine!"

"Well, that's it then," said Cooper.

"Except for delivery."

"Oh, yes. We would need everything no later than the first of the month. Can you manage that?"

"Hm." Goldie said again. There'd be no problem having everything made by then. He could probably deliver the entire order in a week or less. What he was mulling over now was how much to ask. He never knew what value to place on his things. Ten dollars was too low. Was fifteen too high?

The *alcalde* saved him. "We have thirty dollars allotted for furniture."

"That's funny. That's the exact figure I had in mind."

"Well, then. Appears we're all set."

"Yep. Walnut all right?"

"Fine."

Goldie glanced around. "Say where's your stove?"

"Never fear," said the mayor. "The new Franklin will be along in plenty of time for winter."

Annie commented that it was hard to think about it being cold enough to require a fire, especially when it was so hot.

Cooper smiled. "That may be but you'll be glad of a fire come January."

Then Goldie asked, "What're you gonna do about stove wood?"

Cooper replied to that. "Come fall each family will be asked
to bring one wagonload per child."

Three loads of wood! And that was in addition to their normal
needs. Goldie rolled his eyes at Jack but Jack was looking at
the teacher who was red-faced and looking at her shoe.

Goldie and Lloyd Cooper were talking about wood but Annie
was hearing the uncomfortable silence that ran beneath their
conversation.

She had become terribly aware of Jack Dare's relentless
regard and was beginning to feel awkward and flustered by it.
He had hardly said a word but he had not taken his eyes off
her. They were very discomforting eyes. Predatory and all-
seeing.

She had not intended to look directly at him again but of
course, she did. Now he was giving her a little half smile,
leaning against the wall with his arms folded and his ankles
crossed, as if he were supporting the building with his shoulder.

Which of course he could. If he so desired . . .

Impassive-faced, she directed her attention elsewhere, to the
open doorway where she could see the Dare mules munching
on the patchy grass under one of the trees.

This is the best way to handle someone like him. Even a
dull-witted man could not miss the fact that he was being
pointedly ignored.

A small bird hopped close enough to cause one of the mules
to lift his head. When the bird kept coming the mule snapped
at it and the bird flew right between his ears, startling the mule
so that he splayed his legs like he'd just hit ice.

She covered her mouth with her hand but not in time to
silence an unsophisticated, un-schoolmarm-like giggle. She
glanced around to see if the others had heard and caught Jack
Dare looking at her chest!

Her color rose and so did her hackles. Rude crude lout! At
the first opportunity she intended to tell him exactly what she
thought of him. Staring at her, grinning at her, throwing her
that knowing look. Yes, indeed she would! She did not like
the man and never would. Not ever. And she would not hesitate

to tell him so. In no uncertain terms. Just as soon as her throat no longer felt like she had swallowed a cotton ball.

Meanwhile Jack was deciding that he liked everything about Miss Annie Mapes. Her pride, her womanly ways, her beautiful face and fine figure—oh, yeah. Everything. Hell, he even liked her prickly nature.

"Well, then," said Cooper. "I guess I'll head on back." Cooper waited a minute, but no one said anything about going with him. "Miss Mapes?"

Belatedly she realized the mayor was leaving and had offered her a ride. "No, thank you, Mr. Cooper. I have a bit more to do here."

So the mayor left but the Dares stayed. Why? She lifted her eyebrows and looked at them. They looked back. Outside some crows were making a terrible racket. Inside there was dead quiet. Did they need a nudge? She offered Goldie her hand and said, "Thank you, Mr. Dare. I look forward to seeing you again in a few weeks."

Imagine that! he thought. Shaking hands like a man! But when he took her hand and shook it he felt it tremble and thought: Why, she's nervous as a bastard at a family reunion.

She turned then and offered her hand to Jack. "And good day to you as well, Mr. Dare." After a moment's pause Jack accepted her hand, but he didn't shake it. Instead he held it and looked at it and thought how small and fine it was! And white as a curd.

Annie was also looking at their hands. She saw the contrast in the color of their skin, how long and callused his fingers were and how wide and thick his palm. And then that her hand had been laying in his for a long, long time. She jerked it back and held it at her waist. "Well . . ."

Jack snicked tinder on flint and lit his pipe. He knew that she felt the pull between them, but he wondered if she recognized it for what it was. *Suppose there's only one way to find out.* Between draws on his pipe he said, "Goldie . . ."

"Yeah?"

"Wait in the wagon."

"Awright."

Before she could register a thought—much less an objection—Goldie Dare abruptly walked outside, strode to the wagon and tossed his things in back. She watched him lay his armpits on the wagon sideboard and fold his hands under his chin. His back was to her and his brother, who was also a murdering knife wielder. A voice behind her said, "Well, now." She turned and stared up at him with wide and very wary eyes. "Miss Annie Mapes."

"Yes? Mr. Jack Dare." He was giving her that easy smile again, which she did not return because she was looking at a deep dimple that indented his right cheek and then at his teeth, which were shark white, large and none too straight. One was chipped. On the bottom, left side.

"So."

"So."

"Guess you been askin' around about me."

"Certainly not!" She could feel red points rising on her cheeks like two hot boils.

"You asked Cooper my name."

She gave a chuckle that sounded strangled. "You misunderstand. I asked the cabinetmaker's name."

"Same difference."

"Well, I didn't know that." She found the wall at her back and pressed her clammy palms to it. How had she gotten over here? How had he gotten over her? Square white teeth grinned down at her and her heart did crazy leaps.

"And when he told you the woodworker's name you thought it was me."

"No, not until you came by the house that night."

"Then you were glad. 'Cause you'd get to see me again."

"Certainly not!"

"Hm!"

Jack couldn't be more pleased. He interested her, but then, that wasn't surprising. He was used to being appealing to women.

"But now . . ." He walked one way. He walked the other.
". . . now you do."

"Do what?"

"Know which Dare I am."

"Now I do."

"So. Anythin' you'd like to know about me?"

Sarcastically. "Well, let me think." She put one finger to
her cheek and looked up at the ceiling. "No, can't think of a
thing."

"Liar!" he said and walked closer. Too close. He put one
palm on the wall behind her. "Tell you what, Miss Annie
Mapes." With his other hand he took the sleeve of her dress
between thumb and finger and rubbed it and turned her nipples
into hard, tight nubs.

"Why don't you ask me about me?"

"Why should I?"

"Why not? I promise that I'll tell you everythin' I want you
to know."

If she hadn't stepped aside she thought he might have taken
her in his arms. "And what if I say that I know all I care to
know about you? Mr. Dare."

"I'd say you were fibbin', Miss Mapes."

"And then I would say that you have overstepped your
bounds! Which you most certainly have. Good day, Mr. Dare!"

Jack looked at her back which was stiff as stove wood and
chewed on his lip. Now he'd done it. He'd figured that a little
lighthearted teasing would loosen her up. Maybe make her less
. . . fearful? Skittish? Whatever she was. Instead he'd made her
madder'n hell. He flip-flopped over what to say next. Finally,
he decided he'd simply say that he'd meant no disrespect.
"Miss Mapes, I . . . uh, ma'am?"

Apparently he would not get a chance to say anything. She
was acting like he didn't exist.

She finally heard him move toward the door. After a quick
look over her shoulder she let out a relieved sigh and collapsed
against the wall. She had to steady herself. She was as breathless
as if she had been running. What on earth was the matter with

that man? Had he been born that way? Was he one of those people who intentionally set out to put others on their ear? Or had he been standing too long in the sun?

She did not go to the door until the sounds of their departure had grown faint but the image of his smile remained with her long after the wagon had disappeared from view.

Riding back, Goldie glanced at his brother then back at the road. "Looked t'me like you were pretty taken with the schoolmarm."

"You blame me?"

"Hell, no! I'da gone to school myself if I'd known that's what the teachers looked like."

"I think I'll marry her."

"Yeah?"

"Yeah."

"Kinda sudden, ain't it?"

"I don't know. Comes a time when a fella gets tired of hellin' around. A man can't be a fiddlefoot all his life."

"Huh!" They rode a ways in silence, then, "Got any idea when?"

Jack shrugged. "Soon as she's ready. Girls need time."

"Yeah. Gettin' their dress ready an' all."

"Awhell, far as I'm concerned, she could wear the one she had on. You see that pretty dress she had on?"

"Uh, yeah." Goldie tried and failed to picture her dress. "That's what I thought when I first saw it. My, ain't that a pretty dress!" His brother gave him a cuff on the shoulder. "So then when'll you be leavin' for the mountains?"

"What mountains?"

The ensuing masculine laughter was loud enough to jolt the mules into a trot.

Annie watched the road until the snarls of smoky dust settled. She was so frustrated she could . . . spit. She knew she had not convinced him that she wasn't interested in him. Quite the contrary, the idiot thought she was fascinated.

All right. Maybe she was fascinated. But really, why should that be so surprising? The man was completely different from anyone she had ever met before. Why, it would be like seeing an elephant for the first time. Of course a person would be intrigued!

She needed some air. She was getting a headache.

Taking up her hat, she stepped outside, jumped off the log and briskly started walking back to town.

If she read human nature correctly—and she had always been able to do so before—she was quite certain Dare was one of those men who had gotten too much female attention too early in life. It had made him overly aggressive and brash. Picturing his handsome face and dancing eyes she had no doubt he'd had plenty of attention in his later years as well. Well, fine. She knew how to handle him. She would treat him as she would a child with the same disposition: act thoroughly indifferent.

Of course, it worked better if the person was not looming over you like a meat-eating animal. He was most unsettling and she did not like feeling unsettled. Actually, she would be perfectly content to live the rest of her life without ever feeling this way again.

Immediately upon reaching home, she sought a return to sanity by re-reading the letter she had written to Abel earlier. It was light and interesting and struck, she thought thankfully, just the right chord.

It was fortunate that she had composed the letter prior to her encounter with Dare. She doubted her frame of mind would have allowed her to write it now.

It wasn't until she was finished with the letter that she realized she had not set down one word about the human residents of Sweet Home.

Dearest Abel . . .

Well, we've seen no bees the size of strawberries, nor did the broom handle we stuck in the ground sprout leaves . . . but

*we have seen some wonders! A favorite of mine is a wild bird
that can run faster than a dog! I've learned they are called
paisanos or chapparel cocks. One of them (and I have become
convinced that it is the same one) has twice challenged our
wagon on the ride over to the school.*

*Imagine my chagrin when we rounded a corner and almost
ran over the alcalde's wife! The near mishap was entirely my
fault, urging Charley to race it as I did.*

*Another interesting critter is a breed of wild cow with long
horns that stand straight out on either side of its head. Invariably reddish in color, they are remarkably fleet and quite tasty,
(though I have never caught one myself) and I understand that
their fat is highly prized for the making of candles.*

*On a less pleasant note, I was collecting some stove wood
one day and saw a thing that looked like a three inch lobster.
I asked around and was told the lobster is called a scorpion
and that it carries a painful sting which it delivers via its tail.*

*I had no sooner learned those unpleasant facts than Nona and
Mittie unknowingly cornered a bigger and far more dangerous
insect right in our own backyard.*

*Abel, you cannot imagine the size of the spider they found!
(You know how I hate spiders! Remember the one that was on
my skirt in the garden that day? The one you said had died,
no doubt, of pierced eardrums?) I do not exaggerate when I
say that this spider was at least as big as a saucer! It had a
big, black, bloated body covered with thick hair and eight huge
hairy legs. Worst of all, when we attempted to swat it with a
broom, it jumped at us! The result was instant. A stampede for
the house where we corked ourselves in the back door! From
the safety of the window we watched it saunter off unharmed.
God knows where it lives. None of us have been in the backyard
since.*

*Oh, Abel, we all anxiously await your arrival so you can
dispatch these things for us. Of course, that's not the primary
reason I wish you were here. I miss you terribly! (But I must
admit an added benefit of your arrival will be your ridding us
of these most undesirable creatures.)*

That last was underlined three times. She added a fourth. Then she sat for a while, idly tapping the paper with her quill. Finally she walked to the door. The sky was slashed with red and blue and appeared to be moving toward another spectacular sunset. She stood listening to the sweet harmony of the song-birds and wondered why they seemed to put forth their best effort right before they quit for the night. Could it be because there were so many night hunters around that some suspected they might be singing their swan song?

Death seemed closer here in Tejas. Of course, death also occurred in Philadelphia but immersed as they had been in the ordinary routine of living, it had always seemed far removed from them, a disaster that struck others less fortunate than they.

Not so here in Tejas where only the most hearty could expect to survive, and then only if extremely lucky. She imagined that most people here were happy to wake and find that they had made it through another night. Then there were those like Jack Dare—to select a name at random—who relished tempting fate.

He had certainly had a strong grip.

She realizing that she was clasping her hand as he had but instead of stopping herself she closed her eyes and without any effort she heard his slow, easy way of speaking and saw the shine of his hair and the square set of his teeth.

That these images appeared so smoothly and easily was disquieting. Even more disquieting was how readily she had slipped into this newly acquired habit of fanciful musing and dreamy reveries. Was she beginning to welcome these escapes? Maybe even to encourage them?

She sat and put her head in her hands. Perhaps she should urge Abel to hurry here to dispatch another demon as well . . . the big dark-eyed one who had apparently taken up residence in a remote corner of her mind.

Chapter 7

Evie came out onto the porch to shell peas. She had no sooner set herself down and arranged her bowl and gunnysack than Jack walked by with his saddle over his shoulder. She saw several things at once. That he had shaved for the second day in a row. That his hair was slicker than green grease and that his mustache had been trimmed so that it no longer curtained his lips. He also had on his best shirt and his good twill pants. She saw these things and her heart stumbled . . . what if he was . . .

Oh, Lordamercy! He was! Her Jack was going courting. Finally! She drew in a chest full of air and she could just about smell the sweet baby scent of her first grandchild!

She straightened her face; he was leading his horse out of the corral. She called, ''Goin' to town, Jack?''

''Yeah. Gonna see if the pay has come in.''

''Huh.'' She smiled a secret smile.

He looked at his mother. ''What?''

''Nothin'.''

''You want somethin' from town?''

''No, nothin'.''

As Jack was disappearing into the trees, Goldie came walking up the rise from the other direction. He swung five dead prairie hens by their legs. "Where's Jack goin'?"

"He says he's gonna see if Austin's sent the fellas their money yet." Evie gave Goldie her one dropped eyelid look. "But I ain't so sure that's all he's gonna do."

"What d'you mean?"

"I got fifty dollars that says he's also goin' in to shine the new schoolmarm. What do you say?"

Recalling the things he had seen and felt at the school, Goldie replied, "I'll make you the same bet and give you five-to-one."

"Golden Jack Dare! Do I look like a turnip to you?"

Jack did stop at the freight office to see if the rangers' pay had come in. It had, but Hap Pettijohn had delivered it to Lloyd Cooper that morning. It turned out to be three months' worth, when they were owed five, but it was better than nothing.

Hap had some fresh tobacco, so for a time he and Jack chewed and smoked and talked about those things they knew the most about: mules and horses, Indians and bandits, the parsimony of Stephen Austin, the lack of safety on the Bahia Road.

Hap was a small, wiry man with bowed legs and a grizzled face. He had been in Tejas for over twenty-five years, which made him an old-timer. A very old-timer. Jack liked him. He was an honest, hardworking man who kept his own counsel, and what he didn't know about mules had not yet been discovered.

They say he had been married to a landed Tejana woman a long time ago but that after she died he had let his ranchero go back to his wife's people. Just couldn't handle the memories, they said. He said he'd wandered around some, found Sweet Home and liked it and started up the cartage company.

At one point during their conversation Jack noticed a man who was leaving Dirty Dave's and crossing over to the bank. He looked vaguely familiar. "Who's that fella yonder?"

Hap squinted. His eyes weren't so good any more. "Looks like Bob Graham t'me."

"Bob Graham?" Jack looked again. "Well, I'll be damned! I'd've never guessed that's what he'd look like after a bath."

"You know, I don't know if you noticed but there ain't hardly any gone-to-hell fellas around town anymore."

Jack looked at him and nodded. "You're right. Why is that, do you think?"

"Marryin' fever. Nobody wants to get caught lookin' normal. Case there's a new woman in town an' they can get first shot."

"Hard to believe that a fella'd go to all that trouble on an outside chance like that."

Hap stepped back and looked Jack over from toe to hat and Jack threw his head back and laughed and Hap did likewise and almost choked on his cud.

It was when Jack was leaving that Hap asked him to take a crate over to the new schoolhouse.

"Aw, Hap! That's clear outa my way!"

"You can take my wagon."

"Well . . ."

"That schoolteacher's been here purt near every day to ask about this here box." Hap squinted up at the sun. "About this time she oughta still be up there, but you can jus' set it inside the door if she ain't. Well?"

"Well . . ."

Of course, he agreed. It was just where he was going next and now Hap had supplied him with a good excuse.

That afternoon Annie'd had another meeting with Lloyd Cooper, the purpose of which was to make sure she understood her duties. He counted his fingers as he went through them. Her job, he said, included building a fire in the morning, cleaning the school at the beginning and at the end of each day and, of course, teaching whatever children attended. Since they might range in age from seven to seventeen he suggested she would be wise not to get too "carried away with your curriculum."

"I'm not sure I understand."

He replied that in this part of the world most parents are

happy if their boys know how to read a land grant and add and subtract well enough to count their cows. By the same token, if their girls are proficient in sewing, weaving and spinning, cooking and the preserving of food, they should be able to realize their goal in life: marriage. Keeping those things in mind he suggested that she confine her teaching to the alphabet, spelling and writing, and very simple arithmetic.

She would have liked to say that she would take his suggestion under advisement. Instead she nodded and to herself added: what he doesn't know won't hurt him.

Next they discussed methods of punishment for willfulness, tardiness and so forth. He said his motto was spare the rod, spoil the child.

"Frankly, Miss Mapes, discipline was a grave concern of ours before we sent you your contract. Some of the boys will be at least as large as you are."

"Don't worry. I will be firm but fair." She believed that sometimes a look of silent reproach was enough to quell an unruly student, but she did not say that either. As she had hoped, Mr. Cooper moved off discipline (not her strong suit) and onto lunches.

Lunches?!

Those children who wanted could bring their own lunch and most would probably do so. Some few, however, might want to cook an Irish potato or a sweet potato which could be put right into the fire and set to bake at the beginning of the day. Still others, he continued, would expect her to provide them with lunch.

This was news to her, but she did not interrupt.

For twenty-five cents a week—a silver dollar cut in half and then halved again—a child had a right to a lunch provided by the school. "As long as they bring their own bowl and spoon from home."

To prepare this meal she would be supplied with a hundred-pound bag of pinto beans once a month. At night, after cleaning the schoolroom, she was supposed to bring in wood, including brush kindling. He indicated the new Franklin stove and pointed at the woodpile outside the window. "Maple or oak for a hot steady fire. Brush and pine knots for kindling." Last thing to do was set a pot of beans on to soak overnight so they would be ready to cook the next morning. That's it? she had asked. Beans? Yes, he replied. "Why?"

"Well, it just seems that beans by themselves wouldn't be terribly nourishing. Or would they?"

She'd tried Mexican beans several times and found that they didn't agree with her. Put plainly, they did not have what you would call "staying power." Further, in the short time they did stay, she'd had a most unpleasant gaseous reaction to them. One could only imagine how disastrous it would be if ten children had the same reaction.

There's a particularly repugnant thought!

To her question Cooper replied that a bowl of beans was probably more than most of the children got for lunch at home.

Appalling! she thought. And while Cooper expounded on types of wood for heat, she thought about lunches for hungry kids.

Maybe she could bake some corn bread the night before. Or perhaps she could buy fresh tomatoes and potatoes to supplement the children's diet until she could harvest some from Emma's new garden. At least she could add a bit of ham or some onions.

She had heard someone say that wild onions grew everywhere in Tejas. Now all she had to do was ask someone where "everywhere" was. While Cooper rattled on she considered other possibilities.

Maybe the children could have their own garden right here at the school. There's a thought. It could be a class project.

No, she would never get away with calling it a learning experience. All these children knew more about growing produce than she did.

Maybe the simplest thing would be to buy some food already made. Alma Cooper recently told her that Maude Stone, the woman who owned the rooming house on the edge of town, had added a cabin to the side of her house and had started serving breakfast and lunch. More importantly, Alma said Mrs. Stone intended to sell bread, pies and cookies.

Children love bread, pies and cookies.

Teachers love bread, pies and cookies.

Of course, the major problem with that idea was money. Her monthly salary was seventy-five percent of the students' attendance fee plus ten dollars. With the seven students who had enrolled thus far, she would earn just over fifteen dollars a month. Buying prepared meals could knock that down as much as two-thirds.

It was at that disheartening moment that they were interrupted by a man named Simmons whose son would be attending the school. He had stopped to see if it was all right to pay the fee for his son in gunnysacks of corn, or in fresh deer meat. She had a disgusting mental picture of her with a half a bloody deer carcass slung over her shoulder, but while she was shaking her head, the mayor was saying, "Yes, yes, of course. Miss Mapes can take the produce or meat to Bowie Garlock and sell it to him!"

After Cooper left she sat slumped against the wall. All in all, it had not been an auspicious day. What she could not know was that with respect to her own peace of mind it was destined to get worse. A lot worse.

By the time Jack headed for the schoolhouse the sun had made the day too bright for a wide eye. He tugged his hat down and slowed the mule to a walk.

Not much was moving. A cow lay under a tree chewing her cud and tossing her horns at the flies. Two turkey buzzards made a slow circle to the south and closer in, a red-tailed hawk flushed a young rabbit that barely made it into the safety of the brush.

Where the road curved into the creek he saw a family of ducks with their tails upturned and their bills buried in the mud, looking for crayfish or small frogs. A little further on he saw a big brown copperhead taking the sun atop a rotted tree trunk and on a flat rock nearby there was a washtub-sized brown turtle doing the same.

He saw all these things and thought he couldn't recall a nicer day, until he pulled up in front of the school. Things were so quiet he thought she had already left for home and he was cursing his luck when he looked inside and saw her there.

His first thought was that if he was a buck Indian he would have had her slung over his horse by now. His second thought was: *This is the first time I've ever wished I was an Indian.*

She stood with her back to him, apparently so engrossed in washing something in a bucket she had not heard the clanging bit chains and creaking wood that had signaled his approach.

He looked with admiration at the curve of her butt and the shape of her back and shoulders, so straight and yet so softly rounded. She wore an apron and a serviceable dress made of sprigged calico and she had her hair in a thick braid that hung past her waist. He tilted his head and grinned. She stood in her stocking feet and one of her stockings had an inexpertly mended hole on the heel.

She still didn't know he was there.

Poor thing would be dead in a day, in the woods.

He scuffed his foot and she turned with her hand over her mouth. Her shirt was opened to expose a two-button length of white slim throat and there was a water spot near where her navel ought to be. He thought she looked mighty fine. Oh yeah! Might-tee fine! It was a moment before she removed her hand from her mouth and clasped it tightly to her.

"You are a very quiet moving person, Mr. Dare." She was so glad she sounded composed!

"Sorry if I startled you."

He was stretched out in the doorway with hand on the jamb and one knee cocked which simultaneously filled the opening and emptied her mind.

Later she would easily recall every single thing she had intended to tell him which was expressly designed to set *him* on *his* ear . . . for a change!

Unfortunately, at that moment she couldn't tell time.

He threw her that easy, careless smile and hitched a thumb over his shoulder. "Hap Pettijohn at the freight office asked me to bring that case over to you. I told him I was glad to. That maybe you wouldn't toss me off the premises if I did."

She came close enough to see in the back of the wagon. And close enough for him to smell the clean woman scent of her.

"My books! Oh, I thought they had been lost in route."

"You want 'em in here?"

"Yes, please."

He went to the wagon and hauled the crate up on his shoulder. He and Hap had been surprised at its weight. Damn thing felt like it was filled with rocks!

"Oh, I'm so glad they've come!"

Look at her, he thought, joy smitten over such a little thing as a box of books. He suddenly wished he could go on carrying that box in and out forever.

Then his eye fell on something strange and since his hands were occupied, he used his chin to point. "Say, what is that thing?"

"What?" She looked around. "Oh, that. That's a slate board for writing on." Her face became brighter still. "When you wipe the writing off, you can use it over and over again."

He set the books down. "Naw!" He really didn't give a rip. "Over an' over again?"

"Yes, watch." She scribbled something, flashed the slate in front of his face then wiped it clean. "See?" She handed him the piece of chalk. "Now you write something."

He handed it back to her. "There ain't nothin' I do that requires writin'."

She looked at him, at the heavy guns at his waist, the knife butt sticking out of his boot top and wished that one day she could remember to think before she spoke. Of course he could not read or write!

The thought that she might have hurt him bothered her a lot. (And the fact that hurting him had bothered her would bother her even more later!)

"I'm sorry. I hope I haven't . . . offended you."

"Cause I can't write? Hel- . . . I mean heck, no. Not atall." Jack didn't know many men who could.

"I'm glad. I . . . I know that at least in this part of the world there are many things that are much more important than writing."

He folded his arms and cocked his head at her. "What do you think's important, Miss Annie Mapes."

"Well, a man has to be a good hunter and protect his loved ones from the Indians and . . . and lots of things. Of course, I have only lately become aware of these things since we arrived." She glanced at him then away. "However, Tejas will not always be like this . . ."

"Let's hope not."

"And when that day comes and you decide you're ready to learn, um, well, you know, you're never too, ah, old . . ."

Her face flushed and she would not meet his eye. She sure was a taking little thing. "You sayin' you could teach this ol' dog a new trick?"

"Of course." She looked at him earnestly. "You know, it is actually quite common for a teacher to be younger than some of her students."

She was waiting for his response. He folded his arms and put a thoughtful look on his face. "You know, mebbe I'll take you up on that sometime." She smiled and there was a look in her eye like the one he once saw Earl Durrell get when he shot a skunk dead while drunker than one hisself. *So that would make her happy, eh. Teaching me to write.*

Annie longed to unpack her books but still he stood there staring at her through another long silence, one that did not seem to bother him in the least but one that made her mouth dry and her palms wet. Flustered again she turned away and began to struggle with the crate's lid. "Here, let me." He pried it off then sheathed his knife. She removed a book and blew some dust off. If she could find a market for dust here in Tejas, she would be a millionaire.

"You could learn to read any one of these books, Mr. Dare. This one by Thomas Paine or this one by Herman Melville or

Washington Irving or Ralph Waldo Emerson or Henry Thoreau or Edgar Allan Poe or Nathaniel Hawthorne.'' She looked up at him and gave him a bright smile. ''Wouldn't that be something?''

''Mm.'' He could look at her forever.

''Well, it's, um, something to think about.''

''It is and I think I'll . . . think on it.''

She kept her eyes on his face while a squirrel scolded something outside. And while he looked at her like a new species. ''Mr. Dare.''

''Hm?''

''Do I have dirt on my face?''

''Why?''

''You're staring.''

''I am?''

''Yes, you are, and you do that all the time!''

''I do?''

''Yes!''

So that annoys her, eh? ''You know . . . you actually do.''

''Do what?''

He touched his cheek. ''Have a little dirt.'' When she lifted her hand to her cheek her breasts nuzzled the fabric of her dress and caused him a bit of trouble breathing. ''Ah, no, ma'am. The, uh, other one.''

She had both hands on her cheeks before she noticed the twinkle in his eye. ''You're teasing me, Mr. Dare.''

''Yeah, I am. Say, why don't you call me Jack?''

''I'm sorry but that's quite impossible . . .'' Her eyes met his and danced away. The thumping in her chest was so loud she could hear it in her ears. Could he hear it too?

Her hand was shaking. She set the thick text aside lest she give herself a clubfoot.

''Please don't let me keep you, Mr. Dare. I'm sure you have something much more important to do than stand around here and watch me dust.'' She did a poor imitation of a laugh.

''I can't think of what it would be.'' He continued to study her. ''You know, I never saw nobody with eyes like yours.

One time I'll look at you an' your eyes'll be the soft blue of a summer's day, then the next time they'll be as gray as a dove's feather."

Her eyes looked into his for a long minute and then she seemed to find a point of interest far in the distance.

"Mr. Dare."

"Jack."

"Mr. Dare," she said determinedly. "I must tell you that . . ."

"Yeah?" He moved a little closer.

". . . that I am affianced."

"Aaf-eye-anced, eh." He touched an errant curl on her cheek. "That the same as a lunger?"

"What?" She moved away but he followed.

"A lunger. You know . . ." He tapped his chest. "Bum lungs."

"No, no. You misunderstand. Saying that you are affianced means that you are promised to be married." She looked at him and twisted her fingers. It wasn't possible to tell anything from the expression on his face; there was none.

"An' you are?"

"Yes, I am."

"Huh! So where is the af-eye-ance?"

"In Pennsylvania. He intends to come down here as soon as he has finished his preceptorship."

"He's a seaman?"

"No . . . Why?"

"You said somethin' about a ship?"

"No, no. Abel's going to be a lawyer."

"On a ship?"

"No, here." *Good heavens!*

"Ah. I gotcha now."

He pulled on his hat. He was smiling slightly and did not look particularly heartbroken. It bothered her a little that he didn't.

"When did you say this fella's due?"

"No later than the first of the year."

"Six months, uh?"

"Yes." He catwalked to the door then looked over his shoulder at her.

"You gonna write him about this?"

"About what?"

"What's between us."

She tried to laugh. "Mr. Dare, there is nothing between us. Believe me. Nothing. When Abel arrives we will be married."

"Six months, you say?"

"Yes."

"Well, that oughta be plenty of time."

She knew she shouldn't ask but she did. "Plenty of time for what?"

"For me to change your mind."

"Change my . . . ? Really, Mr. Dare, I must insist that you believe me when I say that I have no intention of . . . of . . ."

But he had already passed through the door, strode across the yard and was climbing into the wagon.

Jack had returned Hap's wagon and was two miles out of town before he realized that he'd forgotten to stop at Lloyd Cooper's for the rangers' pay. He had been riding along, grinning about the look on her face there at the end and thinking about what a stir she'd been in.

Guess he'd been the one in a stir! Riding off without taking care of business like he had. Well, he supposed he might as well start getting used to it. They say once a fella falls in love he's worthless as . . .

He stopped the wagon. Now that's damn interesting. As if saying it had made it true, he'd just accepted the fact that he had fallen in love with Annie Mapes. He would have never believed it if it hadn't happened to him. Just like that!

Wait'll Goldie hears. Jack knew just what he'd say: Hell, you're worse'n a Mexican!

They'd talked about it not a month ago. They were in Dulce's, listening to her guitar player and Goldie said he'd always wondered why Mexicans are so silly about love. "Well, think about it. You don't see any Anglos goin' around singin' about stuff like that—at least not any we know.''

Goldie was right. That sort of music was about all the *guitarristas* at Dulce's liked to play. And it was all the Mexicans ever requested! ''Love like Lightning.'' That was one of their most requested tunes. Goldie figured it had to do with their fiery food. ''All them green chili tamales an' bowls of chili cabrito.''

Not that a Mexican did not tend to business. In Jack's opinion a man can have no better friend—or no worst enemy—than a Mexican. They'll fight long and hate forever, but what Goldie'd said was fact—every one he'd ever known had been silly as hell about love.

Let there be no misunderstanding. He had no intention of carrying on like a Mexican but he *was* more simpatico now that he knew why he'd been hanging around in Sweet Home, wondering what was missing in his life.

Annie Mapes was the unknown ''something or someone'' he'd been waiting for. The one who would set him on the path his life was meant to take. And she didn't even know it! He grinned and urged the mule into a trot. He could hardly wait to tell her.

Of course, it went without saying that nothing known to man was going to keep him from having her.

Chapter 8

Twilight the next night found Annie following the narrow path that ran alongside the creek. She had started out being especially careful. She had walked there before and knew the path was as crooked as a barrel of snakes and strewn with roots and rocks. But as happened often of late, her mind kept drifting and she'd already paid for it with a stocking that was torn beyond repair and a skinned knee that felt the same.

Ever since the incident with Jack Dare she'd not been herself. She'd been alternately edgy, moody, forgetful and weepy. This wasn't like her and it *must* cease. She'd thought that a walk would clear her mind and help bring her thoughts into some semblance of order.

So far . . . not so good.

Apparently her problem with Jack Dare had no solution—other than marriage to Abel. Not once in his presence had she successfully articulated her objections to his cavalier attitude, because, quite simply, every time he appeared, her presence of mind disappeared. Yesterday, for instance, she had been so taken aback by his bold-faced statement about changing her mind that afterward she wasn't able to remember a word she'd said. She'd meant to strongly and firmly set him straight. Apparently she failed because he definitely left her with the impression that he intended to court her.

Actually she'd never been courted, period, and so had only a sketchy idea of what it might entail but the mere thought of being courted by a man like Jack Dare was extremely upsetting.

Abel and she had decided to marry when he was eighteen and she was sixteen. It had been a well-thought-out decision on their part, one they had talked over and agreed upon as calm, careful adults. But it had not been the culmination of a courtship. When soup came to nuts, they had really decided to marry because neither of them could imagine spending their life with anyone else.

That's not to say that in the intervening years she had not had any misgivings. She loved Abel dearly but she did not relish the thought of being intimate with him. The idea just didn't set right with her.

But then since there was no one else and no other situation where it *did* set right, she'd assumed that was just the way she was. Reserved. Self-possessed.

Sometimes she wondered if the institution of marriage was suitable for her. Perhaps it simply wasn't in her nature to be passionate about . . . passion. The mere thought of being naked with a man was a most disconcerting idea, but when over the passage of time she learned that most women never removed their night garments in their husband's presence, she'd been relieved. But now that same reassuring revelation was the precise reason for her concern. The previous night she'd had a dream in which she readily—no, gleefully—removed every stitch of her undergarments in front of her husband whom she addressed as Abel but who looked exactly like Jack Dare!

If that weren't enough, he and she then rode through town bare-butt naked while the townspeople threw flowers in their path and chanted strange pagan melodies! She'd awakened feeling hot and feverish. Her breasts were hard and needful-feeling while another part of her—heretofore unnoticed but never to go unnoticed again—was slack and dewy and terribly . . . demanding.

What was going on with her? That's what she'd really like to know. Physically, mentally and emotionally—there was no part of her that was not experiencing some sort of unwanted transformation. Why? If only she could reason it out!

She had to. She intuitively knew that not to do so was the end of the serene state of mind and mental equilibrium that she had always enjoyed.

So far this meditative walk had not helped a bit. Her mind was in a worse jumble than the path. About the only gain was an opportunity to observe the beautiful scenery.

As with many nights, a spectacular sunset had been followed by a clear night sky with a big yellowy moon that gleamed through the trees and flickered gently on the water. Swarms of fireflies had strung themselves in the bushes where they glittered like tiny candles.

Lost in thought she continued to stroll along until she realized that she had gone much further than she had intended. No sooner had she had that thought then she noticed how very quiet it had become. She paused and looked around but she was unable to distinguish between shadow and substance. Was there something over there? Just off the path?

From the limb of an alamo overhead came a loud screech that was immediately echoed by the one that rose from her own throat. She pressed a hand to her galloping heart and looked up just as an owl unfurled its wings and took flight. Her knees almost buckled with relief.

Chiding herself for being such a sissy, she retraced her steps but she hadn't gone ten yards when she heard a soulful howl behind her. She paused and listened. Another came from her left and yet another from her right. Then as if a wilderness conductor had raised his baton, a ghostly choir of concerted baying pierced the night. As her scalp crawled and her arm hairs danced on end, an inner voice screamed: Wolves!

Oh, for heaven's sake, said the sane one. Relax! You know

how sounds travel at night! Why, those wolves are probably way way out on the prairie.

She whispered, "I don't care where they are! As long as I am inside the cabin and they are not!" With that she hoisted her skirts and—as they say in Tejas—lit a shuck.

She was watching her feet, trying not to trip and hit her head and be found in the morning and have to be identified by her buttons. Naturally she was scared silly when a voice said, "This is the second time this week that I've wished I was an Indian."

"Mr. Dare!"

He was leaning against a tree with his long legs stretched out in front of him and crossed at the ankles. Aromatic smoke circled his head.

"What *are* you doing?" She held her hand at her throat to keep her heart inside it.

"Leanin' ag'in this here tree."

She looked to see how far she had come and more importantly, how far she still had to go. Quite a ways. She could barely see the cabin window through the chokeberry bushes; certainly she could not be seen by anyone from the house. She supposed her next concern should be: would anyone in the house hear her if she screamed?

Then, irrationally, his lounging there like a big lizard made her furious. Curse him, scaring her out of all hope for a ripe old age! She balled her fists and wished she were a man. She would march over there and poke him right in the eye!

"I would really appreciate it, Mr. Dare, if you would . . . quit . . . sneaking . . . up on me." That last part had been forced out between bared teeth.

"Sneakin' up on you?" He looked pained. "But I didn't. See that horse yonder?" He pointed. "Somethin' spooked 'im and he took me right through that prickly thicket." He sniffed and pointed to a three-cornered rip on his sleeve. "About tore my clothes off, to say nothing of a layer of skin. Didn't you hear me yelp?"

She folded her arms. "All that . . . just so you could lean against that particular tree?"

"Sure. This is my favorite spot for checkin' out the stars. I have to see if they're tendin' to business."

Devil! In the soft light she could see the flash of his teeth and eyes. She looked up at the sky. "It appears that they are. Well, good night, Mr. Dare."

"Hey, hold up a minute."

"I'm sorry. I really can't stay."

"Aw, c'mon. Can't hurt to pass a little time together."

"Actually, it can. I'll soon begin teaching the young people of this community—unless my reputation is in ruins and I am discharged from my position—and that's precisely what will happen if I am observed talking to you. Especially out here and especially at this hour."

"Wanna go talk some place else?"

"Absolutely not!" She turned to go but again he called after her.

"Say, watch out for that snipe."

She paused. "What snipe?"

"The one that just ran by. Didn't you see it?"

"No. I'm not sure. I've never seen one before."

He nodded. "Don't feel bad. Not many have."

"What do they look like?" She was pressing on her skirts so she could see her feet. "Is a snipe a big black spider with long furry . . ."

"Aw, no. A snipe looks sorta like a ferret only smaller."

"Is a ferret a big black spider with long furry . . ."

"Naw, let me think a minute. They're sorta like . . . Heck, I'll bet you've never seen a nutria either!"

"No."

"A vole?"

"No. Say, do any of these things bite?"

One minute his arms were folded across his chest, the next minute they shot out and capped her shoulders and pulled her to him. She puffed up like a bullfrog. "I'll thank you to unhand me!"

He was lowering his head. "You can thank me all you want, but I won't unhand you till I've kissed you."

"I assume you're joking. I gave you no indication that I would welcome your attentions." She turned her head.

"Aw, c'mon, you knew I'd come."

"I did not!" She felt his mouth on her nape and bit off a moan.

"You musta felt this thing between us."

"No."

"You musta wanted to know what it is." His eyes probed hers then he drew her even closer and whispered, "You wanna know what it is?"

"Revulsion?"

"This." He pulled her flush against him and laughed gently. "Relax. It's just a kiss."

Just a kiss? repeated a voice in her head. God help her!

She knew she could extract herself from his grasp if she wanted to but she didn't push him away. It surprised and it shamed her but she wanted him to kiss her. Only once. She had never been kissed by anyone but Abel. What would one kiss hurt? Acting completely on their own, her lips parted and she waited. He lowered his head.

Oh, God, he was going to kiss her. Sanity returned. "Wait!"

"Lady, I been waitin'. I think mebbe all my life. Miss Mapes—Annie—I am compelled by the violence of my feelings to marry you as soon as possible."

And then without further ado his powerful hands held her head for an openmouthed kiss that was deep and long and unlike any she had ever known before.

A kiss was not supposed to be like this! A kiss had always meant two pairs of closed lips pressed lightly together. It had not meant a questing tongue and nibbling teeth and a hard body tightly pressed to hers.

"Annie!" he said. His lips moved over her face then returned to her mouth.

When he kissed her a second time, it was a gentler but no less thrilling kiss and once again she never imagined anything could be so potent, so indecent and carnal. So . . . intimate. A queer feeling gripped her stomach, but other than an insistent banging under her ribs she seemed incapable of movement. Her knees were jelly and she experienced a disturbing turbulence . . . like nothing she'd ever felt before. She had not even known such feelings existed! She forced herself to wrench her head aside, but he followed, slowly chasing her mouth with his until he caught it again. And again.

Jack pressed his lips to the milky softness of her neck and his heart hammered in his chest. It was like she was the first woman he had ever touched! His desire was a raging thing, emptying his mind of everything but the way she felt in his arms. He kissed her mouth lightly and tasted its soft wetness and then he looked at her. Her eyes were closed and her chin was lifted. She seemed to have stopped breathing. "Funny," he whispered, "Not a week ago I thought I wanted to see the world, and now here I am . . . starin' it right in the face."

She knew she was stretched across his thighs like a wanton yet it felt so good, so right. The hard cold tree behind her, the hard warm tree in front of her.

Control failed her and she had to touch him. She had to know if his body was truly that hard and that warm. Oh, it was! And it too was in a terrible turmoil! Beneath her palm his chest was pounding like crazy!

"Annie, you've never been out of my mind. Not from the moment I saw you." His voice was ragged. "Darlin', I want you so much, my teeth hurt."

His knowing mouth was relentless and his hands were everywhere and when he got several buttons of her shirt undone, his lips were burning a trail above her breast.

"God, you're so damn pretty you pull the breath right outa me."

Her head was spinning. She was very close to losing her virtue here . . . now . . . pressed against a tree. She gathered her reserves and punched his shoulder. The result was instant. Pain. Hers.

Jack didn't even notice. All her twisting and turning had drawn every drop of his blood to one core part of him. He cupped her breast and felt the hard little bud poke the center of his palm. He made a sound of satisfaction then lifted her breast and rubbed his thumb across her nipple while he kissed his way to it.

Somehow a whispered plea breached his consciousness. He lifted his head. She was holding his wrist away from her breast. Bright circles graced both her cheeks and her eyes glittered wetly. His lips were a hair's breadth away from hers, wrestling with conflicting impulses as well as his conscience.

His eyes were black as the night but she imagined she saw an earnest appeal gleaming in their depths: Please, they said. Let me! "No," she whispered. "I cannot. I must not."

She saw a softening but it still seemed that at least an hour went by before he straightened and released her.

She was out of his grasp in a shot.

Some feet away she paused and they looked at each other. His arms hung at his sides, empty and useless. Damnit! Now she was all haired up again. "I didn't mean for that to happen. All I meant to do was ask you to marry me."

"Marry you?" She spat. "Are you insane?" She was holding her shirt under her neck like a noose. "You would ask someone you don't even know to marry you?"

His mind was starting to come around. Maybe some blood had returned to it, although a part of him cried: *No! I've got all the blood I need! Hell, don't waste it! Let's go! I'm ready!*

He concentrated on making his point. "That's how things work down here. Fast!"

"Then you're all crazy!"

He ignored that. "A girl arrived in town last month. Fella married her four days later an' took her off to the hills. Ain't nobody seen neither one of 'em since."

She could just imagine what they were doing up there in the hills. Exactly what he had just been doing to her! The nerve of him. Putting his hand on her chest when she wasn't looking!

"A woman needs protection an' a man can provide it. A man needs a home an' children an' . . . stuff that a woman can provide. Seems like a good bargain all around."

"It occurs to me that the only thing I need protection from is you!"

"No, ma'am. I am the least of your worries. Why, you don't know half the things'll go after a girl down here."

"What, for instance?"

"All manner of things. The Indians or grizzlies. Snakes or mad animals. Some've had trees fall on 'em. Or they've been buried by loose snow or trampled by horses. I've known 'em to starve t'death, freeze t'death, get caught in high water or poisoned by bad meat or shot by another woman."

"Shot by another woman? Why would one woman shoot another?"

"For a good man."

"Oh, really!" She looked at him. "And I suppose you consider yourself one of those 'good men'?" If she hadn't been so mad she might have laughed at the pose he struck.

"The best. For any harm to get to you it'd have to get by me first. That's fact, ma'am. No boast."

"Mr. Dare, you are absolutely beyond the pale."

He grinned. "I figured you'd notice."

Amazing! Impossible! Imbecile! "Mr. Dare?"

"Yessum?"

"I have only one thing to say to you."

"Yessum?"

"Don't ever ever touch me again!"

He watched her run to the cabin and grinned. Not a chance. Miss Annie Mapes.

Annie gained the sanctuary of her room and leaned her forehead on the door. Her head was spinning and her insides were in a tumult. The way she felt, he might as well have a hold of her still.

She stiffened. Something had caught her eye across the room.

There was a wanton reflected in the mirror. Someone she had never seen before. Her hair was wild around her face and her eyes glittered fever bright. Her lips looked loose and rubbery. She let her shirt fall open and imagined that she could see the marks his kisses had left. She stepped closer. She could see marks!

Good grief was that how married people kissed? With tongues and teeth and twisting lips and mashed noses and neither caring about anything but getting closer? Then why hadn't she ever heard about it before? How had all the married people in the world managed to keep something as momentous as that a secret? She licked her lips and she could taste him still!

She limped to the bed—she had stubbed her toe and now it felt like a potato. She stretched out Christ-like and let her head hang over the edge of the bed; it never failed to clear her head. Except this time.

Oh, God, the feelings she'd had when she was in his grasp. Just remembering made her stomach flutter and her palms moist.

Jack Dare, a total stranger, had just seen and touched parts of her that no one had ever seen or touched before. It had been terribly intimate . . . shockingly indecent . . . shameless and immoral.

Wonderful!

She was forced to acknowledge a very uncomfortable truth. Though she had never experienced it before, she intuitively recognized this emotion for what it was: physical lust, and it was, without question, the most powerful feeling she had ever experienced.

She couldn't have been more surprised at herself. Prior to tonight she would have described herself as an optimist and a pragmatist. A little independent, a bit too impulsive, but basically a sensible person with a logical mind. Never would she have used words like wanton or passionate and yet, apparently she had just been both. Within minutes he had moved her from mild curiosity to senseless, shameless passion. All with his kisses.

Oh, but what fine kisses they were! So completely different from Abel's, which were sweet, cherished, chaste and . . . She groaned and punched the pillow. What had she done? She had never thought of Abel's kisses as dull before. In her mind they had always been perfection.

But what—asked an annoying inner voice—about in your body?

Aye, there, as they say, is the rub. Her body had not had an opinion one way or another. Until now. Now apparently her body had grown a mind of its own because her body had wanted Jack Dare to go on kissing her more than she had ever wanted anything in her life.

Her spirits plummeted and an awful sense of guilt closed in. She had betrayed Abel. Her best friend. Her affianced. She was despicable. Degenerate. Detestable. Desperate! Extremely desperate! *What am I going to do?*

She sat on the bed and buried her face in her hands. In time her insides settled and she was able to think rationally again. Soon a plan evolved. Her backbone stiffened and her tear-streaked face became resolute. She must guard against this flaw in her nature. She must be at all times vigilant so she is never alone with him again. Never. But more importantly she must do nothing to hurt Abel. She swore she would never allow that to happen and she would not. She would marry Abel the day he arrived in Sweet Home. In the meantime, she would stay away from Jack Dare.

She went to bed but it was a long time before she slept and when she did, she dreamt hot, unsettling dreams that she couldn't recall in the morning. Emma Fuller heard her moan in her sleep and thought the sound was like the low hopeless one of an animal in terrible pain.

Chapter 9

In preparation for their first day of school, Annie took Nona and Mittie to the dry goods store. She wanted to buy each child a hair ribbon and maybe a nice lace collar. Lest she stand before Mr. Garlock with a blank mind she carried a note listing those two items. She'd been having trouble concentrating lately. Of course, she knew why.

That entire episode with Jack Dare had lasted only five minutes yet it must have been indelibly etched in her mind, because it had replayed itself there at least a hundred times. Vividly and when she least expected it. Instantly its return had the ability to freeze her to a spot with her eyes slitted and her mouth open.

Apparently others had noticed. At least Emma had. Earlier that morning she had laid her hand over Annie's and asked her what was wrong. Why, nothing, she had replied. Only then did she realize that she was staring into the mirror with her arms folded so they pressed against her breasts.

Hastily she leaned close and patted her hair. "I guess I've been a little absorbed lately."

"To put it mildly! I just spoke to you twice and for all the response I received, I might have just been moving my lips."

And that was but one of the problems she had been experiencing. The day before she had narrowly missed being run over by a team of four horses. The red-faced teamster had crawled off his wagon, stomped over to her and stuck his face an inch from hers. "Didn't yuh hear me yell?" It looked like he had a rock in one cheek.

"I'm sorry, but I didn't."

"Yuh better start listenin' up, girley, or yuh'll end up lookin' like that cow pie right yonder."

Dutifully Annie looked where he pointed and saw a wafer-like object in the road. "You're right. Thank you. Sir?" He was stomping back to his wagon. "Please?" He turned. "Mr. Pettijohn?"

"Yeah?"

"Remember me? Annie Mapes, the new schoolteacher?"

"I see that now." He looked at the curled toe of his boot. "I don't see so good no more. Well . . . sorry I hollered at yuh, miss."

"Thank you! Thank you very much." She beamed. An unexpected apology! From a Texian! "Mr. Pettijohn, we have some more things coming in. Some furniture and more books. Personal books. It would be nice if we could have them delivered at home instead of at the school."

"I can do that."

"Thank you. Would you like to know where we live?"

"I know where you live. Over at the old Katy place."

"That's right."

"Yore things might be a bit delayed, miss. My driver, Ned Kirby, died a few weeks back so I'm one man short."

"I understand. No problem. And I'm sorry to hear about Mr. Kirby. Was it a long illness?"

"No, real quick. About a one-second illness."

"How unexpected!"

"Yeah. Well."

"Thank you, Mr. Pettijohn."

"Yuh better watch yerself, miss."

"I will. I promise."

She had every intention of following Mr. Pettijohn's advice but by the time they neared the store she was looking around instead of paying attention to her surroundings. A laxness she would soon regret.

"Well well well." The voice grated like a rasp. "Lookee here, Dutch."

Two men stood before her, one with a sneer under a dirty oxbow of hair, the other a horribly scarred man with lips like a slit in a leaf. Both men wore hats with feathers stuck in the band. One of the men removed his and swept it before him like a gallant. Unfortunately the maneuver was ruined by the half-moon stain under his arm. The other man had his hands on his knees and his face in Mittie's.

"Howdee do, little missy. My name's Dutch. What's yourn?"

Mittie answered, "My name's Mittie and this is Nona."

"An' your big sister's name?" He leered up at her and his parted lips revealed teeth so stained they looked serrated.

"Oh, she's not our sister. She's . . ."

Annie interrupted Nona. "I'm sorry but you'll have to excuse us. We're in an awful hurry . . ."

Quickly she skirted the men and pulled the girls inside the store. Never was the click of a latch more reassuring but through the closed door she could hear them laughing and saying awful things. She shuddered and held a hanky to her nose but she could smell them still.

She was one of only a few single women in the area. Not surprisingly there had been many men who had gone to great lengths to get themselves introduced to her. Some who stopped by the house had used the ruse of business, telling Emma and Annie what services they offered at the livery or at the apothecary or at the tin shop. They had actually come to see if they could come again . . . with hat in hand and far more serious things in mind. Of course, all had been politely and kindly discouraged.

Without exception her callers had been hardworking men who were obviously uncomfortable with their newly shorn heads and never-seen-before necks. They had been tall, short, fat, thin, as old as the hills and as young as Charley Walters. But none of them had been dirty and scary like the two men outside.

"Annie?"

Gathering herself, she replied, "All right. Now we'll shop."

She scanned the interior of the store and was glad to see a slight, narrow-chested man standing behind the counter. He smiled and she immediately felt better. "Can I help you, ma'am?"

"Yes, please. I am Annie Mapes and this is Nona and Mittie, and we need some new things for school."

"You're the new teacher."

"Yes."

"Well . . ." He came around the counter to offer his hand. "Pleased to meet you. I'm Bowie Garlock, the proprietor. Just a minute while I call my wife." He parted the striped curtains behind him. "Rutha, come out here a minute, will you?"

Soon a woman much larger than her husband appeared. She had a florid complexion and sharp, coffee-bean eyes. She was wiping her hands on her apron. "What is it, Bowie?"

"Rutha, this here's the new schoolteacher."

Rutha smiled. "Good. I'd been hoping I'd get to meet you soon."

"I too. I wanted to thank you for the pickles and honey. We've eaten some of both—not together of course—and they were delicious."

Several women had come by to welcome them to Sweet Home, and none came empty-handed. They had received all manner of things: cakes, several loaves of bread, wheels of cheese, butter and eggs. Pies.

The Garlocks told Annie that they had a son, aged nine, who would be attending her school. Another shout in the back produced said son, Alfred, who proved to be an unkempt and listless-looking boy with his mother's ruddy complexion and his father's slight stature. But he was another student, which meant she now had eight.

After Alfred had slumped back to whatever he had been doing earlier—certainly she did not care to know what that might be—and after they had chatted about one thing and another, Annie said she had better get her shopping done.

"You want help findin' somethin'?"

"No, thanks. I'll just wander around on my own if that's all right."

"Sure. Make yourself t'home. But be sure an' holler if I can help you."

"All right. Thank you." Nice people, she thought as she looked around.

The left side of the store was a well-stocked grocery with staples like flour, lard, beans, and coffee as well as shelves with assorted utensils for cooking and eating. The right side contained tools and implements such as hoes, rakes and plow-shares while the rear of the store was reserved for ladies' personal items which included bolts of material, ribbons, trim and pins and needles.

Shelves with guns, powder horns, and shot pouches climbed the wall behind the counter while unwieldy things like traps and wash buckets hung overhead from the roof beams.

Her meandering around finally brought her by the front window. And an alarming sight . . . those men still stood on the boardwalk outside the store! She backed out of sight before they spotted her and saw Jack Dare striding along across the road. One look at that smooth-as-butter walk and all that had happened between them returned in a rush. So did a pounding pulse and a flaming face. He had disappeared down the road before she composed herself and approached the counter. "Mr. Garlock?"

"Yes?"

"There were two men who were just leaving as I came in . . ."

"Bittercreek Clarke and Dutch Elliott. They live at a place south of here called the Crow's Nest."

Now she remembered. They must be part of the group of men that Mrs. Cooper had described as the blight on their community. Now that she had seen them she thought her description was most apt. "One's face was horribly scarred."

"That's Bittercreek," Rutha said. "He's been branded with H on one cheek and T on the other. Means he's a horse thief."

Garlock nodded. "There's some places in Tennessee and Arkansas where branding is still the penalty for horse stealing. First offense."

"How awful!"

"Oh, I don't know. First offense in Tejas is hangin'!"

"Oh . . ."

"Looks to me like he tried to blur the letters. Probably used a knife or something hot."

"Good Lord!" Annie couldn't imagine such a thing.

"They were here to look at new pistols," said Garlock. "I tell you, I unpeel my eye when there's someone like that in the store."

"I don't blame you a bit."

By the time they were done Annie had purchased two hair ribbons and two tatted collars. And candy. But she'd also bought a bag of salt, some fresh coffee beans recently shipped in from New Orleans and a sack of flour . . . too much to carry home. She asked Mr. Garlock if she could send Charley Walters by to pick up her purchases later.

"Fine. Or . . ." He pulled a little slat-sided wagon out from behind the counter. "You could use this and bring it back tomorrow."

"Sure you don't need it?"

"I'm sure."

It would be good to have a fresh cup of coffee when she got home. "All right. Thank you."

They set off after Garlock loaded the wagon and after Annie had settled the girls' argument about who would pull it first.

"If you both hold the rope you can both pull the wagon. Watch. See?"

They were off the boardwalk and bumping down the road before she saw Clarke and Elliott. They were on opposite sides of the road, strolling along at such an angle that they would intercept them just beyond the edge of town.

It is broad daylight.

But they look so malevolent.

It's your imagination.

Is it? I'm not so sure.

Better to be safe than sorry. All right. Should she go back to the store? Or stop now and seek someone's help? Or keep going and act unconcerned?

They were level with Durrell's livery when Jack Dare stepped outside. The lesser of two evils? Absolutely! she thought and flashed him a smile that made him lift his brows.

"Yoo-hoo! Mr. Dare!"

Jack had not seen her since that night by the creek, almost a week now and at that time he definitely got the impression that she didn't care if she ever saw him again. Now here she stood, smiling so wide he was almost blinded by the glare.

He saw Clarke and Elliott then. Aha! So that's it! The lady's in need of a good man after all.

He gave her a devilish grin, and after a heart-stopping pause, he sauntered over.

"Well, if it ain't Miss Annie Mapes!"

He removed his hat and made the sort of bow that on anyone else would have looked ridiculous. "Mr. Dare."

"Want me to pull your wagon for you?"

"Well, actually . . ." Pasting on a silly smile, she slid her eyes back and forth between the two louts who were watching them like vultures. He leaned close enough for her to feel his breath in her ear. "You makin' eyes at me, Miss Mapes?"

"Certainly not!" she hissed. "Can't you see that those ruffians are stalking us?"

"Them?" He lifted his hat. "Howdy, boys. How y'all doin'?"

Without bothering to respond, Dutch Elliott and Bittercreek Clarke turned and walked back toward town.

"Huh!" Jack said with feigned hurt. "Wonder what's got into them?"

Nona and Mittie insisted on pulling the wagon so Jack and Annie fell in behind. "I don't think those fellas would've tried anything. Not in broad daylight in the middle of town."

"It was broad daylight when they accosted me in front of Garlock's." He had stopped walking so she did too.

"What's that mean 'accosted'?"

The look on his face frightened her. "I'm sorry. My tone was unnecessarily alarming. Accost merely means to speak to someone uninvited."

"They spoke to you . . ."

"Yes."

"An' said what? Exactly?"

"Well, nothing, really but . . ."

"Nothin'? They must've said somethin' that bothered you."

"Well, it was more the way they spoke than what they said." She looked over her shoulder. "And the fact that they are so revolting."

"Does this mean that I am not?"

She looked at him frowning, "Not what?"

"Revoltin'."

Hardly, she thought but said only, "Yes."

"Am I forgiven then?"

"No."

"What would it take to be forgiven?"

"A solemn promise never ever to do that again."

"Do what again?"

He was smiling. That he enjoyed watching her squirm made him every bit as intimidating as those other two! "You know exactly what I mean!"

"All right."

"You agree?"

"Yeah, sure."

She looked at him with surprise. Or perhaps it was disappointment. He had given in so easily. "And do you always keep your word, Mr. Dare?"

"Always."

"So do I."

She'd laid on those last words and had given him a hairy eye in case he had missed her meaning. Which he had not.

"So . . . let's make sure we have an understanding of our agreement. You promise never to, um, accost me again."

"Unless I'm invited." *An' then watch out, lady!* "Right?"

"Right."

A wary silence fell as they approached her gate. The peace of dusk had settled. Lanterns were being lit and cookfires stoked. From somewhere came a woman's voice, calling in an unseen child. She saw that Emma had lit a lantern within but now she was in no hurry to go in. She turned and looked up at him and she could see the light that danced in his depthless eyes. He finally must have heard her silent plea to speak.

"So do we have a deal?"

He was offering her a safe bet since she never intended to invite him to "accost" her. "We have a deal."

He nodded but neither moved. A killdeer gave its sharp shrill cry and in the nearby hills some coyotes began their nightly serenade.

"We best shake on it."

"All right."

"We can leave out the part about spittin' in our palms."

"What?"

"Nothin'." As he offered her his hand, he was thinking about that eager little nub he'd felt when he held her breast.

Reluctantly she placed her hand in his and thought: how hard it is! Which was exactly what she had thought when his hand slid inside her shirt. Her throat slammed with a bang, but her concern was unwarranted. This time he shook her hand like he was priming a pump. As his hand slowed their eyes met and he smiled and all the feelings that were so close to the surface welled up once again.

She wrenched her hand away. "Good."

"Fine."

The girls had carried most everything inside. She picked up the few remaining items in the wagon.

"Want me to take the wagon back for you?"

"Charley Walters will do it."

"That's all right." He picked up the rope. "I'm headed that way anyhow." He tipped his hat. "Ma'am."

"Mr. Dare."

"Don't forget our agreement."

"Ha! Not likely! Don't you forget!"

He stood there a minute. "Well, all right."

"All right."

She watched him go off down the road pulling the wagon behind him and she thought she had never seen such an incongruous sight. Apparently she wasn't the only one. When he rattled by a man on horseback, the man reined in his horse and sat staring after him. She chuckled, and then as Jack disappeared so did her smile. Of course, she had no way of knowing it but an expression of utter hopelessness had adorned her face.

Her father used to pull her around in a wagon. It was one of her earliest and fondest memories of him but one that she didn't allow herself to think about very often.

She never knew her mother and older brother. Both died when she was three but her father she had known well and loved dearly. He was a tall, dark-haired man who smoked a pipe and smelled good and he used to call her Snitten. In the beginning it had been "Sweet Kitten" but as she aged it somehow got shortened to Snitten. The memory brought intense heartache, but interestingly enough it also brought a glimpse of insight that came and went just that fast. She stood there, trying to recapture the thought then she shook her head and walked toward the cabin. Too bad. Something having to do with how much it hurts when you love too hard. Later she would try to reason it out, but by then its meaning had become even more vague and hazy and . . . surprisingly painful. It was therefore easy to tell herself she would think about it another time and then forget about it entirely.

That night Annie told Emma about the two thieves, Clarke and Elliott and felt vindicated by Emma's shocked reaction when she came to the disfigurement part. "The Garlocks spoke so matter-of-factly that I was beginning to wonder if I could ever 'harden' up enough for this country."

"I suppose the real question is, do you want to harden up that much?"

More than anything Annie was worried that her perception of danger had been a product of her overactive imagination. Which would mean that she had called Jack Dare over to her when she really did not have to. Which would mean she had no control over herself where he was concerned. Of course, she hardly wanted to speak to Emma about that!

They were sitting together in the main room. Emma had her slippered feet on a pettipoint stool and the lantern trained on her work. She was knitting for Christmas, a pastime that occupied her all year long.

If Annie were to hazard a guess, the finished product would be a sweater for Abel. The blue yarn was almost the exact color of his eyes.

Just that random thought of Abel plunged her back into the guilty morass in which she had been wallowing ever since her moonlight tryst with Jack Dare. She looked at Emma, blithely knitting away and thought: if I don't put that night behind me, I'll go crazy.

Nona and Mittie came in to say good-night, and effectively ended her mental torment. She buttoned Nona's nightdress the rest of the way and tied Mittie's hair back the way she liked it. Then Emma opened her arms wide enough for both girls.

"It's probably wishful thinking on my part, but I think you girls have grown an inch taller since we arrived."

"I believe you're right, Emma, but best of all is that Nona has not suffered any more of her spells."

"If the change of climate has healed her, it will all be worth it."

"Even the spiders?"

"Even the spiders!"

After Emma kissed each downy cheek, Annie took the girls off to tuck them in and hear their prayers. When she returned, she paused in the doorway a minute. Emma felt her gaze and met it. "Do you feel all right, dear?"

"Yes, fine. And you?"

"I've been feeling positively renewed! And look!" She stretched her fingers. "My hands hardly ever ache anymore."

"Good!"

Annie had been pleased with how Emma had improved since they arrived. She had been the Emma of old which meant she had boundless energy and was brimming with ambitious projects again. At present she had Charley hard at work at her latest undertaking . . . a garden of new potatoes, beans, peas and squash. And she'd taken up knitting again.

Which was, Annie told herself, what she should be doing, knitting herself some new stockings. Every pair she owned was patched, and poorly at that.

Emma's hands stilled. "You know I don't mean to pry, dear, but you don't seem yourself lately."

Annie looked up and flushed. "I know. I've been worrying about school tomorrow." She smiled nervously. "Guess I've got first-day jitters."

"Don't give it a thought," said Emma. "You are bound to be the best teacher this place has ever had."

"I'm the only teacher it's ever had."

"You know what I mean."

"Yes, I do, and I certainly intend to try."

Emma studied her young companion, the soft curve of her cheek and the long tendril of hair that had escaped her pins. She knew her well enough to know that she had not been honest with her just then. Why? she wondered.

Annie Mapes was very dear to Emma Fuller. Since she had never been blessed with children herself, she had felt very fortunate to have her late husband's son by his first wife to raise. Then when she was given Annie she had felt doubly blessed. And now Annie and Abel had fallen in love.

It had been almost too much good fortune when the two people she loved most in the world had informed her that they intended to wed.

However, after the initial euphoria wore off, it was easy for Emma to envision the future and see Annie and Abel moving away to set up their own household. That was the real reason she offered to take Nona and Mittie . . . pure selfishness. She could not bear the thought of being alone again.

"Emma, would you like me to read Abel's letter to you?"

"Yes, dear, if you don't mind."

"Not at all. I'll go get it."

Annie paused in the doorway. "Would you like me to get you a cup of warm milk while I'm up?"

"That would be nice. You know how it helps me sleep."

"Yes, I know."

Annie left and soon sounds came from the area they had screened off with a tall boy chest. Emma's hands stilled again. If the truth were known, it bothered her a little that Annie could read Abel's letters to her in their entirety. It seemed to her that there should be something too personal and private to read aloud.

A part of her was glad to know that Annie and Abel's love was not solely based on physical attraction, but upon common goals and intellectual compatibility. But there was that other part of her that wished Annie had to seek a locked room and lowered lantern.

"Here we are."

Annie had returned. She set the cup of warm milk beside Emma and resumed her seat. "Thank you, dear."

Without hesitation Annie tucked one leg up under her and unfolded the foolscap and began to read.

My dear Annie—
I received your last letter in only twenty-eight days! Isn't

that amazing! Anyway I hasten to respond in time for this afternoon's mail because I have an interesting tidbit of news to share regarding that spider in your backyard.

I went to Loganian Library first but without much luck I'm afraid. I then paid a visit to Professor Wellman—you probably remember him. He's the one who has every obscure book ever published and has memorized them all. Anyway he had a book concerning all such crawling creatures and he believes your spider is a tarantula. Here's what else he found.

The word "tarantula" comes from the Latin word Tarentum, which has now been modernized to Taranto, a word that originated in southern Italy. It refers, apparently, to any of a number of large venomous spiders.

The true tarantula was the European wolf spider whose bite brought on an affliction which was apparently characterized by melancholia, stupor and an uncontrollable desire to dance! A lively Italian dance called the tarantella is supposed to have originally come about as a remedy for the spider's bite.

Professor Wellman thinks those afflicted with the venom believed they could dance it out of their system. (More than likely they simply wanted to have a good time before they crossed over.)

I don't see how this will be of any use to you but that's Professor Wellman for you—a veritable fount of worthless information.

Does he believe that this is the same spider? Professor Wellman is pretty sure it is but he cannot say without seeing one face-to-face. He suggested that I have someone send him a live specimen for experimentation. Apparently a spider of that size would have no trouble surviving the trip without fresh meat! Can we count on you to capture and ship one? I imagine that I can hear your answer from here! Oh, well, I can't say that I blame you.

One more thing. In case I arrive there and find you dancing uncontrollably, I have arranged for lessons in Latin dance. At least we can go together, Annie dear, clicking our heels and yelling "arriba!"

Kiss mother for me and watch yourselves at all times. I miss and love you both much more than you know! Yours, Abel.

P.S. What makes you think I am brave enough to kill your spider for you? Better hire one of those ranging fellas. I don't think I'm up for it.

Annie folded the letter and stared at it. "Twenty-eight days. Imagine."

Jack had decided that this love business fit him like a pointed foot in a square boot. Why the Mexicans were so crazy about it was beyond him. Hell, he'd had a mule bite that felt better!

Yet, once again, here he was. Standing by the same tree, at the same time, same as he had been every night this week, waiting for Annie Mapes to take another walk by the water. He wasn't happy about it. Not a bit.

He hadn't asked to be in love. He hated it. Hated the way it had taken over his life. Hated the things it made him do. Hated the way it made him feel.

It was not a bit pleasant to go all soft and unsteady at the sight of her. Or to walk into things 'cause your mind was on splashy gray eyes and a figure that most men only saw in their dreams.

He was acting like a damned simpleton. He wasn't used to it and he didn't like it. He'd rather just get over her, but with the same certainty that he knew every man has to die sometime, he knew that he'd not be getting over Annie Mapes in this lifetime. He was hooked. Line and sinker. And that made him mad. Hell, there were times when he almost hated her for making him into what he'd become!

Why her, anyway? Sure she was an eye-full, but fifty bucks said she didn't know squat about what went on between a man and a woman in the hay. He'd have to start right from the git go. Show her how to kiss right. Teach her how to touch him . . . and where. Probably have to spend hours coaxing her into letting him do this little thing and then that little thing . . . Hell, the process could take the rest of his life! Holymanaliveboywow! He straightened in order to adjust his vitals, and thought: So much for talking himself out of love.

About the only thing that would give him relief would be to win her. He was determined to do so, only there wasn't much that he could point at and say: well, at least I did that much right. So far he'd done nothing right. That's what had him tied up in knots.

And yet, there were other times when he didn't think his chances were all that bad. Especially when he recalled when they kissed . . . the soft sounds she made and the one brief moment when the tip of her tongue had touched his before it darted away.

God, she might be untried but she was ripe! There had been a minute or two when she'd been stuck onto his lips like a leech! He was holding onto that memory like a rat in a hell-rushing river.

His only chance was to make himself irresistible to her. She already wanted him. Couldn't hardly take her eyes off him . . . now if she would just let him see her so that she could see him!

He waited until the last light was extinguished. He was pretty sure now that the back window was hers. He stood there for a while, watching the cabin, the woods, the sky and then he retrieved his horse and started for home.

Annie blew out the candle then lay looking up at the play of moonlight on the exposed beams. Tomorrow was the first day of school and in many ways, it was also the first day of her life. From tomorrow onward she vowed that this new beginning would be one without guilt and self-recrimination. She would not continue to allow her thoughts to meander at will. She would take herself in hand and hold on! She had to. Her future—her very life—depended on how well she did in handling this new . . . challenge.

She took solace in the fact that she had not committed any

sin—either against Abel or against her soul—and vowed that she would never do so. ''So help me, I will not!''

Renewing her vows had soothed her, and by concentrating on only uplifting thoughts, she soon drifted off to sleep.

Chapter 10

Finally, after a seemingly endless wait, today was the first day of school. Wearing her best dress and with her hair braided into a matronly coronet, Annie was as ready as she would ever be.

The schoolroom was ready as well, having been thoroughly scrubbed and dusted and judged from every conceivable angle. The furniture had been delivered and positioned and then repositioned and then pushed back into the original configuration. Early this morning she had distributed supplies to each student's place.

About half the children would have feather quills and ink bottles or charcoal, and the rest would have slates and chalk. Each child would have a book which they would make themselves by taking two pieces of rough paper and folding them to make four pages. After one edge was sewed, these homemade affairs would become their copy books.

She was fortunate that Mr. Cooper had allowed her to order twelve *McGuffey's First Readers*—they were awfully expensive—but they had not yet arrived. She did, however, have a few old hornbooks which at least contained the alphabet, the

numerals from one to ten and the Lord's Prayer. For texts there
were six *American Spelling Books,* also called the blue-book
speller, two almanacs and of course, the Bible.

She looked over the students who were present so far.

The first to arrive had been the Cooper girl, Electra, a primly
dressed blonde with a giant pink bow pinned to the back of
her head. She had been escorted by her mother—who had
stayed so long Annie thought she intended to spend the day.

According to Annie's information Electra was only thirteen,
but either she was already using starch on her face or she was
unnaturally wan.

Next to Electra sat the Williford girls. She smiled at them
and got brief shy smiles in return. Then their small faces became
very serious and they looked around, worried that some of the
other students might have seen what they did. After all, she
was their teacher now and not just Auntie Annie.

Since they had not wanted to get up as early as she did, she
had asked Charley Walters to bring the girls to school with
him and they had just arrived. They sat up front, scrub-faced
and big-eyed while Charley sat slouched in the last row with
his arms folded and his eyes like blanks, the picture of boredom.

She frowned a little, thinking about the distressing news she
had heard about him. News that she had not had the heart to
share with Emma yet.

In his free time Charley had taken to hanging around Hap
Pettijohn's place doing odd jobs for an extra coin or two, and,
apparently, learning how to shoot. There'd been nothing said
but then the week previous when Goldie Dare delivered the
new furniture, he mentioned that Charley had recently asked
him how old a person had to be before they could join the
ranger troop. Further, Charley had told Goldie that he had been
saving his money in order to buy a gun and that he intended
to join up as soon as he met the age requirement. He was
delighted—Annie and Emma equally distressed—to learn that
there was none!

Knowing what she now knew, she'd be surprised if his attendance in school lasted the month. It was a terrible shame; this

was no doubt Charley Walter's one chance for an education but, unfortunately, she had no say in his life.

Seth Haggard and the Garlock boy, Alfred, arrived next. Seth had a scar above his right eye, a double tooth in front and an Adam's apple that protruded on his throat like a burl on a tree. He told her he lived on a farm two miles south of town and that he had an older brother who might come to school later in the year, provided he was no longer needed at home.

Apparently Alfred Garlock and Electra Cooper were friends because Alfred immediately abandoned Seth in order to sit next to her. After a hurried whispered conversation, Electra raised her hand and informed Annie that they—"Alfred and me"—already knew how to write. As she sat down she shot a look around the room to see who had heard her announcement and judge how impressed they were.

Electra seemed to be a bit haughty, which one might expect given her affluent background and the position her father held in town. Annie was prepared to take that into consideration—up to a point.

In order to test their level of writing expertise, Annie asked each of them to write a short paragraph about an exciting thing that had happened to them.

"This year?" asked Alfred.

"No," Annie replied. "It could have happened at any time in your life."

Freckled Zick—short for Ezekiel—Simmons had red hair that formed a frizzy halo behind his ears not unlike a drawing of a saint at sundown. His face, however, was that of a habitual rascal. It was Zick's father who had promised to bring a slaughtered carcass to her for his son's fee, an event she awaited with bated breath.

Abner and Rebecca Yates were brother and sister and aged nine and twelve respectively. As soon as they gave Annie their names and ages they told her that their brother, Billy, was one of the rangers who rode with Black Jack Dare.

Their tone was the same that one would use to say: "And He sittith at the right hand of the Father . . ."

Making it eight were Juan Rivera and Josh Phelps, two boys who said they both had sisters at home but that neither girl would ever be coming to school since there "weren't no need for girls t'learn nothin'."

She bit her tongue lest she ask him what about the girls already present. *Or more importantly, what about me?*

Almost on cue, three girls tumbled into the room, handsome ones who looked vaguely familiar to her. Moving to greet them brought her by the window where she saw Jack Dare uncurl his leg from his saddle and slide to the ground.

She should have known the girls were his kin, for they all had the same strong jaw and the same dirt black hair.

The jangle of spurs became louder until there he was, standing in the doorway. He removed his hat. "Good day, Miss Mapes," he said softly and just looked at her.

She had to resist the urge to smooth her bodice. "And to you, Mr. Dare. Ah, who do we have here?"

"These hellcats're my kid sisters." Walking behind them he touched each one in turn. "This here's Britain—call her Brit—and this one's Irish. If you get 'em mixed up, that's okay 'cause everybody does. An' this little girl here . . ." He laid a hand on the smallest one's shoulder. ". . . is Miss Denmark Dare. Sometimes called Markie, sometimes called Goober." The little girl rested the crown of her head on his stomach and gave him an upside-down-backward grin.

"She's blind."

Blind! Annie's stomach fell. She had no experience teaching the blind! Recovering her manners but not her wits, she said, "Welcome! Please come in and take your seats. Except you, Mr. Dare."

"Awheck! You mean I can't stay?"

The other children giggled and looked at him in awe.

The nearest sister—Annie thought it was Irish—took Markie's hand and led her to a bench.

The first thing Markie did was touch all the things on the desk in front of her. The ink bottle, the quill pen, the folded papers, carefully, gently and holding her mouth in a perfect O. Then she scrunched her shoulders and grinned.

The little one looks more like her oldest brother than any of them. No one could miss the intensity in those black eyes. Looking at her, it was hard to believe that she was blind. Oh, Lord! She's blind!

Jack took some coins out of his pocket. "Here's for their first month. Three dollars, right?"

"Yes, thank you." She dropped the coins in her pocket without counting them. She hated this part of it.

"They've got fried chicken and half a dozen hard-boiled eggs for their lunch." He indicated an oddly shaped basket which one of the twins had hung on a whittled-wood coat peg. Already hanging there were the tied sacks, pails, and pine-stave buckets containing the other kids' lunches.

"Fine. That's fine."

"Jack!" Markie had her mouth cupped. "Don't forget to ask what time we'll be done."

"About four," Annie replied, then to Jack. "All right?"

He shrugged. "Okay by me."

"Maw just wanted to know."

That was Markie again and Annie was thinking: She might be blind but she's not shy. As if he'd read her mind he pointed at Markie and grinned. "Shy as a mail order bride, ain't she?"

"As if that were something to be proud of."

"What?"

"Nothing."

"Well ..." He pointed outside where a spotted pony munched grass under a tree. "They can ride that horse home."

Noting that the horse was not tied, she said, "Won't he wander off?"

He grinned. What a town girl! Doesn't even know the difference between a mare and a stud. Boy, she would if he had anything to say about it. Oh, yeah, you bet she would!

"Normally *she* won't but if something spooks her, Irish can run her down. She's faster'n a wolf on a three-legged deer."

"I see . . ." A particularly repugnant image. It seemed that every Texian had a hundred.

"Well . . ." he said.

A hush settled. One that lasted long enough for a few of the kids to look at each other and then at the two grown-ups. First one. Then the other. Only they weren't doing anything much. He turned his hat in his hand. She brushed at a horsefly and shifted her feet. Zick gave Joshua a look that said: Ain't grown-ups strange!

"Anythin' else they'll need?" Jack was running out of things to say to drag this out.

"No. Thank you. We'll be . . . fine."

He pointed at his sisters. "You girls be good now. You know what Maw'll do if you get yourselves thrown outa school."

He looked back at her and grinned and kept looking. Her mind was running wild again. She imagined that he was thinking about pulling her to him right then and there! She felt her face heat but he merely put on his hat, tugged it down and said, "Ma'am."

"Mr. Dare." Having followed him like the trail of a comet, she was standing in the open doorway when he touched his hat to her one last time and then walked to his horse.

Feeling oddly let down, she proceeded to the front of the room and looked at the faces that looked back at her. Her mind had been wiped clean. The blind girl, Markie, had her head cocked birdlike.

"What's she doin' now?" She had a whisper that would wake the dead.

Her sister shrugged. "Nothin' so far."

"Huh!" She'd cupped her lips to her sister's ear—which did nothing to diminish her voice. "Well, tell me if she ever does somethin'."

Annie cleared her throat. "First I will call the roll. Please say 'here' when your name is called."

"She's walkin' over to the desk . . ."

"All right, now. The first thing we are going to learn is that there is to be no talking during lesson times."

Markie asked her sister, "How're we gonna learn if we can't talk?"

"I don't know."

"Unless you are called upon," added Annie.

"Aha!"

"That'll work, won't it, Markie?"

Annie glared. "Irish!"

"I'm Brit."

"Whoever you are, I just said there is to be no talking. It disturbs the rest of the class."

Markie asked, "Does whisperin' count the same as talkin'?"

"Yes!" Annie cried. And instantly regretted it. Poor thing! "No! One of your sisters may tell you—very quietly—what the rest of the class is doing."

"That'll work, won't it, Brit?"

"Oh, yeah, Markie. That'll work jus' fine."

Annie looked at that grinning, sun-smitten face, so eager, so happy . . . and then she looked at the rest of the class. This will never work. It simply will not work.

"I'll be back in, uh, just a minute. Please remain in your seats until I return."

There was a flash, a collective whiplash of the pupils and teacher was gone.

Annie had raced outside just in time to catch the sight of Jack Dare's hat disappearing behind a little hill. He would pass another little hill next and that's where she headed, cutting across the field then running down the tree-walled path. Of course, the children all came outside to watch her.

"Ooohwee!"

"Gee willakers! Look at her go!"

"Like the milltails of hell!"

"Like somebody'd turpentined under her tail!"

Jack Dare popped into view the instant the teacher launched herself from the little hill yelling the Kiowa war cry. Zick blinked and said, "Holy cow!"

"Look at her hang onto that stirrup!"

Thinking he had been attacked by a panther, Dare's horse

shied and ran from their view with teacher gamely hanging on. The kids exchanged a look. "You see that?"

"Yeaaa!"

Short of killing a greased Comanche in a knife fight there wasn't much she could have done that would have won them over faster. Meanwhile, beyond the brow of the little hill . . .

"Miss Mapes!" Jack was still trying to control his horse. "What t'hell . . . ?"

"Mr. Dare! Please." She had a hand on her chest, trying to still her heart. Her coronet was a loop on her back and she had lost a shoe.

"I have to talk to you!"

"I ain't goin' no where 'less I drag you with me."

She only then realized that she had a death grip on his pant leg. She let go and brushed ineffectively at the crimp.

"What's wrong?" He climbed down off his horse.

"Mr. Dare, I don't have any experience teaching a blind child."

"You have a lot of experience teachin' other kids?"

"Some," she replied defensively then slumped. "All right, none. But all of my training has been geared toward teaching sighted children. Little Markie will not be able to grasp anything without being able to see the lessons and I'm sure it will be terribly boring for her."

"You want me to take her home with me?"

"Would you? Could you?"

He walked off a ways then walked back and she could see that his expression was that of a man who had just shot his dog.

"She's gonna be mighty upset. Maw said she didn't sleep all last night, she was that excited. This mornin' Maw said she was sittin' in her chair a good two hours before daybreak, washed an' dressed an' ready to go."

"I feel awful but my hands are tied . . ." She shook her head. "I can't think of what else to do."

"If you won't keep her then there's nothin'."

"I'm sorry but there are the other children to consider. I do hope you understand."

"I guess." God, he hated to tell Markie she couldn't stay. "I don't think the twins'll stay if Markie can't."

"Oh . . ." Three students lost. Mr. Cooper would kill her!

Some time went by. While she chewed her thumbnail and looked at the dirt, he looked at her and thought: if she only got to know Markie . . . "Look, how about givin' it a coupla days? Let her listen to what's goin' on. She's pretty smart, you know. If she can tell she won't learn anything, she'll decide to leave on her own."

"Well . . ." Jack waited while she stared at something far away. It seemed a long time before she said, "All right. I'll give it some time."

"Good! Well . . ." He mounted up. "It's settled."

"Yes."

Poor girl! The look on her face would make a glass eye cry. "Good-bye again, Miss Mapes."

It wasn't much of a smile she gave him. "Good-bye, Mr. Dare."

She looked so forlorn. He watched her limp away and her shadow made a shepherd's staff on the slope of the hill.

As Annie rounded the corner she looked up just in time to see all the kids scurry inside. She couldn't really blame them. She guessed she had made quite a spectacle of herself. And all to no avail.

She was not stupid. She realized that Jack Dare had pulled a fast one on her, and that he knew enough about her to suspect that Markie would be her student as long as she wanted to be.

What was she going to do? She couldn't let the poor child sit there while everyone else learned. She regrouped and started making plans. Tonight she would write to Abel and ask him to send her every book he could lay his hands on that had to do with teaching the blind. Good Lord, help me! Twenty-eight days there and twenty-eight days back. What would she do with Markie Dare in the meantime?

She paused momentarily at the front door then nonchalantly strolled down the aisle.

Thump Slap. Thump Slap.

She had reached the front. She turned and faced the class. Three children were hanging out in the aisle, apparently trying to see what was wrong with her foot. She ignored them and smiled. "Well," she said. "Shall we begin?"

"About time," grumbled Markie.

"Miss Markie Dare! You confine yourself, please! From now on, anyone who has anything to say *must* raise their hand and wait to be recognized. Is that clear?" She paused to modulate her voice. "Now, everyone please stand and we will recite the Lord's Prayer." A hand shot up. "Yes, Markie?"

"What about the roll call?"

"The . . . roll call? . . . oh, yes. All right. All right!"

Rounding the desk she sat and loudly raked her chair forward. She opened the attendance book with a slap and dipped her pen in the ink jar. Zick nudged Alfred and pointed under the teacher's desk. Looked like a sick turtle head was sticking out of her stocking.

"All right. Miss Electra Cooper?"

"Here."

Markie whipped her head around to the sound of Electra's voice. Alphabetically the Dares were next.

"Brit?"

"Here."

"Irish?"

"Here."

A pause then . . . "Miss Markie Dare!"

"HERE!" She stood up and clasped her hands over her head. "Oh, yeah. Here I am. In school right here. Markie Dare."

"Thank you, Markie. You may take your seat."

"Thank *you*."

"And lower your hands."

"Yessum. Ma'am?"

"Yes?"

"Did you put a check next to my name?"

"An X."

"Ah!" she whispered. "An X!"

Looking at the sheer joy on her face, Annie couldn't help smiling, but she soon found herself on an emotional edge, teetering on the brink of crying. Such a winning child. Such a terrible shame.

At the end of the day she was sitting with her stocking feet (actually half stocking, half shreds) on a pile of books, feeling like she'd just fought a war. And lost. Her desk was a mess and so was the schoolroom and so, no doubt, was she. And she still had to clean, bring in stove wood and set the beans to soak. She was ruminating about all the extra work when her eye fell on the burnished brass bell that Abel had sent her. It brought a tired smile. Dear Abel! She had written to him after she received it to say that it had become her most prized possession.

Abel said that he had purchased it at an estate sale and that it was purported to have been cast by a bellmaker in Drohndorf, Germany. It was quite old—the date etched on the clapper was 1682—and had a sweet tone that reminded her of the traditional English hand bells played by Christmas carolers.

She sat twirling a strand of hair around her fingers, remembering Christmas, snow and carolers . . . until she realized how much time had slipped by. *This is not getting the rest of your work done.*

She sighed and stood then sat that fast. Two slates lay facedown on her desk. Alfred and Electra's special project about an interesting event in their lives. She started with Alfred Garlock, curious as to what he would consider exciting. She read his first—and only—sentence which was: *I Aynt Had Won Yet.*

She set the slate aside, once again admonishing herself for letting her expectations soar above reality. Surely Electra's would be better. But instead of being heartened, her hopes were dashed. Electra's was worse. Her narrative began: *The Spectikle of the Sircus.* And it went on for a full page with scarcely a single correctly spelled word.

Annie sighed and rubbed her eyes. Clearly she had her work cut out for her.

There was an apothecary in Philadelphia who used to carry a powder that not only calmed one's nerves but simultaneously cured one's head pains. She better write to him tomorrow.

Chapter 11

On the second Tuesday in June, a day when school had been in session about three weeks, Bittercreek Clarke and Dutch Elliott bought a new gun at Garlock's store, walked outside and shot a stray dog that had been trotting down the street.

Annie heard the shot, which was a common sound after sundown but an unusual one during the day. Since she had just released the children for the day, she went to the door and looked down Main Street and saw the storekeeper, Bowie Garlock, Markie and the Dare twins standing in a loose circle around something that lay on the ground. She pulled the school door closed and fastened the latch and then hurried toward them.

Arriving breathless, she saw that Bittercreek and Dutch Elliott were standing on the boardwalk under Garlock's covered vega, looking at a pistol Dutch Elliott held. The dog, a spotted mongrel, lay dead in the street. Irish was comforting a teary, blotch-faced Markie. It wasn't her dog or anything, but Annie would later learn that Markie considered any animal her animal. "What an awful thing to do!"

"There was no call for it atall," said Garlock.

Annie looked over her shoulder at them. Dreadful men!

A large blond man walked up. He was visibly angry and carried a squalling child under his arm like a sack of grain.

"Who was that shooting in the street?"

It sounded like he said: "Who vass dat shooding in da street?" and suddenly Annie knew who he was: The German millwright. Everyone had been talking about him. Some said he would be building a lumber mill, some said a gristmill. Both were much needed. Schumacher, yes, that's his name. From Leipzig, they said. Unless she was mistaken, that same someone had told her that his wife was ill, which would explain why he had his son with him every time she saw him. Annie pointed behind her. "It was those men right over there."

He scowled. "We were crossing the road. We could have been shot."

Bittercreek Clarke and Dutch Elliott came over, brazen as could be. "I was 'shooding in da street.' Tryin' out my new gun here. A Harper's Ferry .54 caliber flintlock pistol with a rifled barrel."

Schumacher did not appear to be a bit intimidated. "You cannot fire a pistol in town!"

"Sez who?"

"Says me. Emil Schumacher. You could have killed someone!"

"Ain't no turd kicker like you gonna tell me what I can or can't do!"

At that Mr. Schumacher handed Irish his son and doubled up his fist—which turned it into a ham—and hit Bittercreek with such force that his manure-flecked boots appeared to meet the sky.

Since everybody was watching Bittercreek land hard enough to lift dust, nobody noticed that Dutch Elliott was drawing his weapon until Blue came up behind him and fetched him a smart rap with the butt end of his pistol. Elliott crumpled like a house of cards and joined Bittercreek on the ground.

Blue Dare was rubbing his finger along his gun until he looked up and noticed the shocked expression on Annie's face.

"Hey, I coulda hurt my gun! Last time I hit 'im with my fist I busted my hand."

"You did gut!" The millwright was offering Blue his hand. "I am Emil Schumacher."

"Blue Dare, an' you did pretty good yourself. Your fist all right?"

"Vhat?"

"Your fist. You didn't bust it on 'im, did you?"

"Oh, *nein*." He gave Bittercreek a none too gentle nudge in the side with the point of his boot. "Next time I will open his head like a melon."

Blue blinked, then grinned and pounded the German on the back. "Good man!"

Two kindred souls, Annie thought.

Dutch Elliott was weaving a bit but he gained his feet first and then helped Bittersweet Clarke to stand. One was rubbing his jaw and the other one held a filthy rag to his pate. Clarke pointed at Schumacher and said, "I ain't gonna fergit yuh, mister."

"Me neither," said Elliott. "Yuh better watch out fer us, yuh damn kraut belly!"

"Gut! You watch for me! I watch for you!" said Schumacher. Having removed his hat, he turned his head first to one side and then to the other. "See this face, yah? Remember face, yah? Und remember where I live so you can find me." He pointed. "House's right down that road."

Since she had been watching this volatile exchange, Annie did not see Jack Dare come up until he was beside her.

"What in hades happened here?" Jack picked up Markie, who was still sobbing.

Clarke and Elliott shook their fists and bared their teeth but apparently the new odds didn't suit them because they collected their chewed-brim hats and stalked off.

"What's the matter, Goober. Are you all right?" After Blue told him what happened Jack threw a look after the retreating figures. "Jus' lookin' for a laugh, were they?"

The Dares would not tolerate cruelty to animals, but they had even less patience with human beings who acted like animals.

Blue cracked his knuckles and started off after Clark and Elliott.

"Where you goin'?"

"T'have a talk with those fellas."

"What about?"

"Firin' a weapon on the street."

"There ain't no law against it."

"Hell, Jack. I'm gonna take an axe haft to 'em. I don't need no law for that . . ."

"Watch your language."

To Annie, Blue said, "Sorry, ma'am."

"We'll take care of them later. Right now somebody's got to bury this dog."

Blue noted the direction of Jack's gaze and got a pained look on his face. "Aw, c'mon, Jack!"

"Bowie'll loan you a shovel. Won't you, Bowie?"

"Yeah, sure."

"Good. I'll take the Goober home."

Blue laid his head back between his shoulders and asked the sky, "Why me?"

Jack nodded to Annie. "Miss Mapes."

"Mr. Dare."

Annie saw several things as he walked away. Markie's red face over his shoulder. How her arms and legs clasped his neck and waist. How his gloved hand cupped her head and how his lips moved against her ear.

Jack Dare might be uneducated and unpolished but he certainly understood the meaning of love.

She would not realize it until later but it was with that episode that her feelings toward him started to soften. She was no longer angry about what had happened by the creek that night. After all, he was not aware of the mores of society. Besides, it was as much her fault as his. She intuitively knew that nothing else would have happened if she had not allowed that first kiss. She watched Jack and Markie until they were lost in the shadows of the vega. He was a rough, unlettered frontiersman, but he was also a fine brother.

Meanwhile Schumacher had rounded on Lloyd Cooper, who had just arrived. "Is there no law against shooting off a pistol in town?"

Cooper blanched. He could not afford to lose this particular immigrant, a skilled specialist and well heeled to boot. "No, but we can make one."

"Gut! You moost arrest people like dat."

He leaned down to take back his son and his shoulders blocked Irish from the sun. "*Danke*, little missy." Irish nodded but forgot to speak because she was thinking that his were the palest blue eyes that she had ever seen.

"I'll say good day then."

He lifted his hat and showed them his wealth of white blond hair and the band of lighter skin that ran across the top half of his forehead. As a group they watched him stride off. Irish was still tongue-tied but not Brit. "Is it true that Mr. Schumacher is married to a leper?"

"What?" Cooper was shocked. Where did these rumors begin? "Certainly not! But his wife has been very ill."

"I could hardly understand him," said Brit. "But he sure is handsome!"

With Schumacher's departure, the little gathering scattered. All except for Irish, whose eyes followed the man until he rounded the corner.

Lloyd Cooper went home and told his wife that the new millwright was dead right. It was high time Sweet Home got itself a sheriff.

Not a man to dillydally, he immediately put in a petition for money from the Vice Governor in Bexar and within days after receiving the go-ahead, he hired a man named Ernest Goodman as the new Sheriff of Sweet Home, a childless widower who had been living in Nacogdoches.

Goodman had proven himself against the Creeks in the war

of 1812 and again against the British at New Orleans. More recently he had done some peacekeeping work and had even driven for Hap Pettijohn on occasion.

He was in his mid-fifties which some said was too long in the tooth for the job. Not the mayor, however, since he and Goodman were exactly the same age. Nowadays maturity is a far greater asset than speed and agility. Or so said the mayor to those who would listen.

When Goodman arrived in Sweet Home, the townspeople saw a rooster-chested man with an ever-flushed face, close-cropped, sooty hair and pale, watery eyes. They also saw a man who looked a good ten years younger than Cooper.

Chapter 12

The next week marked the start of high summer, traditionally a time of long light and short tempers. Seeing as how it was the first of the month, it was also . . . "Time to pay the teacher." Evie Dare scarcely got the words out of her mouth when Jack vaulted onto his horse's back and headed for town.

Jack was oblivious to his mother's measuring gaze. He was thinking that the country looked particularly pretty. The glitter of the creek water. The sun through those oak limbs yonder.

Strange, but he had found himself doing that a lot lately, looking at everyday things as if he had never seen them before. Somehow he had missed the way the treed hills moved down to bushy clumps and then rolled into tall wavy grass. Yonder was another good place to take Annie, that splotched place with the red and yellow wildflowers. He'd have to make sure he remembered that one too.

In his mind he had lain with her a hundred times in a hundred different places. It wasn't hard to find a likely spot. Most of them looked good to him. In that little abandoned cabin or in that sweet-smelling straw . . . Beneath a full sun and under a leafy tree. In the creek and beside it. In the schoolhouse and in some stranger's bed and high atop a mountain where the wind whipped their loving into a wild and frenzied thing.

He looked back at the meadow of wildflowers and imagined how it would be. *Such a pretty dress, he'd say. Sure be a shame to dirty it. And she'd say, Well then, I suppose I better take it off.* And when she did, she stood before him, smiling and willing, long-legged and lean as a tendon . . .

He'd had to stand off his horse and air cool for a time. As a result, it was lunchtime when he arrived and all the kids were in the field behind the schoolhouse. He looked for the twins and saw Irish playing leapfrog with some boys—no surprise there—and then he spotted Brit, strolling slowly beside the creek. That a redheaded boy danced attendance on her was no surprise either. A covey of quail rose out of a clump of bushes and squeals of laughter were followed by the appearance of Markie and another little girl. Finally, the figure he sought walked into sight, holding something in her skirt.

She hadn't seen him yet or she would not have left her dress hiked up like it was. It was pale green, like the grass, but he was too busy admiring shapely calves and well-turned ankles to notice more than that.

With her hands thus occupied, she turned into the wind to get the hair out of her face and that's when she saw him. He knew the instant it happened because her head went up and her hem went down.

The day previous Markie had proudly informed him that they had shown Miss Mapes how to find wild onions so, naturally, he'd thought they were at it again until he saw what dropped out of her skirt. Flowers.

Annie could not control the leap in her chest when she saw the buckskin figure. Twice before she had seen him like that, sitting motionless with his carbine across his pommel. Both times it had been late in the day and he'd been atop the hill across from the school. She purposely had not acknowledged his presence. Just locked the door and started for home.

Of course she knew who it was and the thought of his eyes following her never failed to give her that queer feeling in her stomach . . . the same queer feeling she was experiencing right now. He urged his horse closer. Determined to be cordial—and nothing else—she smiled up at him from behind a strand of wind twisted hair. "Hello, Mr. Dare." That smile greeted her from beneath a lustrous shelf of mustache.

"Miss Mapes."

She pointed. "Look at all the flowers we found!"

"Yeah," grinned Markie. "Jus' look at 'em all."

The Cooper girl said, "Can we take our pick, Miss Mapes?"

"By all means, take any you want. But you better wrap them in a wet rag so they'll last until you get home."

"You help us, Miss Mapes."

"All right."

Jack sat his horse and watched her sit on her heels and parcel out the flowers until they were gone. She stood, and a half smile formed on her face as she watched the children run to the creek for water. He followed her line of sight and saw Markie running at breakneck speed to keep up with the pack. One hand was clutching her flowers and the other was hanging onto the back of her sister's skirt. She was howling like a wild Indian.

Jack was watching Annie Mapes with the same intensity that she watched Markie, and especially he watched the way the wind held her clothes against her. When she finally turned and moved toward him, it was with the grace of a deer, and he thought she looked better dressed than any woman he had ever seen naked before.

"What can I do for you, Mr. Dare? Mr. Dare?"

Suddenly his purpose escaped him. Oh, yeah. "Markie says you want her to stay after school."

"Just for an hour or so and only a couple of days a week. I want to spend some time reading stories and exercises to her. See, much of the work the children do involves reading a lesson and then memorizing it. Markie excels at memorization but the exercises have to be read to her more than once and that may be boring to the sighted children."

She turned and started walking toward the school. He stepped off his horse and kept pace, walking with his hat in one hand and his reins in the other. His manner seemed relaxed and easy while hers was anything but.

As usual his slick hair was poorly confined by a rawhide tie. But oddly enough she no longer found the effect unkempt. When she looked at him now she only saw how the sun lit his hair and how the wind ruffled it.

In truth everything about him had become the height of manliness to her. His fierce mustache, his big teeth and rough hands and the way he talked and walked and laughed. Even how he had tasted.

She stumbled a little then and he touched her elbow.

"All right?"

"Uh, yes. Thank you."

"You were sayin' . . . ?"

She looked at him with stark eyes. "What was I saying?"

"About Markie?"

"Oh, yes. I was saying that Markie has a fine mind."

"We always thought so."

"You know, I once read an article in the paper about a fifteen-year-old student at the Institute for the Blind in Paris who had developed a system to allow a blind person to read. I didn't pay much attention at the time, but I've written away for some more information."

She was looking up at him and squinting a bit from the sun. Her loose hair was pulled back by a green ribbon and hung halfway down her back. He thought about parting it and kissing his way down the bones of her spine to the dimple he was sure to find on her butt . . .

They had reached the school and he'd reached his limit for those kinds of thoughts.

"I know if anyone could learn this method, Markie could. Think of what this could mean to her."

"It would mean a lot to her an' to us. 'Course we'll pay you extry for your time."

"I won't hear of it!' She turned angrily. She was on the stump-step which made her about his height and he thought about how easy it would be to cup her buttocks and bring her close to him.

And then walk around this side of the building away from any small prying eyes and lift her skirts and drop his pants.

There he went again!

"This is something I'm doing because I want to, Mr. Dare. Not because I expect to get paid extra for it." Red dots circled her cheeks and sparks lit her eyes.

"No need to get sand in your gizzard," he said as he followed her into the schoolroom. What he really wanted was to take her in his arms and kiss her silly. Instead he lit the pipe he had prepared earlier.

"I'm concerned about her getting home alone."

"That's no problem. Another hour of school won't hurt the twins."

"They aren't needed at home?"

"Naw, I'll talk to Maw. It'll be all right. Through the smoke he watched the sunlight move in her hair. He'd always admired the way her ears lay against her head and the fine hairs that grew on her neck. He knew how she smelled right there. Like a flower he'd never smelled before.

She glanced up, saw the look in his eyes and turned to the open window.

Markie was standing in the center of a long piece of board laid over a fat log, throwing her weight from side to side to enhance the ride for Rebecca Yates and Electra Cooper on the opposite ends. She was crying, "See Saw Margery Daw!" and everything on her was in motion: Pigtails. Arms. Legs. Her smiling face looked lit from within.

"Was Markie born blind?"

"Maw doesn't know. She said she didn't notice that anything was wrong with her until she was some weeks old."

Annie turned. "She didn't?" Her tone added: Impossible!

"Markie was her twelfth, you know. She said by then all she had time to do was count fingers and toes and see if any of their limbs were crooked. Any more than that had to wait till later. But she said Markie seemed alert and knew where to find . . . what she needed to find.''

Annie turned her flaming face to the window, but her discomfort left after watching Markie some more. ''Oh, she's such a girl! I would love a child just like her, blind or not.''

''Ma'am, I'd be happy to give it everythin' I got.''

He had come closer, so close she felt his breath stir her hair. She moved away then turned and looked up at him. ''Please. I'd hope we could be friends.''

''You don't get a kid by being friends.''

''Mr. Dare, you promised you would not do this . . . !''

''All right.'' He held up a gloved hand. ''All right. Friends.''

''Fine.''

''Well, one friend to another, how about if you teach me to read.''

She tossed her head. ''Oh, really!''

''What?''

''Shame on you!''

''Why?''

''You are not interested in learning to read.''

''Huh! I jus' thought I said I was.''

''Well, you're not. You're a big fibber!''

''Fibber!''

''I recognize one when I see one. Especially one as brazen as you. You know, I may have just the thing for you.'' She knelt and started rummaging around under her desk. ''In Normal school we were told that an appropriate punishment for a liar is to sit him in a corner with this sign on his head.'' She held up a piece of peeled bark. Something had been written on it in charcoal. She pointed. ''This says STORY TELLER.''

He pushed himself off the wall. ''You know what?''

She dropped the bark hat. He had that look about him again. ''No, what?''

''I think maybe you're scared . . .''

She scurried around the desk. ''Scared of what?''

''Of tryin' to teach me to read. You're scared cause you're not sure you can do it.''

"I know I can do it."

"Hah!"

She got a sly look in her eye. "Mr. Dare, I will not fall for your ploy. You said there's nothing you do that requires reading or writing, remember?"

Ploy? Sometimes she might as well be speaking another language but this time he got the gist of what she was saying.

"Okay, what is my . . . ploy?"

She blushed beet red. "You know what it is . . ."

Yeah, he did and the thing was, she was right! "Well, all right then. Don't teach me." He turned and walked toward the door. "I was only gonna do it for Markie's sake. I thought if I learned to read I could help her study at home. Maybe read her some stories. Hear her lessons. Whatever. But if you don't have the time." He checked the impact of his words and saw that her face was stricken. "Well . . ." He made his voice sound terribly sad. He heard a horse then and went to the window. It was Billy Yates, riding up fast. Damn his bad timing! He walked outside.

Annie followed, and Billy touched his sweat-stained hat to her. "Howdy, Miss Mapes."

"Hello, Mr. Yates."

Billy was a clean-shaven young man who bore a strong family resemblance to his younger kin, Abner and Rebecca. He had been one of many who had come "calling" in the beginning. Though he had seemed disappointed to learn about her impending marriage, he still sat and talked with them until late that night. They'd both liked him and though Annie didn't see it, Emma said he reminded her of Abel.

Abner and Rebecca had come running as soon as they saw their brother ride in. He grinned at Abner and pulled Rebecca's braid as they beamed up at him. "All right. Y'all scat. Jack an' me need to talk."

The two men put their heads together, Billy by leaning on his pommel and Jack standing beside him and patting his horse's neck. Unabashedly curious, Annie tried to hear what they were saying but they spoke too softly.

"Trouble, Billy?"

"Yeah. Comanches. Stole Ramón Allende's horses. Shot his cattle and work oxen. Luckily he wasn't at home, but the tracks looked like they were headed for the Hart place. Clyde's gone to round up the others. Blue's bringing your gear."

"All right." He walked to his horse. "Well, Miss Mapes, I guess we have to continue our talk another time."

"Do you really really want to learn?"

"To read? Yeah, I do. Really."

"Then we'll begin when you return."

"Really?"

"Yes."

"You won't chicken out, will you?"

Annie's nose pinched shut. Chicken out, indeed! "Never fear that, Mr. Dare."

"Good!" He turned his horse then reversed direction. "I almost forgot." He stood in his stirrups to dig in his pocket. "Here's two months for the girls. By the way, they said that you're the nicest, kindest person they've ever met." He smiled down at her and let his eyes add what he thought.

Chapter 13

The following Saturday Goldie was getting ready to make a trip into town when Evie asked him to take Irish along with him. "I need a paper of pins and some spirits of turpentine at the store."

"All right. Go get your shoes on, Irish." Goldie gathered a half dozen deer and wolf skins which they would trade at Garlock's for some of the things they needed and by the time he had them in the back of the wagon, Irish had climbed up on the seat. As they pulled away, Evie cupped her mouth and yelled, "Irish, you tell ol' Bowie Garlock that if he ever comes down on that red wool I'll buy some of it off 'im. Then you an' me'll make the boys some new drawers."

Irish waved and nodded to her mother, like she always did. As if she would ever have the nerve to tell Mr. Garlock that!

They were halfway to town when Goldie told her he was going to stop at the new mill to see what that German fella would charge him for cutting some wood.

"You recall his name?"

"Emil Schumacher," Irish said and then turned to stone.

"That's it. Shoemaker."

Goldie explained that his visit had to do with a new settler who'd asked him to build a cabin for him! Floor to ceiling. Furniture and everything and the man's offer was so good and the work so easy Goldie couldn't hardly turn him down. Plus he'd promised a bonus for a fast completion, which prompted Goldie to ask Blue and Jack if they would lend a hand. When they were not out rangering, of course.

"Did they say they would?" She surprised herself by the calmness of her voice.

"Heck, yeah. Why wouldn't they? With that kind of money!"

"Maybe us girls could help too."

"Probably be plenty to do. The man appears helpless and his woman's likely to be the same way. They're from a place called Bermont or Kermont. Something like that. When I told him he sure did talk funny he comes right back at me an' says: "You sure do talk funny too! Hah!"

While Goldie went on like that, Irish's thoughts turned to Emil Schumacher, something that was getting to be old hat to her. Matter of fact he'd hardly been out of her mind ever since that shooting incident. She kept wondering how he was making out with a sick wife and a new business and a little baby. He sure had his hands full.

Her next thought was so unusual that she almost told Goldie about it. She had just wished that she had taken the time to fix her hair!

She knew exactly what he'd say. "You? Ha! I'd sooner believe you if you said you'd just seen a three-legged fox."

She glanced at her brother and knew he wouldn't understand why she would be interested in something she'd never cared one whit about before. Maw wouldn't understand either. Probably the only one who would was Brit. After all, she'd predicted it would happen just this way. "Sooner or later." But then Brit added, "Knowing you, it'll more'n likely be later. Probably much later."

Brit didn't have to explain that. She'd been careful about how she fixed herself and her hair for over a year now. Irish had always been slower on the things that Brit considered important while Brit was behind on what Irish considered important.

"Well, there it is," said Goldie.

"I see it."

"Gonna come in?"

"Nuh-uh. I'll wait here."

Goldie looked up. "Ain't it somethin'!"

"Uh huh." She joined him in looking over the big building that housed Sweet Home's newest business. Of course she'd seen it many times before but it was still something to admire with its two stories and ten tall narrow windows.

The rear of the mill backed up to the creek and when viewed from that side, she thought its huge wooden wheel looked like it wore a shagbark hat.

More often than not there'd be a loud squealing sound coming from within, caused, she'd been told, by two huge stone wheels fixed up so that they ground against each other. Rutha Garlock'd told her that the wheels were powered by creek water and that they were what ground the corn into meal and the wheat into flour. The miller's apparatus could grind a bushel of corn into meal in less than ten minutes. Rutha said it would sure be a time-saver for those who hand-pound their corn and Irish'd thought: like the Dares.

Goldie wrapped the reins around the whipstock. "I'll jus' be a minute."

"I'll be here."

Goldie went up the stone stairs to the open door and after a minute the squeaking noise slowed then stopped altogether and a deep silence fell.

Irish looked around. A fat calico cat lay sprawled on a second-story window ledge, absorbed in washing its two-toned face with a white paw. If its job was to kill the mice that were attracted by the corn, it acted like it knew its business. Fat and sassy, that's how it looked to her. ldly she looked upstream where she could see the miller's house beneath some oaks.

Like the mill, it too had two stories but it had been fancied up with a deep, pillared porch and a roof of split wood. Word was that it had eight rooms, including an indoor room for cooking. Imagine that!

Since no one had yet laid eyes on Mrs. Schumacher, there'd been a lot of speculation about her, especially about her alleged illness. A few weeks back a rumor had circulated that she was a leper, but the definition of a leper was murky. Someone claimed that a leper's important body parts kept dropping off of them until finally they died. Sometimes there'd hardly be anything left to bury . . . a potato-sack-like body, armless, legless and faceless.

Mrs. Schumacher was already pretty far gone. Zick Simmons's second cousin True Purfle had seen the Schumachers riding in a wagon one night. He'd been walking along the side of the road when he heard someone coming and dove into a gulley. The Schumacher wagon was directly in front of where he was hiding when they hit a bump and half her face rolled off and lay on the side of the road! One of the kids had asked what had happened then but True Purfle said he couldn't see anything more because he was occupied with running in the other direction.

Irish shivered. Obviously everyone's next question had been how a person becomes a leper. Brit said only from the bite of a leopard but Brit was rarely right about that sort of thing. Irish wanted to ask somebody who knew. Miss Mapes maybe.

She no sooner had that thought than a flurry of white drew her eye to one of the upstairs windows at the miller's house. She stared at the spot while her mind came up with a hundred possibilities for the vision, all of which were gruesome and life threatening. She was almost disappointed when the girl-eating-twin-preferring monster turned out to be a windblown curtain.

Right then she heard something behind her and barely kept from vaulting over the mule's head. Then she heard it again and a side-eyed peek between the seat-back slats showed her that it was Schumacher's baby who was in a basket just inside the mill door. She sat up and smoothed her hair.

Such a nice baby! Rosy-cheeked and bright-eyed. Looked

like he could grow up to be almost as handsome as his paw. He had his paw's eyes and hair. Matter of fact, she couldn't see any of his maw in him at all. He was fussing about something. Maybe the way the sun was slanting in on him.

Unfortunately he also had his paw's skin. The cheap sort that never acts right in the sun.

She jumped out of the wagon and went up the stairs. Chucking the boy under the chin got her a toothless grin in return. Poor motherless thing! He sure was good-natured. She momentarily forgot her apprehension and went in search of his father.

The mill smelled like fresh corn, trampled wood dust and soured grain. Sacks of ground meal stood in a line against one wall, each tied and tagged with a name. Emil Schumacher and Goldie were standing on the far side of the mill, beside a pit.

Irish stood there, chewing her thumb. She hated in the worst way to call attention to herself, but she didn't see any way around it. Hearing the baby fret, she squared her shoulders and walked closer and as she neared she heard Schumacher say, "If I had known you built houses I would have had you build mine."

"I ain't built none but our own so far. Well, I have helped some of our neighbors' with theirs, but this is the only time I've ever built a cabin an' been paid for it."

"But you build furniture and get paid for it."

"Well, yeah. Sometimes."

"I heard you are the best cabinetmaker in Tejas."

Goldie's color deepened beneath his tan. He scratched his chest and then the back of his neck. "I do a little here an' there."

Irish had to interrupt; the baby had started crying. "Mister, um, Schumacher?"

He turned and gave her a big grin. "You are the girl from the other day . . ." To Goldie, he said. "She held my boy for me."

"I heard about that. This here's my sister, Irish."

"Say, is it all right if I move the baby out of the sun? I think it's bothering him."

"Please!" He looked relieved. She certainly was, and promptly removed herself.

The men went back to their conversation. She walked around and talked silly talk to the baby, but she couldn't help overhearing some of what they said. Goldie was very interested in how everything worked. Schumacher pointed to a pit and explained that it was built expressly for sawing logs. To Irish it looked like an ordinary hole in the ground but apparently not to Goldie who walked all around it and then stood with his hands on his hips, staring down into it.

Schumacher went on, telling how one man stood beneath the log and another one straddled it on top. Each man took hold of a long saw and then slowly walked down the length of the log, sawing as they went.

Goldie pushed his hat back. "Ain't that somethin', Irish?"

She nodded and moved off a ways. Only a man could make a big to-do about a hole in the ground.

"I want to hire a cooper next year," said Schumacher. "Then I can make casks, barrels and hogsheads."

"In addition to the grist work?"

Their words faded as Irish walked to the far end of the mill. "Hey!" she whispered. "What're you doin'?" The baby had stuffed as much of his fist in his mouth as he could and was working it over pretty good. "Are you getting a tooth?" She gently pushed up his lip and saw a bruised looking spot on his gum. "Well, no wonder you're so cranky. Let's see if we can't find something for you to gnaw on." She wandered around until she found what she was looking for. "Here we go." From a discard pile she selected a piece of wood that was about as wide as her finger. She dipped it into a bucket of water then gave it to the baby who clamped it in his jaws like a hunting dog. By then she had circled back to where the men stood talking. Schumacher glanced at them, saw the stick and immediately took it away. The boy started whimpering. "Stick is not good for baby."

She looked at Goldie then at Schumacher. "He needs somethin' to chew on. He's teethin'."

"Is that what is wrong? New teeth?"

"Uh-huh. Look here." She rolled up the child's lip. "See that place right . . . uh . . . there?" He'd leaned down so close their heads were almost touching.

He sure smelled good! Like the mill but also sort of minty, as if he'd just had himself a nice swim in the creek.

She wondered how he'd look when he went swimming. Her brothers looked all brown and hairy. Maybe he'd look the same only all blond and hairy. Maybe like he'd been speckled with gold.

"You're sure it's safe?"

"Uh-huh. It's too big to swallow and that kind of wood doesn't splinter."

"I do not need a little miss to tell me about wood."

Goldie chuckled. "I guess not!"

"But I thought you might not have this kind of wood where you come from."

"We have this wood."

"Well, all right then." Talk about cranky!

He gave the stick back to the boy then raised one of his eyebrows and examined her with a new look in his eyes. "How would you like a job?"

"Doin' what?"

"Just what you are doing right now. Once in awhile I need someone to take my boy for a couple of hours."

Under the heat of those silver blue eyes, all thoughts of leopards and lepers flew right out of her mind. "I will. If Goldie says it's all right." She looked at Goldie who stood with his hands in his back pockets. He was staring into the pit again. "Goldie?"

"Yeah?"

"Mr. Schumacher wants to know if I can take care of his baby after school sometimes."

"Fine with me."

"It's fine with Goldie."

"I heard." Schumacher had been about to smile but she

looked so serious. As he watched her a line appeared between his brows.

What was it, he wondered, that struck him about her? There was something vaguely unsettling but what? She looked wholesome enough. Her square face was scrubbed and spotless and her hair hung to her waist in one fat braid. Her figure was slender but on the verge of being womanly, her gaze direct and clear, and her teeth the color of fresh milk.

All in all she looked very . . . healthy. She was also very young. Too young. Too nubile. Too something. Perhaps he should reconsider. But when Goldie Dare said he didn't see a problem with a couple of hours a day, he heard himself say, "It will help me quite a lot, having some time to myself."

He spoke to Goldie but he was idly watching his son nuzzle the front of the girl's dress. She didn't seem concerned that the boy was wetting it with his open-mouthed searching. With a low laugh she said, "Hungry little beggar!" and gave the baby the tip of her pinkie finger to suckle. Then she smiled up at him and it was like a mule kicked him in the stomach. His heart thumped and his face felt hot. It had been so long since he had felt passion it took a full minute for him to recognize it for what it was. He was physically aroused. He turned aside and moved some things on a counter. The brother said something and he said something back but he had no idea what.

The fact that he felt desire for this young girl both appalled and slightly sickened him but at least there was a practical benefit to his reaction. He was relieved to learn that after the events of the past two years he was still a healthy virile male.

The girl, however, was completely inappropriate as the object of his desire.

Again he told himself that the best thing to do was retract his offer but, yet again, when Goldie said, "Have we struck a deal?" something inside him formed his reply. "Is fifty cents a time acceptable?"

Irish's eyes widened. Fifty cents a time! That would sure add to the family cache.

"All right with me," said Goldie.

Emil looked at Irish and then away. "Why don't you take him up to the house? Tell my housekeeper, Mrs. Von Blucker, who you are. She'll show you where his food is kept."

"All right. Say, what's his name?"

"Helmut."

She tried not to roll her lip. "Helmut?"

"Yes."

"What do you call him for short?" Goldie asked with a grin. "Mutt?"

"I call him Helmut."

Goldie was still grinning. Schumacher, however, was not so Goldie said, "No need for flaring your nostrils at me. I was jus' kiddin'." Appears this fella has the same appreciation for wit as that stone yonder.

Irish broke in there. "Mr. Schumacher?"

"Yah?"

"What's the boy's middle name?"

"Johann. John."

"Johnny!" She nuzzled the boy's neck. "That'll work."

Goldie called after her. "I'll be around for you in a bit."

"All right."

Emil watched the swing of her rear as she walked up the slight rise to the path and then looked at Goldie Dare who was eyeing him knowingly. "She's a good girl, Schumacher."

"Good," replied Emil, purposefully mistaking his meaning.

"An' she's only sixteen."

"That old?"

"You know what I'm sayin'."

Schumacher's jaw came out at that. "No, what are you saying?"

"That if anythin' happens to her while she's under your protection, I'll be all over you like stink on shit! You understand stink on shit, don't you?"

"Perfectly!" Hotly, he added, "I remind you, Dare, that I am a married man!"

Goldie barked a laugh and Schumacher's lips thinned further still. "Mebbe you're the one who needs remindin'. There's an ol' sayin' where I come from . . . if it weren't for married men, whores'd have no business atall!''

"I do not dally with whores!''

Dally? Goldie's brows closed. "I've done a lot of stuff with whores but I ain't never dallied one.''

Schumacher shook his head. How exasperating! "What I mean is: you need not be concerned about your sister.''

"Good!'' Goldie gave him a clap on the back that would have staggered an ordinary man. "Long as we have an understandin'.''

Plans for a jail with attached living quarters for the sheriff were drawn up and the land was acquired between Sloane's apothecary and the barbershop. Construction was set to commence immediately.

Emma, for one, was irked that Sweet Home was to have its jail before its church. That was not the way Lloyd Cooper had told them it would be in his letter. *For the time being salvation is chancy because we have to depend on traveling circuit preachers. (Unless you are a Roman then you can go to the Mexican mission, three miles up creek.) But rest assured, a church will be the next building erected in Sweet Home.*

Emma complained about it to Annie. "I may have to give Mr. Cooper a piece of my mind. Honestly, as if Sweet Home needed a jail more than a church!''

Annie didn't think Emma knew what all went on during the nighttime hours. Maybe she didn't know what went on in the daytime hours. But Sweet Home probably needed a jail at least as much as a church.

The square, free-standing building would consist of two rooms on the jail side; one that was for conducting business and one that was for housing prisoners. The latter's windows would have iron bars set six inches into the wood.

The other side would be the sheriff's residence, built shotgun style with a sitting room first, then a sleeping room—with a connecting door that led into the office side of the jail—and finally a room for cooking and eating.

Before the walls went up, Annie was walking by one day and couldn't help but notice that the fireplace was clear in the back. She later asked Sheriff Goodman if the sitting room wouldn't be too cold in the winter. He replied that he didn't think he would be doing much sitting in his sitting room since he had no chairs.

Annie mentioned the conversation to Emma that night and Emma decided to donate two old stuffed chairs to the sheriff. "It's not his fault that a church has fallen second fiddle to the jail. Besides I've wanted to get some new chairs for years. This will give me a good excuse." She smiled over at Charley who was eating a cookie and drinking a cup of milk. "Charley, will you be so good as to put those two chairs in the wagon tomorrow morning?"

"All right."

"I'll go over there with you and take Sheriff Goodman some of those molasses cookies." She hard-eyed Charley over the top of her glasses. "Provided there are any left."

Charley put the half cookie he hadn't eaten back on the plate and dusted his hands. "See you tomorrow, then."

"Good night, Charley."

After the door closed, Emma and Annie looked at each other and had a good laugh about that!

That same night Jack and Blue returned from the fruitless search for Ramón Allende's horses. Telling Allende that they had failed had not been fun. Allende was already poor as a bald whore.

Afterward both Dares headed home, starved, tired and wet to the bone. With their feet close enough to the fire to singe their toe hairs, they sat on their spines and ate with their plates on their chests. All they wanted was dry clothes, food and sleep . . . pretty much in that order.

Chapter 14

The passage of a couple of days found Jack up on the hill overlooking the schoolhouse—which would have looked abandoned if not for a curl of smoke from the chimney. He leaned against a tree, unconsciously slapping his horse's reins against his leg. He had half a mind to go down there and find out what in the sam hill was going on! Class had been let out a half an hour earlier than usual. The kids had all peeled off in different directions—including Brit and Markie who generally stayed after school on Wednesday—and now the door was closed— which it never was—and Annie Mapes was still inside.

At least that was what he thought until he heard certain noises from the woods behind him; branches rattling, twigs snapping, a loud crack and a muffled "Ow!" He smiled then straightened his face but it was hard to stay deadpan when birds were taking flight and alarmed squirrels were loudly scampering from tree to tree.

It seemed to go on forever but somehow he kept right on doing what he was doing until he felt a finger tap him on the shoulder. He jumped a foot and let out a little yelp. He turned. "Miss Mapes!" He had one hand over his heart. She had a

smug look on her face, which was sheeny and blotched from
exertion. It looked like a welt was rising on her forehead.
"Where did you come from?"

"I came up through those woods." She pointed. A twig
stuck out of her disheveled hair like an Indian feather.

"Boy, you sure caught me nappin'!"

"I know," she replied smugly.

"Why didn't you jus' . . . ?" His wave encompassed the
cleared hillside that ran down to the school.

"Because I didn't want anyone to see me talking to you . . ."
She looked around as if she were checking for someone
crouched in the bushes. So did he and his heart missed a beat.
She'd gone to a lot of trouble to talk to him alone! "About
what?"

"About your standing up here all the time. It's got to stop!"

His heart settled back to its usual pace. "Why? It's a free
country."

"Because you are going to give me a reputation unbefitting
a woman of my station."

"A woman of your station." His gaze swept over her. She
was wearing a plaid skirt and a white, yoked, shirtwaist blouse
and looked about twelve. Except for certain shapely lumps here
and there.

"Yes! If I can see you standing up here, then so can others.
Electra Cooper asked me if we were courting!"

"What did you say?"

She continued as if he hadn't spoken. "I've already explained
that I can't keep my job unless I have an absolutely unsullied
reputation . . ."

"Hey! Can I get a word in edgewise?"

"What?" She smirked, as sure of herself as she'd ever been.
He smirked back. "You got somethin' in your hair."

"What?" She went rigid as a tree. "Oh, God! Is it a spider?"

A spider? He went slit-eyed and leaned close enough to smell
her sweet womanly scent. "Uh-oh!"

"What?"

"It's a Midnight Millie."

"A what?"

"A kinda black walking stick, only this baby's got over three hundred legs with a stinger in ever' one."

"Oh, God! Are they poisonous?" She wasn't even moving her lips.

"A bite from one of 'em means instant death."

She whimpered. "Please, please get it."

He came very close, looked and bit his lip. "I don't know. She's really got a hold there."

"Can't you jus' . . . squash it?"

"I daren't take the chance."

"Why not?"

He shook his head. "I saw a fella try it. One minute he was walkin' around, next minute his feet were reaching for heaven. Looked jus' like a dead sheep."

"Please! You've got to try."

He moved close enough to feel her breath on his neck. "Hold very still. We don't want 'er falling down your collar." He almost laughed at the pitiful sound she made. "Hold it! Hoooold it . . . ah, got'er." He plucked out the stick and threw it into the woods, then he devoted all his attention to holding onto Miss Annie Mapes, who had sagged bonelessly against him. He pressed his lips to her hair and murmured soothing sounds, but she was in la-la land. Her head lolled to one side, offering his lips an especially juicy piece of neck. He accepted and cupped her breast and thumbed her nipple through her shirt.

He had his hand up her dress when she started to come around. He removed it just in time to slap her lightly on the cheek. "Miss Mapes!"

"Mumpft!"

"Are you all right?"

She raised her wrist to her forehead. "I felt dizzy for a minute."

"I think you swooned."

She looked around and realized that he was supporting her with an arm around her waist, which pressed their legs together in a way that was not at all fitting. She pushed him away. "Quit it!"

He stepped back. "I was only holding you out of the Millie's reach."

She glared suspiciously at him. "I wonder if there truly is such a thing as a Midnight Millie."

"You think I lied?" He steepled one hand on his chest. "Me?"

She sniffed. "I wouldn't put it past you."

"Well, it's easy enough to prove. We'll jus' mosey over there an' find that little killer . . ."

"I do not want to find it. Nor spiders or scorpions or redbugs or snakes or snapping turtles."

"Those snappin' turtles'll make a nice house pet. Once you get 'em trained."

"Trained!" It was only when he put his finger across his lips that she realized she had screamed.

"I thought you said you didn't want the town . . ."

"I don't!"

"We are sorta out in the open." He looked around. "Wanna go into those bushes over there?"

"No. I do not want to go in those bushes." She only barely refrained from stamping her foot like a petulant child. "Mr. Dare, why are you here?"

"I was waitin' for you to finish up so I could talk to you about settin' up my lessons." He bent down in order to see her face. "You already agreed, 'member?"

"I've had second thoughts."

"Why?"

"I question your motives."

"Uh-huh. Just as I thought."

"What?"

"You're scared."

"I am not!"

"Haven't I kept my word?"

"Except for watching me all the time."

"I didn't know it bothered you." He swept off his hat and

slapped it to his chest. "I apologize. Now. Can't we be friends again?"

She stared off. There was no reason why she could not be cordial to the man. Good heavens, she was teaching his sisters. She glanced at him, looked away then looked back and frowned. "What happened to your head?"

"Nothin'."

"Nothing! There's a large, angry-looking bruise on your forehead."

"Oh, that."

"It looks awful."

"Naw. Jus' a little bump."

"How did it happen?"

"Blue an' me're helpin' Goldie build a cabin." She nodded. The girls had told her that. "Blue was up on the roof an' I was on the ground, sawin' shingles an' handin' 'em up. Everythin' was goin' great guns 'till Blue got bothered by the flies an' mosquitoes. He climbed down and slathered himself all over with bear oil an' vinegar then climbed up, ready to work." He chuckled. "He set a nail but when he lifted the hammer it flew backward an' nailed me instead! Next thin' I knew I was starin' at the sun an' seein' stars!"

"Good grief! I fail to see the humor in that. You could have been killed."

The words were out before she could check them.

"Would you care?"

"Of course I'd care." She looked away in case the truth showed on her face. "The girls would be terribly upset . . . it would affect the entire school." She sighed and faced him. "Of course I'd care."

He looked at her silently saying: *c'mon, c'mon* and she looked at him silently saying: *no no no.*

"Bet you'll be the kinda mother worries herself sick."

"I have no idea what sort of mother I'll be," she said and blushed. Discussing babies with him made her very uncomfortable.

"Early on maw said she didn't have the time to worry about

what we kids were into. She figured we'd be doin' dangerous things an' we'd either live or we'd kill ourselves, an' if we killed ourselves, it'd be a good lesson to whatever kids were left.''

"All right. Come on Tuesdays and Thursdays at four."

"I'll be here. If I'm not out on a scout, I'll be here."

"And the rest of the time, please refrain from being here entirely. In particular do not stand up here on this ridge."

"Why?"

"You ride your horse along this ridge until I reach my house. Almost every night you're in town. Isn't that true?"

He nodded. "Sometimes . . ."

"Aha!"

"I watch for Markie and Brit. Dusk is when the wolves prowl and the Indians like to carry people off."

"I am not afraid."

"Oh, yeah you are." He mounted his horse and sat looking down at her. "You're scared of lots of things."

"Like what, for instance?"

"Spiders for one an' . . ."

"And?"

"An' me." He rested his wrists on the pommel, and looked intently at her. "Maybe if you were honest, you'd 'fess up to being scared of one other thing."

"What?"

"Yourself."

There was a long minute in which their gazes locked and she feared he read concurrence in her eyes.

"So long, Miss Mapes."

"Good evening, Mr. Dare."

Annie leaned against the tree and watched him ride downhill, slanting across the steeply pitched grade toward town.

She always felt so drained after an encounter with him, like she'd had to use every fiber of her being just to keep her head about her.

Probably because she had. Only a minute ago she had come so close to asking him to hold her again. As usual, it was only after he'd left that sanity returned. She had, however, managed to resist the urge. At least that was something!

After another few minutes of reasoning with herself, she headed for the school—taking care to remain a good distance from the bushes and whatever lurked within them—and thinking about how gratifying it would be when Jack Dare was her pupil and she was the person in control. He wouldn't be putting Miss Annie Mapes on her ear anymore. Not when he was in her territory and under her power. No sir! Let him try one thing and she would find her tongue and she would use it. If words could blister that's what hers would do. Blister him senseless.

She was imagining certain situations and favorable resolutions to them all when she heard a yell and saw Hap Pettijohn sitting on one of his mules in front of the school.

"Oh, Mr. Pettijohn! I'm sorry! Have you been waiting long?" Oh, God! Had he witnessed that episode on the hill?

"No, ma'am, I only jus' got here."

"Did you want to see me?"

"Yes, ma'am, I did."

"How nice!" His sun brown face flushed a little darker. My, he's shy, she thought. "Please come in."

He paused at the door to dispose of his cud and to draw the length of his sleeve across his facial pelage. Then holding his hat by its chewed brim, he stepped gingerly inside and looked around. Obviously he was another who had never seen the inside of a school. "Can I get you some water, Mr. Pettijohn?"

"No, ma'am?"

"There may be a bit of cider in the well?"

"No, ma'am. I wouldn't want to put you to any trouble."

"Why, it would be no trouble at all."

She took a tin cup off the wall and went outside. He watched her draw up the jug with the top half of her body down the well and her toes pointed at the sky. He moved back to the center of the room and shook his head. Pilgrims!

She returned red-faced and smoothing her hair. "Here we

go! A nice drink of cider.'' He took the cup and mumbled his thanks.

They looked at each other for a minute then he looked into the mug, swirled it and took another swig. "Well . . .''

She cocked her head and smiled sweetly. "Is there something I can do for you, Mr. Pettijohn?''

No sense beating around the bush. "I come about Charley Walters.''

"Oh.'' Her smile faded and a line appeared between her brows. Charley had not been in school for two days.

Hap Pettijohn picked up one of the hornbooks, scrutinized it upside down for a minute and then carefully laid it back on the desk. "I imagine you heard about the robberies the freight line's been havin'.''

"Yes.''

"I been robbed twice. Last time my best man got killed an' I still ain't found nobody to take his place.

"What does this have to do with Charley?'' She asked the question but she had a feeling she already knew the answer.

"Charley got hisself a gun a month or so back. In the beginnin' about all he could do with it was drive tacks but he's been practicin'. He ain't as good as some, but he's better'n many an' he'll get better.'' He looked at her square. "Anyhow, I've hired him and Blue Dare to ride guard for me. We're gonna try again t'bring in Bowie's guns.''

"Mr. Pettijohn, Charley is only sixteen.''

"He's a month shy of seventeen. Blue started rangerin' when he was younger.''

"But Blue Jack Dare grew up in the wilderness . . .''

"Charley tole me some about that place where he lived in Pennsylshire. Sounded jus' as wild as Tejas to me.''

She folded her arms and walked around her desk. He had her there. In some ways the slums in Philadelphia were every bit as dangerous as the frontier. "Oh, I wish he wouldn't!''

"Ma'am, you gotta face it. That boy's gonna to do somethin' to make a livin'. It's part an' parcel of becomin' a man an' he's ready for it. If he don't do this, he'll more'n likely find somethin' else an' it might be somethin' that ain't near as honest as the job I'm offerin'.''

"What do you mean?"

"Well, I ain't sayin' nothin' one way or t'other but I seen him talkin' to Dutch Elliott twice last week."

"Oh, Lord." She thought a minute then sighed. "You're right, Mr. Pettijohn. It is better that he have an honest job with you than one with those criminals."

"Most of the time he'll be ridin' with Blue. He'll be all right."

"What about when the rangers are out on a scout?"

"Then it'll jus' be Charley and the driver."

She shook her head. "If I were a robber that's exactly when I would make my move."

He nodded. "You're right. Alls we can do is try to call off a trip if it looks like he'll be ridin' alone but . . ."

"But you can't guarantee that it won't happen?"

"No, ma'am. I don't see how we could."

They walked to the door together. "Thank you for coming to tell me."

"Yes, ma'am." He untied his mule.

"Mr. Pettijohn, is it all right if I walk along with you?"

"Yes, ma'am! You bet."

He waited while she gathered her things and secured the door. She smiled at him then clasped her hands in front of her. He led his mule.

"So, Mr. Pettijohn. Have you seen many Midnight Millies lately . . . ?"

That night she related their conversation to Emma Fuller and Emma insisted that they try to do something. After all, it was she who had guaranteed Charley employment. Honest work that didn't require laying his life on the line. If he thought he had to have a better job then perhaps she could offer him one.

"But he could make as much as fifteen or twenty dollars a month working for Hap."

Emma blanched. "If we scrimp a bit here and there, I suppose I could offer him ten."

"I can add to that. I have four students more than I originally expected." She looked at Emma. "But that still won't be as much as the Pettijohn job."

"No, but our fifteen dollars is guaranteed, don't forget. Hap Pettijohn's is not."

"What will Charley be doing?"

"Just what he's been doing right along." She fluttered her hand. "Little things here and there."

In other words Emma was willing to bribe the boy to keep him out of danger's way.

"It'll be like a nice easy job for him. I'm sure he'll take it."

Charley turned them down flat. He also informed them that he was moving into Maude Stone's rooming house as soon as he made his first trip and got paid. They knew then that it wasn't merely the money. Hoeing their garden didn't hold half the appeal that riding guard with Blue Jack did. Emma did get him to agree to continue driving for them, for money of course. But, he specified, only if he was not previously committed to his job for Pettijohn.

They watched him strut off and thought the gun in his belt looked huge against his slender body. "Well," said Emma sadly. "We tried."

Annie had some rules for Jack Dare concerning his reading lessons. She had some for herself as well, but those she would not vocalize to anyone but herself. Those for Jack Dare she vocalized in no uncertain terms.

First, he was to honor the terms of their agreement by not coming around the school on any days other than Tuesday and Thursday and then only at four o'clock. She intended to hold him to that. Second, if she was the least suspicious that he was not serious about learning to read she would toss him right out on his ear.

She told him all that and then waited for his response but he simply raised the hairy shelves that served as his brows and looked at her.

They had already spent one entire lesson fighting about whether or not he was going to pay her for tutoring him. He insisted. She refused. They argued, hers being that he was already paying extra for Markie's after-school studies. Paying the same for himself meant he was giving her the equivalent of two full-time students' fees.

And his argument? Non-existent. However, they finally compromised and met each other halfway. Only the look on his face made her wonder if she hadn't just been had. "So . . ." he said. "Here's this month's an' next . . ."

When he stretched his leg so he could get in his pocket, he sent her thoughts back to that night when she had been stretched across his leg just like that buckskin. Only closer.

She handed him the slate without meeting his eye.

"It's got writin' on it already."

"Yes, it does." She had written "Jack Dare" on it. He turned it toward her and tapped it.

"You write this?"

She meant to look at the slate but instead she saw big black-haired hands with callused palms and scarred knuckles. A lot of scars and she wondered how he had hurt himself so. Suddenly she thought about pressing her lips to each scar and her voice came out wobbly, "Yes, I did."

"What's it say?"

"Your name."

He looked at it then at her. "Jack Dare."

"Yes." He gave her that terrific grin.

"Imagine somebody comin' up with these slate things. About handy as a pocket, ain't they?"

He smiled at her again and she thought: This will be hard. This will be very, very hard.

She was right.

Almost immediately she started missing him on the days he wasn't scheduled to come. She would sit on the stump supposedly watching the children at play when what she was really doing was counting the days until his next lesson. Thursday to Tuesday seemed like an eternity instead of only four days. Every time she realized what she was doing, she would shake herself out of it, but it never lasted for very long.

As for Jack it would have been very easy for him to forget what he had promised and take her in his arms. Naturally he had not, but any physical contact, however slight and meaningless to her, had been torture for him. Her hand over his as she helped him form a letter. Her shoulder to his as she looked at his work. Her breath on his cheek as she bent to check his progress.

One day he had been waiting for her to lock up when she slipped on the rain-slick stump and plastered her body against his, and he had been that close to throwing her down and having at it, right there in the mud.

He might've gotten to that point but for one little hitch. Whether it was by design or not, they were almost never alone. Markie and Brit often stayed because they wanted to. Sometimes another kid would stay too but it was usually anything but voluntary. One day it would be Zick Simmons sitting in a corner with a sign that said Johnny Dawdle because he had been late to school three times in a month. Next time it would be Josh Phelps doing teacher's chores for an entire week (hauling wood, sweeping the floors) because he'd dropped a frog down the back of Electra Cooper's dress. (Markie told Jack that doing teacher's chores after school was Miss Mapes's favorite punishment.)

One day Jack came in and saw two boys sitting with their faces to the wall and Annie said that Seth and Juan Rivera would be staying after school for the entire month. "Perhaps even longer." She glared at them. "They climbed up on the roof and stuffed a rag in the chimney and smoked all the children outside."

Jack looked at them with changed eyes. Coupla skinny little runts. He wouldn't've thought they had it in them.

"Well, Mr. Dare, should we begin?"

"Whenever you're ready."

He was leaning on the window ledge with his legs stretched out and his arms and ankles folded. She was standing at the desk, shuffling her papers and trying not to look at him. "Last week we were learning about the five most important traits."

"I think I can read that myself now."

She looked up, surprised. "Really?"

"Yeah, I think so."

It would be quite an accomplishment if he could. Nonetheless, she handed him the book and returned to sit at her desk. She smoothed her skirt and folded her hands primly in her lap. He held the book up in front of his face and read . . . "The five most important traits are truthfulness an' honesty an' cleanliness."

Jack had no trouble hearing Markie's whispered words but she was going way too slow! Unfortunately he couldn't figure out any way to tell her so.

"Number four is punctuality an' number five is . . ." He kicked the wall behind him with his heel. Annie looked up. "Excuse me," he said, rubbing his leg. "Dang knee injury. Let's see . . . Um, number five isss . . . kindness."

Annie smelled a rat. She pointed him to a neutral corner of the room and went to the window. Leaning out, she looked down and sure enough, there was Markie Dare, sitting under the window.

"Miss Markie Dare!"

There was an out-loud soft: "Dang!" Then louder, "Yessum?"

"Are you prompting your brother on his lessons?"

"Mm, sorta."

"Either you are or you aren't."

"I am."

"Come in here this instant!"

"Yessum."

Damn, thought Jack. That had to be worth a month. Now I'll have three big-eared kids listening to everything I say.

Within a few weeks Jack didn't need his sister to prompt him with the answers, which made Annie pleased as a parent.

He was bright and inquisitive and learned very quickly. He wasn't always a biddable student, however. Sometimes the mindless repetitions bored him. Other times it was the tedium of the material. Take, for example, the exercises in McGuffey's Reader.

> Do you see that boy?
> There are two girls with him.
> The name of the boy is John.
> Jane has a book in her hand.
> They can all read from the book.
> They must keep the book clean.
> They must see how fast they can learn.

When he finished he asked her, "Where am I apt to see these words strung together like this?"

She tried her quelling look—the one she had practiced in the mirror with such great satisfaction—and discovered that it did not work on Jack Dare at all. He dropped his eyes, looked her over from tip to toe and then raised his eyes to hers again. The message they sent needed no translation.

That was the end of their lesson anyway because that was the afternoon that Harold Simmons arrived with a bloody deer carcass on the back of his mule. Annie could not bear to look at it much less toss it over her shoulder, so Jack took it to Garlock's and sold it for her for two dollars.

Chapter 15

"Miss Mapes?" Annie looked up and saw Markie Dare in the doorway. Behind her stood the twins. The rest of the children had gone for the day.

"What is it, girls?"

"Maw wants to know if you can come to supper Sunday."

"We're supposed to wait for your answer," said Brit.

"And not take no," added Irish with a smile.

She should accept. She had already had Sunday supper at the Garlocks' and the Coopers', and she could be expected to be invited to dinner by all her students sooner or later. Besides, for some perverse reason she found that she wanted to accept. Just the thought stimulated her and got her juices going. Perhaps she wanted to show Jack Dare how well she could deal with him in his own territory.

Then again, maybe the person she wanted to show was herself.

"Tell your mother that I am pleased to accept."

"Good!" said Markie. "Maw says she's gonna have Jack pick you up and Goldie drop you off. That'll help you decide which one of 'em suits you best. "

She felt her cheeks flame. This child is impossible. "Picked up by Jack and dropped off by Goldie?"

"Uh-huh."

"What about Blue?"

"Blue says he ain't never gettin' married. The mere idea of seeing the same woman naked for the entire rest of his life gives him a flutterin' fantod that won't quit."

"Markie, I swear!" Even Irish blushed at that.

"Ow!"

Brit had pinched her on the arm. "For pity's sake, Markie."

"It's all right, girls. I'm getting used to it. Now, what time shall I be ready?"

"Noon on the nose" said Markie, rubbing her arm. "That's what Maw said to tell you."

At noon on the nose on Sunday she heard a wagon pull up in front of the house. Since she was as ready as she would ever be, she collected her shawl and reticule and walked outside. Jack Dare was leaning back on the wagon with his weight on the heels of his hands and his long legs stretched out in front of him. He gave her that smile that gave her the usual accelerated heart rate and cottony mouth and asked, "Ready?"

"As I'll ever be," she muttered.

A strong gust of wind caught her bonnet, but she snatched it back and tugged it down and tucked her head and went on.

Though the idea of his scrutiny made every step a peril, she managed to put one foot in front of another without an embarrassing mishap. At the wagon he took her arm and assisted her into it.

"All right?"

"Yes, fine. Thank you."

"Want me to tuck in your . . ."

"No, thank you. I can manage." She pulled her skirt in and smoothed it and then checked the bone buttons on her high-necked blouse. Why did she always feel undone around this man?

That obnoxious inner voice answered: Because you were that close to being undone . . . literally . . . and you would be wise to remember it.

As they drove off, grave-faced Nona and Mittie waved to her from the front porch. Emma paused in pruning a bush on the side of the house and solemnly did likewise. After thumbing up his hat, Charley Walters rested his wrists on a hoe handle and looked at her like she was leaving for an extended stay in a sanitarium. She put on a great act, smiling and waving gaily at them.

Once beyond the house she snuck a side-eyed look at her escort. He had obviously spruced up for the occasion; his face glistened from a recent shave and his hair was damp on the ends. All futile efforts. No matter what he did, he would always look like what he was: a frontiersman.

She never imagined that she could be so aware of someone else's person but she was always aware of his. Oh, yes. Always. He wore coarse spun pants and deerskin moccasins and a buckskin shirt which was loosely tied closed with rawhide whangs. She wasn't aware of consciously looking, yet she could unequivocally say that a patch of black chest hair was showing through a tented opening in his shirt. She could also readily describe the furry, heavily muscled forearms that stuck out of his rolled-up sleeves, or his wide, gloved hands, or his rock-hard thighs.

She sat there, stiff as a hat tree and remembered exactly how those thighs had felt when they were pressed against hers.

They passed the three Coopers on the street, all of whom waved and then stopped to stare after the wagon. Next they passed a black and tan dog who was trailing Abner Yates. Annie made the mistake of waving to Abner when they drew level, which the dog must have taken as a challenge because it ran after the wagon for at least a mile barking furiously and snapping its jaws with Abner right behind yelling, "Chico! You quit that, Chico!"

An auspicious beginning, she thought.

"It'll be all over town by tonight."

"What will?"

"Where teacher had Sunday supper today." He was grinning at her again. "Amazin' what little some people can find to talk about."

She might have said: exactly my reason for asking you to leave me alone, but she hated to dredge all that up again.

At the Y outside of town they took the arm that followed the river. It was a high sunny day, as usual a bit breezy, but nice. Birds chirped in the bushes beside the road and powder blue clouds lazed about overhead. She could smell the prairie flowers and the ripe sun-warmed scent of grass. She began to relax and enjoy the ride.

In a while he turned in at a fencepost with a cow's skull nailed on it and drove along until they came to a little ledge where he stopped the wagon. Apparently he intended to admire the view. After a questioning glance at him, she did the same, for there was an abundance to appreciate.

Below was a little valley centered by an island of trees and surrounded by a sea of grass that was splashed with wildflowers. Twisted across it from east to west was a swift-moving stream that was as sleek and shiny as a strewn pewter ribbon.

She saw these things and a peaceful feeling settled over her. Sounds became hushed and muted and the world and its problems seemed a long way away. It was lovely and she said so.

"I think so too."

"Is it yours?"

"Yeah, that ridge off to the east there marks the tail end of our property." He tamped tobacco into his pipe. "I've slept right down there. Laid there an' looked up at the stars an' moon. Smelled the wild honeysuckle an' heard the frogs croaking down by the water an' I guess it's about the most peaceful spot in the world."

The idea held sudden appeal. She had never slept beneath the stars before.

He used his pipe stem to point. "I've always thought I'd like to build a cabin on that little rise. There's plenty of good green grass and the ground's dry.'' She saw the spot he meant, but she also saw the line of his jaw, the girth of his arm and his left ear—which for the first time she noticed was quite large and not very flat to his head. ''Tuck it right into those trees yonder.'' He turned to her and saw that she had been looking at him and not the view.

''I jus' might do that someday. When I find somebody I'd like to share it with.''

He was about as subtle as an oriental gong. ''I hope you do, Mr. Dare. Truly it is a lovely setting but . . . shouldn't we be going?''

''There's a protected pond behind those trees.''

''Oh?''

''Got lily pads all around the edges and a big rock square in the middle. I saw a swan in it.''

She looked at him. ''Really? A swan?''

''Trumpeter. Wanna take a look at it up close?''

''The swan?''

I love these little games we play. ''The pond. The land.''

''Another day perhaps.''

''Really?''

She sighed and looked away. ''No, Mr. Dare.'' She picked at a place on her glove. ''Never.''

''Never say never, Miss Mapes.''

Quite suddenly a small herd of antelope bounded out of the woods and veered off across the prairie. ''Somethin' spooked 'em,'' Jack said. ''See how their shoulder hairs're raised?''

''How could I have missed that!''

He looked at her but she was studying the woods. A minute later a lean coyote trotted out of the same break in the trees. A long pink tongue lolled out of one side of his jaw as he glanced warily around.

''No antelope supper tonight.''

''Good!''

''Good?''

''I don't want him to kill one of those beautiful animals.''

''What's he supposed to eat? Dirt?''

"I don't know . . ."

"A rabbit? A deer?"

"Grass?"

He laughed. "Poor fella's jus' doin' what comes natural." He propped one boot on the splashboard. "It's always interested me, how animals know what they're supposed to do. When I was a kid I heard about a fox that was raised by human beings an' yet it still knew that its favorite food was chicken and I recall thinking: I wonder how it knew?" He looked at her. "How do you think it did?"

"Instinct, I suppose."

"Huh!" He studied the land for a minute then, "You believe humans have the same sort of instincts?"

"Yes, I do. I believe most of our spontaneous actions are motivated by instinct."

"Spontaneous actions, huh. Think that'd cover the draw one human bein' feels for another? Like, you know, when that fox recognized the chicken as somethin' created jus' for him?"

Shaky ground ahead, she thought and said, "I think we should stop right here."

"But Miss Mapes . . ." He looked around, the picture of innocence. ". . . we are stopped."

"You know what I mean."

"I do?"

"I know where you're going with this . . . conversation."

He looked at her. "You do?"

"You're about to claim that man acts with the same basic instincts as an animal but I will tell you right now that the difference between man and animal is that man is supposed to control his baser instincts."

"Why?"

"Why? Because if he didn't he'd be an animal." She jerked her chin. "Really, we don't have enough time to go into this now. Aren't we going to be late?"

"Basic instincts, eh." He looked at the coyote, which was now only a speck on the prairie. "Miss Mapes?" He looked at her and she recognized the gleam in his eyes. "I don't suppose it'd be all right for me to accost you right now?"

"No, it most certainly would not."

"That's what I thought. Well, I'll wait." He looked off a ways and then back. "You know, you're about this close . . ." He held up two gloved fingers. ". . . to lovin' me."

"Really?" Her heart pounded against her ribs and she hoped she looked calmer than she felt. "And what . . ." She gave her eyebrows a contemptuous lift. ". . . makes you think that?"

"I call it gut feeling. You call it instinct. It sounds like the same thing to me."

"You know what our problem is, Mr. Dare?"

"Yeah, I do. Want me to tell you? Or show you?"

She ignored that. "We think nothing alike."

Probably a long time had gone by since Annie had spoken truer words. Because of the influence of her pragmatic father, she had always tried to remove all feeling from her thinking. If she suspected her decision was based on emotion she would fight it tooth and nail. Whether the decision was right or wrong was immaterial.

Jack, on the other hand, was a straightforward man who acted instinctually most all of the time. If he had the time, he would ponder a decision, but often as not he did not have that luxury, especially in his line of work. So he heeded his gut feelings and had been well served by them.

Neither would ever understand the other's way of thinking but if asked, both would say that the other one was the one with the better judgment. And then Jack would add: except in matters of the heart.

He looked at her. "Guess we're back to how you feel about giving your word nowadays."

"Nowadays, Mr. Dare?"

He folded his arms. "Would you keep your word even if it meant ruining the life of the one you gave it to."

"I'm . . . I don't understand."

"I know. That's what I've been waitin' for . . . for you to understand."

He grinned at the expression on her face and clucked to the horses. "Well," he drawled as they rattled on. "I jus' wanted you to see my favorite place."

"Thank you."

"Now, there's no need for you to start throwin' your head around."

"Mr. Dare, it would be quite impossible for me to throw my head around."

"You always do when you get haired up."

"Haired up?"

"But first the tip of your nose gets red as a buzzard neck."

"How amazingly observant."

"Huh?"

"Never mind."

The rest of the ride—which was thankfully short—was spent in silence and in no time they were splashing across the creek, going up a little rise on the other side, skirting a huge live oak and there was a big double-winged house with an open passage in the center.

About thirty dogs met the wagon, circling, barking and jumping around. Jack told them to shut up and there was instant silence, though they continued to run around the wagon. One was as big as a horse. They pulled up in front and he stopped the wagon. "We're here."

The deep porch had weathered wood furniture on one end and a long table with potted greenery on the other. The open windows all had small pots on their ledges and a mending basket sat next to the deepest chair. It looked very homey.

"You want a blindfold?"

She only then realized that he had come around to her side of the wagon and was looking at her with that half smile on his face. "A blindfold?"

"You act like you're about to be stood up against a wall."

"Not at all, Mr. Dare. I'm looking forward to this."

"Yeah, I'll jus' bet you are."

"I am!" He laughed and assisted her down. With his hand on her elbow, they went up steps bounded by fragrant lilac bushes and the door flew open. "They're here!" hollered Markie.

The people on a farm five miles distant had just looked at each other and said, who is?

"Thank you, Markie." Acting on Markie's wide-flung invitation, she entered. The plank flooring surprised her. She hadn't expected that.

She looked around and immediately thought of a medieval dwelling because of all the skins that covered the floor and walls. Lending even more credence to the impression was a deer rack over a sawed-log mantel that held a half-dozen weapons, fringed bags with intricate beaded designs and powder horns of all types and sizes.

Built into a corner were a row of jumbled shelves containing jars of yeast, salt and spices, bags of dried fruits and raisins, jugs of sorghum, molasses, honey and melted fat, and sacks of sugar, cornmeal, potatoes and pecans. Hanging off whittled pegs on one end was a gourd dipper, a rack for drying fruit and a huge string of dried chili peppers.

Bracketing a river-rock fireplace were two barrel-backed chairs made of stretched cowhide, and in the center of the room there was a long table with two squat candles on either end. She noted that the table's two companion benches were remarkably similar to the ones at the school.

A door stood ajar in back allowing her a partial view of a clay oven. From without came the sounds that cooking makes and the smell of good things to eat. It was from there that a woman entered, one with a face tortured by a hard life but arranged in that winning Dare smile. She was wearing a hat with purple flowers.

"Welcome to our home!" she cried and took Annie's hand in both of hers. They were knotted, very warm and a little damp. "Thank you."

"You're Annie Mapes!"

"Yes."

"Lord, you're everythin' I heard you were. I'm Evie Dare an' I'm glad you came."

"I was delighted to be asked."

"Good! Well, is everyone here yet?"

Annie looked around. There was Goldie grinning and looking handsome. Irish and Brit looking pleased and proud to have her in their home. Markie, of course, doing her gleeful little shuffle and Jack, looking at her as if she were on the menu.

Blue came in then. "Miss Mapes! A vision of loveliness as usual!"

Since he was still slicking his wet hair with his hands, he hooked a chair with his boot and pulled it backward. "Did any of these clods offer you a seat, Miss Mapes?"

"Thank you." She sat and then rose like a jack-in-a-box. "Unless I can be of help to you, Mrs. Dare?"

"No, no, sit. We'll eat in jus' a jiffy." She dropped an eyelid and gave Blue a look. "Now that we're all finally here."

The twins followed Evie outside while the three men—and Markie—sat or lounged around, grinning at her but saying nothing. She smiled.

From the oven area she heard Evie say something and one of the twins respond. She smiled at Goldie. He smiled back. Someone's stomach growled. My stars! Really loud! Like a rumble of thunder! She pointedly avoided meeting anyone's eye, but when it happened again she experienced a queer tightening in her nether regions and realized . . . *it's me!*

"Miss Mapes?"

"Yes, Markie?"

"Jack's told me all about how you look."

"How . . . nice." These next minutes could be the longest of my life.

"Took about three hours!"

"My heavens!"

"Said you're about the prettiest thing he's ever seen."

Her cheeks turned rosy. "Thank you, Markie. And . . . thank you, Mr. Dare."

"An' then Goldie reminded Jack that he'd said that very same thing about the colt Judy had last month . . ."

"Oh? Thank you, Goldie." He scuffed his foot and turned bright red.

"Markie!" Mrs. Dare was back carrying a steaming platter. "That's enough, now. Let the grown-ups have a chance to speak."

"I was jus' tryin' to drown out Miss Mapes' stomach . . ."

Annie groaned. Mrs. Dare glowered. "Markie!"

"Didn't you hear it out there? Y'all have t'be deaf as a door."

"Markie, you hush!"

"But they weren't sayin' nothin' an' it was real . . ."

"Markie!"

Brit came in with a bowl of something. "Maw, don't let her get goin'."

"I don't see why I can't talk if they don't."

Blue threw Annie a grin and said, "Markie'll talk the hind end off a mule."

On her way back to the oven, Evie Dare gave Goldie a rabbit punch in the kidney which frogged his eyes and prompted him to say, "Sooo, Miss Mapes . . . how's that ol' furniture workin' out?"

"Fine, Goldie. Not one complaint."

"No splinters?" asked Blue.

"None that I've heard of."

Markie lifted her voice so her mother could hear. "Now they're talkin' so stupid I can't believe it!"

"Markie, I swear! Come sit at the table, Miss Mapes."

Annie found her feet and stood, but how she would never know. Her face, torso, everything felt marbleized.

With the help of the twins, Mrs. Dare served dinner. Wearing her hat. Wild turkey with giblet dressing, haunch of venison, fried catfish, black-eyed peas, sweet potatoes and biscuits.

No beans! Thank heavens! That would be all I'd need.

For sweets Mrs. Dare announced that she had two pumpkin pies and two apple pies in the warmer and demanded that everyone save room for each.

The table was set with wooden platters, cane forks and pewter spoons. Some of the spoons were a little dented but not the one at her place.

Everyone clasped their neighbor's hand and bowed their head. Annie clenched her insides so hard that her bottom would be sore for two days.

"Lord," said Markie.

If Markie talked the Lord's hind end off too, Annie was in trouble. She frantically eyed a nearby loaf of bread.

"Thank You for this food to eat, and thank You for us all being here together and thank You most especially for our company, Miss Annie Mapes who is our schoolteacher. But if You didn't already know that then I guess You wouldn't be God now would You? Ow! Amen! Maw! Brit kicked me under the table fore I was done!"

"But you were done, Markie," her mother calmly replied. "You jus' didn't know it."

Goldie let go of Annie's hand but Jack did not . . . not until the venison platter stopped in front of her and could proceed no further. She tugged and he grinned. She tugged again openly scowling and he let go. But he was still grinning.

Food started disappearing with amazing alacrity, explaining the need for all the staples on the shelves, and Annie shuddered. Imagine having to cook for this tribe every day!

The men cut their food with their hunting knives but she noticed that she had been given a small delicate knife with an elk horn handle. Each person had a tin cup or one made of a halved wild squash shell that had been scoured until it was as clean and smooth as clay. A jug of apple cider was passed. Annie had never tasted better and said so.

"Hey!" said Markie. "How come I didn't get passed any peas?"

While her mother shook her head, her brother Blue handed her the bowl. "Markie!" Mrs. Dare said. "What have I tole you about bawlin' at the table?"

"Everybody knows how much I like black-eyed peas an' they always pass 'em behind me outa pure meanness!"

Indeed Annie had seen the pea bowl go from Blue to Irish

behind Markie's back and from the look on the culprits' faces, this was a regular prank. With pride Mrs. Dare said that not much gets past "our Markie."

Annie laughed. "I know. She can sense what she cannot see. Last week she marched up to Zick Simmons and unerringly punched him square on the eye."

"Why'd you do that, Markie?" her mother asked.

"Cause he called me a pissant," Markie replied calmly between bites.

Irish asked, "What's the difference between us callin' you Goober and him callin' you Pissant? Both are little and puny."

Markie worked her mouth, thinking, and everyone was grinning at her answer before she said it. "Cause you're kin and he ain't."

"He's not."

"Not."

Everyone laughed and Blue tugged on Markie's braid and Annie experienced a stab of envy. Such a nice big family. And so close. Their fierce love for each other was almost palpable.

"You know, Mrs. Dare, I've discovered that all of your children have their own special talent. Irish, for example, drew a picture of your place that was so precise and exact I would have known it anywhere."

"She draws real pretty. She did that picture right there."

Mrs. Dare was indicating a thin piece of wood nailed to the wall. It was the likeness of a man done in charcoal. "I noticed it earlier. Who is it?"

"Her father, Otis Dare. She drew it from memory but dang if it don't look jus' like 'im!" Irish was blushing prettily.

"He certairly was a handsome man."

"That he was."

Mrs. Dare's eyes were a little wet so Annie waited a minute before she went on. "Goldie makes furniture as fine as any I've ever seen and Brit . . . why I can't recall ever meeting anyone who is faster with their numbers."

"There's more to my Brit than she wants people to know.

I never have figured out why, but don't let her fool you. She's sharp as mustard, our Brit.''

"Maw, I jus' hate when you talk about me like I'm not here!''

"It's jus' so hard to get her to speak up,'' said her mother drolly.

"A problem they all have,'' Annie said. "That terrible shyness.'' There were guffaws and snorts all around. Then she looked at Jack. "Your eldest has done so well in school that I doubt if he'll have to come much longer . . .''

That brought Jack's head up but before he could say anything, Blue jumped in. "An' what about me, teacher? What do I do best?''

"Well, I don't know. I guess that remains to be seen.''

"Ha!'' His mother shook her head. "Believe me, Miss Mapes. You don't wanna know.''

Over pie and strong chicory coffee, Mrs. Dare talked about her plans for her family. The Dares had definitely put down roots.

"We have nearly eight thousand acres now but my goal is ten. That oughta be jus' about right.''

"Just right for what?''

"All my gran'kids.''

"Do you have any?

"Not yet but once we get goin', watch out. We Dares run to big families.''

"So you're planning ahead.'' Talking babies with Evie Dare was almost as unsettling as talking to her eldest had been.

"Not that far ahead. Markie claims somebody's thinkin' about startin' almost any day now.''

Jack stood at the hearth getting a stick to light his pipe. 'Better hold your horses, Maw. None of us is married yet.''

He turned and his eyes caught and held hers. One corner of mouth lifted and she felt her skin change color. He knew at he did to her and it pleased him.

She picked up the thread of the conversation and soon wished she hadn't. Blue was explaining Markie's prediction. "Somebody'd get married tonight if they could. Ain't that right, Markie?"

"Right. Maw, is there any more apple pie?"

Goldie winked at Annie. "She's good at tellin' when our animals are ready to, ah, marry. Ain't that so, Markie?"

"Uh-huh."

Blue again. "She says they smell different."

"Uh-huh. Sorta yeasty. Like fresh bread risin'. I can't believe y'all can't smell it!"

Mrs. Dare returned with a pie balanced on her palm. "Markie!"

"Whut?"

"It ain't polite to talk about how somebody smells."

Markie's face fell. There was no mistaking her mother's tone of voice now. "Nothin' I ever say is right!"

"That's not true."

"Is too."

"Markie!"

"I'm so tired of gettin' hollered at all the time! Sometimes I wish I was borned deaf too!"

"Shame on you, sayin' such a awful thin'!"

Annie had to speak in Markie's defense. She was on the edge of tears. "Mrs. Dare, if there's anyone to blame for Markie's indiscretions, it is her brothers."

"What?"

"Hey!"

"Who? Me?"

". . . they brought up the subject and they egged her on."

Markie cried, "Miss Mapes is right, Maw! They egged me on."

"It would help greatly if they would treat Markie like a lady . . ."

"Yeah! They oughta treat me like a lady!"

"Perhaps then she would act like one."

"I doubt it," muttered Jack.

"Markie knows how to shut her mouth. I've seen her do it."

"When she's asleep . . ."

"I can't hardly ever say the right thing." Markie stood. "I'm never talkin' again!"

Well, thought Annie, I have always wondered what the word caterwaul meant. Half laughing, she drew Markie close and said soothing things until her body stopped jerking. Finally she gave a huge last shudder and whispered, "Miss Mapes?"

Markie had her lips close to her ear. "Yes, Markie?"

"It's you."

"What's . . . me?"

"It's you that's got the matin' smell."

When she looked up, naturally her eyes locked on Jack's. "Um, Markie, do you suppose we could keep this between the two of us?"

"Sure."

"Our own little secret."

"Yeah! Right."

Holding a fixed smile on her face, Annie set Markie back on her chair and petted her back quite firmly, but not as firmly as she would have liked. Not on the location she would have liked either.

Food continued to move around the table but Annie was afraid to move her arms and so would shake her head when anything paused in front of her. Blue helped himself to a second piece of pie and passed the plate to Goldie who did the same.

Evie leaned closer to Annie. "I expect my girls'll marry well. They're pretty enough an' like I always tell 'em, it's as easy to love a landed man as a poor one." She took a big swig of cider and then leaned close again. "I've about decided I can't depend on my boys for gran'kids. I don't know what the trouble is. I never met any men who liked wimmin more and ain't none of 'em shy . . ."

Now's the time, Annie thought, before Evie Dare propositioned her on behalf of one of her sons. She clasped her hands tight and when Evie took another swig of cider she said, "I will be getting married before the end of the year myself. My fiancé's an attorney and though I would love to have some land we'll probably live right in town.''

Evie Dare narrowed one eye and stared at her with a scrutiny so disconcerting she had to check the alignment of her plate in relation to her fork and knife.

''Well, you know what I always say?'' Annie shook her head. ''That there's many a slip twixt the cup an' the lip. That's what I always say.''

Chapter 16

After supper Evie said that the twins would help clear the table while she washed the dishes. This she said while she was already pouring heated water in an oaken tub. Meanwhile the "boys" were to take Annie for a walk. "An' take Markie with you!" Since she would brook no argument from anyone, off they went, Annie and Markie, and the three brothers.

They walked without speaking for a while. Annie listened to the night birds' songs and the sound of the leaves rustled by a cooling breeze from across the creek.

It was one of those long summer nights, warm but not uncomfortably so. A full moon hung like an orange ball in a blue-black sky that looked splattered by stars.

"Comanche moon," said Blue to Goldie.

"What does that mean? Comanche moon?" Annie asked.

"It's a favorite killin' time for the Comanche. When the moon's like that."

"Oh."

From somewhere came the tinkling of a small bell and the sound of cows lowing, such peaceful sounds that they—and

Sweet Home—seemed far removed from the Comanches and their killing time.

Goldie had spoken so matter-of-factly about death, but then they all did. That's how they lived life, taking each day as it came, doing whatever they had to do to survive.

There was an ageless quality to the Dares, a timeless aspect that would have allowed them to look as at home on the Crusades as they were in Tejas. They were the sort of people who had been born to struggle, those adventuresome few who, throughout the ages, had gone into strange lands before all others and there had fought, bled and died so that those weaker could follow and survive. Without people like the Dares, places like Tejas would never be made safe enough for scribes and arbitrators like herself and Abel O'Neal.

At the end of a tree-lined path they came to a shaggy two-rail fence and almost immediately a little donkey separated itself from the shadows and trotted over to them. "Oh, look at the little donkey! Isn't it adorable?"

"It's a hinny," Blue said.

"Really? It looks just like a donkey." She sensed an exchange of looks behind her back. "What is a hinny anyway?"

"A cross between a donkey and a stallion horse."

She would have given anything to be able to say: I knew that. "Whatever it is, it's adorable. What is its name?"

"Roxanne," said Markie who was rubbing its neck through the rails.

"Roxanne!" scoffed Blue. "Imagine a male hinny named Roxanne!"

"Miss Mapes, is Roxanne a girl's name?"

"Yes, it is."

"See, birdwit," said Blue. "What'd I tell you?"

Markie looked determined. "Miss Mapes, is Denmark a girl's name?"

"No, not normally but because it is your name and you are a girl, it automatically becomes a girl's name."

"Ha!" cried Markie. "So if I name a boy hinny Roxanne, then because it's a boy, Roxanne becomes a boy's name?"

Annie gave Blue a look that said: *clever!* and he returned one that said: *Ain't she though?*

"Ah, yes."

"Aha!" She cried again.

Annie leaned down and looked into the hinny's eyes. "Hello, Roxanne. You sure are pretty!"

"Give it this, Miss Mapes." Markie offered something she'd taken from her pocket.

"What is it?" It looked like something she tried to avoid in the road.

"A sorghum ball."

"Oh!"

Do hinnys bite? she wondered and had a brief vision of herself with a hook strapped to her arm. She switched the ball from her right to left hand, closed her eyes and stuck out her hand.

Velvet-like lips snuffled around her palm until it found the ball. "Oooh, it tickles!" It let her scratch it between the eyes. "I can't remember ever seeing a white donkey."

"It won't stay white. This kind gets blue when they get older."

"Won't get a lot bigger either," said Goldie.

"Unfortunately hinnies don't have a lot of strength."

Markie was pulling her on. "I want you to meet my chickens, Miss Mapes." Markie pushed up the hide covering that served as a door and disappeared inside.

"It will be my pleasure, I'm sure . . ."

To Goldie she whispered that a chicken was not high on her list of Pets I've Always Wanted to Own and he replied that Markie would make a pet out of a rock.

To no one in particular, Annie said, "You know, you've only got yourselves to blame for Markie. You have spoiled her silly."

"Wouldn't you?" said Blue.

She looked at him a minute, then nodded. "Yes, I would."

Markie offered her a young chick that was just losing its

down. She tried to get away with just stroking it with her finger but had not a chance of that.

"Here, hold it, Miss Mapes."

"It's so soft!" She hadn't expected that. She held it next to her cheek. "I don't know what I expected but it certainly wasn't some . . . uh!" Suddenly she looked rosy and foolish.

Markie cocked her head. "What?"

"It, uh, you know in my, ah, hand."

The chick's reaction to being squeezed affectionately must've been expected because Jack had already gone to wet a rag in the stream. "Thank you!"

"Any time."

While Annie watched him kneel by the creek to wash out his pocket rag, Goldie and Blue jiggled their brows at each other over her head. Jack rejoined them and from close by came the intense shrill cry of a whippoorwill. As if it had been a signal, they all walked on.

A deep breath brought Annie the smell of wood smoke mixed with just a touch of mule manure and it struck her that it all pleased her—the land, the trees, the Dares, even the mule manure—and for the briefest moment she allowed herself to flirt with fire. Just on a lark, she let herself imagine that she was affianced to Jack Dare instead of Abel O'Neal. It was a breath-stealing thought. She could just imagine what would be afoot now. He would want to get her alone, of course. Perhaps she would want him to. Maybe they would have made a plan to be together. Maybe he would signal her somehow and they would drift away and lose themselves in the deepening shadows. Or maybe they would brazenly tell everyone else to go on ahead without them. Maybe if none of their plans worked, they knew there would always be the drive home. Knowing Jack Dare, she imagined that he would stop the wagon at some private place, tie the reins on the whipstock and turn to her and . . .

She abruptly walked into Goldie because everyone else had paused atop a little hill. "I'm sorry. I was looking around instead of where I was going."

"This is a nice spot, ain't it?"

It was. She could see all of their farm that the trees and moon allowed. "I can imagine what you thought when you first saw it."

"It looks pretty much like it did that day," Goldie said.

"Except for that rye hayfield yonder an' the buildings," said Blue. "An' that well over there an' . . ."

"All right, Blue. You made your point."

Annie pointed at her feet. "I hate to change the subject but there's a dog that keeps throwing itself down in front of me."

"Son of Sally!" crowed Markie.

"Another one of Markie's babies."

Annie bent to scratch the dog's stomach and it jerked its hind leg in response.

Blue said, "Maybe you can solve something for us, Miss Mapes."

"Of course . . ." she said as she stepped over the dog for the seventh time. ". . . if I can."

"Would you say, Miss Mapes, that you're pretty good at spottin' smartness?" He gave her an exaggerated wink.

She nodded, playing along. "Very good, even if I do say so myself. Why?"

"Well, here's the thing. A critter has to pull its weight around here. If it don't, then we do one of two things . . . eat it or drown it." He pointed at the dog who was working its way to the front of the group. "Now, everybody in this family—'cept for one—says that that is the dumbest, sorriest, most useless animal that they've ever seen, but Markie claims we are just trying to get her goin'. Now that sure wouldn't be the case with you . . . would it? So here's my question: What do you think? Is this the dumbest, sorriest, most useless animal that you've ever seen? Or not?"

"Dumb and sorry? Oh, heavens, no." Blue groaned. "Matter of fact, this animal appears exceptionally intelligent for a canine. Far far above average."

Markie cried, "See, ol' Blue Jack Dare. You can jus' bite my . . ." Her words were cut off because Jack's palm was clapped over her mouth. Annie missed it entirely because she was smiling at Blue, who was glowering back and pretending to be furious.

She liked him. Why, she was willing to bet that half the scurrilous things people had said about him were simply not true.

However, if even half of them were . . .

Goldie showed her his work shed next, which was a roof and three walls, all of which were covered with tools hung on huge rusty nails. Centered square in it was a long scarred table with pieces of wood stacked neatly underneath it.

"Show 'er the rattler, Goldie," said Markie.

"Rattler! As in snake?"

"Yep." Goldie stepped outside and pointed. Warily Annie followed and saw a snake head the size of a doubled fist nailed to the long beam of the roof.

"Measured five feet ten inches," said Markie and pulled Annie around the side of the shed so she could see the tip of the tail dangling off the end.

"Good Lord! Where did you find it?"

"A few feet from where you're standin'."

Within her shoes Annie's toes and heels tried to touch.

Blue took something from his pocket and showed it to her. The snake's caudal appendage. "Had thirty-four rattlers," he said.

"You don't say!" she said and tried not to roll her lip when he laid it in her palm. It was dry and raspy feeling. Certainly not something she would carry in her pocket.

"Goldie said it had a full-growed jackrabbit in it."

She looked at the thing with horror. "Euu!"

"That's enough, Goober." Jack slung Markie over his shoulder and they started toward the cabin. "Teacher's obviously got a cheap stomach."

"Teacher does *not* have a cheap stomach." She was crow hopping along behind Blue with her hand extended like a beggar. She wanted him to take his "thing" back but he was striding along with both hands in his pockets. She couldn't exactly stuff it up his nose, although the thought had merit.

"Well, in that case, you'll never guess what else we found inside it . . ."

"All right!" She held up her hand. "I lied, all right? I have a cheap stomach."

Blue's teeth flashed at her and she felt admiration in his gaze. She dropped the rattlers in his palm and folded his fingers over it. "Miss Mapes, when you are ready to leave, may I have the pleasure of escortin' you home?"

"I'm takin' her home," said Goldie.

"Awheck. Well . . ." He wore that Dare grin, wider and more but familiar nonetheless. "Mebbe another time."

She was going to say "Maybe" when his oldest brother muttered, "When frogs grow fangs!"

Evie came out onto the porch where Jack was leaning against the post. Goldie and Annie Mapes were about out of sight. They watched the wagon until it rounded the bend and then Evie slapped her eldest son on the back. "Well! Anythin' you wanna tell your ol' maw?"

"No."

Her smile faded. "Nothin'?"

He thought a minute. "Good eats tonight."

"Good eats? I was talkin' about the girl. I can see she's crazy for you an' you're crazy for her."

"Think she is?"

"Of course she is!"

"I think you're right.

"I know I am."

"But she still says she's gonna marry that fella from Philadelphia."

Evie looked incredulous. "Yeah? An'? Ain't you gonna do nothin' about it?"

"It's up to her now, Maw." He stepped off the porch and walked down the path to the creek.

Evie closed her mouth. Her Jack . . . not fighting for something he wanted. "Well, I'll be!"

Full dark had fallen by the time Goldie and Annie started back. The moon cast long, silvery streaks on the land and the trees along the road threw dark shadows across their path. In the sky the stars flickered like candles and Annie thought how peaceful and gentle the country looked at night, like it never looked in the daytime.

Unlike his brother, who drove with his legs loose and open in careless arrogance, Goldie drove leaning forward with one foot on the crossbar and his elbow on his knee. Every once in a while he would turn his head and smile at her and she would smile back. She liked him too. Like his brothers he was a good-looking, well-proportioned man but he was quieter and less brash. There was something sure and steady about him. She suspected that he was much like the things he built: solid, sturdy and serviceable.

"My, but I like your family." It surprised her, popping out like it had but it was true.

"Did you get the idea that Maw wouldn't mind if you joined up?"

"Aptly put, but I had already been warned."

"Markie?"

"Markie."

"Figures." After a while he added, "You know, you're right about Markie. It's pretty much our fault, the way she is. We've always teased her half to death. Tryin' to get her t'cut loose with somethin' funny."

"I gathered that."

He looked over at her then back at the road. "Is that true what you said about bein' promised to another?"

"Yes." Now, why did saying that make her feel so melancholy? It was uncharacteristic of her to be so pensive and gloomy.

Goldie drove for quite a while without speaking and she assumed that they had finished with the topic until he said,

"You know, I was thinkin' about that lawyer fella. O'Neal, right?"

"Yes. Abel O'Neal."

"Well, I can't tell if Jack's got his sights set on you or not. But if he has, you might jus' as well write the poor fella an' tell 'im."

"Tell him what?"

"That you're a gone goose."

She knew she closed her mouth about a mile from town because that was when they drove through one of those little clouds of insects.

After she was assisted off the wagon, she mumbled something by way of thanks, to which Goldie lifted his hat and petted her arm and then she walked stiffly into the house.

She politely but firmly fended off Emma's questions about how the evening had gone and went directly to her room. She felt queasy and light-headed. Perhaps she was coming down with something, but then, what did she know? Perhaps her symptoms were those of a gone goose.

Chapter 17

Sure enough, that night's moon had been a forewarning; there was a Comanche raid that sent Jack and Blue riding off before dawn. "This damn Indian business's gettin' worse insteada better."

Blue was right. The Comanche and Kiowa had been giving the settlers nothing but trouble all summer. Stealing horses and killing stock. Murdering people or worse, taking them off to burn.

Jack had a lot of respect for the Comanches as fighters. They were tenacious and wily, and, as far as making war from horseback was concerned, no one could hold a candle to them.

They did not lack for cojones either. Not only were they battling the Mexicans and the Texians but most of the eastern plains Indians as well. And yet with all that warring they found plenty of time to steal. The other Indian tribes' sign for the Comanche was a backward wiggling motion of the pointing finger which signified the snake and its silent stealth. It fit. Jack knew of a man with eighteen head of horses who lost two head a month to Comanche stealing raids. He was at the end of his rope. He'd tried everything. Dogs. Trip wires rigged with bells.

Everything. When he was down to his last two horses, he started sleeping in the corral every night but they came in and took the horses anyway. They could have easily killed the man but chose to bedevil him instead. He considered himself lucky and moved back to Missouri.

Most white men saw the results of a Comanche killing raid and thought there could be only one answer to the Indian problem: total extinction. Jack thought there had to be a solution other than that. God knows why. He'd seen enough Indian barbarity to justify killing every one of them.

But killing to kill went against his grain. All the blame didn't rest with the Indians. The whites had been taking Comanche land and killing every Indian they could. If not with bullets, then with disease. Now the Indians were fighting a war of survival, for an end to their way of living would mean the end of the Comanche. It was a war that they were destined to lose but he doubted that they would ever admit it.

He could not speak for Blue and the rest of them, but he had long ago vowed that he would not kill any Indian—and that included a Kiowa—unless that Indian had done harm to a white person first. He had also vowed not to shoot women and children although there were times when that was easier said than done. Like when a woman stood firing arrows at him or when a kid of ten stuck a knife in his leg. And there had been many occasions when it had not been humanly possible for him to remain cool-headed after seeing some of the things the Indians did to the people they tortured to death.

Shooting a woman or a boy who is about to kill you is one thing. Killing for the fun of it is another. And that was one of the Comanche's favorite pastimes.

The Castenada raid had not been for captives or plunder, but was solely killing for killing's sake and even Jack had been hard put to remember his vow after that day.

José Castenada and his three sons, aged eight, ten and twelve went to get a load of corn from a little field about two miles away from their farm. They had loaded the wagon and started for home when two dozen Comanches attacked them. Castenada whipped his oxen into a run but they were no match for the Indian ponies.

The oxen were not killed and were allowed to make their way home. Castenada's wife heard the wagon and went outside, smiling and calling that their timing was good since she had just finished preparing their lunch.

The ranger troop was notified and set off for the Castenada place at once. They found the woman sitting stone mute, staring sightlessly at a wall. After seeing what she had seen, it was easy to understand why.

The rangers buried Castenada and his sons, and when they left there wasn't a man among them who didn't have blood in his eye.

They picked up the trail easily—maybe too easily. Concerned about an ambush, Jack had He-Coon ride three miles ahead of them and dropped Ed Cox and Jesse McIninch two miles back as flankers. All eyes were busy scanning the land for hostiles. The sky threatened rain but didn't produce.

The next night the low clouds made a black dome over the world but it still didn't rain. They made a cold camp, slept for a few hours then moved on at first light.

They tracked the raiders for two more days and when the Indians split so did the rangers. Within another three days the tracks brought all parties back together again and suddenly the Indians dropped all pretense of covering their trail. Instead they set a northwesterly course and remained on it like a shot arrow.

By then the rangers were deep in Indian territory and each man had to wonder why the Indians had come such a long way to strike fear in the hearts of the homesteaders around Sweet Home.

The Comanches weren't the only ones on the prowl. The rangers found evidence of many unshod ponies and after they passed the second Kiowa war parties, they wrapped their horses' hooves in burlap bags before going on.

Finally, early on the eighth morning they were on a low ridge that looked down on a Comanche village of thirty or forty tepees. It was cooler this far north. A woolly fog hovered above the ground and gray spirals rose from between the tepees' lodge poles. Everything else was dead still.

Several men glanced at each other in surprise. Either the Indians were confident they'd outrun any pursuit, or they were damned sure of their fighting abilities. They hadn't put a guard on their horse herd, which numbered around fifty animals, and many had left their shields and bows propped against their tepees or hanging in the trees.

The rangers could tell that the encampment was not a new one, from the amount of food accumulated. Dangling from low tree limbs were looped intestines, bison paunches and parfleche bags containing pemmican and other stores. A picked-over horse carcass lay atop several others in an earthen pit.

Having seen everything they needed, the rangers pulled back and set about getting ready. There was no need for talk; they all knew what they were supposed to do. First Billy Yates and He-Coon would circle around and herd the horses through the camp to throw things into a state of confusion. The rest of the men would split up in order to come at the camp from two directions.

The fact that there were only ten of them was immaterial. Their intention was not to kill every Indian in the camp but to send a strong message . . . every raid on Sweet Home would bring swift and harsh retaliation.

All their former weariness was gone. They were quiet and serious-faced but resolute. Any one of them might soon be dead but this was war and they got paid to fight.

While the rangers checked their weapons, He-Coon painted colorful signs on his horse. Lightning streaks on its neck for speed. Rings around its eyes for good sight. A radiating mark on its chest for a brave heart.

When he finished with his pony he started on his own face, but for it he used only black . . . the color of death.

Jack clapped the backs of the two nearest men and mounted up. "A guaranteed raise to any man killed."

And as always, the familiar words made hats wobble and teeth appear like slashes of paint across black-whiskered faces.

The rangers approached slowly until the dogs started barking and then they drew their weapons and rode flat out.

At the edge of the camp an old man stepped outside to see what was wrong. All Jack saw of him was a sunken chest and spindley spider legs, but there was nothing wrong with his voice. The Indians ran out of their tepees in great numbers, many were naked, some wore only a loincloth.

Brush encircled the camp. Those who made it there returned fire or let go with clouds of arrows. But many showed the incredible bravery for which the Comanche were known. Standing their ground, they drew their hatchets or knives and met the rangers head on. Several fell dead at first fire.

The Indian horse herd came pounding in from the other direction and the camp became a hell on earth as horses neighed and dogs barked and women sceamed and children cried. The rangers added their own yells and curses while the Indian warriors screamed their war cries or chanted their death songs.

Several women and children took advantage of the confusion to make their escape. The rangers shouted that they would not be hurt, but they kept running up the shallow stream or into the nearby woods. Finally the rangers just let them go.

Early on Jack had taken a bullet high in the leg but he managed to stay on his horse until it was shot out from under him. He snagged the braided horsehair halter of a passing horse but with all the shouting and shooting he couldn't get a leg over it. While Jack was doing a twirling dance with the pony, a roan with a blaze forehead fell nearby and Ed Cox screamed with pain as he went down under it. Jack let go of the halter and limped toward Ed but saw he would not beat an Indian charging with a raised tomahawk. Jack's gun misfired so he threw it and caught the Indian above the ear and they went down in a tangle of arms and legs. Though he was still pinned beneath his horse, Ed pulled his pistol and dispatched the Indian. Jack crawled behind a stretched hide and continued the rest of the fight from there.

Less than a minute later it had gone the rangers' way and the Indians broke and ran but Jack didn't know it. He'd had to stop and tie his neck hanky around his leg and by the time he had done that, it was over.

Long Bob and Blue came over and pulled Ed's horse off him and then everyone took stock. The camp was deserted and eerily quiet. Those men who needed some sort of tending formed a loose line in front of Hector Salazar. The uninjured set about putting some dying animals out of their pain.

Hector took one look at Ed Cox and handed him a goatskin full of pulque. The leg was broken in many places and required better attention than Hector could give it but he had to try and stabilize it.

"Drink until I am finished with the others."

Then he laid his knife blade in a low fire and began to patch the rangers up. Blue had an arrow sticking out of the fleshy part of his shoulder. Hector cut the shaft off, pushed it on through then plugged each hole with chewed tobacco. Jack dropped his pants to his knees and Hector doused his leg wound with water first and then with whiskey and Jack hissed like a snake. But when Hector laid the heated knife on it, Jack threw his head back and filled the air with some incredibly imaginative cursing.

Long Bob and Jesse had minor injuries that were soon tended to, and Hector figured Ed might be drunk enough for him to uncrimp his leg.

Blue was sitting on a log licking his wounds when he looked around. He stood and looked around again. "Hey!" he yelled, "Where's Billy?"

That was the first anyone had noticed that Billy Yates was missing. After a short search they found him where the horse herd had been picketed, dead with an arrow through his heart.

First they wrapped him in his own blanket then they carried his body back and laid it gently on the ground. They stood looking down at him and a stunned silence fell.

Yates's death was a shock to everyone—he'd been well liked by all the men—but Blue and Billy had been best friends. They had drunk, gambled and whored together ever since the Yates family had moved to Sweet Home some five years before.

Earlier, Blue had found a shield with a long red-haired scalp on it. Between that and the death of Billy Yates he'd worked himself into a real temper. Now he was walking around and kicking at things and muttering about the fact that there wasn't anyone left to kill.

Only there was. While looking for booty, Luke Bryant tripped over a body and it moved and he jabbed the faker with his pistol until he stood up only it wasn't a ''he'' but was a gaunt-boned girl with big wet eyes and a wide dark-lipped mouth.

She had been fixed up like a Comanche. Red lines ran above and below her lids and then crossed at the corners. Her ears had been painted red inside and both cheeks were daubed with a solid red circle.

Jack studied her. The crow-straight hair that framed her fine-featured face didn't fit. Comanche women hacked their hair off short; this girl's was long and braided. There was more. She wasn't pale from fright as he'd originally thought but was naturally lighter-skinned than a Comanche. Finer-featured too.

Jack called He-Coon over and told him to ask her if she was a Comanche. There was a pause then the girl shook her head. The girl told her tale of woe to He-Coon and he relayed it to the men. While the girl's voice was soft and her eyes downcast, He-Coon's tone was matter-of-fact and bored-sounding.

She was a Cherokee captive who had been a Comanche prisoner for over three years. Her father and mother and four kids had left Cain-tuck-ee to find land they could keep from the white man. A week after crossing the Sabine everyone but herself had been killed in a Comanche attack. The Comanche had recently traded her to another band. Not out of meanness but because the other band needed young wives. She was to have been married as soon as her intended came for her. She had been painted for a week, waiting.

Some of the men exchanged looks here. She appeared to be only thirteen or fourteen.

Asked why she did not try to run away with the other women

and children she replied that she was afraid. She had seen them kill captives in the past.

The poor kid was looking at the ground and acting like she expected to be killed by them! Jack suddenly felt very old and very tired. "We'll take her back to Sweet Home till we can figure out what to do with her."

Blue wheeled his horse. "You can't take a hell-fiend like that back to Sweet Home! You think you got a tame Indian here? Hell, she'll kill somebody in their sleep!"

Jack managed to mount a horse but his face turned pasty under his brown coloring. "I said what we'll do an' that's what we'll do. Somebody take her up behind 'em an' let's go."

"Not me!" said Blue. "I'll be damned if I will. She probably shot Billy before she laid down and played dead."

If it hadn't been for his leg, Jack would have taken her himself and been done with it. He scanned the other men's faces but they would not meet his eye. "He-Coon! Will you take the girl up behind you?"

The Tonkawa finished winding a thong around his gun barrel, which had been broken off from the wood, and then he walked to his horse and mounted up. Without a word the girl scrambled up behind him.

Long Bob and Jesse rounded up as many of the Indians' horse herd as they could find and started them south. Clyde finished tying Billy Yates's body to his horse and the rest followed.

It was a long miserable ride back for everyone, but for Ed Cox it was pure torture. Hector had splinted Ed's leg with some sticks and then they had rigged a travois by stretching a buffalo hide between two alamo saplings. They would pick up the back end of the travois when they crossed water or rocky ground but it was still a rough ride. In order not to be bounced off, Ed had to hold onto two rawhide loops tied to each sapling. Two days later they had to tie him on, and by the time they got him to Sweet Home he was out of his head with fever. Since the nearest doctor was in Brasoria, they took him to Evie Dare.

Though Jack had padded his leg against the saddle, he had felt every step the horse took. There was nothing he wanted more than to get off that horse and onto a bed. But first he had to take Billy Yates's body home to his mother. And he would sooner be shot another ten times than have to make that ride.

The Yates place had the run-down look of moneyless good intentions. Half the bark roof looked new and the rest looked leaky. A lean-to for wood had joined the pile and the porch was in peril from a good wind.

But the garden on the west side showed promise and on a fence hung a green sheepskin and several beef hides, drying in the sun. There were planted apple trees out back and children's laughter in the air.

Mrs. Yates appeared in the open doorway. She hung a wash bucket on a nail and dried her hands on a sacking cloth tied around her waist.

Her smile of welcome faded when she saw the horse that Jack was leading. There was a moment of stunned silence and then the crying began.

Next day at school Abner and Rebecca Yates were conspicuous by their absence. Also the three Dare girls were late but they were not punished when Annie heard why. Before she crossed the threshold Markie announced that "Billy Yates was killed!"

"Oh, no!" Annie's heart wept for Abner and Rebecca. Their sun rose and set with their big brother Billy.

"Indians got Jack an' Blue too!"

Annie pressed one hand back on the desk and thought she might have to sit down. Objects shimmered and white dots floated in front of her eyes. Later she would think about that moment and realize that then was when she knew she loved him. "Not . . . not dead?"

"Naw! Heck, they've had lots worse wounds'n this. They're jus' all shot up."

"How . . . how badly are they hurt?"

"Blue got an arrow in the shoulder an' Jack took a bullet in the leg."

Brit was looking at her teacher and frowning. Miss Mapes didn't look so good. Not good at all. A white ring circled her lips and her papers rattled in her hand.

"Maw told Jack that if that bullet caught him any higher it would've trimmed his doohicky for him."

"Markie!" hissed Brit.

"What?"

"We were up half the night," said Irish. "Makin' vinegar curds."

"Mixin' soot an' lard so the wounds wouldn't putrify."

"Makin' a red clay cast for Ed Cox."

"Ed Cox too?"

"He's the worst of the lot. Horse rolled onto his leg an' busted it in about eighty-four places."

"Maw's got 'im fixed up pretty good now."

"Only he don't even know where he is."

Annie told herself to take deep breaths: You'll be all right. Just . . . fine. Take deep breaths. Stay calm.

When her equilibrium returned she decided she'd best take refuge in routine.

"Let's all stand and say the Lord's Prayer for those who were injured and most especially for Billy Yates and his poor family. Think of how Abner and Rebecca must feel today . . . and . . . and ask God, uh, ask God to help them bear it . . ." She tried to finish and couldn't. She simply couldn't swallow the sob that was lodged in her throat. She held up one finger and solemnly marched outside.

The kids looked at each other, but no one spoke. Brit went to the window. Her breathy "Gol-lee!" brought the rest of the kids clamoring over. Miss Mapes's skirts were hiked and her feet were flying. "Boy, she's really upset!"

"What's she doin'?" asked Markie.

"She's pressed herself to the big tree an' looks like she's trying to hug it to death."

"Huh!"

"Her shoulders're gonna . . ." Irish sniffed. ". . . shake right off."

That's when Markie started to cry and within seconds the rest of the girls followed suit. Even the boys were swallowing hard.

Annie had never imagined she could feel such pain, nor would she have believed that she could drop to such a depth of depression that in the split second she had thought he was dead she would want to die too.

Oh, thank God he was alive! It was all that she could do not to run to his side right now!

When the outpouring of tears ended at last, she rested her cheek against the rough bark and stared sightlessly into the woods nearby. She was still sobbing but only about every tenth breath.

Well, one thing had come of this. The truth. No longer could she tell herself that she was merely curious about Jack Dare. Or that he intrigued her. Or beguiled her. Or even that he had awakened dormant passions in her. He had done all that and more, but none of those things were why she was always in such a muddle around him.

The truth was that despite every intention to the contrary, her feelings for Jack Dare had grown beyond the boundaries she had set for them and now she was forced to admit that she had fallen in love with him.

This was not easy. Previously, in order to be lenient on herself she'd viewed the episode at the creek as a mature man taking unfair advantage of an immature—and very foolish— girl. Now came the truth. She was far more culpable than he. She who was already promised to someone else had fallen in love with another. In her heart she had betrayed Abel O'Neal. Not only once but many times. A fine, good man. One of the most admirable and exceptional men she would ever know.

Only . . . God help her! . . . he was not Jack Dare.

*   *   *

Annie returned to the school as if she had just made a trip to the necessary, only everyone could see her splotched face and red nose and later the kids would agree that the whites of her eyes had looked like they'd been bleeding.

She fiddled with something on her desk until she had composed herself then turned and faced the class. "Well . . ." She spoke with what she hoped was cool cheerfulness . . . which was far from how she felt. "Let's all get to work, shall we?"

It seemed that midday break would never come, but at last it did. Unwilling to be a part of such a pretty day when she felt so terrible, Annie sent the children out and stayed in. As she wandered aimlessly around the room, she performed mindless acts like picking up Joshua's book and carrying it to Zick's desk and setting it there. At some point she must have dipped a rag and erased the lesson that she had finished printing out, only minutes before. As she passed the window she saw Electra standing below, apparently talking to someone beyond her view. Idly curious, she came closer.

"Then Maw stuck it with her knife."

"Ick!"

"An' green pus ran all down his leg!"

"Ick! Ick!"

"An' then Maw took a burning poker an' . . ."

"Miss Markie Dare!"

Her face appeared below, a little black-eyed flower raised to the sun. "Yeah?"

"Come inside this instant."

Annie waited for her at the door. She walked in with her head hanging and her feet dragging across the floor. She knew she was in for it.

"This is the last straw!"

"Yessum."

"I am at my wits' end!"

"Yessum."

"Something must be done!"

"Yessum."

"Take your seat!"

"I am in my seat." Markie could hear the teacher tapping her foot. Under her desk Markie had her hands piously clasped. *Lord, I could use a little help right about here.*

"What have I told you about unladylike talk?"

Markie cast her eyes downward and swung her leg. "Gol, lotsa stuff."

"Haven't I told you that there are some things you cannot— you must not—say?"

"Yessum."

"Would the, uh, pus in your brother's wound be something a lady would talk about?"

"Maybe." She looked hopeful. "Yeah, I think she might. 'Specially if she had an interest in healin' an' . . ."

"Markie!"

"Well, probably not most of 'em."

Annie knew she was blowing this all out of proportion, but she couldn't seem to stop. "Are you supposed to talk about something like that?"

"No."

"Why did you then?"

"I dunno."

"Yes, you do. Why?"

"To get her to urp."

"You were trying to . . . Oh, ick! That is the most disgusting thing I have ever heard! Why on earth would you want her to do that?"

She picked at her shirtsleeve. "I can't see 'er."

The other kids had come in by then. Brit sized up the situation right away and cut Irish a practiced look that said: time to save Markie.

"Say, Miss Mapes?"

"Not now, Irish."

"But I forgot to tell you about the little Indian kid they're holding over in the jail."

She looked at her. "What little Indian kid?"

Markie smiled. Saved! Good Lordamighty, I am saved again!

"That's right. They're holding her at the jail."

Brit jumped in there. "A Cherokee. Comes from far away from here. Captured by the Comanche an' made a slave."

"Yeah," whispered Markie. "Uh slave!"

Miss Mapes was just standing there staring at them so Irish went on. "They're tryin' to figure out what they should do with her."

Markie added, "Blue says she stinks but I took a big whiff of her an' I thought she smelled kinda good. Sorta like tanned skins an' smoke."

Annie looked at Markie and thought: I give up! "Where are her people?"

"All dead!"

"That's what they say."

"She was supposed t'get married."

"An' she didn't even know the fella!"

"Poor thing! What are they going to do with her?"

Markie threw up her hands. "We couldn't stay to find out any more 'cause we didn't want to be late for school."

Annie scowled at her. You smug little imp! Of course, her scowl did not intimidate Markie but it make Annie feel better.

"She says her name is Jane Yellow Cat."

Chapter 18

Annie and Emma hurried to the jail first, and finding no one there, went on to the temporary council room, which was what Lloyd Cooper was calling the added-on shanty behind his office.

There had been talk about building a courthouse and a meeting place on the land between the school and the edge of town but in the meantime, business gatherings of any size seemed to end up in the tiny former storeroom behind Lloyd's office. As they neared the building they were encouraged to see the several norses and two wagons that were tied in front.

It was so crowded that someone yelped when they opened the door. Bowie Garlock made room for them and then they had to press together so he could shut the door.

The Coopers were there as were the Garlocks and Hap Pettijohn. Charley stood between Hap and Sheriff Goodman. Blue Dare was there as was most of the ranger troop. Smoke hung in the room like the residue of a doused fire, and was joined by the smells of unwashed armpits, tobacco and damp animal skins.

They stood on their toes, but some men were blocking their view of what was going on. Next thing Annie knew Emma had grabbed her hand and was elbowing her way up front, and that's when Annie saw that Jack Dare was across the room. Oh, he looked awful! Hollow-eyed and starved with whey-colored skin. She could just kill him! Coming here when he should be home in bed! Why, he couldn't even stand without leaning heavily on a pine cane.

She intended that he should see how annoyed she was but he was intent on the proceedings and within minutes she too was drawn into the drama taking place.

The center of everyone's attention was a slight, scared-looking figure in buckskin who was sitting in a ladderback chair in the middle of the room. Jane Yellow Cat. Why, she was little more than a child!—Annie thought, and her heart went out to her. Apparently the meeting was only now under way. Lloyd Cooper was speaking.

"Come now. Surely we can put aside our prejudice long enough to decide what is best for this young lady."

Blue snorted his exception to the young lady part.

"We certainly can't give her back to the Comanches."

"Why not?"

"Does she have any people?"

"She says she knows of no other living relatives."

"Well, there ain't no place for her here."

"I say take her back where she come from."

"Kentucky?"

"Naw, jus' take her out yonder an' leave her. Them Indians'll find her. Or she'll find them."

"We'll take her to live with us." Everyone looked at Emma who returned their stunned looks with a wide smile. "Why, we'd be delighted to have her, wouldn't we, Annie?" Annie nodded, but she was trying to judge Jack's reaction without seeming to do so.

Emma's invitation precipitated another loud nose noise from Blue Dare. "What's she gonna do at your place? Practice torture on your family cat?"

That ruffled Emma's feathers. "What does it matter to you

what she does. She can eat, breathe, sleep and play. Same as any other youngster.''

"And she can go to school," Annie added.

"You can't teach a damn savage to read an' write," Blue said hotly.

"Watch your language, young man!"

Clearly exasperated, he said, "Readin' ain't gonna make no difference. Nothin' will. You get all done, she'll be exactly what she is: a stinkin' Indian!"

Jane Yellow Cat looked directly at the man in the fringed poncho. She had not missed the way his deep-set eyes burned with hatred for her. "I can write English and I can read English. Better than you, I'll bet. And the only time I got close to you, you smelled like spoilt meat."

Ho! thought Annie as she watched the sparks fly between Blue's eyes and those of the young Cherokee.

"Well said, my dear!" Emma turned to the mayor. "Is there any law against us offering her refuge in our home?"

"No," said Lloyd Cooper. "But . . ."

"That's all I need to know. Let's go, dear." She went to Jane Yellow Cat and took her hand. "Come along, Annie. Jane, dear, I promise you that you'll be very happy with us."

That ought to have been it only Blue wasn't done yet.

"Has anybody ever told you what happened to the Augustus Katy family?"

"Augustus Katy?"

"Yeah."

Annie glanced at Cooper but he was looking at his shoe. "No."

"No, I imagine they didn't. That's because the Indians got 'em. Four Kiowas crept up from the creek one night an' crawled in through the kids' bedroom window and killed 'em all. The two little girls, three and five. Their mother an' father." He pointed at Jane Yellow Cat. "She'll probably unlock the door for her friends an' lead 'em right to yuh."

* * *

Jane Yellow Cat showed no unease when she entered the cabin with Emma and Annie. Matter of fact, she informed them that it was quite similar to her family's cabin only smaller.

Emma had been a little taken aback by her prideful statement. Later she said, "Impudent little thing, isn't she?" but Annie told Emma she thought the girl's comebacks might mask her fear, and in the days that followed she was proven right.

Jane was entirely too restrained for her age and spent most of her time watching, and listening to others. As a consequence, she did not miss much. She rarely showed emotion, but when she smiled, she was lovely and when she laughed, she was irresistible.

One of Emma's primary concerns—that Jane's presence would make the Williford girls jealous—turned out to be unfounded. Nona and Mittie took to her right away. And they weren't the only ones. Though Charley Walters no longer lived with them, he used to sporadically show up at mealtimes and he was always set a plate. After Jane moved in he was there every night. He claimed it was a coincidence but no one could miss the side-eyed looks he sent her way.

Emma decided that they lacked a suitable place for "a young lady" to sleep. There was the alcove where Charley used to sleep but they had only a pallet there and Emma was determined that Jane have a bed.

"Oh, I wish Abel were here!" Emma worried her bottom lip with her teeth.

"Why?" Annie asked. "I mean, so do I, but why now, especially?"

"So he could make the bed for us. It's such a saving, having a man around the place."

Annie choked back an incredulous sound. Abel!? Abel could not make believe, much less make a bed! Surely Emma knew that much about her son!

Then again, maybe not. Had he actually succeeded in fooling her? Even at this late date? Amazing!

Abel used to promise to do some chore for Emma then after she went out the front door he would sneak the carpenter or repair man in the back.

Annie always thought Emma secretly knew. Apparently she didn't. Since Abel was not very good at subterfuge, it must be an example of the blind might of a mother's love. She hid her smile and said, "A bed would be nice."

Emma turned and pressed Annie's arm. "More than nice. A necessity. I won't sleep a wink with her on the floor, worrying about spiders and those little lobsters."

"I know what you mean."

Actually she did not. Jane had been sleeping outside on the ground where those creatures moved about at will.

"Could you ask the Dare girls to see if Goldie can stop by next time he's in town?"

"Of course."

"Well!" Emma was all business now. "That takes care of that. Now I'll see about fixing something to eat. Want to join me, Annie?"

"Not yet."

"Sure?"

"Yes. I'll fix something a bit later."

She had intended to go outside but instead she sat by the window and tucked one foot under her. Since the flurry of activity associated with Jane's arrival, she hadn't had any time to herself and she wanted to think about Jack.

He had not looked well. Not at all. He was so pale! She could tell by looking in his eyes that he was very sick. Why on earth had he come into town when he should have been home in bed!

She could answer that question. He was so self-important he probably thought his input was indispensable.

No, that wasn't true. He was concerned about the girl. That's why he had come. He had found her. He felt responsible for her well-being. That's just the sort of man he was. Kind. Courageous. Modest and unassuming. Handsome and manly.

Forbidden!

Her face held an expression of utter hopelessness. Emotion welled and her view of the yard shimmered. How long until it stopped? A week? A month? God, surely this wanting would not last a lifetime! No person could live with this agony forever. She was so preoccupied she did not hear Emma come in. She jumped a foot when she felt a hand on her shoulder.

Concern was plain on Emma's face. "Annie! What is it?"

Annie mopped her eyes and gave her a watery smile. "Surely you heard it?"

"No, what?"

"That silly donkey that the Martínezes have. Makes me laugh every time I hear him. All the wheezing and snorting he has to go through before he brays. Listen!" She flipped her handkerchief. "There he goes again!"

Emma cocked her head. "You're right. He certainly makes a production of it." She smiled down at her. "For a minute I thought you were crying!"

"Crying? Me? Oh, no. Did you know, Emma, that the Martínez donkey is a hinny?"

"A hinny? What on earth is that?"

Jane Yellow Cat was watching their exchange from the doorway and thought: So! I am not the only one who acts one way and feels another.

Goldie stopped by the house two days later and it was while he was measuring the space available for Jane's bed that he told Annie that Jack's leg wound had become infected. He said that his maw'd had to reopen the wound, clean it out good and burn it again.

Annie was trembling inside. *Burn it again!* Goldie had said that so matter-of-factly. "How is he now? Much better I'll bet!" *Please say yes!*

Goldie had seen the way she was tying her handkerchief into

a knot and hated to tell her that he wasn't. "Now he's got a fever."

She sat as if her legs had been whacked off at the knee. Fortunately there was a chair behind her.

"A fever?"

"Yeah. Real bad one. Last night we had to carry him down to the creek to cool him off. He gave Blue and me all we could handle. Got us ten times wetter'n we got him!"

Annie spent a terrible four days until finally the girls told her that their brother's fever had broken the day before.

She'd almost worried herself into a fever too but she couldn't help it. She couldn't quit thinking about him. She'd get a tight rein on her thoughts but could never hold on for long. Within minutes she'd have slipped back into the same old pattern. What was almost worse was how she would mentally thrash herself because, once again, she had not been capable of keeping her concern on an impersonal level. She scarcely slept, and as a consequence she was pale and wan herself.

One morning she'd overslept and arrived at school only a few minutes before class was to begin. Since she expected the first of her students any minute she wasn't surprised to hear the sound of a horse's hooves, but minutes later she *was* surprised to look up and see a work-stooped woman peering in at her. She rose, smoothing her hair and smiling. "Come in. Please."

The woman shook her head. "I won't take none of yore time. I jus' stopped to tell you not t'expect Abner or Rebecca in school no more."

"You're Mrs. Yates."

Her head bobbed. "Yessum, Billy's maw."

"I'm so sorry, Mrs. Yates . . ."

Her head bobbed again. "Yessum, but I'd jus' as soon not speak about it now, with the hurt so raw."

"Yes, of course. I . . . I truly hate to lose Abner and Rebecca. They are fine children and good students. Very bright and curious."

"They been cryin' all mornin'. About Billy. About school. About life, I guess."

"Mrs. Yates, if conditions change, will you let them come back?"

"Oh, yeah. I believe in learnin'. But I'm guessin' that conditions ain't gonna change an' if they do, they're jus' as likely t'git worse as better. We already seen hard times aplenty." She looked down a minute. "Well, Abner and Rebecca said t'tell yuh that yore a real good teacher an' that they liked school a lot." Finished, she nodded and started toward her horse.

"Mrs. Yates, wait. You're, ah, due a refund on the fee."

Going to the desk, Annie took out two coins which represented what Mrs. Yates was due then she added two more, guessing that Mrs. Yates might not know the exact amount Billy had been paying. "Here you are." She laid the coins in the woman's callused palm and folded her hand over them. "Please let me know if there's anything I can do for you, Mrs. Yates."

"Thank yuh but I don't know what it would be." She smiled. "Unless yuh can make a miracle?"

"I . . . no. But I would if I could."

"Me, too. When we first come here I had five kids an' a good man. Over the last four years either the ague or the Indians've whittled at us till there's only me an' the two littlest."

"I'm so sorry."

Mrs. Yates looked up and the sun struck her face just so and suddenly Annie didn't see a wrinkled woman, old before her time. She saw clear blue eyes and a strong dimpled chin. Why, Billy Yates's mother had once been a pretty woman.

Mrs. Yates stood there for a long while staring at something far away. Annie heard the Spanish church bell and watched a hawk disappear behind the crown of the hill before Mrs. Yates finally spoke. "Windy as a dollar preacher, ain't it?"

"Yes, but then . . . it often is, isn't it?"

"It's the nature of the land, I guess." She seemed to gather herself and she looked at Annie. ''Well, we live up yon a ways. Yuh come see us, hear?''

''Thank you. I will.''

''Good-bye, Miss.''

''Good-bye, Mrs. Yates.''

Apparently Annie had been walking an emotional tightrope because Mrs. Yates's visit sent her to the bottom like a dart. It was a good thing her students started to show! The way she felt she might have cried all morning.

Chapter 19

Emma held a handkerchief over her face. "What on earth is that smell?" They were passing a house where in back a thin woman and two girls moved around in some rising curls of steam.

"I think the woman of the house is making lye for soap. See that big kettle and that barrel."

"Imagine! Oh, Annie," Emma shook her head. "Sometimes this place makes me feel so inept."

"You, Emma? Why?"

"Because I have never made lye soap or my own candles or stuffed my own tick or slaughtered my own hog."

"Thank heavens!"

"But it does rather bother me that I cannot do half the things that the women here do routinely. And readily. That's one thing about this country. It certainly points out one's shortcomings. I never felt inadequate in Philadelphia."

"Shouldn't we consider ourselves lucky?"

"I suppose, but with the price of soap and candles here, I feel like I should ask someone to show us how those things are done. Why, even those Dare girls know how to do that stuff.''

''Emma, I don't care to learn how to kill a hog.''

''You're right. But let's at least try candle making and ticks.''

''All right. I'll ask them if they'll show us.''

''I think we're here, dear.''

They stood in front of Maude Stone's rooming house, a square sturdy two-floor structure that was wider than it was long. A narrow porch ran all along the front, and crooked cypress posts held up its steeply pitched roof as well as some wooden flaps on the second level where there were three dormer-style windows.

They ascended the porch stairs and knocked, and Annie for one was surprised at the youthful appearance of the woman who opened the door. Maude Stone was barely thirty and quite attractive in a frazzled sort of way. She wore a calico dress with a stain on the curve of one generous breast, and her apron could have been used to clean up after a hog slaughter, but she had a wide winsome smile and a full head of hair that was a lovely shade of red.

Was it burgundy or currant-colored? That's what Emma and Annie would argue about on the way home.

They were shown into the public eating area which had been grafted onto the side on the main building like a wart. It was still unfinished, with sawdust on the plank floor and a large skin-covered gap in the back wall, but there were four tables and enough chairs for two of them. As they were shown to their seats, Annie said, ''My, it smells wonderful in here!''

''You must like the smell of lime wash!''

''You can't fool this!'' Emma tapped her prodigious nose then wagged her finger. ''I smell more than lime!''

Maude Stone smiled proudly. ''I did get a raisin pie and an apple cobbler done earlier and there's a peach pie in the oven.''

''Good!'' Emma settled herself and folded her gloved hands on the edge of the table. ''We'll have a piece of each!''

Annie looked at her, shocked. ''Emma!''

''Well, I mean a piece of raisin for Annie and a piece of

apple cobbler for me and we better take the peach home for supper tonight.''

"My stars!" Annie said, shaking her head.

Both pieces of pie were delicious as was the coffee. "It hasn't been stretched," Emma said after a sip.

"No, it's wonderful!"

Shipments down the Bahia Road were so precarious even the relatively affluent people would stretch their coffee with rye or barley. Annie and Emma had refused to do so when they first arrived but it only took three weeks without any coffee at all for them to be converted to the practice.

Actually, if they could have laid their hands on some coffee during that period of forced abstinence they would've stretched it with dirt.

When Mrs. Stone returned, Annie said that she had heard Maude was planning on serving breakfast and lunch to the public. "By public I mean those other than your roomers."

"As you can see," she waved at the room. "I was hoping to serve a few." She tucked an errant strand behind her ear and it sprung out as soon as she released it. "Now I'll be lucky to get my roomers served on time."

That brought a gleam to Annie's eye. "Trouble finding good help?"

"That's it in a nutshell. The best girl I've ever had left just last night."

"Oh, how unfortunate!"

"Yes. She was a little negro gal who'd come here with a Georgia family. They no sooner arrived than the entire family sickened and died and left her all alone. I bought her papers for ten dollars and we got along famously until this big black fella came through town. I could tell by looking at him that he had run off from someplace. You could see that in his eyes. He was headed south, of course, further into Mexico. I used to see him hanging around outside and I almost said something to Addie but I couldn't do it. It was her life and now she's gone and done it. Left with him just this morning."

"Are you sure?"

"She couldn't leave me a message, but she had all the food ready. Crusts rolled out and everything and she left me this." Maude drew a primitive doll from her pocket.

"May I," Annie asked.

"Sure," she said and handed it to her.

The doll's body was a corncob. The arms, skirt and kerchief were made of husks and the hair of corn silk. It looked like she had drawn on the face with a piece of coal. "Isn't it pretty, Emma?"

"It certainly is! And very cleverly done!" said Emma.

Maude took it back and put it carefully in her pocket. "Guess it was her way of saying good-bye. And you know what, I really can't blame her. If they can get through the Comanche and Kiowa she'll have a chance for a life as a free person."

Emma wiped her eyes. "A heart-touching story, dear."

"It is," said Annie. After a moment's pause—which gave Emma time for a healthy blow—Annie said, "You know, Mrs. Stone, Abner and Rebecca Yates used to bring the most wonderful lunches to school. They gave me a round of bread one time and it was simply delicious! Believe it or not their mother had made the bread in an outdoor oven on a shovel."

"Huh!" Maude said. "My old granny used to bake bread that way. Best bread I've ever eaten."

"Mrs. Stone, I don't know if you heard that Billy Yates was killed last week."

"I heard about it. I didn't know him well . . . just to say hello to . . . but he sure seemed like a nice young man."

"He was and his dear mother's only grown boy. Now his mother has her back to the wall." She took a breath and plunged ahead. "Mrs. Stone, I was wondering if you plan to replace Addie?"

"I guess but I suppose they'll jus' leave too. Addie's the second girl who's up and married on me, you know. I guess that's to be expected. Sparse as females are in this country."

"Maybe this time you would consider hiring someone more, um, mature."

"Heavens, yes! You bet I would."

"I haven't asked her but I'm sure Mrs. Yates would be willing to try out for the job."

"You think so?"

"I hope!"

"I'll send word to her. You think? Ask her to come an' see me?"

"Oh, that would be wonderful. But don't let on that I . . ."

"No, no. Of course not."

Before they left, they bought baked bread as well and by the time they reached home, Emma had forgotten about making candles and ticks.

Jack Dare arrived at the Yates place about an hour after Charley Walters had delivered a question from Maude Stone and then ridden back to town to relay a positive answer.

Jack had come out to tell Mrs. Yates that she had five horses in Hap Pettijohn's feed yard, Billy's share of the horse herd that they had taken from the Indians She didn't bother to hide her relief at the news of this windfall.

Jack said that Hap was interested in buying one of the geldings and he thought she might ought to keep one for herself. He said there was a nice mare in the bunch. Looked like she could be a good breeder.

Mrs. Yates asked him if the mare was gentle enough for her to ride it into town to her new job. Jack replied that the mare was, and what new job was that?

When Jack got back to town it didn't take much to find out who had arranged for Mrs. Yates's new job. His heart swelled with pride and love and he thought: That's my Annie!

Hearing a horse, Annie walked to the door and saw Jack Dare swinging off his mount, a sight that both gladdened and alarmed her. She wasn't sure she was strong enough to cope with him without giving herself away.

He came forward moving gingerly, still using the pine-knob

cane. He was pale beneath the stubble that covered his jaw but he looked wonderful to her. Her heart was fluttering and a good breath seemed hard to draw and she suddenly had the urge to touch him so bad it hurt. He looked up at her and removed his hat. "Good morning, Miss Mapes."

"Mr. Dare! I didn't expect to see you up and about so soon."

"Soon? Seems to me like I've been laid up all my life." He looked up at her and smiled. "But it's doin' wonders for me already."

"What is?"

"Seein' you."

Unable to prevent the tears from welling, she turned aside. "It's good . . . good to see you too."

His brows ran together "Hey, what's wrong?"

"Nothing. I . . . I just feel unwell today."

Annie did not seem like the sort of a woman who was prone to spells but Jack was prepared to believe her. He'd known a lot of women who'd had strange spells come on them. Made some of them snaky as hell!

"I just realized how very ridiculous it was of me to say that when you are the one who's been ill." Her voice was muffled by her handkerchief.

"How are you?"

"Fine. All healed up. Just a few twinges occasionally."

"Please sit down."

"I'll stand, thank you."

She looked at his face. Leg. Face. Leg. "Is it your wound?"

"Mm. Throbs like crazy when I sit."

"I see." She blushed furiously. "Well . . ."

He leaned against the wall. "Markie's been telling me about you."

"And Markie's been telling me about you." Annie walked to the desk and leaned against it. She laughed ruefully. "That little rascal!"

"She in trouble again?"

"Not really, but I did have to speak strongly to her."

Jack doubted that she was ever harsh with Markie. Or for

that matter, with any of the kids. From the hill he had watched her with them, especially the littler ones. He'd seen her pick them up and dust them off and make a big to-do over the ratty things they'd bring her. He'd seen her make the big kids bring into their games any little one who'd been left out. Why, he'd even seen her kneel and play London bridge herself.

The older kids got their share of attention too. One day she spent an hour picking a sticker out of Zick's foot and more time than that sitting under a tree while the Cooper girl cried on her shoulder.

Finally he strongly suspected that she was spending her own hard-earned money to buy food for the kids. He'd often seen her carting in something by the boxful but it wasn't until he asked the twins that he found out she was buying lunches for those who couldn't afford to bring a good one.

The girls then told him that about the worst any kid had ever got from Annie Mapes was a wagging finger stuck in their face. Or a seat in the corner after school.

He sighed. "What'd she do this time?"

She sighed. "Her feelings were hurt. She thought Seth had ridiculed her."

He frowned. "Does ridicule mean make fun of?"

"Yes."

"Did he?"

"Not really, but she thought he did."

"Why?"

"Exactly my question. She said that Seth told the other kids that her drawers were made of sacking cloth."

"They probably are. So?"

"That's what I said to Markie. So what? Well, she thought about it and said, 'Don't you think I oughta fight 'im for that?' and I told her I didn't see how she could fight someone for telling the truth."

"That was good!"

She blushed under his praise. "Then she asked me how I figured he knew that her drawers were made of sacking. I said it was probably just a lucky guess. Or maybe it was because his were made of sacking too! She thought that over, and then set her face in that fierce scowl of hers. 'Well, I better not find out he's seen 'em. That's all I gotta say.' '' They both chuckled. "She is such a little firebrand"

"That's our fault. We told her not to ever take any guff from anybody. Taught her how to protect herself an' all. Probably overdid it, but there's some people who . . . like to hurt those weaker'n they are."

"As far as her spirit and mental view of life, I would not change a thing about her. Not one thing." They looked at each other for a long minute and then each looked away; Jack to a place on the floor; Annie to the configuration of her fingers. A deep silence had rolled down and covered the room like a harbor fog. It seemed a long time went by before he said, "Say, how's the Cherokee kid doing?"

Annie was relieved to keep the conversation rolling. And impersonal. "Jane's just fine. No, more than fine. She surprises us all the time."

"How."

"Well, I for one was very surprised to learn how well educated she is. She said that her family had lived in a house that was very similar to ours. She said that they had two slaves, and that most of the members of her tribe owned slaves!"

"I've heard that's how come they call the Cherokee one of the civilized tribes, though I guess I don't see how havin' slaves makes a person civilized."

"Me either."

Jack moved toward the door. "You know, I'd like to talk to her about that band of Indians she was living with."

She cocked her head? "Why?"

"All the Comanche who raid Sweet Home seem to return to the same area." He made a circle. "I'd like to ask her if she knows why?"

"Of course! When would you like to see her?"

"Tomorrow all right?"

"Fine." The next day was Sunday and there was no school. "Would you like to come by the house?"

"Yeah. About four?"

"Fine."

It was late afternoon, time for her to go home only he hadn't seen her in so long he hated to leave. "The other kids're probably readin' way ahead of me by now."

"It doesn't matter."

"Mebbe not to you."

She shook her head. "You don't need to know how to read."

He tried to see her face but she kept it turned away. "I thought you said readin' was about the most important thing a man could do."

"I was wrong."

"Wrong? You mean I spent all that time sweatin' over my lessons for nothin'?"

"I once thought it was important. I suppose it still is, if a person lives in New York or Philadelphia. But not here." Their eyes met and held and she looked away first. He was looking at her with an intentness that she had never seen before. She kept herself busy, tapping some papers on the desk, blowing some dust onto the floor.

"You've sure changed your tune."

"Me? I suppose I have. I guess I've been here long enough to realize that most men would never make it in this country."

"Like who?"

"Well, like the ones who compare everything here with the place they came from. Or the ones who have received all their knowledge from between the covers of a book. Of course, neither description fits you. You make the best of every situation and have learned everything you know from experience. Which is, of course, the ideal way to learn."

"An' all this time I thought you didn't approve of me."

"To the contrary, I wouldn't change a thing about you." Too late she added, "I mean there's no need for you to change anything about yourself. You are just . . . fine as you are."

His wound was killing him but he still felt like making love to her. He'd always feel like making love to her. *Damn but that's one helluva powerful pull.* "Sounds to me like you're tryin' to get outa teachin' me to read.'' There was a long moment before she answered, and her voice sounded wet and strangled.

''I don't dare.''

''Annie!''

He had come up beside her but she moved away. ''I'll expect you at the house at four tomorrow,'' she said, facing her desk.

''But . . . !''

''Please go now.''

''We need to talk.''

''There's nothing to say. Just . . . go.''

''Damn it!''

''I am asking you to leave.'' She turned and looked at him and he'd seen warmer eyes beyond the bore of a gun. ''Are you refusing?''

At the door he paused. ''I know what you did for the Yates family an' I want to say that you are a damn fine person, Annie Mapes.''

After she heard his horse she went to the door and wished she hadn't because he had turned for one last look at her. She stared back at him for a long time. She thought he was going to say something else and she was almost ready for him to.

Jack would remember none of the trip into town.

She had been so damn close to saying that she loved him, that he had almost taken her in his arms and used better methods of persuasion. Luckily he hadn't. He had done that once before and almost ruined everything. Obviously the only way to get to Annie Mapes was to quit pressing her. Let her come around on her own. Hell she already loved him! She'd almost said it. What he did not understand was why she didn't?

He had tied his horse in front of Garlock's store and didn't realize he was there until someone called to him from a wooden-wheeled caretta across the road. It was Hector Salazar's brother, Navidad, and he had his family with him. Navidad's wife waved.

When Jack had eaten at their home not long ago Navidad's wife had been as big as a barrel. Now here she was holding a swathed bundle and grinning like a cat. He went over. She'd unwrapped the baby and he could see the peanut between its legs. "Not another boy?" exclaimed Jack.

"*Sí!* Yet another boy!"

The four black-eyed sons that trailed the wagon looked like they were standing on different stairs but they bore no other distinguishing characteristics. Shoeless and whip-thin, all had bowl haircuts and wore bleached cloth camisas with baggy pants held up by frayed ropes. Navidad and his family were as poor as churchmice . . . and Jack was jealous as hell.

"Navidad, you are a very fortunate man."

For a second Navidad wondered why Jack sounded so solemn but then he felt a great swelling of pride and forgot. "I know, señor. *Muy fortunato!*"

They spoke of unimportant things for a time and before they parted Navidad made Jack promise to come to dinner soon. Jack watched them for a time and then crossed over to Lloyd Cooper's office.

"Jack! Glad to see you up and around. Come in and take a seat."

"That's the first thing everybody wants me to do an' when I do, it feels like I've a tied boulder swinging off my cojones."

"Good grief! Then by all means, stand!"

Cooper sat back and patted his girth, a self-satisfied habit that Jack recognized. He leaned against the wall and studied him. "You're actin' mighty pleased with yourself."

"That's because I am. I've just made the final arrangements for a new courthouse and a new church. And I've applied for Sweet Home to be a judicial district."

"What's that mean?"

"That means we'll be assigned our own judge and that people will come here from all over the district to settle land claims and do their legal business. I'll tell you, Jack, this could be big. We're liable to have a town here yet!"

"Mebbe. If the Indians don't kill all of us off first."

"Yes. Well." Subdued now. "It was a shame about Billy Yates."

Jack nodded somberly. "Yates'll be damn hard to replace an' not just with the troop. His mother's a widow woman who depended on Billy's help and earnings to get by. She's still got two youngsters to bring up an' she's worried about making it without him."

"Will she?"

Jack shrugged. "On the day of the funeral she talked to us about buying her out. The Yates property backs up to ours on the north."

"Are you buying it?"

"We told her not to do anything hasty."

"I figured they were in trouble."

"Things are some better now. She's got Billy's share of the horse herd which Hap is gonna sell for her an' Annie Mapes got her a job."

"She did? Where?"

"Maude Stone's."

"Good idea! I'd heard she was adding on."

"We also talked to Miz Yates about her taking in some young fella who's willin' to trade meals an' a place to stay for helpin' with some of the chores around the place."

"Another good idea. I can think of ten men who would go for that in a minute."

"In the meantime," Jack said. "Something's got to be done about the Indians."

"I thought you were doing something about them."

"If you mean kill them off, the score's probably about even."

"What more can we do?"

"I'd like to talk to 'em."

"What?"

"Ask 'em why they pick Sweet Home to raid when there's other nearer an' smaller settlements . . ."

"Liberty?" He brushed at something on his knee. "That's nothing."

Liberty and Sweet Home had received their land grants from Mexico's land commissioner, Francisco Madera, at about the same time. What was not known to the *alcalde* of the other town was that Cooper had been in a race with him ever since.

"Still I'd like to ask one of 'em . . ."

"Jack, you can't ask anything of an Indian! At least, nobody I know has ever done it."

"Mebbe it's time somebody tried. Way we're goin' now, we'll both keep fightin' till one or the other is wiped out."

"Nobody's ever negotiated true peace with any tribe. At least not one that lasted more than a month or two."

"I can't make peace with them. I haven't that authority. But mebbe we could make a little side deal."

"What sort of side deal?"

"You leave us alone an' we'll leave you alone."

"An agreement between Sweet Home and all the Indians who've been attacking it?"

"Not all Indians. Not the Kiowa. Not even all the bands of Comanche. Just the Comanches in that one area."

"I don't think it will work."

"Why not try? We can't jus' keep killin' each other off."

"Jack, we're not dealing with an advanced society, you know. These are primitives. Raiding and killing is a way of life with them. Why, any one of them would sooner kill you as look at you. I know I don't have to tell you that."

Jack stood staring at an old map tacked to the wall. It had been drawn on an antelope skin so long ago that it showed only rivers and very few of those. Beyond the northernmost one there was a large blank place. Indian country.

"Jack?"

"Most all the raiders who attack Sweet Home . . ." He tapped the map. " . . . come from there." He looked back at Cooper. "What if we gave 'em something they want?"

"Like what?"

"They want the white man out of their range. Which is this big area right here." He tapped the map again. "What if we made 'em a deal . . . told 'em that if they'll leave off stealin' our stock an' killin' our people, we will discourage future settlers from moving onto their land."

"How?"

"For one thin', tell anybody who crosses that river that they're doin' so at their own risk."

"I don't know if Coahuila . . ."

"They don't even have to get involved in this. This is a deal between Sweet Home and the Indians who live right here." He tapped the map again.

"I don't know. How would we stop Americans and other anglos from going across that river?"

"We can't. All we can do is tell them that if they insist on going, we can offer them no protection beyond that point."

"Who would you talk to?"

"I don't know. I'm goin' to talk to Jane Yellow Cat tomorrow. I want to find out if she knows the name of the man who organizes most of the raids. He's the one to talk to about a truce."

Lloyd thought about it. Mexico City would never approve of little Sweet Home negotiating its own truce with the Comanches. But if it stopped the fighting, who cared? He'd long ago learned that what Mexico City didn't know, didn't hurt them. "What would you need?"

"Wampum. Conchos. Mirrors. Blankets. Knives. Pots. Glass trade-beads and cloth. A few mules to carry stuff on."

Cooper took paper from the desk drawer, dipped his pin and scratched a short note. "Give this to Bowie." He finished a second sheet. "And give this one to Durrell at the livery."

Jack folded the papers and put them in his back pocket. "All right then."

Cooper stood and offered his hand. "Jack, at the least you're wasting your time and at the worst, you're risking your life. But I wish you good luck."

Chapter 20

At four on Sunday, Jack arrived to talk to Jane Yellow Cat and found Annie and the girl waiting for him behind the house, sitting in the dappled shade of an apple tree.

A siesta-time stillness had settled over everything. June bugs buzzed in the bushes, and chickens softly clucked as they scratched in the dirt.

Jack sat on a fallen log and the girl sat Indian style in front of him. Annie Mapes and Blue Dare stood apart but nearby.

Blue had made it quite clear that he disagreed with Jack's intentions and had come along purely out of curiosity. Annie knew nothing of that but she would not have been surprised to learn that more than anything he had come because he knew his presence would annoy Jane Yellow Cat. She had never seen such open hostility between two people!

Jack was trying to decide what was different about Jane, without committing a breach of Indian conduct. He didn't know about the Cherokee but staring was an insult to a lot of tribes.

It was more than a lack of paint and the fact that her braids were tied by ribbons instead of wrapped with strips of deerskin. He was fixing his pipe when it finally hit him what it was. She had lost that hunted animal look. The beaten way she stared at the ground and never met a person's eye was gone now. Matter of fact, her gaze was so level and direct that it made him feel a bit uneasy.

"I am pleased that you're well."

She lowered her head. "I am pleased to see that you are the same."

There followed a few minutes of the Indian equivalent of small talk before Jack got down to business. "On the day we attacked your camp, our scout He-Coon says he found some tracks showing that many horses had ridden away from the encampment the day before."

She nodded. "Hunters."

"Some of those men were on the Castenada raid." It was a statement of fact and she did not dispute it. "Matter of fact, the one who led that raid was among those hunters." She nodded then. "I'd like to have a word with that fella."

Most Comanche bands never designated a head man or a chief. As a result, almost any warrior could cook up what he thought was a good strategy and if the other warriors agreed with him they would follow him. Or maybe they wouldn't, as they wished. However, the leaders of successful raids were highly honored, and respect for their decisions grew with each triumph.

The man who led the Castenada raid was the one Jack wanted to talk to. By a warrior's standards his raid had been successful. He had killed Texians and taken scalps, but the aftermath of the raid had been very costly because of the retaliatory attack by Jack and his men in which many Indians died.

Jane Yellow Cat asked why he wanted to speak to that particular warrior.

Jack shrugged. "Three Tejano boys and one man cost them upwards of twenty lives, one slave and forty-eight horses. I'm thinkin' mebbe the time to talk to him is when the loss is still fresh in his mind."

She was obviously surprised. Any warrior was willing to

give their life if it meant whites' lives were lost too. "Men fight and die all the time," she said. "That is a man's purpose"

"Every time a red man kills a white man, I kill some red men in return. Then they kill some white men and on and on."

Yellow Cat nodded. As warriors, neither side could allow a raid to go unanswered. "Why is that a problem?"

"Seems senseless to me. Forever ridin' back an' forth an' rubbin' each other out. I'm sick of it. I'm ready to try somethin' else. Maybe he is too."

"A little talk and the Comanche will be ready to quit making war?" Doubt—maybe even derision—was evident in her voice.

"In at least one area. I'll tell 'em . . . if they'll quit killing the people around here, where I live, then I will quit killing the red man where he lives."

Using her chin she indicated Blue, who stood with one booted foot back against a tree. "His face says you are thinking like a fool!"

Jack grinned. "He'll come around."

The way she raised one eyebrow suggested that he better not hold his breath, and once again Jack was struck by how old-acting she was.

"The most important warrior of that band is named Crying Hawk. His brother, Red Horse, was killed on the day you found me."

Blue pushed off the tree. "Well, that's that then. That redskin ain't about to sit down an' palaver with his brother's killer."

"Just a minute, Blue. You're sure about the brother?"

She nodded. "I saw him dead."

"That ain't good, Jack."

"No," she said and smiled sadly. "Just as you want revenge for your dead people, Crying Hawk will want revenge for his brother."

Blue said, "Guess we'll have t'call the whole thing off."

As Jack stood a look of pain crossed his face and he grasped his leg with his hand. Annie almost went to him but he straightened and accepted his cane from Blue. He ran his fingers through his hair and pulled on his hat. "I ain't ready to quit yet."

"You ain't?" Blue was incredulous. "Hell, those Indians'll be madder'n a buncha bees in a jar!"

Jack clapped his brother on the shoulder. "I never said it'd be easy."

Annie had listened to all that Jack had to say and she thought any endeavor to end the killing was admirable, especially after she'd met with Billy Yates's mother and witnessed her anguish firsthand. But like Lloyd Cooper she questioned his insane decision to ride into a Comanche camp unarmed. He would, of course, be placing himself in terrible danger, but as much as she would like to ask him not to go, she refrained from doing so. It was not her place to ask Jack Dare anything. She had no ties on him.

Once again before they left, Jack told Blue that he did not have to be a part of the scheme and Blue got plenty hot about that. He said he was not going along because he thought Jack's idea held any water but because somebody had to see that he got out of the Indian compound alive.

The three brothers were near the work shed. Jack was leaning against it to keep his weight off his bad leg and Blue was pacing the bank, pausing every so often to toss a rock into the water. Goldie had his arms folded and his legs spread and seemed intent on a slowly circling hawk on the opposite bank of the creek. "Where do you think they'll be?" he asked.

"Not at the campsite we burned. Further up north somewhere." Jack shifted his weight. "Yellow Cat only knew the Comanche names for the various campsites but I'll bet ol' He-Coon knows where they are."

Blue turned. "Think he'll take us in?"

"Why wouldn't he? He's taken the troop everywhere else."

Goldie looked at Jack. "I better come along this time."

"So Maw can lose us all in one day?"

"You plannin' on not comin' back?"

"Don't worry, I plan on comin' back."

"Then what's the problem?"

"The problem is that I can only worry about one harebrained Dare at a time."

Blue turned but by the time he'd figured out he'd been insulted, Jack had talked Goldie into staying.

"Well, all right."

Blue pitched his last pebble in the water. "Guess we go talk to He-Coon."

Jack pushed off the wall. "Yeah, I guess."

"First thing tomorrow morning?"

"Naw," Jack said. "About midmorning. I got something to do first."

First thing the following morning Jack was at the school asking Annie if he could speak to her alone for a minute. She told the children to remain in their seats, but of course as soon as she walked outside the kids layered themselves at the only window that faced in their direction.

They stopped beneath the big tree and faced each other. Jack was working his hat brim over pretty good. Teacher looked like a sleeping bird with her head turned and her chin tucked. The kids strained their ears but couldn't hear a word.

"You're leaving."

"Yeah. This morning."

"I wish you weren't."

"Why?"

She shrugged. "I don't want you hurt."

"Why?"

"You know why."

"Annie . . ."

"Please don't."

"But . . ."

She looked at him. "Just leave it be. Please"

"I can't do that."

She turned and put a hand on the tree. Above them a mocking-

bird was running through its medley of songs but neither heard
a note.

"Annie, you love me. You know you do."

"No."

He came up close behind her and softly said, "Liar!"

"I am already promised to another."

"So you're gonna go ahead an' marry a man you don't
love?"

"Yes"

"You can't."

"I must. And I do love him. I have all my life."

"It's not the same." She turned. "All right . . ." He held
up his hand. "I'm willin' to let it go till I come back but the
least you could do is allow me to speak my piece. Annie, you
know how I feel."

She looked left then down at her feet. The sight of all the
kids hanging out the window had not even registered with her.
"Jack, you don't even know me."

"I know all I need to know an' I like everything I see."
And what I don't.

"If you had the opportunity you'd see a lot you wouldn't
like about me."

"What? Something like . . . you never cut your toenails?
Stuff like that?"

"Don't be silly. I wouldn't be able to wear shoes."

"You love me, don't you?" He waited for her to shake her
head but she never did. It was enough for now. He put on his
hat. "Will you be worried about me?"

"Yes, very."

"Will you think about me?"

Slower now. "Yes."

"Will you kiss me good-bye?"

"No."

"I didn't think so." He put on his hat. As for the expression
on his face he tried for the saint-being-tortured-on-the-rack
look. "Well, Annie, if we never meet again, remember that I
loved you until the end of my life." He snuck a look at her

and was gratified to see that she looked quite stricken. "Good-bye, Annie Mapes."

A choked sob followed him to his horse. He grinned.

At about dusk they arrived at He-Coon's *ranchería,* which was a scattering of several cone-shaped huts made from grass, brush and branches and then patched with skins. They were shown to the scout's hut and invited to enter. They had to step over a horned buffalo skull to do so.

Once inside they saw He-Coon sitting beside a rock-banked fire. He directed them to sit on woven grass mats while his woman prepared a ceremonial pipe. It was quite warm, but then it was outside as well. While they waited, Jack looked around and recalled what he knew about the Tonkaweya—which loosely translated meant "they all stay together."

They called themselves the Tickanwatic which meant the "most human of all people." It was a pretty universal belief. The Comanche, Apache and Kiowa all thought of themselves in the same manner. Jack had always wondered if it eased their conscience when they killed members of their own race.

In general Tonkawas were a tall, slender people though not as tall as the Karankawas. They had never practiced agriculture but rather had always hunted, gathered and fished for their sustenance. Unlike other Tejas tribes the Tonkawas had no taboos against eating fish or oysters. They were also the only Indian tribe that had almost always been an ally of the white man, not because of the white man's charm and goodwill but because the Tonkawas had almost always been the enemy of every other tribe in Tejas.

After everybody had smoked, the pipe was returned to He-Coon whose eyes almost closed completely as he drew deeply on it.

A woman offered them a length of intestine into which meat and pecans had been stuffed. Jack bit off some and passed it on to Blue who kept right on passing. *There is no way in hell*

I'm eatin' anythin' made in this place. Damn meat's probably dog!

But Blue was quite taken with the bare-breasted girl who was doing the serving. Circles had been drawn on each of her breasts, smaller near the nipple and growing larger as the breast did. The only other female in the wickiup was an ancient woman whose head had been flattened, a practice supposedly discontinued long ago. She also was bare-chested; but unlike the pert breasts of the girl, the old woman's dugs hung flat on her chest and were nipple-less. Blue would later ask He-Coon about her and he'd say that she had cut her nipples off herself, one for each of the sons she had lost in battle.

He-Coon's face was wreathed in smoke but when Jack told him that he wanted to talk peace to a Comanche named Crying Hawk, He-Coon's eyes flew open and he came as close to smiling as Jack had ever seen him. He replied that the Mexicans had been trying to make peace with the Comanche for five thousand moons. What made the white man think he could succeed when all others had failed? Jack had no answer to that question, only that he thought it was worth a try.

He-Coon said he was sure the effort would fail. He would, however, go along so that when the peace talks did not work, he might have an opportunity to kill a few Comanches before he died.

As they rode away, Blue said it sounded like He-Coon wanted to start a war. Jack replied that he didn't care why He-Coon came along as long as he came. Blue said he cared quite a bit. Especially if he started something just for the hell of it. "He's always said that as long as he takes a Comanche with him, he's happy to throw himself away."

"Jus' so long as he doesn't throw us away at the same time."

Jack fell silent then. Blue looked at him and shrugged and did the same.

They left the next day, Blue, He-Coon and Jack, following the general directions that Jane Yellow Cat had given them.

They didn't think that it would be easy to find the Indian camp and it wasn't, although Jane's information was surprisingly accurate once they realized that when she said "one day's travel" she had not meant on horseback but afoot with a dog-pulled travois.

By the eighth day they had ridden into a land of rolling prairie and shallow creeks, a land that had a deficiency of settlers and an abundance of Indians . . . ones who knew they were there. They'd seen smoke signals behind distant hills and had found the tracks of unshod ponies across their path and on the trail behind them. They were riding alongside a narrow gully when four Indians suddenly appeared on the opposite side.

They carried long lances and shields or bows and quivers of arrows but they were not hunting—at least, not for food. Their faces were ocher-streaked and their horses' tails were tied. In their hair were ceremonial war feathers that fluttered in the wind.

These were not young braves trying to count coup. These were seasoned warriors looking to add some more scalps to their collection.

The Dares and He-Coon sat their horses and watched them, and when the Comanches rode into the gully and up on the other side they left their long guns tied to their pommels and stepped off their horses. The Indians began to circle them. He-Coon folded his arms and spoke with derision. "It is the Comanches' foolish belief that if they can run around an enemy they can win a fight with him."

"They probably can," Blue said, "seeing as how we've left our carbines on our horses. God, I feel naked as a scalded hog."

When the Indians rode closer still, Jack made the sign for peace and told He-Coon to tell them they were looking for Crying Hawk. One man gigged his horse forward and He-Coon nodded toward him: "That man says you have found him."

Crying Hawk had a well-knit frame and keen lashless eyes. His coarse black hair was slicked to his head, parted in the middle and braided into two plaits that hung to his waist. His part was painted red. He wore bison-hide moccasins and a breech clout. He was probably close to Jack's age.

"Tell him we have gifts an' want to talk."

After He-Coon relayed that, Crying Hawk motioned that they were to follow on their horses. One of the braves rode by each horse and collected their rifles and then they mounted up and fell in. Two Indians led and two followed.

Blue muttered, "Well, Jack, I sure hope you're right about that first-visit stuff."

He referred to the fact—or the myth—that the Indians will always grant hospitality to an unarmed man approaching their camp for the first time. It was the way traders had been able to make contact with different bands for many hundreds of years. Walk in with your goods and no arms and supposedly the Indians would let you walk out unharmed. When you left you were either told you would be made welcome the next time you came or you were told that you would be killed on sight. A wise man heeded.

"If I'm not right, we can look forward to a hell of an excitin' minute or two an' a bullet to the head. If we're lucky!"

"An if we're not . . ."

"We all learn how to yodel."

Blue took some comfort in the fact that the Indians had not taken their knives, but after he thought it over he decided the Indians hadn't taken their knives because they believed that no white man can best a Comanche in a knife fight. In most cases they were right, but those Indians had not yet fought a Dare.

As usual, the Comanche *ranchería* had been situated alongside water, this time a fast-running, rocky stream. It was a good-sized village with upwards of fifty tanned-hide tepees strung out on both sides of the water.

Moving slowly and keeping his hands in sight, Jack took the booty off the mules and spread the things out on several good-quality blankets.

They had brought skinning knives and fighting knives, axes, awls, rebozos, mirrors, silver conchos, colored glass beads, mantillas, cast-iron pots with tripods, combs, brushes, ribbons and the blankets on which everything lay.

It was a fine array of goods and several Indians looked over everything very carefully. Apparently Crying Hawk saw nothing that warranted a closer look. He remained standing with his arms folded.

Jack was glad now that he had brought along the burning glass that he had bought in St. Louie. It had been damned expensive and he had planned on keeping it for himself but one look at Crying Hawk's expression told him this might be a good time to part with it.

He gathered some punk and made a production of getting set up, making people stand back and drawing a circle in the dirt, showing everyone the small round glass and waving his arms over the mound of kindling.

He pointed at the sun . . . everyone stared at the sun. Then he pointed at the punk. He knelt and held the glass over the punk.

Of course, nothing happened for a long minute and he could hear some impatient grumbling behind him. *It worked in St. Louis; it damn well better work here.*

Time crept by, then finally a piece of straw caught fire.

There was a rumble of interest then and several Indians had to put their hands above the flame to see if it really was a fire. Most could not hide their fascination, especially when the pile burst into a roaring fire.

Crying Hawk's face remained impassive but Jack sensed it wasn't easy for him.

Once the gift giving was over, they were led to a tepee that had a rising sun and a spread-winged hawk painted on it. Inside they sat on a pallet that had been made of grass and then covered with a deer hide that was laid fur side up. The wood smoke was almost overwhelming and Jack's eyes were smarting in seconds. Crying Hawk sat across the fire and stared at them with eyes that were as pitiless as a snake's. It was a toss-up which gave the most heat, the Indian's eyes, or the fire.

While looking around Blue had caught the eye of a young

Indian who sat in the shadows behind Crying Hawk. He was eighteen, maybe nineteen, too old to be Crying Hawk's son but they looked enough alike to be brothers.

Once Blue got his night eyes he saw that the kid featured himself a dandy. He was wearing three white womens' rings on his fingers and had a woman's lapel watch pinned on his breast plate.

The young brave sat with pride. He knew where the white man's eyes had been and he was glad. When the white man's eyes rose to meet his, he offered him an unmistakable challenge. Blue shortened his neck and glared an answer that required no translation.

The Indian signaled that there would be no small talk so in the simplest words he could use, Jack explained why they had come. He-Coon translated Jack's words then Crying Hawk's reply. "He says that you offer them the safe use of land that is already theirs."

Jack replied, "Just as the Comanche once took this land from the Apache, the white man will one day take it from the Comanche. Unless we make a pact to live here together without bloodshed."

"Crying Hawk asks how the white man will keep other white men from traveling into the area reserved for the Comanche. If he were so foolish as to agree to such a thing."

Jack replied, "Ask him how he will keep his young men from stealing our horses? Both are difficult tasks."

Crying Hawk listened to He-Coon and nodded. "He says not stealing horses is impossible for a good Comanche. He himself would rather steal horses than breathe."

"Tell him that we can't make the white men stay out of Indian land, but we will tell 'em that they travel there at their own peril. And that we will try very hard to convince everyone to settle elsewhere."

He looked at Crying Hawk, who was shaking his head. He spoke for a long time. When he finally finished He-Coon obviously gave them a condensed version of the speech. "He says he used to have many people in his family, so many he had to use two hands twice to count them. Now all are dead except his brother, Runs With the Wind.

"He says you may be brave and honest men who want very much to do what you say you will, but you are also fools because you are promising that which you cannot do.

"He says you may take your weapons and go, but if you ever come back here again, he will make you wish that you had died inside your mother's belly."

Chapter 21

At last Annie received the information she had requested from Abel on the Braille reading system for the blind. Immediately after she finished reading it over, she went in search of Charley Walters who still did a few chores for them when he was not riding guard for Hap Pettijohn. (As he reminded them practically daily, nothing took precedence over that.) Half an hour later they were rattling across the creek to the Dare place.

The Dares greeted them cordially and insisted on giving Charley a turkey leg to gnaw on and Annie a cup of cider cooled in a crock raised from the well. Goldie and Evie were the only ones home. Jack and Blue were still off on their peace seeking mission with the Indians and the three girls had gone fishing.

There followed some obligatory small talk including questions about how the girls were doing in school. Unlike when she was asked that question by some of her other students' parents, she did not have to prompt herself to be diplomatic. She could honestly say that the Dare girls were her best students.

It was cooler on the porch but still uncomfortably warm and when the girls returned with their stringer of black bass Annie envied them their bare feet more than their catch. (She hated hot feet. Given half a chance she would remove her shoes in a heartbeat.)

"Nothin's hotter'n Tejas in August!"

Evie's comment was interrupted by a snort from Charley Walters who had fallen asleep with his back against the porch post and his head crooked at an impossible angle.

Annie took that opportunity to ask if they'd had any word from Jack or Blue. She tried not to sound too anxious.

"No word yet," answered Evie, "but I'm sure they're fine. I believe I've learned how to tell if they aren't."

Ridiculous as that sounded, Annie believed her.

"Why?" Evie gave her a shrewd look. "Did you need to see Jack about somethin'?" Her voice held a hopeful note.

"No," she replied. "Just concerned about their safety."

She hoped she had stressed the word "their" enough to nip Evie's expectations in the bud, but just to be safe she diverted Evie by bringing out the sheaf of papers from Abel. "Actually I came to see Goldie."

"Me?" He sounded surprised but pleased.

"Yes." She unfurled a piece of paper that was so large she had to ask Irish to hold down the top edges. "Goldie, I came to see if you can make something to help Markie in school."

"Sure. What do you want me to do?"

"Could you put these sixty-three dots on a flat board in a way that fixes them there permanently? It's important that they be spaced exactly like these are."

He looked at the pattern of dots but they made no sense to him. "I can't make head nor tail out of that."

"I know. Neither could I until I'd studied them." She pointed to one grouping. "If you look at them closely you can see that there are six basic dots, three down and two across and that all these symbols are variations of those same six dots. When they are put in a certain order each one represents a letter. Like this one here is an *F* and this one an *M*. Letters put together make a word. Words strung together make a sentence."

"What's it for?" asked Evie.

"If Markie can commit these basic patterns to memory, I think I can teach her to read!"

She looked up at Evie and Goldie and was disappointed to see how confused they looked. Then she heard Markie breathe, "I could read? Really?"

"Markie, I am almost positive you can." Certainly she was smart enough to grasp the concept. If she heard a word she remembered how to say it and how to spell it as well as what it meant. Annie was betting that she could memorize the dot alphabet too, and if so, then all she had to do was recognize them in their different configurations.

"While Goldie is copying the dot alphabet onto a piece of board, I am going to translate a story into Braille and after you've memorized the sixty-three signs, I'll put the story on a board and we'll see if you can read it."

"I'll bet I can!"

"I'll bet you can too."

Thinking out loud Goldie said, "The dot alphabet needs to be permanent . . ."

"Yes."

"But the story does not?"

"No, the same board could be used over again unless she wanted to save each story. But what I need to know is what could be used to make the dots stick."

"Hm. Let me think about it," said Goldie. "Would it be all right to punch holes in the board rather than make them raised?"

"Yes. All she has to do is be able to feel the pattern with her fingers."

Goldie was looking at the dots. "Be more permanent that way."

"Good." She took Markie's hand. "Oh, Markie, I'm so excited I can hardly stand it. Just think! Maybe you'll be able to read!"

After Annie Mapes and Charley Walters left, the twins went to clean the fish and left Evie and Goldie sitting on the porch alone. They could hear the excited tone to Markie's voice.

Evie said, "She's sure a good woman, that teacher."

"That she is."

"Jack fancies her a lot."

Goldie nodded. "I know but a person doesn't always get what they want outa life."

Evie looked at him. "I don't see why not."

A day later Annie heard that the two Dare brothers had returned unharmed and the weak-kneed relief she experienced made one thing painfully clear: her plan to fall out of love with Jack Dare was not working.

She had not even succeeded in getting him out of her thoughts. When she least expected it, his face would flash into mind. Obviously she had to try harder, but how? Every attempt had failed. Even guilt.

Which should have been fairly easy since she *was* guilty.

No matter how long she studied her predicament and no matter how hard she'd tried, she'd been unsuccessful in whitewashing the situation; she had not been forced. She had willingly allowed a man who was not her husband—not even her fiancé—to put his hands all over her and kiss her in a most shameless manner.

Apparently even raging remorse was not enough to turn her against him because ever since that night she had been obsessed with the man. She thought of little else and her thoughts were far from pure.

Only one saving fact remained: while it was true that she was a weak-willed person with a hundred character flaws, she was *not* someone who gave their word lightly. At least she had continued to be steadfast in her vow to Abel O'Neal. She had promised herself to him and she would marry him. No matter what.

Abel was her dearest friend. As God is her judge, he would be her loving husband as well.

Once she was married to Abel she was certain she could learn to be content. She simply had to convince herself that she was happy with what she had. And stop yearning for what her foolish heart kept telling her she was missing!

Chapter 22

Abel O'Neal arrived in Sweet Home about two o'clock on a Friday afternoon, weeks before he was expected. He intended for his appearance to be a complete surprise, and it would be.

Since he had ridden in with one of Hap Pettijohn's drivers, Hap was the first Sweet Home resident he met. The second would be Goldie Dare, who would soon arrive to pick up some hinges he had ordered from Little Rock.

It was late August and hot enough to peel paint, which was probably why there were so few people out and about. He could hear a barking dog and the munching of the mules in the feed yard, but otherwise it was deadly quiet. A slow steady wind cartwheeled a piece of trash into a wall and dust spirals rolled down the narrow road that was the main—and only—street.

Apparently the dry conditions were not unique. The block-like buildings that lined the road looked sand-scoured and everything, including his teeth, was covered with a fine layer of grit.

Abel had directions to his mother's place but now that he had finally arrived he felt strangely unwilling to hurry things, so he dawdled a while, talking to Hap and getting a feel for the town. That's when Goldie Dare rode up.

Goldie saw the tall, alert-looking young man who was standing in front of Hap Pettijohn's depot and then he saw the carpetbag at his feet and he knew who he was, just like that. Sure enough, soon as he walked over Hap said, "Abel O'Neal, this here's Goldie Dare."

As the freight line owner introduced him, Abel offered his hand. A vise took it and squeezed it numb. "I figured that's who you were," the man said. Thanks to Annie's letters, Abel knew who Goldie was too, having heard all about the Dare clan, beginning with their unusual names and ending with their unusual natures.

Abel took in the breadth of Goldie Dare's shoulders, and the face that looked like it had been chipped out of a hard rock and he concurred with Annie that the Dares were very impressive. "You're the fella who made the furniture for the school."

"Unh," Goldie looked at him. "An' I guess you're gonna be Sweet Home's new lawyer . . ."

"Unless I'm mistaken, I'll be its only lawyer."

"Could be. Yeah, I believe you're right."

"Good! I hope there's enough business to . . ."

"Abel!"

Abel looked over Goldie's shoulder and saw a vision of loveliness approaching fast, a veritable whirlwind of fluttering skirts and waving hands. Annie.

"Annie!"

"Oh, Abel! Charley said he'd heard you rode in with the freight wagon!"

Abel O'Neal went to meet her and Goldie frowned at the sight of them hugging and kissing each other. Hap leaned close. "I thought Jack was sweet on the schoolmarm."

"He is."

"This could mean trouble."

"This could mean a lot of trouble!"

"Good thin' Jack ain't here to see this. He'd be madder'n hell!"

Goldie muttered something about not being sure Jack's reaction was going to be anger and he was right. At the Y in the road Jack Dare sat his horse and watched the stranger and Annie walk off, arm and arm and smiling into each other's eyes and what he felt inside was about as far from anger as a person can get.

He sat stock-still until the couple passed beyond his view, then he turned his horse and rode slowly away.

Over his mother's and his fiancé's objections, Abel took a room at Maude Stone's little boardinghouse on the other end of town. He insisted—and he could be quite stubborn—that he needed to maintain a separate dwelling until he and Annie could get married and afford to have something more suitable built.

As he said that he had looked at Annie and smiled. He said he was sure she could see the need for that.

Annie could not. She wanted him to stay with them at their house. That wouldn't be proper, he said. Why, she asked. We lived in the same house in Philadelphia. Where's the difference? The difference, he said with his usual patience, is that Philadelphia is a big city and Sweet Home is a small town. It wouldn't look right. People would talk. All right, she said, then let's get married right away. Tomorrow if possible.

"Nobody can say anything if we live here then . . ."

He steepled his fingers. "All right, Annie. Let me see if I understand the plan. We get married, right?"

"Yes."

"And we live here."

"Yes."

"With mother and Charley and Nona and Mittie and Jane Yellow Cat . . ."

"Well, no doubt it will be a little crowded but . . ."

"A little crowded!" He shook his head. "Annie, Annie! Please! There's no need to rush things, is there?" He smiled winningly and Annie wanted to slap him. "Chances are you and I will marry only once in our lives. Please let us wait and do it right.''

Doggedly she pressed on with it. ''But Abel, it would only be until we can afford our own place.''

''No, I'd rather get our own place first, Annie.'' He took her hand in his. ''It won't be long. A few months at the most. What can happen in a few months?''

What can happen in a few months? Oh, if you only knew!

That night Annie lay in bed with one arm crooked back behind her head and a deep frown on her face. Abel looked well. Healthy and happy and . . . young. Terribly young! She had never noticed that before. Which was ridiculous when she thought about it. He had always been only two years her senior.

And another thing. He was so . . . complacent. Perhaps he was *too* easygoing. Where was his fire, his passion?

Apparently he'd left it back in Philadelphia. The only time she'd seen the evidence of any fervor was when he was talking about where he thought he would set up his new office.

She had pinned all her hopes on everything falling into place when Abel arrived. His touch would thrill her, and his words of love would remove all doubts from her mind—to say nothing of removing Jack Dare from the same spot—and they would live happily ever after.

Happily. Ever. After.

Now she feared the worst, namely that Abel loved her but did not desire her. At least not with the fire that Jack did. And what's more, she feared that she loved Abel . . . but not with the fire with which she desired Jack!

Once she saw Abel she was sure she could wipe the memory of Jack's kisses from her mind by replacing them with the heated ones she would receive from Abel. Only she hadn't received any heated kisses from Abel. She had made a point of being alone with him twice. On both occasions they had been quite isolated and completely private. (In the same situation an unrestrained Jack Dare would have had her clothes off her in five minutes.) Abel had held her hand.

She had counted on Abel to bring an end to all her uncertainty and put her heart at rest. Why hadn't he? They were supposed to be in love. Why didn't he at least act like he was?

Once when he was sixteen he had written her a sonnet that was quite ardent. Of course she had been fourteen at the time and perhaps what seems ardent at fourteen is not so ardent at nineteen. However, in retrospect it did prove that he had once been capable of passionately expressing his feelings. How thrilled she had been then! And how unthrilled she was now.

Since Abel arrived she had felt a prodigious amount of affection for him but she had not been aflutter with desire.

The question was: Had he outgrown his passion? Or had she?

An uncharacteristic gloom had settled over Jack Dare. No one outside the family would have noticed, but everyone within it did.

He went hunting and was gone for three days. Nothing unusual about that but when he came back, he was empty-handed! Goldie couldn't remember a time when that had happened to any of them.

Jack was home a day and left again and this time Goldie followed him and found he'd camped at the little place where he had always said he would like to build a cabin one day. He lay next to a smokeless fire with his hands cupping the back of his head and his legs crossed at the ankles. He was either sleeping or counting the stars. Goldie would have ridden over but something told him his company might not be welcome. He returned the next day and heard the sound of an axe ring in the stillness. He crept close enough to see that Jack was clearing land as if he were building a homesite, splitting and stacking wood, dragging brush into a pile.

God, he hated to see his brother like this. It was so unlike him that Goldie thought he might be reading more into this

thing with Annie Mapes than there actually was. Having never
been in love himself, he just couldn't imagine Jack's being all
that het up about it. Must be his imagination. But that very
night he found out that if it was imagination, it wasn't just his.
Apparently others'd had the same thought.

Evie and Markie were sitting near the light. Markie held
yarn on her spread hands while Evie reeled it in.

"Markie, I think I know what's wrong with Jack, but there
ain't nothin' you or me can do anythin' about. An' it ain't none
of our business neither."

They had apparently forgotten that Goldie was sitting on the
far end of the porch, fitting a new handle on the hoe.

"But can't you tell me what it is? Is he sick?"

"Sorta. He's fallen for your teacher, but she ain't fallen for
him.'

Markie breathed, "Poor Jack!"

Neither said anything more for a minute then, "He's plain
crazy for her, ain't he?"

"Mm, I believe he is."

"Like Blue was crazy for Lucetta?"

"Who's Lucetta?"

"The girl who helps Dulce at the cantina."

"Oh."

"If it's like that then it'll go away in a week or so."

"No, it ain't nothin' like that."

"How come?"

"How come?" Evie repeated. Then she sighed. "Your
brother Blue's hell on women. Likes 'em one day. Can't recall
their name the next. Jack's different. I don't think he's ever
known a woman who's appealed to him like Annie Mapes
does."

"I feel sorry for him!"

"Never thought I'd say it, but so do I."

Chapter 23

Abel's new office above the mayor's council room was reached by a narrow set of steep stairs that angled up the south side of the building. The former occupant had been a gambler who sold also an "elixir of life" as a sideline. He had obviously been poor at both occupations because the previous winter he'd been labelled a cheat and a charlatan and had been run out of town.

Apparently he had not been given an opportunity to take along his product because Abel had found several elixir bottles laying in a dusty corner. They were murky brown in color and smelled like cat scat to him.

After delivery of the few pieces of furniture he had purchased, Abel had hung out his sign and settled in to wait for the world to find him. Of course, he had no clients yet, but he was pragmatic. And very patient. He expected it would take months before he would have enough business to support himself, much less a wife. It's true that he had some savings put aside but making it stretch until his practice got rolling meant the sort of belt-tightening he would not think of subjecting Annie to. He also refused to use the fruits of her labor to support them.

Yes, he supposed he was old-fashioned and stubborn and everything else she had called him. But he had made up his mind before he left Pennsylvania and that's how it would be. Understandably Annie was disappointed but he knew his Annie; she would come around.

A week after he had arrived, his books did. It was a warm day and he had rolled up his sleeves to unpack them. He had barely gotten started when he heard a knock. My first customer, he thought, and opened the door. There stood that Dare girl. The blind one that Annie had pointed out to him. What had Annie called her? "Eager, curious, intelligent . . ." Markie! Yes, that's her name. Markie Dare.

She was wearing a yellow dress, a braided straw hat and no shoes. Crooked on one of her arms was a pine-stave basket containing three puppies. "Hello, Miss Markie Dare. Who are your little friends?"

"They don't have names yet. We thought we'd let their new owners name 'em. Say, how'd you know my name?"

"Your teacher, Miss Mapes, pointed you out to me. She said you were her prize pupil."

"She dee-ud?"

"Yes, she did."

"Well, I'll be . . . ! Say, are you Abel O'Neal?"

"I am."

"Good! You're jus' the person I was lookin' for. I brought you a nice doggie to keep you company."

"Me? I can't have a dog."

"Sure you can! Well, not till they're done suckin' but you can pick yours out now and I'll hold it for you till they're weaned. I'm givin' you first choice, seein' as how you're new in town an' all."

He folded his arms, mostly to resist picking up one of the puppies. "You're quite a salesman, ma'am."

"Oh, no. There ain't . . . isn't any charge."

"I . . . see. Well, come on in and we'll talk it over. "

She put out one toe and felt for the step. Thinking to help, he reached out and took her arm. In an instant a narrow lethal knife appeared in her hand. He had no idea where it had come from. Suddenly it was simply . . . there.

"Sorry!" He removed his hand and stepped back. "I didn't intend any harm."

"I didn't figure you did but my brothers say I have to be extry careful, you know, being blind and all."

The knife disappeared and she walked in. "It sure smells good in here." She stood in the center of the room and took a deep breath. "Like fresh sawed wood. Like Goldie's work shed."

"Does it? Yes, I imagine that it does. I bought some new furniture from your brother."

"I know. Maw really liked that chest a lot."

He looked at the chest which he had placed near the window so the light would fall on his work. It didn't look like most desks but that was why he liked it. "You mean that belonged to your maw . . . your mother?"

"Sure, but don't feel bad. Most everything Goldie makes we only get to keep for a week or so."

"Why?"

" 'Cause somebody always comes along an' buys it out from under us. Maw put her foot down about our big table or we wouldn't have anyplace to eat. You've been cleanin' with beeswax, huh?"

"You're right." He folded his arms and studied her. "You know, Annie was right about you."

"When she said I was her prize pupil?"

"Oh, she said a lot more than that."

"She dee-ud?"

"Mm. She said that you were as quick as a whip."

"Am I?" she said, shamelessly fishing for more.

"Mm. And pretty as a picture. You know, you look just like a big daffodil in that yellow dress."

"I got it in St. Louie almost two years ago. Maw's had to add onto the bottom." She stuck out one dusty foot. "See?"

Indeed there was a border of flowered fabric along the bottom, shirred so that it looked like a ruffle.

"I don't have any shoes on."

"I saw that."

"I have some, but I'd rather be horse bit than wear 'em."

"I . . . see." Abel looked at her sweet, sturdy face and thought she was every bit as fetching as her puppies. "You still look very nice."

"Like a big . . . what did you call me again?"

"A daffodil."

"I don't know what that is."

Of course you don't, he thought and cursed himself inwardly. "It's a long-stemmed yellow flower that looks sort of like a trumpet."

"What's a trumpet look like?"

Damn! he thought. "It's a musical instrument that has a flared bell on one end and a mouth thing that you ah . . . blow through on the other. Say! One of my favorite poems is about daffodils."

"A poem?" A line appeared between her winged black brows. "What's a poem?"

"A poem is ah . . . a lovely saying that rhymes. Well, not always. Sometimes they don't rhyme at all."

Markie detected a bit of desperation in his voice and figured she had been asking too many questions again. Maw said that jus' drives people nuts!

"Wait just a minute. If I can find my book, I'll read one to you. Please sit down. Here . . . Let me move . . . There."

Markie sat on the edge of the chair and quieted the puppies by scratching behind their ears. She quieted herself by pressing her lips together hard!

"I had that book not five minutes ago . . ." There was a loud thump and a muffled ouch then, "Here it is! Now if I can just find the right page . . . I have it!" He sat on an unopened box across from her. "This poem was written by a man named Wordsworth." He cleared his throat. "It's entitled: 'I Wandered Lonely As a Cloud.' "

"I'm ready."

He looked at her and smiled. She did indeed look ready with

her head slightly cocked, her small face set in a serious and intent expression. What a strange little thing!

"Here goes then." Resting his elbows on his spread knees, he began to read.

> *"I wandered lonely as a cloud*
> *That floats on high o'er vales and hills,*
> *When all at once I saw a crowd,*
> *A host of golden daffodils;*
> *Beside the lake, beneath the trees*
> *Fluttering and dancing in the breeze."*

He looked up. "Well, what do you think?"

"Aah!" She let out a long breath. "That was the prettiest thing I've ever heard! I wandered lonely as a cloud that floats on high o'er vales and hills when all at once I saw a crowd, a host of golden daffodils um . . . Beside the lake beneath the trees."

He joined her here, his voice an awed whisper. "Fluttering and dancing in the breeze. Markie!"

"Yeah?"

"You remembered that entire stanza!"

"Uh-huh. I figured it would please you if I said it back."

"Please me? Please yourself! You're remarkable. That's what I'll call you: Remarkable Markie Dare!"

"Ha!" she said and blushed prettily.

Suddenly he was very curious about her. "How do you fill your time, Markie? Aside from going to school."

"Me? Oh, I got a lotta off an' on interests."

"Like what?"

"Well, I catch fish for supper an' knit suspenders for my brothers, an' I braid straw hats for my sisters. An' me." She touched her hat.

"Very nice."

"Thank you. I weave mats for the table an' mats for the floor. I pick berries in the woods an' pick bugs in the garden. I feed the animals an' take special care of their babies. An'

I'm learning to read!'' Of course he knew all about that. ''An'
sometimes I play the fiddle.''

''You can play the fiddle?''

''Jus' a few songs.''

''That's wonderful. I'd love to hear you play sometime.''

''I could go home an' get my fiddle, if you want.''

''Er, no. That would be too much trouble.''

''Nuh-uh! No trouble atall.''

''Maybe the next time you're in town.''

''All right. Say, is there any more?''

''More what?''

''Any more poem?''

''Yes. Wait. All right. Here's the rest.''

She listened carefully and when he finished she was silent.
''Did you like it, Markie?''

She nodded gravely. ''More'n anything I ever heard up to
now.''

''Thank you, Markie. Thank you very much.'' He set the
book aside, strangely touched by her.

''You know what your voice reminds me of?''

''My voice? I can't imagine. What?''

''My fiddle.''

''Your . . . fiddle?''

''Yes, when I am playing the low part and it sounds sorta
like runny sorghum.''

''Thank you!'' *I think.*

''It turns my innards all funny. Like the time I had the colic
only I don't feel like urpin'. You know how I mean?''

''Uh, yes.''

''I feel the same way when the sun first comes up an' starts
to get warmer an' warmer an' I feel it on my face an' under
my feet an' on my arms an' in my chest an' it feels sooo good
I can't hardly stand it!''

He only realized that his mouth was open when he tried to
swallow and couldn't.

''Well, I guess I better go. Can I come another time to hear
some more poems?''

"Absolutely. Please do!"

"Good." She thrust the basket at him. "So which dog do you want?"

Sighing with resignation he reluctantly examined the puppies. They were flop-eared and long-nosed, one brown, one a muddy white and one a combination of both colors. He would have to keep the dog at his mother's place temporarily. Lord knew what she would say about the addition of a dog, but he knew what reaction he would get from Annie, Mona and Mittie. They would be delighted. Maybe even Jane Yellow Cat would be pleased. He had a sudden thought: God, he hoped she wouldn't eat it!

He picked the splotched one up. It wagged its tail violently and tried to lick his face. It really was a cute little dog. "This one, I guess." He handed it to her.

"This is my favorite one too!"

"Really? But how do you keep track of which dog is which?"

"Easy." She felt between the puppy's legs. "This one here's the boy."

"Oh?" Abel watched her busy fingers and felt his cheeks redden. Silly, he told himself.

"Yeah. There's two girls and a boy and the brown girl has an extry toe on her left back foot. See?"

"Yes, I do. Very good. Well . . ." He had another sudden thought. "Say, how did you get here?"

"My brothers Goldie and Blue brought me. Goldie went to see the miller and Blue went to see the new girl at Dulce's."

Abel felt his face heat. He had seen Dulce's new girl, Lucetta, when he and Lloyd Cooper had a beer there. "How do you know about, um, Lucetta?"

"From Blue and Jack and Goldie. She dances for money." Abel had moved to the window but he noticed that she turned toward him wherever he went. "Wouldn't that be about the best job ever? Dancin'?"

"Mm, yes." There was no wagon in front of his place. Nor any mountain-like men standing around. "I better see you to wherever you're going next."

"No, I can go alone. I thought I would try Hap Pettijohn next. His old dog got killed by a runaway wagon about three months back. I figure he's about ready for another one."

"What happens if you don't find a home for all of them?"

"Jack says he'll drown them."

"Will he?"

"Naw. He's all wind an' no weather. He'll holler a lot but we'll keep them."

"I see." He smiled to himself. She was already pretty confident of her control over the men in her life. Probably with good reason.

"Did you mean it when you said I was pretty?"

"Absolutely," he said and meant it. "You will be quite lovely some day."

"When?"

"When you are grown."

"When will that be?"

"Oh, when you're sixteen or so."

"Will all the boys want to kiss me then? Like they want to kiss Brit and Irish?"

He nodded then remembered that he had to speak. "More. They'll be buzzing around you like . . . like . . ."

"Flies on fresh hooey?"

"Precisely!"

"You too?"

He laughed. "You bet me too."

"Will you want to marry me . . . Like all the men want to marry the twins?"

"Yes, of course."

Her face fell. "You lied right then."

He had hurt her! "Oh, Markie . . ."

"You jus' said that to get rid of me."

"I'm sorry, Markie. I thought you knew that I was only joking." Why didn't he tell her he was going to marry Annie? He put his hand on her shoulder and felt like a class A cad. "When you grow up you will probably have your choice of every man in Tejas and you will not want me."

"Yeah, I will."

She said it so convincingly he almost believed her. She was testing the edge of a scab on her knee and looking quite forlorn.

"Tell you what. Let's make a date to discuss it then."

"When?"

"When you're seventeen."

"You jus' said sixteen before."

"All right." Exasperated. "Sixteen."

"All right then. It's a promise. Say, can I feel your muscles?"

Abel came over to his mother's to eat that night. Earlier he had asked if he could take his meals with them, thus saving some of the boarding fee at Maude Stone's. Of course, they were delighted to have him.

After dinner Annie thought he might join her for a walk down by the creek. She was interested in testing her theory about the romantic setting. She wanted to see if kissing Abel there would thrill her like never before. If it did, then she could be certain that Jack Dare's kiss had excited her for that exact same reason: a conducive setting. Oh, if only that would happen! It would be such a relief!

She made plans. She would have to take the initiative. All right. She could do that. If she had to. Thanks to Jack Dare she now knew how to light a fire under Abel that would rage right out of control!

When she finished with the dishes, she went looking for him and found him chopping stove wood in the backyard. He was really going at it!

"Abel?"

"Yes?" He paused and drew his sleeve across his forehead.

"What are you doing?"

"Chopping stove wood."

"But Charley comes over and does that for us. A couple of times a week."

"That's all right." He set another piece of wood on the stump and gave it a resounding smack. "I can use the exercise."

* * *

Markie came home full of praise for Abel O'Neal. He was about the nicest person she had ever met! And so smart! He was a lawyer. And he knew all about trumpets and daffodils and just about every single thing a person wanted to know. Why, he even knew poems!

After Blue had showed everyone his open mouth, he said, "You know, that's downright amazin'! I was up all night, worried about jus' that very thing!"

Markie looked confused. "Worried about what very thing?"

"That nobody in town knows any poems! I was jus' sick about it. Jus' sick!"

Goldie snorted. "Blue, you wouldn't know a poem if one slapped you upside your head."

"An' I suppose you do?"

"I don't, but I don't have no trouble sayin' so flat out."

"Hell," Blue said. "I've probably had ten-twelve of 'em poems an' didn't care. What's one look like anyway?"

"It ain't a thing," Markie replied testily. "It's a sayin'!"

"I knew that."

She recited the daffodil poem for them. Brit, Irish and Evie all loved it. Blue said, "Hell, why didn't you say that's what you meant! I know a lot of them."

"Say one then."

"Mary went to town one day but she took a wrong turn and lost her way . . ."

"Blue!"

Blue looked at Jack. "Whut?"

"You know what." Jack stood up and left Blue staring at the slammed door. "I was only gonna say it to the next line. Say, what's got into him lately anyway?"

The next afternoon Abel got another knock on his door, but this one was quite loud and manly sounding. A customer for sure.

His visitor was a man all right, though not necessarily a reputable one. He was dressed all in skins and wore a floppy-brimmed hat whose purpose was to either shade his eyes from the sun or shade them from the scrutiny of others. Either way, it did both.

He was not shaven and his shirt was open to show a wide expanse of hairy chest that was shiny with sweat.

Abel decided that if he was a customer, he was looking for a defender, probably against the charge of murder.

"I'm Abel O'Neal. Can I help you?"

"My name's Blue Jack Dare."

"Pleased to meet you! Please come in."

Dare leaned and looked inside. "Naw, I'd just as soon talk out here. 'Case I have to tie into yuh, I don't wanna bust up Goldie's stuff while I'm at it."

"Bust up Goldie's . . ." Abel looked inside then stepped outside and pulled the door closed. "I'm afraid I don't understand. Have I offended you in some way?"

"I wouldn't say that."

Dare unsheathed a fifteen-inch fighting knife and started paring his fingernails. The blade flashed in the sun and little half moons flew everywhere, pinging off the cow-horn boot scrape and falling onto the plank platform. *How can he do that without de-fingering himself?*

Abel watched this demonstration for a while and then folded his arms. "All right, Dare. What's this really about?"

"It's about my little sister." He stopped paring and held out his hand to check his nails. Apparently the length suited him because he turned his hand palm down and looked at Abel. "Stands about this high. Little blind kid named Markie."

"I've met her. A delightful child. She came to see me about a dog."

"Uh-huh. Well, her and me got to talkin' yesterday."

"Yes?" Abel's first impression had been correct. The man was a murderer . . . of the English language.

"An' she tells me the two of you're gettin' married."

Abel blushed red and gave a croak that was supposed to be

a laugh. "She asked me if I'd wait for her until she grows up and I said yes. You know, I didn't want to hurt her feelings or anything."

"Huh." Blue Dare was giving him a strange look, judging his sincerity he supposed. "When she grows up?"

"Of course. Well, no, not actually. I was, like I say, trying not to hurt her feelings . . ."

"But if you two *was* gonna get married it'd be when she grew up. Not next week . . . an' not in your back room."

Instantly Abel hated him. "You low-minded . . ."

Blue held up the hand with the knife in it. "Now don't get all het up. I jus' wanted to make sure you ain't like some fellas we ran into once."

"What are you talking about?"

"Well, I'll tell you."

Abel did not bother to mask his sarcasm. "That would certainly be nice."

"We visited St. Louie a few years back an' one night me and Jack and Goldie went to this place where there's women for sale. Well, not for sale but for rent. You've been to one of those places, ain't you?" He waited for Abel to nod. "Well, we was havin' a few drinks, lookin' over the merchandise an' tryin' to relax. We'd all had a very tryin' day. You ever been to St. Louie? Well, I'll tell you right now—you don't need to go. Worst place I ever been. There musta been a hundred people for every square mile. Awful!

"Well, anyway, like I was sayin' . . . we musta been takin' too long to make our selection 'cause pretty soon a woman sashayed over to us an' says that if we didn't like what was showin', they had some younger stuff upstairs. Jack asked her how young an' when she told him, he got red-eyed mad an' started makin' kindlin' outa the chairs an' tables an' then a couple of the owner's men pulled pistols on us an' we had us a damn war goin', which we won, of course, but Jack said we weren't done with 'em yet an' we better put the upstairs outa business an' so we did an' we was jus' about ready to leave when Goldie wanted a drink to cool 'imself down an' damn if some fellas that worked for the town didn't show up. Called 'emselves, um, constipators I think . . .''

"Constables."

"Yeah! Well, they tried to get us to come with 'em peaceable-like and Goldie says . . . do we look like we're the peaceable types? an' damn if one of 'em fellas didn't try to knock Goldie in the head with his stick!''

Abel held up one hand. "I think I get the idea."

"You do?"

"Yes, I do and had I been there, I would have joined you. I think that sort of thing is despic-, uh, atrocio-, um, terrible."

"Us too. It ain't human. A man who'd do somethin' like that ought to be shot like a mad animal. Don't you think?'' Abel nodded. "You sure as hell wouldn't ever do somethin' like that, right?''

"I would not."

"Good. We understand each other then. Poor little ol' Markie jus' found out that there ain't a stork, you know. Smart as she is she only now discovered that humans must do it sorta like the animals do. I'll bet you get my meanin'."

"I think I do."

Blue Jack Dare sheathed his knife and touched his hat. "Welcome to Sweet Home."

"Gee, thanks." As Dare was pedaling down the stairs, Abel called, "Sure was nice meeting you."

Chapter 24

Something was happening up at the school. No doubt about it. People stood in town and speculated about it. What on earth is goin' on? Orange daubs of lantern light came from every window and tar flares had been nailed to all the trees along the path. (As usual, whatever illumination the flares provided was almost completely negated by the clouds of billowing smoke which they produced.)

"Looks like it's on fire."

"Hey! That's an idea. We could pretend we thought there was a fire, an' tear up there with a water bucket."

That earned the speaker an odd look from his companion. "Why?"

"So . . . butthead . . . we can find out what's goin' on. Why do yuh think?"

Butthead continued toward Dirty Dave's. "Tomorrow's soon enough for me."

The other man, by nature extremely curious, but a craven coward, stared up there a minute and then sighed and followed his buddy.

Inside the school Abel chuckled as he pushed the benches

back into a line after Annie had mopped each area. "I feel like we should have strung bunting out front."

"Saying what?"

"Markie Reads!"

She looked up. "We could still do it!"

"Annie, I was only kidding!"

"Oh." She made a few swipes with the mop and stopped again. "Oh, Abel, I hope I haven't made a mistake."

"What mistake?"

"I have invited her entire family here."

"Yes, I know."

"What if she cannot read the fable?"

"She'll be able to read it. You said she had the key down pat."

"Yes, she did that almost immediately."

Annie remembered the day Goldie brought the board to her. He had bored the holes in a piece of polished wood. Sixty-three arrangements of the six core dots along with twenty-five letters of the alphabet. In addition there were arrangements for five common words: *and, for, of, the* and *with,* nine speech sounds and the letter *W.* Every afternoon for three weeks Annie had gone over all the letters and signs with Markie. The last week she had been studying them on her own.

Goldie'd had a devil of a time finding something Annie could use to make the "book board." He had cut pieces of pine and experimented forming clumps of dots with several different concoctions, hoping to find one with staying power. Some drew flies. Some crumbled after a week. Some melted. Most all of them drew ants and others did not hold their shape when touched. In the end perseverance finally paid off. Along with the finished alphabet board Goldie also presented Annie with a narrow-necked jar with a corncob stopper. "This stuff'll work for droppin' on your board and makin' your letters."

"This will do it?" she asked.

He nodded. "That'll do it."

Using a sliver of wood, she dipped it in the mixture and dropped a dot on the slate of wood. It stuck and did not run.

She shook the board and it stayed raised. "So far so good!" She waited several seconds then felt it and it remained a round, raised hard little dot.

"Perfect!" she cried. "What is it?"

"A combination of corn meal . . ."

"Yes?"

"Flour."

"Yes?"

"A bit of isinglass melted in two egg whites."

"Yes?"

"And horse piss."

"Euu! How did you ever think of trying that?"

"Somebody once told me he'd watched some Indians mix horse piss with buffalo hooves to make paste."

"I wonder who first thought to try, ah, it. And why?" She imagined trying to collect the horse's . . . contribution. Did someone just sit beside the horse with a bucket on the end of his raised arm?

He shrugged. "I don't know an' I don't care. I'm jus' glad that a little bit goes a long way."

"I certainly will not waste any!"

Dryly, he said. "You'll have my undyin' gratitude, ma'am."

Everyone arrived at seven and took their places, solemn as funeral goers. Throats were cleared and feet scraped against wood but there was little conversation. This was a serious occasion and everyone acted accordingly. Indeed, the only person who did not seem affected by the importance of the event was Markie, who sat waiting to begin, her eyes bright as buttons and her hands clasped tightly in her lap.

Aside from the Dares the only outsiders were Jane Yellow Cat and Abel O'Neal. Both were present at Markie's request. She considered them her very special friends.

"If everyone is ready . . . I'd like to explain what is going to happen. We hope." Annie held the "book" in both hands so that everyone in the room could see it. "Barely five years ago a blind Frenchman named Louis . . ."

Blue cupped his hand and leaned closer to Irish, "Don't look like nothin' I've ever seen before."

"It's Braille," she replied reverently.

"Could be Greek."

"Shh!"

Annie went on. "I understand he's quite young but apparently very brilliant . . ."

Annie's eyes often fell on Jack who sat near the back on a chair that was propped against the wall. He looked quite comfortable with his legs splayed and his arms folded across his chest.

She faltered and looked away. Since he didn't stop at the school and had abruptly discontinued his lessons, she hardly ever saw him anymore, and she missed him with a pain that was almost physical.

"Markie is going to try to read one of Aesop's fables tonight. He was a Greek writer . . ."

Blue jabbed Irish with his elbow and gave her a look. *Tole you it was Greek.*

". . . who lived in the sixth century B.C., uh, six hundred years before Christ."

"Wow!" whispered Irish.

"I changed a few words in the fable because I knew Markie would not be familiar with them but other than that, nothing has been altered. I also included a few of the more difficult words that are contained in the fable in Markie's lessons but there weren't many. Of course, she has never read or heard this story before."

She looked at her feet for a long moment and Jack could see her throat moving from where he sat.

"You know, we sighted people really cannot imagine how difficult it would be to have been born blind. If you ever want to put your life in perspective, just put your hands over your eyes and try walking around. Try doing anything." She looked at Markie who was grinning because everyone was talking about her. *Little imp!* "I have never known a more independent little girl nor have I ever seen a harder worker. You, her family, must take credit for that. The greatest gift you gave her was never thinking of her as helpless. As a result she doesn't think of herself that way either." When she looked back at the crowd everyone noticed that her eyes had filled. "With that, um, I guess I will just let her begin."

She handed the slate to Markie and moved away. For a long minute the only sound was the willow-moths beating around the lanterns. A confident smile was fixed on Annie's face but she grasped her arms above her elbows so hard she would find bruises in the morning.

Solemn now, Markie held the slate by its top and brushed her hand down one side, a movement that reminded Abel of the innate grace of a concert harpist. She tilted her head slightly and ran her fingers over the first row and then the second and then she returned to the beginning. Everyone sat forward in their chairs.

"The . . . Lion . . . and . . . the . . . Mouse."

There was a collective sigh from the spectators. Evie Dare stared at her youngest over gnarled knuckles and started crying. Brit put her arm around her mother's shoulders and shushed her, but her eyes were just as wet.

Markie spoke slowly and softly. Often there were long pauses between words while she moved her mouth to silently sound out each syllable. Sometimes the word came out mispronounced anyway. No matter. Everyone acted like they were witnessing a miracle. And in a way, they were.

"A lion was asleep in his den one day when a playing mouse for no reason at all ran across his paw and up his nose and woke him from his nap. The mighty beast clapped his paw on the little mouse and would have made an end of him. 'Please!' squealed the mouse, 'Don't kill me. Forgive me this time, O King, and I shall never forget it. A day may come, who knows, when I may do you a good turn to repay your kindness.' The lion, smiling at his little prisoner's fright and amused by the thought that so small a creature ever could help the king of beasts, let him go. Not long afterward the lion, while ranging the forest for his prey was caught in the net which the hunters had set to catch him. He let out a roar heard through the forest. Even the mouse heard it, and knowing the voice of the lion, ran to the spot where he lay in the net of ropes. 'Well, Mr. King,' said the mouse. 'I know you did not believe me once when I said I would return a kindness, but here is my chance.' And without further ado, he set to work to nibble with his sharp little teeth at the ropes that bound the lion. Soon the lion was able to crawl out of the hunter's snare and be free.

"The meaning of this story is: No act of kindness, no matter how small, is ever wasted."

Markie looked up and her face was that of an angel who has just been conferred its wings. "I can read!"

The room went wild. Blue stamped his boots and Goldie gave an ear piercing whistle and the twins squealed and hopped in place like snared rabbits. Evie went to Annie and they held each other and cried like babies. Markie ran/hopped around the room until Jack snagged her and held her until she complained that he was "squashin' her to death."

Meanwhile, across the room of bobbing heads Jack saw Abel O'Neal near the window, honking into his handkerchief then daubing at his wet eyes.

Damned if he wasn't beginning to like him in spite of himself!

Cookies and coffee were served and it turned into quite a party. Evie got Markie aside. "Read it to me again, Markie." When she finished, Evie said to the room at large. "Ain't that about the best story you ever heard?"

"Read it again, Markie."

Later Abel and Annie stood by the door as the Dare brothers left. Each spoke to her in turn. Jack took her hand. His eyes held hers and he said simply: "Thanks." She had to turn to his brother or start crying again. "Goldie," she said. "I could have never done it without you."

"An' nobody would've done anything without you. We won't forget this night, Miss Mapes."

"Nor will I, Goldie."

Blue tried to hold onto his usual cross attitude but she could tell he had been moved by his sister's recitation. "You did good, teacher."

"Thank you, Blue."

Evie came next. Annie was standing by the open door accepting her thanks again when she heard Blue's voice outside. "Wanna see if we can get a game."

"At Dirty Dave's?" That was Jack.

"Yeah, sure."

"I figured you'd be visitin' Lucetta." Jack again.

"Naw, hell. I'm done with that girl."

"Why's that?"

" 'Cause when I feel like fightin', I like to pick my own. An' I don't feel like fightin' tonight."

"Huh!" Jack said. "Somebody oughta have a talk with that gal. Get her straightened around . . ."

The rest was lost in the creak of leather and the sound of moving horses and Annie had a pain that felt like she had been jabbed with a burning stick. She had seen the girl one day, leaning against the cantina wall and smoking a corn-shuck cigarillo like a man. She had on a loose blouse and a colorful skirt that stopped at her ankles—and obviously not much more. And now Jack was going to see her and the mental image of them together proved almost unbearable.

It was immaterial that she had no right to be jealous of that girl—or any other for that matter. She was, and a lot of the joy of the evening was gone because of it.

As they might have anticipated, Markie wanted a story a day, an impossible task. Why, just making the fable had taken Annie over two weeks of painstakingly putting the dots into just the right configurations.

Brit came to the rescue. Although she was not an advanced

reader yet, it was a simple matter for her to copy the correct configurations onto a new board. Sometimes it took Brit an hour to do a word but she wanted to do it for her little sister and that was half the battle.

Frankly, Annie had been a bit surprised when she volunteered. She had thought Brit was too preoccupied with herself to help another. To find that she was wrong had been an unexpected and most heartening surprise.

Chapter 25

Dulce's new girl, Lucetta Valmonte, was supposedly another of her cousins from Sonora, but skeptics wondered, since all of Dulce's girls had been cousins from Sonora.

Dulce's two previous whores had both been of simple peasant stock, young girls who had hoped to better their status in life and apparently they had—both had married within a year.

The new girl was young, exceptionally pretty and enthusiastic about her work. As a consequence she made a lot of money for Dulce, but she was also a lot of trouble because what Blue Jack had said was true. It excited her to play one man off another and it excited her even more when she gave herself to the bloodied winner. Most men who frequented Dulce's thought nothing of it. As one put it: "Hell, I'm gonna end up in a fight anyway. Might jus' as well be over her as over how many times the cock'll crow tomorrow."

Sooner or later her proclivity to violence was bound to result in a death and it happened shortly after Markie's victorious night at the schoolhouse.

A young man was enjoying Lucetta's attentions when Gil and Earl Daggert came into Dulce's with Bittercreek Clarke.

They had been drinking at Dirty Dave's since midafternoon and it showed. They were beyond the feel-good stage and fast approaching the stage where they peed in their boots and didn't realize it until they tried to remove them.

All three men immediately offered to fight the young man for the girl. Those who had been enjoying a quiet drink grabbed their glasses and pressed their backs to a handy wall.

Generally nothing stopped the Crow's Nest boys once they had decided to fight, but this time Lucetta did.

It was uncharacteristic of her, but she actually liked the young man. He had held his whiskey well and had treated her with kindness. In addition he had no visible sores, plenty of visible dineros and all his teeth. He might even be able to remove his boots before he climbed into bed!

Lucetta allowed him to purchase her services for the entire evening. And he did not have to lift a hand.

Unfortunately, come dawn he was found in the weedy alley behind the cantina, stabbed in the back. Someone—presumably the murderer—had also emptied his pockets. Sheriff Goodman was called.

Of medium height and build, the stranger had been about twenty-five, with a shock of mahogany-colored hair, and pale skin that the Dares would've called cheap because it was the kind that never did right in the sun.

It was impossible for Goodman to tell if he had been unarmed when he was murdered, but he was when he was found.

When Sheriff Goodman talked to Lucetta she told him that the young man had told her his name at the time but that she could not recall it for the sheriff. The stranger had also told her where he was from but she couldn't recall that either. She did remember that he had been carrying a lot of money, and a big round watch with writing on the back. Unfortunately aside from an unusual accent there wasn't anything else to distinguish him from any other man.

Public funds buried the man in the small but growing cemetery situated at the horseshoe bend of the creek. Although Sweet

Home was a relatively new town, the young stranger was the third John Doe to be buried there.

Shortly thereafter another stranger came to town. He was well dressed but not flashy, a confident-acting man who was broad across the shoulders and taller than most. He told Hap Pettijohn—who had given him a ride to town—that he had tracked his younger brother as far as Brasoria where his brother had mentioned to a saloon owner that he thought he might go to Sweet Home next. The stranger said his name was McDuff and his brother's name was Duncan.

Hap Pettijohn wondered about that name business, because McDuff had the swart face of a mixed-blood and spoke more like a Frenchie than one of those skirt-wearing fellas.

At Dulce's, McDuff met Blue Dare who remembered McDuff's brother well. Murders were not uncommon in Sweet Home. Same for strange-speaking people. But there had been something about the young murdered man that had set him apart.

Blue said that on that fateful night they had walked out to the privy together and then stood outside, talking for a while. Blue said the man offered him some Turkish tobacco which he found very strong yet very smooth. They first shared some dirty talk about women and then compared the games of chance at Dirty Dave's with those at Dulce's. They'd talked about other things too but the particulars had been so trifling Blue couldn't recall them.

He said he never did ask the man his name but that he had thought him a real likeable fella. Which was why he had warned him to grow some eyeballs in the back of his head. That given half a chance those Crow's Nest hombres'd jump him and beat the living crap out of him. That was the last time Blue saw him dead or alive. When asked, Blue was able to describe McDuff's brother to a tee.

With a sinking heart, McDuff then talked to Lucetta. The young whore remembered nothing until some coins exchanged hands, then, as with the sheriff, she remembered the accent, the money and the watch with the writing on it. McDuff promised her another coin if she would make a list of everyone who was in the cantina that night. She darted her eyes around like she was afraid of being overheard and said she would try. Later.

When McDuff asked about a place to stay, Blue Dare suggested Maude Stone's rooming house and it was there that McDuff made the acquaintance of Abel O'Neal. After he told his story once more, O'Neal suggested that he talk to Sheriff Ernest Goodman. Goodman had taken up his duties only a short time before the killing but he was sure to know something about it.

McDuff and Abel O'Neal walked toward the jail. Simply to fill the time, Abel asked McDuff what J.P. stood for.

"Jean Pierre."

"That surprises me. French first names with a Scots surname."

McDuff laughed wryly. "My father was the Marquis de Montceau. My mother was his Scottish mistress. I was named for him but, of course, she retained her maiden—and only—name." They paused while three mounted men rode by and McDuff took the opportunity to light a thin black cheroot.

"Their affair was long-standing, but as with all things, it did finally end. While I remained in France and continued my education, my mother moved to a small town on the Firth of Forth, married a Scotsman and had Duncan. When my father died he left funds and instructions that I was to attend the Medical College at the University of Edinburgh." McDuff ground out his smoke after only a couple of drags, the height of waste in this tobacco-poor place. "I favor my father and speak with a French accent. Duncan favored our mother and, having grown up in Scotland, spoke with the burr of a true Scotsman."

Abel noticed that he spoke about his brother in the past tense. "How many years between you?"

"Nine."

Abel stopped and pointed. "There's the jail. If Goodman isn't in his office, he lives right next door. Feel free to go over and knock. He's a very affable fellow."

"*Merci*," McDuff said and touched his hat.

"I hope he can help you."

"So do I."

Sheriff Goodman heard McDuff's story in silence and listened carefully to his description of his missing brother. When McDuff was finished Goodman said, "I think I have some bad news for you."

"I expected as much."

Goodman pushed himself out of his chair. "Come with me and I'll show you where I found him." He took his hat off a whittled peg and seated it just so. "I can tell you what I know while we walk." And so he did.

He said that the murdered man was approximately twenty-five years old, and that he'd had a medium build, a fair complexion and a full head of reddish hair. The man had spent the evening at Dulce's with a whore named Lucetta. He had paid her well and when he left she swore he still had plenty of money. She also said that he carried a battered stemwinder that looked expensive but old. However, when he found the young man's body there had been nothing in any of his pockets. "Not even lint," said Goodman.

They were standing in the knee-high weeds behind the cantina. Wind-drifted refuse was caught in the weeds and the air smelled like piss. A rusted wagon wheel lay canted against the building's back wall which had no windows—and hence no illumination—on that side. A narrow footpath led off someplace, but otherwise the area had an untraveled look.

McDuff had been thinking that it was an ignominious place for a life to end until he realized that he was thinking thus because his brother had died here. He had seen worse. Much worse.

By the time they reached the cemetery Goodman had finished telling what he knew and both men had fallen silent. As they walked through an opening in the cypress-rail fence, the lantern flashed on a marker that read: *He had sand in his craw but needed work on his draw . . .*

"From what you've told me, I'd be willing to bet that this is your brother's grave." Goodman'd paused beside a plain cross marker with John Doe 3 burned into the wood.

McDuff said nothing in reply, just stared at the ground with his hands flat in his back pockets and his head thrust forward like a bull. From the side Goodman thought he looked like an old coin he'd seen once.

"I must dig up the grave."

"Dig up the grave?"

Goodman looked at him and McDuff looked back. "There is no other way to know for sure."

"You can't do that."

"Did you not say that no one claimed this man as kin?"

"Yeah."

"Then there should be no one to complain about disturbing the grave. Correct?"

Goodman pushed back his hat and scratched his head. He had him there but it still galled him. In all the time he had spent knocking around here and there he had never heard of anyone digging up a grave.

"Sheriff?"

"I guess."

"You have no objection then . . ."

"I don't see how I can object, but it seems so . . ."

"What?"

"Disrespectful . . . you know, a person's eternal resting place an' all."

McDuff nodded. "I agree, but if my brother's body rests there, then I am the one who has to live with that. If it is not my brother, then yes, I have disturbed some poor unknown man's rest. However, as I said, there is no other way to know for sure."

"When . . . ?"

"Tonight. When there are no children about and no mourners are likely to visit."

"Good idea."

"Would you like to be present?"

Goodman shuffled his feet and thought that over good. "I suppose I better. What time?"

"Midnight, of course." McDuff gave him a wry smile. "When else?

In town, McDuff purchased work gloves, a sturdy long-handled spade, a claw hammer, and a pickaxe from the local emporium. He could sense the proprietor's questioning glances but he ignored them, paid for his purchases and left.

Back at the rooming house he ate a light supper with the young teamster Charley Walters, and the proprietress, Mrs. Stone—an excellent cook but an inexperienced flirt.

The only other roomer, the young lawyer Abel O'Neal, apparently took most of his meals with his mother and fiancée.

Afterwards McDuff retired for a few hours rest, but it wasn't surprising that he could not sleep. Images of Duncan kept moving through his mind.

Moments before midnight he dressed in the oldest clothes he owned, put two extra handkerchiefs in his pocket and silently descended the stairs. Outside he collected the things he had purchased at the emporium and found Sheriff Goodman waiting for him at the gate. Goodman took the hammer and pickaxe and they headed out of town. The heat of the day had lessened at sundown but McDuff knew he would be warmer than he wished once he started digging.

At the grave, Goodman offered his help but when it was refused, he stepped back and watched McDuff. The lack of rain had hardened the dirt and it was a long hour before McDuff's spade hit something solid. He turned and laid the spade aside. As Goodman passed him the hammer, McDuff offered the sheriff his extra handkerchief. Each man secured the cloth over his nose and mouth and McDuff set about prying open the lid on the simple pine coffin. Goodman glanced down then moved away; the stench that rose was almost overpowering. Within a moment or two he heard McDuff re-seating the nails.

"Was he your brother?" he asked as McDuff pulled himself out of the grave.

"Oui."

"Damn! I'm sorry."

"Thank you but I had prepared myself for the worse." McDuff raised his neck hanky and spat. "Where can I get a marker made?"

"Goldie Dare'll probably do one for you."

"Any kin to Blue?"

"Brothers. You know Blue from somewhere?"

McDuff shook his head. "I only met him tonight."

"Their farm's out of town a ways but Goldie can generally be reached there."

"Très bien. I will see him tomorrow." He looked at the narrow band of light that stretched across the eastern horizon and smiled sadly. "I guess I should say today."

"Then what?"

"Then I will go back to Dulce's and see if, um, Lucetta has recalled the names of those who visited the cantina that night."

McDuff had started filling in the grave but Goodman stayed him with a hand on his arm. "Listen, McDuff, don't go bracin' nobody on your own, hear? If you find something out, come an' get me an' let me take it from there."

McDuff did not acknowledge that he had heard, but resumed tossing dirt onto his brother's coffin.

After McDuff parted with the sheriff he found himself too restless to sleep, and a long rambling walk brought him to Dulce's Cantina where lanterns were still lit within. He entered. A fleshy but shapely woman sat alone at a table in the back. Probably the owner, he thought. There was a drunk sprawled at another table, but his head rested on his arms and he was snoring loudly. No one else—including the girl, Lucetta—was in sight.

As he walked over, Dulce gave him a professional smile and used her foot to push out a chair for him. He sat. Still wordless, she nudged a wide-mouthed jar toward him. He drank deeply, paused to draw his sleeve across his mouth then said, *"Muy bueno!''* A calculating look grew in the woman's eyes. She was not unattractive, maybe even pretty in a florid sort of way. She had a wide sensuous mouth and long lustrous black hair and though a hardness edged her eyes, she was probably no older than his brother was. Had been, he amended. God, Duncan was dead! He still couldn't believe it. Even after seeing him in his grave.

He took another long drink and when he lowered the jar she had pulled her blouse down to show him a melon-sized breast with a dark nipple the size of his thumb. *''Para usted?''* She raised her arm and fiddled with her hair, a practiced but seductive movement . . . if it had not revealed the particularly thick tuft of black hair under her arm. It was dampened, as was his interest.

''Gracias, but no.'' He softened his refusal with a smile. ''I am here to see Lucetta.'' Something crossed Dulce's face. Jealousy? She covered herself, which caused mixed emotions in McDuff. While it was true that he was not in the mood, hers was a most noteworthy breast.

''Why do you want Lucetta?''

''For talk. That's all. It will only take a minute.''

''Lucetta is busy.''

''I will wait.''

''I don't know how long it will be.''

''It will not matter.'' He bowed. ''Time flies in company as lovely as you.'' She gave him a one-sided little smile. ''I will, of course, pay for her time.''

They had slipped into Spanish and he found the Mexican accent melodic and much less contrived than the Andalusian lisp affected by so many Europeans these days.

''Perhaps I have the information you desire and would give it to you if you paid me what you were going to pay Lucetta.''

''If you know who was here the night the stranger died.''

''Quién sabe? Primero, dígame! Who was the dead man to you?''

''My brother.'' McDuff took another slug of pulque and felt

its burn in his heels. "Lucetta says she recalls very little of that night. Perhaps the same is true of you."

Dulce tossed her hair and pointed at the valley between her breasts. "Dulce Martínez forgets nothing. Lucetta Valmonte cannot remember her name."

"You talk. I'll pay." He took out a coin and laid it on the table. It proved compelling; Dulce's eyes would stray to it several times during their conversation.

She gave him the names of the men who had been drinking in the cantina that night but she told him that the only ones who had had words with his brother were the Daggert brothers and Bittercreek Clarke. Gil had been particularly angry about Lucetta's selecting someone else over him and then furious that it was not to be for just an hour or two but for the entire night. When Dulce had offered to accommodate him, he'd slapped her hard enough to split her lip. *"Un hombre muy malo."*

McDuff looked at the curtains that separated the back hallway from the cantina. "How long has he been with her?"

"I did not say he was with her."

"But he is, isn't he?" He slid another coin across the table. *"Sí. Diez minutos más o menos."* As he stood she took his sleeve. "Do not hurt Lucetta!"

"Never fear, madam." He lifted her hand and kissed it, and Dulce's face softened as she watched him walk away.

She wondered if he would stay in Sweet Home. She hoped he would. Hers was the only sporting house in town and he was the sort of man who liked a woman regularly.

She licked her hand, dribbled on some coarse salt, sucked it off, then downed her drink. She smiled. When the time came that he needed a woman, she would lock Lucetta in the privy.

McDuff parted the curtains. He listened at one door then moved to the next. He listened for a moment and then kicked it open. The girl was on top and at first glance it appeared that she was trying to smother her customer with her breasts.

"Wha . . . What t'hell?"

Drunk, the man was only now rolling the girl off him but

McDuff was already beside the bed. He pulled the man's pistol from where it hung looped on the bedpost and placed the barrel between the man's eyebrows. With his free hand, he pushed the girl toward the pants that were puddled on the floor. "Empty everything out on the bed."

"But, señor . . ."

"Do it!"

"A goddamn robbery!" said Daggett. "I'll be damned. Earl! Earl."

McDuff laid the barrel of the pistol across Daggert's face and he suddenly became more concerned about his broken tooth than he was about yelling for his brother.

A watch fell out onto the bed. The girl stood back, looking fearfully from the man on the bed to the man beside it. Wordlessly McDuff pointed at a wall and she went to stand against it, still clutching the man's pants to her body. McDuff bent and picked up the stemwinder and turned it over in his palm.

Each brother had been given an heirloom watch. McDuff's had belonged to his maternal grandfather and had no inscription. Duncan's had belonged to his father and read: To Angus McDuff on his 21st birthday: 12 October 1790.

"Where did you get this watch?"

Daggett might have said he bought it or made up some other such lie but he chose not to. He glared up at McDuff, either too drunk or too stupid to know what kind of trouble he was in.

"I ain't tellin' yuh nothin'."

"Actually, it does not matter what you say. I can read the answer in your eyes."

Unbeknownst to McDuff, Gil's brother Earl stood in the doorway, wearing nothing but a pistol. After being serviced by Dulce he'd fallen into a drunken sleep and had only awakened when his brother called out.

Earl Daggert fired but a second shot came so close after his that witnesses would later say that they could have been one.

Earl had shot McDuff in the back. A reflexive tightening of

his fingers had caused McDuff to fire and kill Gil at almost the same instant.

McDuff fell face forward onto the floor, alive but gravely wounded. What with the girl screaming, and Dulce's breathless arrival in the room, for him the rest would remain a blur, but he would later learn that when Earl Daggert staggered down the hall to get another weapon, Dulce had the sense to shut and bar the door. She then sent Lucetta out the window for Sheriff Goodman who took one look at the wound in McDuff's back and tied him onto a mule pointed for the Dare place and Evie Dare.

J. P. McDuff lay on his stomach on a pallet in the main room as Evie Dare examined his wound. "You need a doctor, mister."

"I am a doctor. Which is why I know that we can waste no time. I believe the bullet is against my spine and therefore must come out as soon as possible." Though in great pain, he lifted his head slightly and looked at the old woman. "Are you willing to help me if I tell you everything to do?"

Evie had to listen carefully. It sounded like he'd said . . . "Aire you willing to 'elp me eef ah tell you evairy t'ing to do?" She looked at him for a time and then she nodded. "All right."

"Good."

"What's first?"

"Is there time to send for my medical bag?"

"Where is it?"

"At the rooming house in town."

"I guess there is." Evie nodded to Goldie who threw himself on his horse and took off at a gallop.

"Set some water to boil."

Brit replied. "We did that already, Maw."

Jean Pierre turned toward the voice. *Sacré bleu!* He was worse off than he thought! Already he was starting to see double!

"Got a good fire goin'?"

"Yessum. An' set out clean rags."

He closed one eye and looked again. He still saw double and his vision was still ill-defined but it was sufficient to see that the speaker was a slender young nymph with a pale oval face the color of *café au lait*. Her lone garment was a nightdress that ended several inches above her bare feet. A thick ebony braid lay between her breasts, defining their generous shape and poorly cloaking dark circles beneath.

God, they were nice! He had seen a generous breast just recently but the old woman interrupted before he could think where.

"All right, Frenchie. Now what?"

"Now we wait," McDuff said and passed out.

Brit and Irish looked at each other and then at Sheriff Goodman who was standing in the doorway working his hat brim over in his hands. Then they went back to studying the injured man—the first they had seen so exposed who was not a brother.

McDuff's hips were covered with a quilt, but his arms, shoulders and spine were bare clear to the curve of his buttocks. He had a splat of freckles across his wide shoulders and a small triangle of fine black hair at the base of his spine. The bullet hole was above and just to the left of it.

As with their brothers, his body carried many old scars. One low on his right side, one high on his left arm, one inches from his neck.

"Brit, you best get outa your bedclothes. You'll have to help me."

"All right, Maw."

It had come as a surprise to Evie to learn that Brit was the best help to her in situations such as this. She had a cast-iron stomach and unflinching hands while Irish, who was so good at so many womanly things, always went faunchy at the first drop of human blood. "Irish, throw some more wood on the fire."

"I already did, Maw."

"Good girl." Evie kept a wad of cloth pressed to the wound and looked up at Goodman. "How did it happen?"

"He shot Gil Daggert in bed. Used Gil's own gun to do it.

If he lives, he will stand trial for shooting an unarmed man and he'll stand it in Sweet Home. I got word just last week. We're gonna get our own judge about any day now."

"In Sweet Home?"

It was true. Not because it was the biggest settlement in the district but because it was the most centrally located. He told her the judge's name was Frederico de la Barca.

Goodman looked at McDuff whose blood was slowly soaking the rag Evie held to his back.

"I warned him. Poor fella. All he had to do was tell me what he found out, an' I'da arrested Daggert. Now, if he's found guilty of murder, he'll hang."

"I know a real good lawyer." Markie felt everyone's eyes on her and guessed their faces frowned. "Well, it's true. I do."

Abel O'Neal had been pleased to hear about the new judge's appointment because it meant that people from all over the district would be coming to Sweet Home to do their legal business . . . and it was only logical that some of those people would require a local lawyer's assistance. He was, however, considerably less pleased when Judge Frederico de la Barca arrived with his family and entourage of eight and declared that all legal matters would have to wait until after he supervised the building of a home worthy of his personage.

Also troublesome—to say the least—was the revelation that the judge did not speak a word of English. Abel did not yet speak Spanish.

They had all planned on learning the language of the land before they moved to Tejas but Annie and Emma never got a chance to attend their classes because Nona's illness had forced them to leave Philadelphia earlier than they had anticipated. Abel had finished one language course and was halfway through a second when his preceptorship was concluded and he was free to leave for Tejas. He could ask for directions to the men's privy and for a cup of chocolate but he could hardly argue a legal case.

Chapter 26

Four new families arrived in Sweet Home in September. So did six new babies. Unfortunately a Kiowa raid resulted in six funerals which just about evened things out again. Lloyd Cooper was bereft. Sweet Home would never grow at this rate!

The days changed little that October, but the evenings were noticeably cooler. One morning the first frost glistened on the grass. Soon after some of the birds started to disappear and the hills around town looked like a wildfire was sweeping across them. Fall had come to Sweet Home and with it, a much anticipated event.

The annual celebration locally known as Founder's Day was traditionally held on the third Sunday in October. Originally its purpose was to commemorate the first settler's coming to the area some sixteen years earlier. The settler, a man named Leo Cates—had moved on long ago and had not been heard from since, but the succeeding settlers—who were decidedly more historically minded than Mr. Cates—were careful to mark the date and site of Cates's cabin and the following year when they gathered to share the fruits of their labor, they named the occasion Founder's Day. A tradition was born.

The picnic was generally held in the long stretch of creek-meadow between the edge of town and the fork in the road, the portion of land that had recently been set aside for the new church.

Weather permitting—and providing the circuit preacher showed—the festivities usually began with an outdoor prayer meeting in the morning followed by games in the afternoon and then a barbecue. A dance was held in the evening.

Annie was looking forward to attending, not only because it sounded like such good fun but because she was a little at odds for something to do. She was still tutoring Markie, and the week previous, Abner and Rebecca Yates had started coming in for a few hours every morning to catch up on what they'd missed, but for all other intents and purposes, school was not in session in October and Annie found she had more free time than she cared to have.

The week before, an anticipatory feeling gripped the town and people could talk of little else but Founder's Day. Finally the day arrived, and it was one for which Indian summer might have been named, for it dawned warm and sunny and stayed that way all day. Town was crowded by nine o'clock with those who lived close in. Others arrived throughout the morning and by noon a person could hardly walk down the road for all the wagons and carts that lined it.

Everyone brought something, still Annie wondered how they would all be fed. Then she saw for herself the magnitude of the feast that had been laid.

In a pit dug for that purpose there was an entire beef and a deer. Both had been slowly roasting since the night before. The planks that had been laid over pickle barrels were bowed because of all the glazed hams and fried chickens they held. Other tables offered every sort of hot dish and side dish imaginable. (Once again Annie noted that the Texian side dish of choice was beans—red, baked, string and lima—done, it seemed, in every recipe known to womankind.) In addition there were biscuits, rounds of cheese, flour-dusted loaves of bread, tortillas and pans of corn bread, and on yet another table, several dessert offerings which included pies, bread puddings, loaf cakes, custards and sliced sweet breads with assorted preserves.

Different from anything she had ever eaten before was a local sweet called *nueces dulce,* which was made of nuts, sugar and cinnamon. The Tejano woman who made it encouraged Annie to try a piece and she found it delicious!

Annie and Emma agreed that everything was splendid except . . . the noise was horrific. Barking dogs and screaming children ran everywhere and the adults were no better, shouting and calling to each other over the tumult. As they strolled amid the bedlam, Annie and Emma passed an area where various home brews were being tested, and Annie'd had to place her lips on Emma's ear in order to ask her if she'd noticed how the noise levels seemed to be rising as the jug levels lowered.

When they were joined by Abel, they moved toward the long-cleared pasture where the contests were about to begin. On the way they observed several of Annie's pupils playing games like hide-and-seek, anty over, fox and geese, fox and dogs, base, blindfold, bullpen, crack the whip, devil in the promised land, field ball and plain old tag.

The adult games were as diverse . . . knife and tomahawk throwing, foot and horse races, arm wrestling, horseshoes and shooting matches with both pistols and rifles.

Since Annie knew several of the competitors she was able to name them and tell Abel a bit about them. Jesse McIninch, for example, who won the knife throw, and Hector Salazar who won the tomahawk toss.

Next Blue Dare put on a one-man demonstration of death-defying feats—all performed while his horse was at a dead run. He stood on his hands then on his feet then hung from his horse's belly and rode backwards with his arms folded on his chest. For a finale he flung himself into the saddle from every imaginable way.

With no more result from his effort than a slightly reddened face and sprung hair, he collected a prize from the *alcalde,* as well as a bouquet of posies from a dark-eyed Tejano girl.

One contestant she didn't recognize was the dark, barrel-chested man who won two of the footraces. He looked Indian but unlike any she had ever seen. Intrigued, she asked Lloyd Cooper about him. "He's Tarahumari Indian, probably the fastest human beings in the world."

"Tara-hum-ari," said Emma. "I've never heard of that tribe!"

"They come from the Tres Casillos mountains in northern Chihuahua. I don't know where he lives the rest of the year but he is always in town on Founder's Day." Cooper looked at him. "Last year the man boasted he could outrun any horse in a race over five miles and he did!"

"My stars!"

"Someone said he'd been trying to get some bets down earlier but I'm sure the word has gotten around."

Even as they watched, the Tarahumari approached a frontiers-man standing beside a fine-looking piece of horseflesh. After a short conversation, it appeared the Indian had found a taker. He insisted that the money be held by a third party. Intrigued, Emma and Annie stayed around to see what happened. Sure enough, sometime later the Indian jogged over to the money holder and collected his winnings.

After the horse races came the pistol competition, which Long Bob Benning won handily.

Not only could he pull and fire his pistol faster than anyone else but he could also do tricks such as placing a poker chip on the back of his gun hand, raising his hand shoulder high, letting the chip fall and then pulling and firing his gun so that he hit the chip before it hit the ground.

"I see it but I still don't believe it!" said Abel with awe.

Not surprisingly Long Bob could not do it every time, but he did it three times out of ten and nobody else could do it even once.

The three Dare men were obviously aware of Benning's prowess with a pistol because they did not even compete. They were, however, clear favorites in the long gun shoot.

The rifle match was the biggest draw for most men because

of the sizeable cash prize—twenty dollars—and because almost every male competed in it. Goldie Dare had won two years running but he would not be competing this year because he had cut his hand the week before. That being the case, most everyone expected Jack Dare to win, but several men had high hopes for an unprecedented upset victory.

Annie noted that many were getting as drunk as possible in order to steady their hands.

The first shots were to be fired at fifty paces, then at a hundred paces and then at a hundred-fifty. If the contest was still not won, then the contestants would shoot at two hundred then two hundred-fifty and so on, until there was a decisive winner. It seemed sort of vague to Annie but apparently not to any of the men.

Earlier Abel had wandered off somewhere but Annie thought nothing of it. Imagine her surprise when he walked up carrying a gleaming long rifle! Crisscrossing his chest was a shot pouch and powder horn and he carried a forked stick. Several men admired his gun. Hap Pettijohn hefted it and sighted down its barrel. "This's a Dickert, ain't it?"

"That's right. Made by Jacob Dickert from Lancaster County, Pennsylvania. Finest gunsmith alive today." Then to the mayor, he said, "Is there any rule against a man using a brace?"

"None at all," answered Lloyd Cooper. "The only rule is to hit the mark by any means possible."

Annie watched as Abel prepared his gun. Gratified by her interest, he tried to teach her how to ready a weapon to fire. "First you pour a charge down the muzzle of the gun like so. Then you push the patch and the ball down using this which is called the ramrod. You have to make sure you tamp it down good . . . that's very important. Next you half-cock the hammer and prime the pan by filling it full of powder. Then you close the frizzen."

"The what?"

"This thing right here."

"Oh."

"Close the frizzen over the pan and that's it. You're ready to fire."

"No wonder the Indians kill so many of us."

"They do have an advantage. They say that any Indian worth his salt can fire twelve arrows in the amount of time a white man can get his gun loaded and ready to fire."

"Wouldn't we be better off if we learned the bow and arrow?"

Abel looked at her. "You know, that's not a bad idea."

Annie did not much like guns. Or bows and arrows. Or knives. "Abel, don't you think you're taking things a bit far? I mean, how often will you use those skills? We'll be living in town, remember?"

Abel sighted down his barrel. "This is a rough land, Annie and it is every person's responsibility to be ready to protect themselves at any time and under any condition."

"Oh, Abel! Honestly!"

She didn't notice that he hadn't really answered her question because she was distracted by some of her students calling to her. As a consequence, she also didn't notice the look on his face that would have told her he was hiding something from her.

Given the chance Abel would have told her about the temporary job that he hoped to get. Then he might have explained to her that this did not have to do with whether they lived in town or on a remote farm, smack in the middle of Indian country. This had to do with holding his own with the other men. She might not understand why that was so important to him but gaining their respect meant gaining his own and that was very important to him.

At fifty paces a cent was used and all the men made that mark easily. Then a board with a concho-sized circle on it was nailed to a tree and fired upon from a hundred paces.

Many men were quite inebriated and could barely walk, much less shoot, nonetheless all but two men advanced to the next stage.

Using his forked stick Abel not only hit the mark at a hundred paces, he hit it at a hundred and fifty paces as well. Annie was pleased and proud. "Abel, look at you! Where did you ever learn to shoot like that?"

"I went to a place where they teach shooting and I practiced."

"You practiced?"

"Every day for four months."

"Every day for four months!" She watched him change his position, tap down his forked stick and she thought: I swear I don't know what's come over the man!

While it was true that he was incredibly accurate, it seemed to take him an unusually long time to get set up as he sighted and then sighted again. She had seen a look exchanged between a couple of men yet one of them yelled, "Good 'un, O'Neal!" after he made his shot.

She supposed they admired his marksmanship but were unaccustomed to all his fiddling.

Jack Dare, however, was just the opposite. He must have had to do the same things Abel did to prepare his rifle but he always seemed ready. While waiting his turn, he would stand loose and relaxed with his arms braced on his rifle. (Invariably he'd have one leg locked and the other cocked—which drew his pants tight across his rear and thigh and which made Annie's cheeks heat because she would notice such a thing.) Then, when it was his turn, he would simply lift his rifle to his shoulder and fire—BLAM—seemingly without even sighting down the barrel.

After two hundred paces only Abel, Jack Dare and Clyde Maxey were still in the running. Then Clyde was eliminated and only Abel and Jack were left.

Annie didn't know how she felt about that. Uneasy, certainly, and not quite sure how to act.

They each made their next shot and advanced. The target this time was another board with a circle drawn on it. Abel hit the circle dead center, but when Jack Dare stepped up his shot went into the exact hole that Abel's bullet had made and it was, irrefutably, the finest shot of the match.

Annie's emotions pulled her willy-nilly. She felt sorry for Abel but at the same time she couldn't help but be glad that Jack had won.

She did not know if decisiveness counted in marksmanship but it should. So should it count in life. Probably through no fault of his own—probably simply because of his youth and inexperience—Abel lacked the clear-cut determination it took to act. Conversely, once Jack Dare made up his mind to act he did so without hesitation and with unmistakable intent. It was, she realized, one of the things she most admired about him. And it was, she also realized, exactly how he'd acted when he made his decision to win her. Without hesitation. With unmistakable intent.

When the sinking sun looked like a bloody yolk atop the hills, those who lived far away or those with small children began to pack up and leave. For the others that must have been the signal for the revelry to begin, for torches were lit and some Tejanos—three guitarists, two horn players, and a gourd shaker—began to play. Their first rousing tune ringed them with people who were clapping in time to the music and shouting encouraging things like *"Eso es! Eso es! Sí Sí, Arriba!"*

When the musicians ended that tune, they immediately began another that brought appreciative whistles and cries of *Hola!* One of the guitarists stepped forward.

The soloist had a beautiful tenor voice and from the moment he began to sing he had Annie's undivided attention. The music sounded unremittingly sad and something about it reached right inside her. She had to know what he was saying.

She asked the Tejano woman next to her to translate and it was just as she thought; a terribly sad song about a young man whose life had been ruined by a lost love. Music to cry by, she thought with a deepening feeling of unhappiness.

She was trying to get rid of a hard lump that had formed in her throat when Abel wedged himself into the spot beside her. "Aren't they great?" Fortunately the music had changed to a loud lively tune which helped to obscure her choked reply.

Rutha and Bowie Garlock stopped to say hello then and

when she turned back to the band she saw Hector's youngest brother Vincente and a young girl, dancing around a hat flung on the ground. Vincente had his hands clasped behind his back and the girl was sawing her skirts in time to the music. Across the way stood the singer of the plaintive song, drinking wine from a goatskin and laughing when he dribbled some on his chin. She felt like a fool, to be so saddened by a song. What's worse, a song she did not even understand.

She gave Abel a bright smile. "Abel, I've decided I must learn Spanish. I mean, take lessons or be tutored. I'm just not picking it up fast enough to suit me."

"You aren't the only one! I've got to learn it ... *muy pronto.*"

He told her then about the new judge who spoke no English. "We'll learn together, provided we can find someone to teach us. I'll ask around tomorrow," he said. "Say, there's another group playing over there. Want to go hear them?"

Annie said, "All right."

They moved downhill to a spot where another bonfire had been lit. There a Finlander family was providing fine entertainment with some very crude instruments.

The father, a widower with five boys, played a banjo made from a long-necked gourd while his boys played a jaw harp, a whittled wooden flute, and a flute made out of a turkey drumstick. Sitting cross-legged on the ground was an old woman who was rapping two cow-leg bones together. She was having a high old time, grinning toothlessly at the crowd and putting a lot of elbow into her work.

Markie stood close to the players with her fiddle under her arm, tapping one foot and rocking back and forth. After a few minutes she settled her fiddle under her chin and started playing along. Soon a little space had cleared around her and people were looking at her with smiling admiration. When the tune was finished, the Finlanders pulled her into their midst and by the end of the next tune, she was standing on a barrel smack in the middle of everything, doing her little jig and playing her heart out. Annie and Abel heard many favorable comments from the crowd.

"Isn't she amazing, Abel?"

"I can't believe her," he replied. "Remarkable Markie Dare! That's what I told her I was going to call her."

When the band took a break, Annie approached the Finlander father to see if he was interested in sending his boys to school. He may have told her how to make a banjo from a long-necked gourd or he may have said the boys had no need of school. She assumed the latter but not because she understood a word he said. His English was terrible! She considered telling him that he might find school useful for himself, but instead she merely said that if he changed his mind, his boys would be made most welcome. Then she rejoined Abel who was telling Markie that if she went East there were people in the big cities who would pay to hear her play.

She shook her head. "I don't wanna leave Sweet Home."

"Don't you want to visit other places, Markie?" Annie asked.

"Naw."

"What do you want to do when you grow up?"

She blushed prettily. "I want to marry Abel."

Annie took her hands off her knees and straightened. "Marry Abel." Eyes twinkling, she smiled at Abel. "Really?"

"Uh huh. I want to have a big cabin and a nice garden, all the babies and animals I want."

"Is that all?" asked Annie.

"I want to play my fiddle all I want and hear all the poems there is."

"Are."

"What?"

"Nothing."

Abel had turned a sort of carroty color and was making fish-out-of-water movements with his mouth. Annie was about to explore this further when Markie was whisked up on top the cider barrel by the gruff Finlander father and the music started again. Annie got the distinct impression that Abel was glad that it was impossible to talk over the noise.

Three more fiddlers showed up—hairy-faced men with floppy brimmed hats—and after several long pulls on their jugs, they joined in and led the Finlanders in playing jigs and reels like "The Double Shuffle" and the "Kentucky Heel Tap," "Virginny Breakdown," and "The Pigeon Wing," "Arkansas Hoedown," and "The Back Balance Kick." Someone said they were all popular back in the States but the tunes were completely new to her, especially "Beer in the Mug," and "Flexin' The Texin'." She suspected them of making up the titles as they went along. If they were, they were sure good at it. Besides, like Abel said, it was sure spirit-stirring music. A circle had formed around a cleared area in which some couples were either dancing or throwing fits.

"How about if you an' me kick up some splinters, ma'am?"

"Abel! Listen to you!"

"I understand that's how they say it down here, by cracky!"

"Abel, I have not heard one person say 'by cracky'!"

He frowned. "I thought I had."

"I'm quite sure you have not."

"Huh."

A few minutes passed and she could feel him watching her.

"Is everything all right, Annie?"

"Yes, of course. Why?"

He looked off to choose his words. "I can't quite put my finger on it. I just feel that something's amiss."

"Don't be silly, Abel." She met his clear and direct gaze and then her eyes danced away. "You know I'll never change."

"I hope not!"

She smiled at him then stood on her tiptoes to scan the crowd. "I think I'll see what Emma's doing. Want to come along?"

He shook his head. "I'll stay here and listen to Markie."

"Mm! It looks to me like I might have a rival!"

"You know there's never been anyone to rival you."

He looked so serious. On tiptoes she kissed his cheek. "Thank you, Abel. See you in a bit."

Abel watched her walk away and thought. Something's changed. I don't know what, but in some subtle way she is different from the girl I knew in Philadelphia.

She never did find Emma but she found Jack Dare, standing across a natural path made between two clumps of alamos. She stood behind a handy tree and let her eyes roam over every feature. The two jaw-length hanks that framed his hard planed face. His broad brow and long nose and menacing mustache. She watched his expression turn serious as he talked to the Coopers and then heard the shouted hello he gave Clyde Maxey and then the polite one that he had for the Yates family. A Tejano man with three boys came along and she watched him buy red chili tamales for everyone. He ate his leaning over so he wouldn't get sauce on his shirt.

All this time she was very careful that he not see her. Not that he would do anything about it if he did. It was a thought that brought her misery to new bounds but she could hardly miss how his manner had changed toward her. Apparently he had taken her at her word and obviously he was a man of his. He had said that he would wait for her to tell him that she wanted him. He had waited, and now it appeared that he was done. She ought to feel relieved. Instead she felt terribly sad and very alone and one thing was clear to her now: she would never be able to see him without feeling hollow inside. Oh, God. Must I give up my love of life as well as my love?

Those were her thoughts when she looked up and beyond the passing people and met his eyes. They stared at each other across the lighted path.

Jack held his face impassive but in his heart he was madder than hell. To see everything she felt for him plainly written on her face did anything but make him happy because he could also see the resolve that was there as well. She still intended to marry O'Neal.

She'd insisted that it was because she was promised to him. He hadn't been happy about it but he'd believed her . . . until tonight when he'd had just enough to drink to convince himself otherwise. Now he was sure that it was because O'Neal had the potential for greater prosperity and of course, because O'Neal was an educated and well-spoken man.

She was a fool for throwing their happiness away, but he was a bigger one for waiting around for a woman like Annie Mapes! Angrily he moved off into the darkness.

Annie watched him go, and felt like crying.

Suddenly a chin-whiskered man she recognized as Zick Simmons's brother grabbed her and pulled her down the lane and into a galloping dance of such fury that it came close to dislocating her shoulders. This went on for an endless period until thankfully the tempo changed. At that point her partner stopped spinning her silly and sawed her arm instead. When her eyes could focus, she saw Emma and Sheriff Goodman bob by. The sheriff was an arm-sawer too! "Emma! Are you enjoying yourself?"

"Yes, immensely. Annie, I've invited Sheriff Goodman to Sunday dinner."

"Fine. Great." She would have said more but the music kicked up then and so did her partner.

When the tune ended Annie was on the opposite side of the dance floor from Abel who was talking to Markie anyway. Emma was nearby but enrapt with something the sheriff had to say. Her eyes next met those of her recent partner. He raised his brows and twiddled his fingers at her.

This is, she decided, an excellent time to use the necessary, which had for obvious reasons been set up downwind and quite a distance from the picnic area.

Once away from the crowd, she slowed her step in order to enjoy the beauty of the evening. And it was a lovely one. Here the din of the gathering was muted and the sounds of the night were in the fore. She listened and heard frogs and cicadas and moving water. Once again the night had softened the land, making the trees dark blotches on the path and turning the swelling hills beyond into lumpy-looking shadows.

She had been thinking about Jack Dare and suddenly there he was by the creek, standing with his back to her and his hand cupping his pipe. Curls of smoke floated in the windless air bringing the distinctive scent of his tobacco. She had tasted it on him that night by the creek, a faint and manly flavor.

It was odd how she could call up every little detail about him and yet could recall almost nothing about her life before she arrived in Tejas! The part of her life that had once been so sharp was now dim and indistinct as if it were seen through a murky fog. Sometimes she'd think of Philadelphia and find herself wondering: what was the name of that greengrocer? Or that pert Irish girl who ''did'' for them once a week? Or their minister's wife?

Oh, she could remember if she really tried but she seldom did. It was as if those details had been pushed far back in her brain in order to make room for much more important memories. It was as if her life began with Sweet Home. With Jack Dare.

She hated that he greeted her only in the polite manner one would reserve for an acquaintance. Was that how it would be between them? Would they avoid each other whenever possible and barely speak when they passed on the street? She couldn't bear that! She wanted to say, Please! Let us at least be friends!

She would say it!

She approached warily but of course, he heard her and turned. She waved gaily. ''Hello, there!''

He inclined his head. ''Miss Mapes.''

''Isn't it a lovely night?''

''Yeah, jus' . . . lovely.''

''I've been listening to the music. I had no idea there were so many talented performers in the area! Were you, um, aware that . . . that there were?''

The creek gurgled and the frogs croaked and the insects buzzed, but from him there came only a steady look. Suddenly he rapped his pipe against a tree, a sharp, angry sound that made her flinch.

''You want to see me about somethin', Miss Mapes?''

''No. I was just going to the, um, you know and happened to ah . . .''

''Yeah. Well, you've come the wrong way, Miss Mapes.''

He walked slowly toward her. She backed up a few steps and felt bark behind her. He came closer, still looking at her. She meant to turn and leave but he'd blocked her with a hand on the tree. His breath smelled of whiskey.

He said, low, "Maybe you came to tell me that you've told him."

"Told who what?"

"Told O'Neal that you can't marry him."

"Why would I do that?" She tried a laugh.

"'Cause you don't love him."

Her jovial pretense fled. "I've told you and told you . . . I will never go back on my promise to Abel." But his next words informed her that she had wasted her breath again.

"You don't love him, do you?" His voice was intense.

"I don't have to answer that."

"No, you don't. I already know the answer."

Her eyes flashed. "Who are you to tell me my feelings?"

"Who am I? I'm the one you've tied in a knot an' made crazy with want. I'm the one that you do love. An' you know what I think?"

"No. What?"

"I think you came down here hopin' to see me."

"Maybe I did. Maybe I don't want it to be like this with us."

"How would you like it to be with us? You want me t'come over for visits an' hold your yarn while we talk? Or mebbe you'd like for me t'come over after I know your husband's gone for the day."

She turned her head away. "Please don't say things like that . . ."

"Maybe you came down here 'cause you thought I might help you make up your mind."

He'd cut too close to the bone. "You're insane!"

"I think you want me so bad, you ache."

"And I think you only want me because you can't have me!" Soon as she said that she wished she hadn't. His eyes flared and shot sparks at her.

"Who says I can't have you? I could've had you that night in the woods. Or at the school. Or up on the hill." He leaned very close. "Or right now. Right here!"

"Ridiculous!" she said but her breath came fast and shallow.

"Ridiculous, is it?" He grabbed her shoulders and pulled her to him.

As soon as he touched her she was lost. Every promise she'd made herself fled. A calmness came over her and again she felt how fitting . . . and how right . . . it felt to be in his arms. She stared up at him and it was exactly as he said. She wanted him all right. Right here. Right now. And it scared her to death.

Music mingled with indistinct words and the sound of laughter, but it and the crowd seemed far away and unimportant. She was aware only of the strength of his hands on her shoulders and of the small distance between their lips. Oh, how she hated herself and oh, how she loved him.

Tears glistened on her lashes. He released her and almost immediately the inner pain and awful aloneness returned. Tiredly he asked, "What is it that you want from me, Annie?"

A long time went by. She looked at him and then away. What did she want from him? That which she could not have. Ever. But she was powerless over the need for some small thing. Something to remember forever. To hold and keep always. A kind word. A warm touch. A kiss.

"Perhaps . . ." Her tongue flicked over her lips. "Perhaps a last kiss . . ."

She finally looked up at him but his eyes were hidden by his hat.

Someone was passing nearby. She heard one man say something and heard another laugh and still Jack did not answer her. She was close to tears when he grabbed her suddenly and held her with paralyzing force.

"Damn you, Annie Mapes. You listen an' you listen good. If you ever ask me to kiss you again, it won't be just once. An' that won't be all that'll happen."

Jack turned away from the kicked-animal look in her eyes and by the time he looked around, she was gone.

Chapter 27

Jack was in the shadow of the tree that grew outside Annie Mapes's window. Though the moon had about finished its sweep across the sky it still lent enough light to silver the trees and cast a gun-metal stripe on the water.

And show a man climbing into a window! Which was why he was sitting on his heels with his back against the wall, waiting for a convenient cloud.

From the road a man's voice rose in a slurred song that abruptly ended in a gargle. Then a second man said something, the tone warning but the words indistinct and Jack grinned. Goodman. Dealing with the last of the revelers. As the evening wound down, Goodman's problems did the opposite. Founder's Day never passed without some thuggery, and this year was no exception. There'd already been three fistfights, one shooting and two cuttings.

And, if Jack Dare had anything to say about it, at least one seduction.

He had a plan that ended with Annie Mapes saying she loved him and agreeing to marry him. That's how things ended up. How he got her to that point was not yet firm in his mind.

What he did know was that this was it. The last time he would
try to convince her that marrying O'Neal was a mistake.

From somewhere in the hills came the call of a coyote. A
second one responded and then a dog on the other end of town.
Jack didn't hear them because he was remembering how Annie
had looked before she ran from him. He saw again her tear-
streaked face and shook his head. He couldn't believe what
she did to him.

A cloud finally accommodated him. He stood and stuck his
knife blade between the two shutters to lift the latch. He shot
a look left then right and was over the ledge like a cat.

Annie Mapes's bedroom had a pine dresser with a china
washbowl and pitcher decorated with pink and yellow vines,
a cane-back chair with a flowery cushion and a brass bed. There
was more but that was all he noticed because lying splay-legged
in the center of the bed was Miss Annie Mapes.

Her nightgown was hiked up to mid-calf and her long silky
hair hung off the bed almost to the floor. Her nose was red-
tipped and her cheeks were tear-streaked and through a partially
open mouth she was breathing like a wind-broken horse. Jack
thought he had never seen anything more arousing in his life.

He came closer, drawn by the little string ties on her nightgown. Slowly he pulled them loose. The one at her neck first.
The one between her breasts next. With butterfly fingers he
drew the folds aside so that she lay exposed from neck to navel.
She was so soft and round and white that for a long time all
he could do was look at her.

Without taking his eyes from her, he removed his shirt, boots,
pants and smallclothes until he was buck naked then he trailed
his finger from her collarbone to the tip of her breast and her
eyes flew open. "You!" she hissed. When she half sat, he
peeled her nightgown down to her waist and trapped her arms
at her side. Then he followed her down, kissing her back into
the bed and covering her body with his. "Stop that . . ." He
grunted his approval of her open mouth and covered it with
his own. She struggled weakly and then she quit.

He kissed her for a very long time—deep, mind-destroying

kisses, while his hands made an intimate acquaintance with every part of her. Between kisses he whispered things to her that she didn't understand but his voice heated her blood as much as his lips. She touched his taut, silken skin.

"Annie!" He pulled back to look at her. Long fingers turned her chin to him and he shook her a little. She was no longer resisting. Far from it. She had surrendered. "Look at me, Annie." She opened her eyes. "If you want this to end, tell me to go an' I will."

"Free my hands," she said.

He sat up and did so and her eyes were filled with solid muscular shoulders and a hard-looking chest with curly black hairs. His skin looked slick. It was slick. She spread her fingers on his shoulders then let her hands drift across his chest. He moaned when she accidentally touched one copper nipple so she did it again, curiously brushing her knuckles across one then the other. "God!" he said and crushed her with his body. His mouth twisted over hers then his tongue opened her lips and plunged within. She arched up against him. He pressed down and rotated his hips. They both thought: Oh, my God! This is wonderful! She groaned. He groaned. They both ached. And between kisses they fought for air like lungers.

He'd known that the task he'd set for himself would be torture. He was already atremble, but he reined himself in and began again, slowly letting his tongue and teeth feast on the hollow of her neck and the swell of her shoulder and the curve of her breast.

Annie sighed. Without conscious thought she moved to give him better access and then his lips were there, laving her nipple with his tongue, gently grazing it with his teeth, drawing it into his mouth and suckling like a babe.

Continuing to pleasure her, he pressed his groin to hers and began to move in slow, sensuous circles. First one way. Then the other. Her legs fell further apart and her fingernails dug into the bed. Her breath turned ragged as her hips began to follow his movements.

Jack had an immense and very painful problem, and a thin

layer of cloth was all that was keeping him from solving it, but his plan was not to take care of himself. His plan was to convince Annie that he could take care of her—and in ways she'd never imagined before.

Annie felt something gather within her, an ebb and flow that was so powerful, it wiped everything from her mind but the blinding pleasure that she sensed was close . . . so close. She caught her lower lip in her teeth, striving with an impatient yearning for something that would not be denied.

She didn't know what she wanted but she knew that he did. And that he knew how to give it to her.

"Do you love me, Annie? Tell me you do!" he quietly insisted.

She could not answer because her heart was in her throat. His heat and hardness had stolen her mind. She couldn't think straight, not with him pressing himself into her.

He lifted her with his hands under her hips and felt her quiver and heard the pleading sounds she made. He continued to move slowly. Threading her fingers through his hair she held his head to her breast then arched her back and pressed the crown of her head into the pillow and cried . . . "Jaaaack!"

Afterwards she lay with her head on his chest. His fingers smoothed her hair and his lips pressed her brow with feather soft kisses. Her bones were mush . . . no her body was . . . and she didn't care. She'd never imagined she could feel so sublime.

Jack touched his lips to the top of her head and let his hand drift down to the small of her back. A little squeeze pressed the arch of her pelvis onto his thigh where it burned through her nightdress and drove him half crazy with want. If someone had told him that a man could experience this high a level of pleasurable pain, he wouldn't have believed him . . . until tonight. Tonight he'd gone beyond simple desire to a place he'd never imagined before. It was a place where nothing else mattered. Only Annie Mapes.

He had not found relief, of course, and so was as erect as

the moment he'd started playing with her. She, on the other hand, was draped on him like a wet rag. He couldn't see her face but she might even be asleep. Relaxed fingers were splayed on his chest and a slender leg was tucked between his. None of this helped his condition but worst of all was the warm air that caressed his left nipple. He bit back a moan. This was heaven and this was hell and he hoped it would last forever.

It lasted about three minutes and then she started to cry.

He had heard that untried women do that sometimes, so he held her and patted her back and said soothing things. "Shhh, Annie. Aw, don't darlin'. Everything's gonna be all right."

Now he'd made her angry! Talking to her as if she were a child with a skinned knee. If only that were all that she had done!

"All right?" she cried. "How can you say that? I can never be right again!" Her eyes glittered wetly in the moonlight. "You purposely came here to . . . to do that"

"Sure I did. You think I was gonna let you marry somebody else when you're in love with me?"

"Oh, God! This is awful!" She buried her face in her hands. "What on earth got into me?"

Not me, thought Jack, a fact that was still painfully clear. He had warned her that he wouldn't stop and then he did. What a fool he was! He attempted to pull her back into his arms but she pushed him away and pointed at the window.

"Go!" she cried. "I want you out of here right now!"

"All right if I dress first?"

"Oooh!" She shot him a look then buried her head in her hands.

He knelt by the bed and tried to hold her but she wouldn't allow it. "Annie, we need to talk . . ."

"I never want to talk to you again!"

God, she was an exasperating woman! He laced his pants and shrugged into his shirt. "You're liable to be sorry you said that. Durin' the fifty years we're married you're bound talk to me sometime an' then you'll jus' be madder'n hell . . ."

"I will never marry you!"

"Damnit, Annie . . ." His ire rose. "Either you tell Abel O'Neal about us . . . this or . . ."

"Or what?"

"I'll tell you what . . ." He put his hands on either side of her head and thrust his face into hers. "I'll be back, that's what. Especially now that I know you can't say no to me." His words lost none of their power for their softness. "Think about that, Annie Mapes. Three makes for a pretty crowded marriage bed." He straightened and went to the window. He looked outside then grinned back at her. "Sleep tight, darlin'." And then he was gone.

She flung herself facedown on her pillow. Everything he had said was true. She hated him. She hated herself, but he was right. She could never resist him and she no longer wanted to try. In spite of the things she'd said to him, the truth was: she would die if she could not be with him forever.

There was something else, the decisive factor. She was no longer pure and could hardly go to Abel as an untarnished bride after tonight. Why, she might even be with child! First she felt terrible and then a thought popped into her mind: no wonder people have such big families!

Oh, God. Her mood crashed. Now she *must* tell Abel about Jack.

"But Annie, of course I still want to marry you . . . You shouldn't even have to ask."

She stood and walked away. Abel stood too. He never imagined he could feel this miserable. "I would marry you even if there wasn't a . . . a child involved."

They were behind Maude Stone's rooming house, standing on the path that ran alongside the creek. Every once in a while Annie would see a white spoon-shape in the back window and know that Maude was looking out at them, curious as to why she had come tapping on her back door even before the cock had crowed.

"'I just don't understand how it could have happened to you. It's so . . . unlike you."

"Am I so dispassionate, Abel?" She made a lovely picture, standing there by the water's edge. That is, she would if it weren't for her eyes and nose. They always turned blood red when she cried.

"No, of course not." It was barely dawn and quite cool, yet Abel mopped his forehead before he followed her.

"At the time it, um, happened, I wanted it very much."

"That's what is so hard to take." He ran his hand through his hair. "You've always been so . . . so . . ."

"Circumspect?"

"Well, yes. I don't see how you could have let yourself get talked into doing, um, it."

As he struggled for the right words, she slowly turned to look at him and she continued to look at him for a long time. "You really don't understand, do you?"

"No, I don't."

She came to him and took his hand in both of hers. "Abel, do you realize what you just said?"

"No. Yes. What . . . ?"

"You just said that you don't love me."

He replied hotly. "I'll thank you not to tell me how I feel!"

She chuckled. "God, I said almost the same thing to Jack!"

"Jack? Was it Jack Dare? His face went tight and ugly. "I'll kill him."

"You won't do anything of the sort." She looked up at him. "Oh, Abel, don't you see? You don't understand because you've never felt the sort of passion that makes you so weak you . . . you just can't help yourself."

"Explain that if you will."

"I can't explain it. All I know is that if you don't want me like that . . . then you don't want me the way a man wants the woman he loves."

"I do too." This reply was hotter still.

"You don't. Believe me, Abel, you don't." She looked away then looked back and smiled slightly. "I didn't want it to be like this. It would've been so much easier to skim through life, a water bug on the surface of a pond, staying just above the deep feelings that I believed would have hurt me.''

''Who would ever hurt you?''

''Abel, losing someone you love hurts terribly. I know. I learned that very young, remember? That's why I sought to avoid loving that way. But now I know that I would have never been happy with half of love and I would have made you miserable as well.'' She stopped him from speaking with a raised palm. ''Maybe not right away, Abel, but sooner or later.'' She looked up at him, her eyes awash in tears. ''Oh, Abel, we might have done very well together.''

''I'm sure of it! Why do you think I asked you to marry me in the first place?''

''I hadn't finished, Abel. I was going to say . . . No doubt we would raise our children and live our lives in relative calm but one day one of us would sense that something was missing. I'm not saying that we would be unhappy just . . . wondering what was wrong. Abel, I cannot explain it to you until you fall deeply in love yourself.'' Ruefully. ''And then, of course, I won't have to explain a thing because it will all be clear to you then.''

''Annie, you have mistaken lust for love.''

Abel paced and tried to choose the right words. How could he tell her that he knew about lust without telling her about the brothel back in Philadelphia? How did he explain the urges that drove him down to Wharf Street in spite of all his vows to the contrary.

He opened and closed his mouth at least ten times but damned if he could make himself speak. In the end he lamely said, ''Trust me. I know what I'm talking about.''

''Abel, I believe a person can have both lust and love and I believe that when they do, they have it all—an uncommon and incredibly beautiful thing.''

He looked at her for a long time. ''You've made up your mind.''

She nodded. ''I'm sorry.''

He made a little bow. "All I have ever wanted was your happiness."

Aching inside she watched him until he disappeared into the rooming house before she walked away. She needed a place to be alone. She had to think. She needed a good cry!

Knowing that no one would be there she went to the school and by the time she arrived she was shaking like a leaf. Her head sank to her desk and rested on her bent arms. Tears streamed down her face.

She must have cried for hours—which changed nothing but the size of her lids and certainly did not alter the fact that she still had to go home and tell Emma Fuller that she and Abel would not be marrying.

Emma! Oh, Lord. How would she ever do it? What would she say?

"Yoo-hoo!"

A passerby I hope!

As she walked to the door she dried her eyes on her hem and fixed a calm smile on her lips. That fled as soon as she recognized her visitor. "Oh, no." Coming down the path was Evie Dare, astride a mule and wearing her hat. "Lord, help me!"

Annie thought about crawling out of the back window and then about closing the door and not answering her knock. Instead she squared her shoulders and stepped outside to meet her. She'd faced worse than Evie Dare today.

She stood on the stump step and fidgeted. Evie Dare was moving so slowly she seemed to be standing still! Just as she drew level with the oak, a flock of pigeons rose in undulating flight and retreated to the tangled boughs of a rugged creekside tree. Annie could see her sitting there with a half smile on her face, apparently waiting until the last pigeon had settled itself before she gee'ed the mule on.

Annie forced a smile on her face. "Hello! What brings you here today?"

"Help me down first. Bony ol' mule! I'd sooner ride a

ladder.'' She mopped her face. ''Whew. The sun gets hot by late day!''

''Yes, it does. Would you like something cool to drink?''

''Yes, please.''

She offered Evie the dipper of well water and she drank deeply and noisily before she handed it back. Then she fixed Annie with a calculating eye. ''Are you alone here?''

''Yes, I was, ah, just finishing up a bit of work that I . . .''

''Good. Let's sit under the tree there.''

They each arranged themselves; Annie sitting with her legs folded under her skirt and Evie sitting like a child, legs poled out and feet forked. She had big feet for one so small.

She did not beat around the bush, as Annie had hoped that she would. Instead she clasped her hands under her chin and looked sly. ''You won't believe what happened earlier today.''

''You saw a two-headed cow?''

Evie frowned. ''No.''

''A tornado went by . . . right above your house?''

''No.''

''You saw a . . .''

''Now jus' a durn minute. When a person says . . . you won't believe . . . like that, you're supposed to say 'no what?' an' then wait . . . without speaking . . . whilst I tell yuh.''

''Sorry.'' Annie sighed. She should've known better. ''So . . . what happened . . . earlier today?''

''Well, Jack an' Goldie an' me went over to the Yates place to do a few odd jobs while Mrs. Yates was at work.''

''That is so nice of you!''

''Weren't nothin'. Anyway, Jack cut some wood and Goldie mended a fence and I tidied up the house and put some supper on. We was jus' about finished when we heard a horse an' yonder comes young Abel O'Neal, sawin' his reins an' ridin' like a madman. Next thin' I knew, he'd throwed hisself off his horse an' onto Jack.''

''Oh, no.''

''Got in a couple good 'uns afore Jack cold-cocked him and sat on his neck.''

"Oh, my God! Is he all right."

"Jack or O'Neal?"

"Both. Either."

"Aw yeah, they're all right. You know, I lose my place when I start tellin' somethin' an' people keep jumpin' in. Now I have to start all over."

"Sorry."

"Where was I?"

"Jack cold, um, cocked . . . Abel." *Oh Abel I'm so sorry.* She covered her mouth and tears flowed unhindered down her cheeks.

"Like I said, Jack sat on his neck an' I thought I'd be a big help an' sit on his legs. Boy, I'll tell yuh, he gave me a ride like I ain't had in a long time! I was thinkin' about it on the way over here, tryin' to recall when I'd had rougher an' I believe it was the time my paw tole me to sit on the hind end of a cow while he an' Gib sawed her horns off. Didn't hurt her none but, boy, did she jump!" She smiled at Annie, saw her tears and petted her arm. "Nobody got hurt, mostly cause all O'Neal could move was his mouth. Ooowee, can that boy cuss!"

"He can?"

"Jus' like a Texian. Anyway, Jack asks him why he's so riled and he says it's because Jack's got you with child. Jack says he's talkin' crazy, he did no such thing an' Abel calls him a liar an' dares him to deny that he was jus' with you last night an' Jack says he was but did not—an' has never—known you in a biblical sense. He says he did. He says he didn't." She fixed a hard eye on Annie. "Why don't you tell me? Has he? Or not?"

Annie looked down at her hands, so ashamed she could die. She nodded. "He has."

"You're sure?"

"Well, of course I'm sure!"

"Don't get all haired up now. . . Might as well finish my story. Where was I?"

"They were arguing."

"Yeah. First Jack looked real confused an' then he looked sorta odd. Next thin' I know, he's started chucklin'. Well, I thought about it . . . what would he find funny about this?"

Huffily. "I'd like to know that too."

"You will, 'cause pretty soon it come to me." She looked at Annie whose face was beet red. "Far as lovin' goes, I'll bet you don't know the difference between a pig an' a sheep . . . do yuh?"

"I don't know what I know. Certainly more than I did before last night!"

"Mm. Why's that . . . ?"

Evie's stare was making her very nervous. "Because Jack came over last night and climbed in my window and he . . . he, um, you know . . ."

"Mated with you?"

"I think so."

"That's what I thought." Evie petted her arm again. "My, dear Annie. If Jack had really mated with you, you'd have no doubt about what happened. An' that's why I come over here today. I think I can explain a few things to you an' get this all straightened out."

Explain! Annie looked at her, aghast. "Oh, please don't feel you have to . . ."

"Oh, pooh! I can help you, Annie."

Annie saw the gentleness and compassion in Evie's eyes and cried all the more. Evie ignored her. "First off, I best begin by tellin' you a few things about a man an' a woman an' when I'm all done then you can tell me if Jack could've got a baby on you or not."

Annie buried her face in her hands and wailed. "Oh, this is awful!"

"Oh, hush! It'll jus' take a minute. Now . . ." Evie had to raise her voice to be heard. "I want you to think of a man as if he were a key an' a woman as if she were a lock."

Ten minutes later Annie still had her hands over her eyes but she had not stoppered her ears and she had quit crying. Evie's hand was patting her knee soothingly, but all she could think was: *There's more to it than what happened last night! Good heavens. There's more!*

"Now then, you tell me. Did Jack open your, er, lock?" Evie leaned forward and waited.

"No," she whispered. "He did not."

"He didn't?"

"No, he didn't."

"I didn't think so. Well . . ." Evie looked away. She looked back. "You love 'im don't yuh, girl?" Annie nodded. "An' you couldn't refuse him, could you?" Annie shook her head. Evie handed her a nose rag and she blew her nose hard and then they sat silent for a time.

While Evie watched the girl stare at something in the distance she was thinking: *My stars! Can you imagine her not knowin' a blessed thin'? An' in this day an' age!*

"Annie, Abel O'Neal'll get over losin' you. Probably better'n he'd get over winnin' you. In time—five mebbe ten years—Jack probably would've gotten over you too. But I know my boy well enough to know that he would've had to leave Sweet Home to do it. I know he wouldn't stay here an' watch you live the life you wanted with another man."

The girl said nothing but then, pretty much everything had been said. Evie stood. "Well, if you'll help me get on my mule, I'll be gettin on home."

"Of course." After one more honk into the nose rag, Annie said, "Come stand on the stump and I'll bring the mule to you."

Annie walked alongside the mule as far as her house, holding one of Evie's hands while she guided the mule with the other one. Each was silent with their own thoughts.

At the gate Evie declined her offer to come in. "I've got to get on home an' fix supper, but first there's one thing you need to know. I'm not tryin' to steal your thunder or nothin', but when I get home I'm gonna tell Jack that you might . . . mind you that I said might . . . marry him. If I have read Jack's feelin's for you—an' I believe I have—an' if I know my boy—

and I believe I do—I'll no sooner get the words outa my mouth
then he'll be on his horse, tearin' up the road to yuh.''

Annie blushed and looked at her feet. Oh, to think that I'll
have to live with such outspokenness for the rest of my life.

Evie looked at the setting sun and then at Annie. ''Near as
I can figure, you need yourself about a hour t'get ready. If I
was you I'd go inside and cool my pretty face an' get that leaf
outa my hair 'fore he gets here. An' I wouldn't say nothin'
when he does. I'd let him do the talkin'. It'll do him good to
get it off his chest. An' it's probably best if you don't eat.''

''Eat! Oh, God! I wouldn't! I couldn't! Just the thought of
food makes me feel like . . .''

''Urpin'. I know. That's why I said that. So you don't start
things off on the wrong foot.'' Annie laughed a little. Evie too.

''Well, g'on an' make yourself all beautiful.''

Dutifully Annie started toward the house but she'd only gone
halfway when Evie called her back. She put her hand on Evie's
leg and it was as natural as sneezing.

''There's one more thing . . .'' Evie leaned close and grinned
into her eyes. ''Welcome to the family, Annie Mapes.''

She told herself that before she washed her face or scrubbed
her teeth or brushed her hair—before she did anything—she
must tell Emma. She'd never forgive herself if she allowed
Emma to hear it from someone else first.

She intended to check Emma's room first, but in the main
room she saw two smeared plates and a man's hat on one of
the chairs. Further on, she saw that the back door stood open.

From the shadowy house she saw the sunlit yard, the pole
beans and tomatoes neatly staked and tied with strips of rags,
the musk melons and squash that had already exceeded their
allotted space by twenty feet in all directions and Emma and
Sheriff Goodman, right in the middle of the sweet peas . . .
locked in a steamy embrace! Her hands were in his hair. His
hands were on her butt lifting her to her toes and into his body.
It was . . . shameless. Just shameless!

Annie covered her grin with her hand. My word! Could it be something in the air?

After Sheriff Goodman left and while Annie was tying back her vigorously brushed hair with a ribbon, Emma and Annie each told the other their secret. Annie was delighted to learn about Emma and Sheriff Goodman and Emma was not surprised to learn about Annie and Jack Dare. Actually she said she had suspected for some time, having noted the way Annie looked at him and having seen the way he looked at her—particularly when he thought he was unobserved.

Then Emma lowered the boom and told Annie that she'd heard them talking last night. Not their precise words, mind you, but enough to know that there was a man in her room and that the man was Jack Dare.

Annie buried her face in her hands. "Everyone in Sweet Home knows what happened last night!"

"The sheriff said he heard about it first thing this morning from one of his prisoners." Annie looked up incredulous. "Just joking, dear. Oh, Annie, what do you care? As long as the people concerned know the circumstances, that's all that matters."

"Emma!" Annie seized her hands. "I hope you can forgive me for the way I've hurt Abel. I would have died first but the way I feel now, I'll die if I cannot marry Jack."

Emma kissed her cheek. "Annie, Abel wants you now but later he would know he had only half of you. I think that would hurt him much, much more than this."

"That's exactly what Evie Dare said!"

"Well, she's right. Take it from me."

"Thank you! Dear, dear Emma."

They embraced and said soothing things to each other until Annie remembered the time.

"Emma!"

"What?" She'd jerked like a trapdoor had been dropped under her feet.

"I've got to get ready! He could be here any minute. You know . . . Jack!"

Emma hid a smile. "I thought you might mean him. I'll help you."

After she'd finished preparing herself, Emma helped her prepare the setting, opening the door invitingly, placing two chairs on either side of the fireplace, stuffing Annie's still unmended stocking under a cushion. When everything was ready, Annie seated herself just so and Emma thought she looked lovely. All flushed and glittery-eyed. She told her so.

"Thank you. Oh, Emma, I'm so nervous."

"I'd've never known."

"Really?"

"Really," said Emma and crossed her fingers behind her back.

"All right, Emma, here's what we'll do. I'll ask Jack to sit there and . . . and I'll sit here. Maybe . . . maybe it would be best if you would leave the door open to your room so that you can see us from there."

Emma frowned a little at that. "You're sure?"

"Yes, of course. It's important to observe the proprieties." Seeing the look on Emma's face, she added, "From now on."

Simultaneously they heard a horse riding furiously toward them. Annie's heart skipped a beat then began to gallop in tandem. "It's Jack!" she whispered and went blank-eyed.

"I expect it is. Well . . ." Turning. "Aha, so it is! Here already, Mr. Dare! How are you?"

"Fine, ma'am." He was standing in the door, bringing wind and wildness to the room. And the willy-nillys to Annie. She gripped her chair arms and half rose.

Emma was standing opposite him in the doorway of her room. He strode over to her, made a little move and said, "Will you excuse us for a few minutes, ma'am? Thank you."

And then he softly shut the door smack in her face.

He spun his hat into the chair where he was supposed to sit and knelt by Annie's side. "Is it true?"

"Is what true?"

"Don't play games with me now, Annie Mapes. Are you gonna marry me or not?"

''I haven't been asked.'' The last word ended in a little squeak as he grabbed her shoulders and brought their faces inches apart. ''I love you. You love me. I want to marry you. Do you want to marry me?''

She nodded but wouldn't meet his eye. ''I wasn't sure you'd still . . . after last night . . .''

''You mean do I still want to marry you knowing how you were last night?''

''Well . . . sort of.''

He threw back his head and laughed . . . big enough for her to see his teeth and tongue and to think of all the places on her body that they both had been . . .

He hauled her clear out of the chair onto his lap. ''That was but a morsel. A hundred years of nights and days with you will not be enough for me. Annie Mapes, will you live with me and be my love?''

She went so boneless she almost slithered off his lap. ''Oh, Jack!''

He kissed her then, bent her over his arm and used his tongue and teeth and hands and body. They were both breathless when it ended.

''Annie! Open your eyes.'' She did. When he put his lips near her ear, her toes curled before he said a word.

''Darlin', come take a little walk with me down by the . . .''

''Oh, no!''

''But darlin'!''

''No! No! No!'' She batted his hand away from her buttons. ''No more of that until we're married, Jack Dare.''

''Aw, c'mon Annie. Have a heart!''

''Absolutely not! No more . . .'' Good Lord! She had almost said the word ''fondling'' right out! ''. . . and that's my final word about it.''

He kissed her again like before then set her back in the chair. Her hair ribbon lay on her shoulder and several buttons were undone. Her mouth was reddened, her cheeks were ablaze and her neck was beard marked. She looked, in a word . . . perfect, exactly as he intended her to look as often as he was able. Way he felt now, he'd be able a lot. Ready and able.

He stood and grinned down at her upturned face. "I'll wait."

She released the breath she'd been holding and gave him a wobbly nod. "Thank you."

The next thing she heard was that of a horse pounding away and then there was a ringing cry that rattled the dried peppers that hung on the porch.

"YEE HAA!"

Chapter 28

Jack was looking forward to a week or so of concentrated courting during which he would talk Annie Mapes into a walk down the creekside path and then a walk down the aisle. The last thing he wanted to happen was exactly what did happen— Indian trouble.

The Comanches hit the Coleman farm in the early afternoon when Mrs. Coleman and the three children were at home alone. At sundown Henry Coleman returned from the field to find his wife and daughter dead and his two sons, aged five and seven, gone. All the stock had been driven off, but on foot Coleman made it to a neighbor's where he borrowed a horse and rode for Sweet Home. The ranger troop was assembled immediately. Coleman insisted on going along and Jack reluctantly agreed. He generally turned down offers of civilian support—especially from the family members of captives—but they were already two men short because Austin had not yet replaced Billy Yates and Ed Cox still wasn't able to ride. They were almost ready to pull out when the word came that the man who'd been hired to replace Billy Yates was on his way.

They were waiting at the Y, some sitting their horses, some

standing around and smoking. At the sound of hoofbeats every man looked down the road to town and saw Abel O'Neal coming.

"It's only that lawyer fella," said Blue and went back to re-tying his bedroll.

Narrow-eyed Jack watched the approaching horse then and he said, "I think we jus' got our new man."

"What!" said Blue. He looked at the rider. He looked back at Jack. "Not him!"

By then O'Neal was with them. Some greeted him but most did not. Abel looked at Jack then briefly scanned the rest of the men's faces. Not one of them could raise a smile. He turned back to Jack. It was a touchy moment. Before this thing with Annie he had been looking forward to riding with Jack Dare. He'd actually liked what he knew of him and admired what he'd heard. Now understandably he hated him. But he still needed this job. At least until his legal business grew.

"Listen, I got hired because I've met all criteria . . ."

"Hold it right there! Who t'hell's Al Criteria?"

Abel ignored Blue but rephrased his speech of self defense. "I have passed all the riding and shooting tests . . ."

"How? Usin' your little stick?"

That was from Blue again, but once again Abel ignored him. "I haven't had any experience yet with hand-to-hand fighting but there was a time when you must have been in the same boat. I can only say that I'm willing to learn . . ."

"Hey, y'all hear that? He's gonna learn on the job. Ain't that jus' jim dandy!"

"Aw, shut up, Blue!" Jack looked at Abel. "Why're you doin' this, O'Neal?"

Abel shrugged. "Originally because I was getting married and needed the money." He hard-eyed Jack who gave him a flat-faced look back. "I still need the money. I'll do the best I can. That's all I can say."

"That's good enough for me," Clyde said.

Blue rounded on him. "What're you, crazy? Fightin' Indians ain't the sorta thin' you learn as you go."

Jack knocked his dottle out against his shoe. "Let's ride."

When the Indians who had raided the Colemans pulled their old trick of splitting into two groups, the rangers did too. He-Coon, Luke Bryant, Jesse McIninch, Clyde Maxey and Hector Salazar followed one trail. Long Bob Benning, Jack and Blue Dare, Abel O'Neal and Henry Coleman took the other.

Blue wasn't happy about riding with the two civilians, but he only complained about Abel. So much so that even Long Bob got sick of it. "Damnit, Blue! I am tired of hearin' about it." They had stopped to let their horses blow and to let the air cool their rear ends.

"Well, that's too damn bad 'cause I ain't done talkin' about it. You boys don't realize how green this fella is. If he don't watch where he squats, the cows'll eat 'im."

Abel finished tying his latigo and let the stirrup drop and then he turned and popped him. Blue didn't expect it from someone like Abel. As a result, he never saw it coming and the punch knocked him down. Hector later said that he didn't know who was more surprised. Blue Jack Dare or Abel O'Neal. Blue got up red-eyed mad and ready to roll but Jack stepped between them.

"Blue, damnit! That's enough. Mount up. Now!"

If the muscle that jumped in Abel's jaw was any indication, he was mad enough to kill. As for Blue, the lump on his cheekbone had grown to the size of a goose egg and throbbed like it had a heart of its own. It was only because of Jack Dare that they didn't go at it tooth and nail. Abel did not want to fight Blue but he found that he hated being beholden to Jack more.

Two days later the two trails melded and they joined forces with the other group of rangers. By late day they'd come to an open draw with treed ridges on either side. Jack made them hold up while he studied the sides. They were all tired and starting to show it, especially the amateurs. Abel looked grim and white-lipped and Coleman looked worse.

The air between Blue and Abel could still be sliced with a knife. They were each sitting there, thinking of all manner of awful things they would do to each other when suddenly an Indian appeared across the valley. He was leading a horse with two kids on it.

Coleman jumped like he'd been stuck. "There's my boys!" he hollered and before anyone could stop him he lashed his horse into a flat-out run and disappeared into the trees.

Jack yelled that it was a trap but Coleman was beyond hearing. "Damnit t'hell! Take cover, boys. They're waitin' up there somewhere."

"That's sure as hell!"

Abel strained his eyes and saw nothing to warrant concern, but since nobody else questioned the presence of the enemy, he sat tight.

"Blue, maybe we can catch a few of 'em in a cross fire. Why don't you and Clyde try to work your way over to that big boulder. The rest of us'll fix a place here." Blue and Clyde crawled off.

A couple of the men were hollowing out a place with short-handled shovels. The rest found something they could fit behind and re-checked their weapons. In time there came the softly repeated call of a whippoorwill which told them that Blue and Clyde were in position.

It was a shock to Abel when the Indians suddenly appeared. One minute they weren't there, the next they were, a wildly colorful mass of humanity streaking both ridges. In eerie silence they rode. Feathers and scalps' locks fluttered from lances and shields, and silver ornaments gleamed in the sun. War paint in vivid garish designs decorated both the men and their ponies.

As he looked at them, Abel knew that he'd never see anything more frightening in his life. And he hadn't even heard their unearthly war whoops yet. That came when they kicked their ponies into a charge then that was all he could hear or see . . . contorted black holes screaming hideous sounds. The hairs rose on his head and his mouth went bone dry. Bronzed bodies blurred by as arrows pinged off the rocks where the rangers crouched. When Abel raised his rifle Jack laid a hand on the barrel. "Just watch the show for now." An apt description thought Abel, for that's exactly what it was: a macabre show entitled prelude to death. The Indians circled and came again.

"Hold your fire till you can almost stick your muzzle in their gut." Jack was stretched out beside Abel.

A few moments later the rangers got their opportunity and Abel learned the order of things. Fire your long gun first then lay that weapon aside and fire another carbine—if you carry an extra. If not, then pull a pistol and fire it, lay it aside and pull another and another until you've fired everything you have. Then reload everything . . . carefully but as rapidly as possible. The air was heavy with clouds of dust, smoke and primitive weaponry.

After ten minutes of withering sharpshooting from the rangers and deadly cross fire from Blue and Clyde, the Indians melted away. During the lull the rangers passed water jugs and ammunition or repaired and cleaned their guns. Some took that time to eat some jerky but the mere thought of food brought bile to Abel's mouth.

Jack signaled to Blue telling him and Clyde to come in. Now that the Indians knew where they were they'd be trying to blind-side them and cut them off.

During the respite Hector crawled around doctoring those who needed it. Miraculously they had suffered only minor injuries. Luke had a flesh wound in his hip and Jesse had a minor arrow wound in his right shoulder. When Blue and Clyde crawled in, Blue had his neck hanky tied around his head. He said a bullet that'd ricocheted off a piece of rock had cut him a new part. It'd bled a lot but was really only a scratch. Hector barely had time to tend to those small injuries before the yelling swarm attacked again.

They beat them back again except for two Indians who threw themselves off their ponies and into their midst. They were dispatched by He-Coon and Jesse McIninch.

With sick fascination Abel watched He-Coon scalp the first downed man. He looked away as the scout approached the second, but he would never forget the sound that comes when a scalp and a skull are separated.

The rangers fought well and were remarkably lucky in their lack of serious injury but ultimately the Indians would overrun them. There wasn't a man there who wasn't thinking about whether he was going to die fighting or with his last bullet. Since it was a question Jack Dare had decided long ago, he was thinking about Annie and the dirty twist that fate had dealt them. Served him right, he supposed. He'd actually been able to see an entire life of happiness. More than any man had a right to expect.

Then the Indians did something that nobody expected. A solitary rider appeared and started riding slowly toward them until he had traveled better than half the distance. Then he sat on his horse and waited. Clyde had an old draw tube telescope which he handed to Jack.

It was Crying Hawk, wearing a buffalo horn headdress and carrying a shield of tanned skins that had been painted red and decorated with feathers.

"Huh!" said Jack. He stood and propped his rifle against a rock then removed his shot pouch and horn and laid them beside it. One man cut a glance at another who shook his head and looked uneasy. Several spat. A few grumbled.

Abel said, "Wonder what he wants?" and continued looking through the abandoned telescope until a second man rode into the scope's range. Abel jerked up his head and saw his eyes weren't deceiving him. There indeed rode Jack Dare, right toward the Indian. To no one in particular, Abel said, "What the hell is he doing?"

"The Indian's made an offer of mano a mano. One ag'in one."

Abel looked at Long Bob, "You mean a sort of duel?"

"Sorta."

Abel looked at the two converging horsemen then back at Long Bob. "To the death?"

Blue snorted. "Naw, they're jus' gonna slap each other around a little."

"C'mon, man!"

Someone said, "Shut up, damnit!"

Crying Hawk rode a patch-painted pony guided by a single piece of rawhide tied to its lower jaw. Jack rode a close-coupled silver roan with long legs and white fetlocks. Of the two, the roan was probably the fastest.

On horseback, Crying Hawk and Jack circled each other until the Indian threw his knife into the ground and Jack threw his in beside it. They raced away from each other about forty yards, wheeled their mounts and raced back for the knives. Jack was drumming his heels in his horse's sides and reached the knives a second before the Indian did but the Indian threw himself from his horse and landed on Jack's back with such force that he had to have knocked the breath out of him! Grappling, they rolled off a ways and the rangers saw that only one of the knives remained sticking in the dirt. Unnecessarily somebody muttered, "One of 'em's armed now." Suddenly something glinted. With the knife gut-low Crying Hawk came at Jack hard and fast. Jack's head jerked aside and he went down with the Indian on top. Then the Indian was heaved ass over teakettle and Jack had him facedown in the dirt but somehow Crying Hawk wriggled free and both rose to circle each other. Jack still had no weapon.

Crying Hawk tripped Jack and he went down, but somehow Jack wriggled free again and as soon as he stood he delivered a horrendous kick to Crying Hawk's crotch.

Amazingly the Indian remained on his feet! The knife went up and then down and disappeared from sight. Somebody said an out-loud soft single curse word but otherwise it was dead quiet.

The two combatants looked like they were embracing. They knelt then went to the ground. There was a long minute and then Jack kicked the Indian off him and stood up. The troop let out a collective sigh.

Too soon! thought Abel. The rest of the Indians were riding

up hard and right at Jack! He sighted on the first one but He-Coon pushed up the muzzle of his gun. "No."

"Why not?"

"They come for Crying Hawk."

That appeared to be so. Two Indians picked up Crying Hawk and put him over his horse. No one even looked at Jack, who was limping away.

Then an Indian raced out of the crowd and shook his lance at them. Blue recognized him right off. Runs With The Wind. The little brother who liked to wear white women's things.

Blue stood up and held his rifle over his head and let out a panther-like scream. The two men glared at each other across the expanse of prairie. The red man raced his horse forward a few feet then backed it up and did it again and Abel thought of a couple of dogs, charging each other to see which one will give first.

"I oughta shoot him right now an' get it over with."

"What's this all about?" said Clyde.

"It's another war a'brewin' but it'll have to keep until sometime when my head ain't cracked."

When Jack reached them he accepted a drink from Blue's gourd. After he wiped his mouth, he said, "You see the rifle that Indian had?"

"Looked like a Hawken," Blue said.

"It was. One of Bowie Garlock's I'll bet."

"Wonder where he got it?"

"My question exactly."

"I hope we ain't gonna hang around and ask 'em."

"Not today. Let's ride."

Within a few hours they found Coleman's tracks and then they found his horse, shot dead. They fanned out looking for his body and were surprised to find him walking along, disoriented from a gash on his head but otherwise unharmed.

They came on his two boys a few miles further on, riding all alone on a wandering horse. There were no hostiles anywhere in sight.

The only thing the troop could figure was that Crying Hawk

had ordered the captives' release if he lost the fight and out of respect for him, his tribesmen had kept his word.

It did every man's heart good to witness the reunion between Coleman and his sons, and in spite of everything that had happened, spirits were high.

With at least another day's hard ride to Sweet Home, they camped amid some alamos growing by a stream. The moon was up, but dense clouds covered it. They had a quick meal of hardtack and coffee over a smokeless fire then unrolled their blankets and prepared to bed down.

They were all used up but Abel O'Neal was the first to turn in. Unaccustomed as he was to riding, he had to be pretty saddle-sore but he had never complained once. The others liked that about him. They would've never tolerated a whiner.

It being a warm night, Abel stripped down to his underwear then spread his blanket and dove in. He fell asleep at once, facedown, toes in, legs slightly apart.

There was more than one man there who thought he wasn't such a bad fella. He might own a new fancy carbine and wear shiny flat-heeled boots but his underwear was butt sprung, same as theirs.

Unfortunately while some were thinking kindly thoughts, others were thinking deviltry.

Jesse McIninch took a braided rawhide rope and tied it in a coil leaving a tag end which he attached to yet another lighter, longer rope. Then he oh-so-gently laid the coiled part of the rope between Abel's legs.

Blue dug in his pocket and gave Clyde his prize set of rattlers and Clyde and Jesse settled themselves just out of the glow of the fire, one holding the end of the rope that was attached to the coil between Abel's legs, the other one holding the rattlers. All this was done without a sound.

Blue and Luke stood where Abel would see them as soon as he opened his eyes.

"Abel! Hey! O'Neal!" Abel came slowly awake. "Don't move, O'Neal!"

"Wha . . . ?" He opened his eyes and saw Blue and Jack

standing some feet away. Blue was patting the air with his palms. Luke looked worried.

"Whatever you do, don't move nothin'!"

"What is it?"

"You got a rattler coiled up between your legs."

"What?"

At that Jesse pulled on the rope and the coil moved between Abel's legs. Abel froze stiff as a pump in February. Later Blue and Luke would claim that they probably could've counted every hair on his head.

"Do something!"

"We can't, man! No! Don't tense up!"

To Abel, the rattling noise that came from the bushes sounded like it came from between his legs. "Oh, God! But you've got to do . . . do something!"

"You're gettin' him all stirred up. Be still while we think."

"Oh, God," said Abel. "God God God!"

Blue drew. "Mebbe I can get a shot at 'im! It'll be tricky but I could try."

Blue's gun was weaving as if following the movement of a snake and Abel thought he was going to puke. What an ignominious end: shot or bit in the ass. "Don't shoot! Please!"

"Well, all right." Blue straightened and bit one of the nails of his free hand. "Damn horrible way to die!"

"Yeah, ol' Sam Hope died jus' like this."

"Oh, God!"

Jesse pulled on the rope and Clyde shook the rattles.

"Snake bit him right on the left cojone."

Abel hoped a cojone wasn't what he thought it was.

Luke looked at Blue. "I thought it was the right!"

"Well, you thought wrong. I was there an' it was definitely the left."

Luke snickered. "Either one's pretty hard t'tie off!"

"Tie off?"

Har, har, har.

"Damn you, this . . . is . . . not . . . funny!"

Furious rattling then.

"Oh, damn!"

"Ol' Sam's cojone swelled up like a watermelon."

"Double damn!"

"Died in less'n an hour, he did."

"Weren't nothin' nobody could do."

Abel was frantic. "I'm going to make a run for it." There was furious rattling then and Abel subsided with what could've almost been called a whimper.

"You've got to quit rilin' him!"

"Damnit, I can't lay here forever!"

"Well, I guess you could chance a bite if you want to but I'll be honest with you, O'Neal. Parta ol' Sam's problem was that nobody wanted to suck the venom."

Abel almost lifted his head then. "Suck the venom?"

"Hold still!"

"Goodgawdamighty!"

Luke turned to Blue. "Somebody'll have t'do it."

"Do whut?"

"Suck the poison."

"Awhell . . ."

"Let's flip for it."

"Awdamn!"

"You got a better idea?"

"Awright Awright!" Blue dug for a coin. "Call it in the air," he said.

Luke snickered. "Tails. What else?"

Blue slapped the coin down on the back of one hand and raised the other. "Awdang! You lose! If that don't beat all!"

"You said two outa three." Luke looked at the others, frantic. "He said two outa three, didn't he?"

"I never did." Blue looked at Abel. "You hear me say two outa three?"

It was right about then that Abel heard Jesse McIninch's laugh.

Jesse had a nose that made him look like he was trying to smell his throat. When he laughed, it made a distinctive noise that once heard was never forgotten.

Then Abel heard a snicker from the bushes. He jumped up, mad enough to kill. He kicked the coiled rope and looked around to see who to do first. There was a long moment when it could have gone either way, and then he started to laugh. Grins cut across several whiskered faces and soon everyone was howling like banshees.

As Blue Jack strolled by, he clapped Abel on the back and Abel didn't think the same approval from Chief Justice John Marshall could have meant more.

It was on the following day that they came to a cabin that was about to slide into the ground. They sat in plain view and called out, but no one answered.

Jack couldn't put his finger on it but something wasn't right. It was too quiet. No people and no stock, but the empty corral was surrounded with tracks and a hemp sack of onions hung on a nail near the cabin door.

"Figure everybody's gone to town?"

Jack shrugged "Let's check it out."

The door stood ajar and a buzzing sound came from within. Blue exchanged a look with Long Bob as Jack's boots sounded hollowly on the raised porch floor. After he disappeared inside the others dismounted and filed in after him.

The three dead men had been shot as they sat around a table eating beans and eggs. Their guns, ammunition and anything else of value had been taken. So had their scalps. Hector took his time looking at the men.

"You know'em, Hec?"

"*Sí!* I know them. They are Comancheros."

Back out on the porch Jack lit his pipe to get the stink out of his nose. Comancheros. Traders with the Comanche and Kiowa and worse than scum, but nobody deserved to die eating breakfast. He-Coon was kneeling, looking at something in the dirt. Jack went down.

"Not killed by Indians," the scout said and pointed at some grain on the ground. Jack knelt in the dirt and looked at a hoof print. He-Coon was right. Somebody had fed their mount there and the horse had been shod.

They fanned out and found more prints. Then they found the busted and half-burned crates that had originally held Bowie Garlock's Hawken rifles and a little further on, another dead man. Abel took one look at his horribly mutilated body, and turned away. "Good God!"

Jack stood. "These're the men who've been selling rifles and goods to the Indians. Who knows what happened. A thieves' quarrel mebbe."

"Are you certain?" Abel said. "I mean, what white man would do a terrible thing like that?"

Jack Dare's face was grim. "I don't know, but whatever they were or weren't, they were definitely white." He shook his head and looked down at the dead man. "Makes you wonder which is the savage race in this land."

While the rangers were riding into Sweet Home, Charley Walters and a man named Ryan had just been discovered twelve miles the other side of town, dead. The killers had left the mules, like they had once before and the mules had come home again, this time carrying Hap Pettijohn with a surprised expression frozen in his lifeless eyes.

Someone had waited for the freight wagon at a narrow place between some rocks and there had caught Hap, Dick Ryan, and Charley Walters in their fatal cross fire. It looked like Hap and Ryan had been killed in the first volley, but it appeared that young Charley Walters had given them a fight. Obviously what they were after was Bowie Garlock's second shipment of Hawken rifles.

It was all too pat. The Coleman raid, which conveniently took the rangers out on a long ride, the elimination of the Comanchero go-betweens and finally, the rifle shipment and murder of Hap and his men.

Without being concerned about pursuit and without having to split the pie, the robbery had netted someone goods that were very valuable to the Indians. Everything pointed to the Crow's Nest boys—they were the only group big enough to carry it all off simultaneously—but once again the rangers had no proof.

Then a couple of the killers could not resist doing a little business on the side.

Chapter 29

Enrique Garza was pumping water for eleven thirsty sheep who crowded around and hurried him, by butting him in the rear like goats. Suddenly over the creak of the pump and the loud baaing of the sheep Enrique heard his father call to him. He looked up and saw his father standing on the porch. He shaded his eyes. There was something about the way he stood . . . "*Sí*, Papa?" His father's lips moved and his arm motioned. Enrique left the sheep and went to him, and his father told him to run and hide in the bushes. Enrique looked around to see why, and his father hissed at him: "*Ahora, Enrique! Hombres peligrosos vengan aquí.*"

So Enrique hid in the bushes and saw his father whipped with a rope ox harness because he would not give an angry Anglo man any money. The angry Anglo wore a pony-hide vest and a hat with a feather in it. A long scar crawled down one side of his face like a centipede.

Another man who also had a feather in his hat took his mother into the house and she did not come out. Enrique was very worried about his mother, who had weak spells and coughed a lot.

It was while Enrique was watching the door and waiting for his mother to emerge that the scarred man shot his father. Enrique's knees stopped working and he fell to the ground. There he lay motionless, just like his father.

The other man came out. He had filled his mother's reboza with things from the house. He tied it onto his saddle and both men mounted their horses. Enrique stared at their faces to remember everything about them. Then they herded the sheep away.

Enrique Garza found his mother, dead too. He covered his parents' bodies with bedding and ran to Sweet Home. He was only eight years old and could not run very fast because of his short legs and because of the great ache he carried in his heart. It took him all of one day. He found his cousin Vincente Salazar working in his field. Vincente threw down his hoe and wasted no time getting Enrique to Sheriff Goodman. Goodman listened to Enrique's story and then sent somebody to fetch Jack Dare and his men.

From the boy's description, they agreed that the two men had to be Bittercreek Clarke and Dutch Elliott. They finally had more than enough proof. They had an eye witness to murder. The rangers left immediately. They took the boy with them.

The following day Jack and the others tracked Clarke and Elliott to a whiskey place south of town and arrested them. The boy confronted them and fearlessly stared them in the eye. There was a long minute then he turned and told the rangers that they were the men who had murdered his parents.

If that wasn't enough, Charley Walters's pistol and Hap Pettijohn's carbine were in their possession. So was a new Hawken rifle.

"That's plenty for me!"

"Me, too!"

Blue pointed. "Yonder's a likely tree."

But Jack shook his head. "We've got a sheriff now. We'll take 'em in to him. An' then we'll hang 'em."

*   *   *

Abel was heartbroken over Annie but he had been so busy he had no opportunity to *feel* heartbroken. First there was the Coleman raid, successful by any standard since no ranger lives had been lost and the captives had been returned unharmed . . . and he had acquitted himself well, even if he did say so himself. Then there'd been the discovery of the dead Comancheros and evidence of a link between the Crow's Nest boys, the Comancheros and the Comanche band that habitually raided in the area.

Obviously the Crow's Nest boys had been supplying the go-betweens with guns and goods to sell to the Comanches. And the Comanches were using those weapons to kill hard-working settlers and their families.

If that weren't enough, Abel had been informed that Judge Frederico de la Barca was appointing him prosecutor on the case against Bittersweet Clarke and Dutch Elliott.

Unfortunately the judge was still too busy supervising the construction of his new house to conduct a lengthy trial now. He said they would first conduct a hearing. The trial would come later.

His first case. He'd love to take it, but he could not.

Abel requested a meeting with the judge at which he explained why he felt he could not—in all good conscience—act as the prosecutor for Clarke and Elliott. First of all, he did not feel proficient in Mexican law yet, mostly because he did not speak or read Spanish well enough to study it. Second, he had been one of the arresting officers.

All of these things were told to the judge's assistant, Señor Peza, and then Señor Peza translated to the judge.

The judge was tolerant of Abel's lack of knowledge of the language, but he disregarded his other objections as immaterial. This is just a hearing. A very uncomplicated hearing.

Abel interrupted Peza there. What about the fact that he was one of the arresting officers?

Peza shook his head. *"Es insignificante"* in Mexican law. Particularly at a preliminary tribunal.

"Solamente a hearing, *comprende? Sí. Eso es."*

Such a hearing, Peza continued, is designed to present the state's case against the men. The four men already selected from the population of Sweet Home would decide whether or not the evidence warranted that the men be held over for trial.

"But they'll have no defense! The panel will only hear the prosecution side of the story."

Señor Peza shook his head. *"Es no importante.* At the trial, *sí.* Now, no. The judge will hear the prosecution side of the case this afternoon."

"This afternoon?" Abel croaked.

The judge was already gone but Peza turned and said *"Sí!* Right after siesta."

Abel was frantic, throwing his law books around his office, trying to write an opening statement plus an evidentiary statement—and all in less than two hours.

But at five o'clock, he was there. So was the rest of the town.

The courthouse was under construction and only half the roof was finished. As a consequence, birds flew freely through the open areas and dropped surprisingly large ash-colored turds on the spectators. The judge sat under a protected ledge as did the "panel."

Abel walked in and set his books and papers down and could not prevent his jaw from becoming unhinged when he saw the four men who made up the panel.

He approached the bench and waited to be acknowledged but he might have been a fly on the wall for all he was noticed by the judge or his assistant. The judge appeared to be watching a mockingbird's soaring flight overhead. Abel hissed at the assistant. "Señor Peza!"

"Sí?" He did not pause in his work, which was arranging a glass and two carafes to the judge's right.

"Señor Peza, the jury or panel or whatever you call them cannot possibly sit on this hearing."

"Why?"

"Because they're prejudiced. Bowie Garlock was a victim of the perpetrators and Earl Durrell was Hap Pettijohn's best friend . . ."

"Jew ess he . . . this Pettijohn?"

"One of the murdered men. And the third man lives at the Yates farm."

"The Yeh farm?"

"The Yateses lost a son during a raid that was a direct result of . . . of . . ."

He could see that continuing would only cloud the issue. "Never mind. By law, either of these men would be sufficient to indicate the dismissal of this panel and the selection of a different one."

"Ees not necessary. Ees no' a trial."

Abel shook his head. "Señor Peza. It is *not* all right. Please explain what I said to the judge."

Peza did, or at least that's what Abel thought he was doing with his lips close to the judge's tufted ear. Finished, Peza straightened and the judge waved him away. To Abel, Peza shrugged his shoulders. "See? Ess all right."

Annie watched Abel slump back to the tiny desk where he had stacked at least thirty books, all of which were sprouting scraps of paper. He was upset. She could tell by the vein in his temple. He looked tired and irritable and dusty. Immediately all these things were her fault. She felt so very awful! *Oh, dear Abel, please please forgive me.*

She sat between Evie and Markie Dare so she could tell Markie everything as it happened.

"How does Abel look?"

"Upset," Annie answered. Odd, she thought, that she did not have to ask who "he" was.

"His hair's funny and his cheeks are red and I have a feeling things are definitely not going his way."

Annie felt someone's eyes and saw that Jack and Sheriff

Goodman had just come in with the prisoners. Both Emma and Annie blushed prettily and sat straighter and touched their hair. Jack gave Annie a searing look that immediately reminded her of the night previous and what had happened when she allowed him to coax her behind the apple tree. Sometimes she'd swear the man had nine hands.

The little rat-faced man who was the interpreter called Abel over. They had a heated but muted conversation after which Abel stomped back to his desk and picked up a sheaf of papers. Moving to the center of the room, he stumbled over a worker's awl and viciously kicked it across the floor. After such a violent act his voice sounded strangely calm and modulated. "Ladies and gentlemen of Sweet Home . . ."

Suddenly Markie was standing, alternately clapping and doing a piercing whistle through her teeth. Abel looked at her and turned so red he looked like he had burst into flames. Evie and Annie pulled her into her seat. Each took an ear and talked furiously.

Peza stepped to the center of the room. "Der can be no interrupcions!"

"Thank you." Abel cleared his throat and rimmed his collar with his finger.

"Ladies and . . ."

Anyone who spoke Spanish knew what the judge said when he interrupted. "What is he doing?"

Peza went to Abel. "De yudge wan' to know wha' are jew doin'?"

"Giving my opening statement."

Peza went to the judge then returned to Abel again. "De yudge sez jew give evidence now."

Hours of work! Right down a rat hole! Abel threw his papers onto the table where several slid onto the floor. A few seconds to gather himself then he selected the second batch of papers and faced the judge again. Without further ado, he told what he knew about the crimes. About the several murders and robberies in the area. About the high preponderance of raids in the Sweet Home area compared to other towns that were closer to Indian territory.

It was here that Abel looked down at his notes—which he had been holding chest-high—and saw the splat of bird shit that decorated the page like a seal. He crumpled the paper in his fist and side-armed it across the room. Everyone watched it spin across the floor and finally come to rest against the wall.

Calmly Abel continued about the probable link between the two perpetrators, the Comancheros and the Comanches, the testimony of the young boy, Enrique Garza and how he had been the unwilling witness of the execution of his parents and finally, the coup de grace . . . he told the panel that the men had been caught with the stolen guns on their person.

It was a masterful job performed under horrible circumstances and Abel thought he deserved a standing ovation now. Instead there was dead silence. The two men, Bittercreek Clarke and Dutch Elliott looked bored.

The judge spoke for a long time and Peza translated thus: The panel of four men were each to be given a piece of paper on which they were asked to write either guilty or not guilty. The judge would do the same and then ask that the papers be collected and assessed by Señor Peza. If three of the five papers read guilty, the two men would be held over for trial. Or otherwise, as the court saw fit.

Annie saw Abel's head come up at that "or otherwise," but she and everyone else was distracted by Earl Durrell.

"I cain't write guilty or not guilty 'cause I cain't write."

Peza and the judge had a hurried discussion after which Peza told Durrell to make an O for not guilty and an X for guilty. Durrell nodded and sat. He licked his pencil. He stood. "Lemme get this straight. The X is for guilty, right?"

"*Sí! Es correcto.*"

"Well, I guess we know how Earl's gonna vote!" said Evie Dare.

The decision was unanimous. Abel had won his first case.

Peza announced that the judge would address the room and he would translate. The judge stood, shook out his robes and clasped his hands mid-chest before he began to speak again. Since the panel vote was unanimous, both men were sentenced to death and were to be given their choice of being hung or shot. Further they were to make that choice now.

Abel was first astounded then furious. "You cannot execute these men. You said that this was only a hearing."

To which Peza replied that he had neglected to mention— in a unanimous decision such as this one, there is no need for a trial.

Dutch Elliott had the kind of murky, featureless face of a simple person. It turns out that's exactly what he was. Once he was convinced that he had to choose, Elliott opted to die as he had lived—by the gun—and several men hustled him outside to grant his wish.

Knowing that there was no scaffold in town, Bittersweet said he'd take the rope and he was taken out as well.

Since he'd come from a civilized and quite conventional town, Bittercreek thought he'd been pretty damn clever, but what he did not know was that the townspeople of Sweet Home were neither civilized nor conventional and had no intention of paying for a scaffold to be built when there was a perfectly good elm right outside the jail.

But fate intervened. Unlike his compadre, Bittercreek would have another day of life. For some unknown reason—perhaps simply to allow more time for the outlying people to arrive—the hanging was set for five in the afternoon on the day following.

Inside the courtroom, Blue had sat with Abel until there was the sound of gunfire, then he uncocked his pistol and stuck it back in his belt. "Listen, Abel. We don't want you to get hurt, all right? We didn't know what you'd do, all riled up like you were." He looked like he might slap Abel on the back but Abel gave him such a look that he thought better of it and left.

Abel watched him saunter outside and then covered his eyes with his hand. A man had just been shot—someone who had walked out of here not five minutes ago—and in some crazy way, he felt that he was responsible.

A small hand slipped into his. Abel looked up and into the

blank eyes of Markie Dare. She was smiling sadly and petting his back with her free hand.

He wanted to pull her into his arms and bawl like a baby. Instead he said, "Thank you, Markie."

"It wasn't your fault."

He nodded. "I appreciate that. Thanks."

Annie watched from the door. She had wanted to go over to him but she wasn't sure of her reception. Apparently little Markie'd had no such worry and for that Annie was very grateful.

Chapter 30

Barely noon the next day Sheriff Goodman and a stranger rode up to the Dare place. Goodman hailed Jack and when they got off their horses, said, "Jack, you better listen to what this fella's got t'say." Goodman put his hand on Jack's arm. "Now don't do nothin' foolish till you listen to everything."

Jack looked at the stranger. "I know you from somewhere. Who are you?"

Goldie and Blue had joined them, and Blue said, "That's Autry. New at the Nest."

"That's right," said the man. "Bernard Autry."

He was narrow between the eyes and squirrel-toothed, a small man made taller by a big crowned hat. Probably the sort who only took it off to sleep.

"All right, Autry. What've you got to say?"

He hitched his belt. "Plenty. Shug's done snatched the little blind kid and the schoolteacher an' took 'em out to the Crow's Nest."

"Run that by me again." Jack's voice had no timbre.

Goodman was getting worried. *Getting? Hell, he'd been worried since the cabin hove into view.*

Goldie and Blue had moved to either side of Autry and were bristled out like hedgehogs, and the mother stood on the porch with a carbine that was bigger than she, but she acted like she knew which end did what.

"Markie and Annie're supposed to be over at the school."

"But I'm here to tell yuh that they ain't. Shug's holdin' 'em till awk . . ." Goldie'd lifted him off his feet by his collar and his words were strangled and jerky from his kicking. "Hey, I am only tellin' you what Shug said."

Blue let loose with some hide-blistering curses but Jack motioned to Goldie to let him speak. "What does Shug want?"

Autry hawked and spat once, then twice, and would've again except Blue hit him on the back hard enough to knock his hair over his eyes and clear his throat both.

"He says if you don't let Bittercreek go he's gonna kill 'em. But I'll tell yuh somethin' right now: If Bittercreek don't kill 'em, Riley Mott will . . . Provided he lives beyond gettin' his parts sewed back on. That little kid about de-balled him!" He made a cutting sound with his tongue. "Heh, heh!" He looked around but when he didn't see one smiling face, he hurried on. "Shug says soon as you let Bittercreek go he'll let your females go."

Again Autry looked from the sheriff to the three Dare men. Now he was starting to worry too. The Dares looked like they would tear him apart with their bare hands and the sheriff didn't look like he was inclined to stop them. He bent to retrieve his hat but the one who'd tried to strangle him put his foot through it. *Damn! My best hat!*

But then something inside said: Better the hat than your head.

He put a wider distance between them. "So? What'd ya want me t'tell 'im?"

Jack spat first then answered in that same flat tone. "You tell him that the Dares are comin'."

"With Bittercreek?"

Jack nodded. "With Bittercreek. An' tell him one other thing."

"Yeah?"

"If he hurts them in any way I will personally kill him an' I'll take a week to do it."

Careful not to show too much of his back, Autry mounted up and lashed his horse across the water. The three brothers exchanged a look and headed for the corral.

"Jack?"

"It's all right, Maw. This won't take long."

They went by the school first and by the blood on the floor they could see that Autry had not been lying. "Little ol' Markie gave 'em a fight didn't she?" Goldie's voice sounded choked and he had to blink to clear his eyes. Blue had to hit the wall before he felt better.

"She's all right. They're both all right."

Jack had been concerned that Shug might be holding them somewhere other than the Crow's Nest but from the tracks they soon saw that the trail led straight there. Now that they knew where Markie and Annie were being held they could make a plan.

They left the farm with every weapon they owned and three extra horses. A bound and gagged Bittercreek Clarke was head down on one.

An hour later Jack, Goldie and Blue were lying atop a ridge that overlooked the Crow's Nest farm. It wasn't much. A tired cabin built beside a few scrawny alamos and a barn that was mostly in pieces. There were a lot of busted things laying around in the yard. Lard pails once used for target practice. Wheel rims and popped nail kegs. Empty whiskey jugs. A shoe folded in half and a three-legged table.

"There's five men strung out in a half circle around the farm," said Blue, and drew X's in the dirt with a stick. "About forty yards apart. There's two more on either side of that brushy hill yonder. Here and here."

Jack nodded and the three headed off in different directions. Within the hour they'd returned.

"I'll get them to bring out either Annie or Markie so we can see that they're all right." Jack checked the load on his pistol and stuck it next to the small of his back. "Which ever one they show us, they'll have to send a man along with her. Goldie, you take him neat and square, soon as you see your chance."

Goldie licked his thumb and ran it across the muzzle of his carbine. "I'll get 'im, all right."

"Where do you want me?" Blue asked.

"Go around back an' come through that rear window the minute you hear Goldie fire." Jack held up a warning finger. "Blue, do not come at 'em yellin' like an Indian. An' for God's sake, don't shoot Markie or Annie!"

Blue's jaw came out a foot at that. "You ever known me not to hit what I aim at?"

Jack looked at him. "No." He looked away then back. "I'm, uh, kinda worried that somethin'll go wrong. You know . . ."

Blue was mollified and mildly surprised; he couldn't recall the last time he'd heard his brother apologize. He nodded, then moving quiet as a shadow, he slipped away.

Jack waited until he heard Blue's signal, then he stood up and walked forward alone. "We're here, Shug."

"I see yuh, yuh dirty bastard! You can stop right there." The voice came out of a crack in the cabin door. "Yuh better've brung Bittercreek!"

"He's here. You bring our people out an' we'll get down to business."

"Show me Bittercreek first."

That fast a man appeared on the hill. Shug shaded his eyes. Looked like he'd lost a fight with a wildcat! There was a rope wrapped around him and his hands were behind his back but it was Bittercreek all right.

Jack didn't even bother to look at him, just kept his eyes on the door. "Bring 'em on out, Shug."

"I'll show yuh one."

"Do it then."

"Yuh'll get the other'n when you bring Bittercreek down."

The door opened and a man walked Markie outside. Jack didn't recognize the man at first glance but he didn't spend much time on him. He was too busy looking for injuries on his baby sister. She looked sort of mussed but mean-faced and full of vinegar like always.

"You all right, Markie?"

"Yeah, but I am sure lookin' forward to your beatin' the tar outa . . ."

Jack moved his hand away from his body and the man automatically swung his pistol from Markie to Jack and that's when Goldie fired.

The man sat fast then fell backward. He flopped once or twice and then he lay still. Meanwhile Jack had grabbed Markie and thrown her to the ground and run for the cabin. A bullet touched the side of his neck like a finger of fire. He hit the ground and rolled and another bullet kicked up dirt where he'd just been.

While this was happening outside, inside the cabin there were two shots fired close together, a pause then a third. The door slowly creaked open and Blue's voice emerged. "We're comin' out."

Jack let out the air he hadn't realized he'd been holding. "Come ahead!" He went to the window and looked in but it was too dark to see anything. "Annie?"

"Here I am!"

And there she was. She looked fine. Her face was blotchy and her hair was flopped down but she looked fine.

Seeing him she gave a little cry and ran to him and he drew her to him and held her. She said he was to never let her go. He told her she had his word on that!

As he was walking away with one arm around each of his females, he gave Goldie a look that said: Burn it!

Chapter 31

The fall of '28 turned out to be unusually cold. By mid-November the grass was already tan and dead-looking and most of the trees were leafless. The steely skies held suns that gave no warmth and the moons at night were frosty white and cold. Everyone complained except . . . Annie and Jack who agreed that they'd never seen such beautiful weather. The skies were beautiful. The air smelled clean and clear. The moon spoke to them and the birds sang to them . . .

Normal humans beings could not bear to be around them.

They were to be married on Thanksgiving Day, which was less than two weeks away. Jack, of course, had wanted to marry immediately, but his plans had been foiled by prevailing—and saner—voices such as his mother's, who said she needed time to plan a big wingding for her eldest's wedding, his af-fianced who said she needed time to get her dress ready, and finally his brother Goldie who said he had to have time to get a cabin built.

It was the last argument that did it. He was so smitten he hadn't given much thought to anything but Annie. But now that he did do some thinking on it he realized that he had to have a cabin to take her to and a bed to lay her on. "How about a week, Goldie?"

"I said when it'll be ready an' that's when it'll be ready." Goldie wasn't talking through his hat. A damn nice cabin could be finished in plenty of time. Provided they had enough helping hands and got some cooperation from the Indians.

The terrible weather was on their side because Indians hate rotten weather just as much as the whites do. Luck stayed with them and it went from bad to worse with a rain that turned the roads into mire and made the creek a murky yellow. A week later it was still raining. Now the creek ran bank-full and was unfordable at most of the usual places.

The rain annoyed the hell out of Blue, who was making clapboards for the roof, and Luke and Jesse, who were the puncheon men, and Long Bob and Ed Cox, who were cutting roof logs, and Clyde Maxey and Hector, who were in charge of chinking the walls, and Goldie who was trying to finish the chimney.

Everybody, as a matter of fact, except Jack who laughed and yelled, "Rain! Let's have some more rain! Yeah!"

Then came four hellish days of alternate freezing and thawing. The whining wind sheathed their tools and rimmed the creek in ice. Unexpected spots became hard and ice-patched, and several rangers found themselves on their backs when seconds earlier they'd been on their feet.

And Jack Dare? Hell, Jack just laughed and helped the men up and went on working like a demon.

It made Blue uneasy, knowing what had unleashed all that terrific animal energy. If it could happen to Jack, it might happen to anyone. It was a scary thought. A very scary thought! He talked to Goldie about it. They were sitting under a lean-to, eating fried chicken for lunch.

"It's hard to understand."

"What is?" asked Goldie.

"That any man should suddenly want to marry that bad! What d'you think does that? I mean, exactly how does it happen?"

"Hell, I don't know. I'm as much in the dark as you are."

"Let's hope that's where we stay."

"Boy, you can say that again!"

Soon as the roof was up and the fireplace was finished, Goldie quit supervising the others and turned to building a bed big enough to fill a normal-sized room. He attached the head and one side of the bed to the wall. Its foot and the other side he anchored with big round oak stumps. Tied rawhide strips would be its base.

Jack took a lot of ribbing about how sturdy his bed would be.

"You can do a lot of leapin' around on a bed like this."

Jack's reply . . . "You leap around on your bed if you want to. This one'll be used for somethin' else entirely!" . . . brought a lot of yucks and hars.

The twins were already making two ticks. The one on the bottom they filled with straw and pine needles for scent. The tick on top and the pillow casings they filled with duck down. To top everything off, Emma Fuller supplied them with a beautiful wedding-ring quilt in blue and white.

When he had finished the bed, Goldie commandeered Jesse McIninch and Ed Cox—Ed was finally walking around without a cane—and sent them to find the wood he would need for making chairs, tables and shelves.

The weather did an about-face and once again the woods rang with the sound of axes. Goldie set to work on a highboy and a closet-chest and a long table with two benches. As the others finished with the cabin, they too were put to work helping him. It was inside work but most of them would just as soon have been back outside in the rain. He was not an easy man to please, that Goldie Dare.

The night before Jack Dare and Annie Mapes's wedding was cool, still and clear. Unarguably a beautiful night . . . to everyone but Abel O'Neal.

Abel had been praying for rain or another ice storm or a

"ragin' norther" (whatever that was!)—any excuse he could use not to go out and see Jack Dare. But the weather was refusing to cooperate. He was going to have to go. If he didn't, he might as well move out of Sweet Home. Which at that moment did not seem like a bad idea. He would still have his conscience to contend with but at least he would not be constantly reminded of his own loss.

An hour later Abel sat his horse at the edge of the clearing. The cabin's peeled logs looked raw and naked but within months it would turn the same gray color of every other dwelling in Tejas. It was a square, solid-looking cabin with a small porch, big windows and a wonderful view. Abel would have been pleased to own it.

A light was on inside, and knowing Jack Dare like he did, Abel knew he had to have heard him ride up, yet no one came outside. Abel was just about to call out when Jack stepped out of the woods behind him, bare-chested, bare-footed and with a long bare knife glinting in the moonlight. He releathered the knife and, carrying his carbine with the bore to the ground, he came closer.

"Abel." He laid his palm flat on the horse's neck.

"Jack."

"Good to see you. Step off your horse and sit a spell."

At the porch Jack set his carbine aside and sat on the rough-sawn steps. Abel stepped off his mount but he declined to sit. Instead he stood threading the reins through his fingers or hitching his belt or examining the toe of his boot.

"Nice night," Jack said.

"Yeah."

"Looks like you're expectin' rain."

"I got caught in two rainstorms last week. My shirt got so wet it turned into a collar. I thought I'd wear my poncho from here on out."

"I see." Jack rolled up and put his arms around his knee. He looked into the woods for a minute and then up at Abel. "Somethin' I can do for you, Abel?"

"Yes, I guess there is. You can listen to me while I get something off my chest."

"Go on then. I'm all ears."

Later Abel wouldn't be able to recall his exact words, only that he'd somehow managed to tell Jack Dare that he had come damn close to killing him several times over the last two weeks.

If Abel expected anger, he was sorely disappointed. Jack slapped his knee and laughed and told him he would have been amazed if he hadn't. "Matter of fact, I've had thoughts about doing the same to you! Only I'd been thinkin' about it for more than jus' a couple of weeks."

"Really?" That gave him food for thought. If Jack had decided to go ahead with it, he wouldn't be standing here right now!

"Yeah, I did. The first time was when you crawled off Hap Pettijohn's wagon. I ain't proud of it. All I can say is I suppose it's a human being's nature to look for the easy way out."

He studied Abel for a spell. "It would've been easy for either one of us to do it. If we'd been really serious. Especially during that Indian attack."

"That's when I thought about it the most."

"Figures. Bullets an' arrows whizzing all around. Nobody payin' a lick of attention to anything but the Indians."

"Why didn't you then?"

"I don't know. Why didn't you?"

Abel just stood there. "I guess I didn't have the guts."

"Guess neither one of us did. C'mon in."

Jack had a hold of his arm and Abel had no choice but to climb the stairs.

"Sit by the fire and warm yourself before you ride back."

When Jack padded over to a cabinet, Abel took a quick look around Annie's new home. It was like many he'd seen only larger and nicer. Big room. Big fireplace. Plenty of shiny new furniture topped with tatted runners. No sleeping area visible but a door leading off to one side.

It even smells good, he thought. Then he saw the pinecones and nettles in a basket next to the fire and some familiar-looking wildflowers in a speckled pot on the table. He turned and found that Jack was watching him.

"I love her more than my life." He used his teeth to uncork a squat brown jug with a corncob stopper. "I couldn't ever do anythin' that would hurt her."

Too moved to speak, Abel just nodded. It wasn't just his words, but his tone and the way he was looking at him.

As Jack collected two tin cups and came closer Abel could smell whatever was in the jug and it almost knocked his hat off. "What is that?"

"Goldie started calling it panther piss an' it stuck." He poured some in a cup and showed it to Abel. "See how yellowy an' foamy it looks?"

"Yes."

"Looks like panther piss, don't it?"

"I imagine it does." And quite unappetizing.

"It's a kinda beer." Jack handed him one of the cups. "Made from fermented corn mash."

In his mind Abel held his nose then he took a sip and thought he'd swallowed live coals and broken razors.

Jack said, "It's got a little bite, don't it?"

"A little! How you Texians can exaggerate about some things and belittle others is beyond me!"

Jack laughed. "Better have another. It gets smoother as you go along."

Abel O'Neal and Jack Dare proceeded to get mildly drunk together.

Well, Jack got mildly drunk and Abel got mindless, but that came later.

While they were getting to their state of drunkeness, they talked. Or Abel talked and Jack listened. And as the night wore on several things became crystal clear to Abel. First and foremost, was that Jack Dare was a damn good listener. Second, that he—Abel—was a particularly good talker! It was not his intention to sound self-centered but he honestly couldn't ever recall hearing anyone speak in a more articulate and intelligent fashion.

Matter of fact, he couldn't recall a time when he'd such remarkable insight or a time that he had such *élan,* such *savoir-faire.* His mind was like a *voussoir* as each thought rolled and curved into the next.

It was right about there that Jack fell asleep in his chair. Which was fine; Abel never even noticed.

There were two consequences of that night. One that Abel would discover in the morning; namely, that a perfectly fit human being can wish himself dead. And second, there was a consequence that he would wrongly attribute to many things but never to that night at Jack Dare's. Simply yet quite strangely, it was at some point during that night that Abel O'Neal began to regain his confidence and regard for himself both as a litigator and as a man. Neither would ever waver again.

By the time Jack Dare walked outside in the morning the sun had come up and burned off the fog and dried the icy moisture on the grass. It felt warm already and the sky was cloudless. He sniffed the air like a dog, then he raised his arms toward heaven and yelled, "Perfect!" Which woke Abel O'Neal like two cymbals simultaneously crashing on either side of his head.

Jack'd planned on heading over to the farm immediately. But then he heard the sort of sound that can only be made by a herd of rooting pigs or a violently ill man and he amended "immediately" to right after he got some food into Abel O'Neal.

Earlier, Annie had suggested that they be married in their new home, but after Jack thought it over—and realized how hard it could be to get rid of some of the guests—he said it would be better if they were married at the Dare farm. He congratulated himself now as he arrived and saw the number of people already there.

Actually most of the town was present by midday, shuffling

around in the fallen leaves to greet friends or to partake of food or drink. There was certainly plenty of both; Evie Dare and her girls had laid a feast.

Tables had been set up on the porch, and food was laid out there as well as in the house. Since there weren't enough chairs, most people stood with their plates balanced on their cups. Evie said that when it came time for the actual ceremony, she sincerely hoped that the new preacher had enough sense to realize that they were all wearing shoes!

The bride had arrived minutes earlier. Jack immediately went to her and held her arms wide so he—and everyone else— could get a good look at her. She made a lovely bride and Evie couldn't recall the last time she'd been so pleased, seeing Annie with her cheeks aglow and Jack with a grin as wide as his shoulders.

"Looks like they're almost ready to begin, Markie."

"Great! Say, Maw, where's Brit and Irish?"

Evie looked around but couldn't spot either. "They must be in the house, but they'll be out pretty quick."

Irish Dare was one of only a few people who saw the person who arrived right after Annie Mapes. It was Mrs. Von Blucker, Emil Schumacher's housekeeper. Irish first wondered why she hadn't come earlier with Mr. Schumacher, and then she wondered why on earth Mrs. Von Blucker would be coming with the Salazar family.

Then she saw the cut on her forehead. She went to her. "Mrs. Von Blucker. Are you all right?"

Mrs. Von Blucker grabbed her hand in a painful grip and started babbling in a language she didn't understand. "Mrs. Von Blucker! Please talk English."

She nodded, trying to draw a good breath. "I must find Mr. Schumacher . . ."

"He's here somewhere . . ."

"His wife has taken the child!"

"What?"

She nodded unsteadily. "It's true and she has already tried to kill him once."

"Her own baby?"

"Yes! Oh, *Gott!*

"Sit and wait right here. I'm going to find Mr. Schumacher."

Brit saw her sister dash by with her skirts hiked but she thought nothing of it. That's how Irish got from one place to another. She ought to make a sampler to hang over her side of the bed. Never walk when you can run.

She, on the other hand, was standing beneath a tree, hoping Dr. J. P. McDuff—who stood a short distance away—had noticed her cool demeanor and her regal bearing and that her new shoes had a lady's heel.

She knew for sure that he'd noticed how the bodice of her new dress pushed her breasts up and out because she'd already caught him looking at them. Which wasn't easy to do, considering how many men were standing around her and screening his view.

She was watching him out of the corner of her eye when she saw Sheriff Goodman join him. Brit lowered the cup of cider she'd been using as a partial shield and unabashedly watched them. They spoke for a minute then McDuff nodded and gave the sheriff his little bow.

Sheriff Goodman went to Emma Fuller, spoke briefly to her and then left. Brit excused herself and went to Emma, who was sure to know something. Brit had recently heard that Emma and Sheriff Goodman were going to get married. She about died when she heard that! Neither one of them was a day under fifty!

"Hey, Mrs. Fuller."

"Hello, Brit. My, you look lovely, dear."

"So do you. And your flock." Brit smiled in turn at Jane Yellow Cat, Enrique Garza, and the Williford girls.

They talked then about the wonderful food, the beautiful day, the lovely bride and the happy groom. Finally Brit thought sufficient time had passed to say, "I haven't seen much of Sheriff Goodman lately."

Emma's face turned. "He was just here. Oh, I feel simply awful!"

"Why?"

"He's been ordered to arrest Dr. McDuff today, of all days! I tell you, I was just sick when I heard that."

Brit hardly heard the rest. She felt sick herself. She had been told this would happen yet she was not ready. Tried for murder! Oh, this was awful!

"Dearly Beloved . . ."

In what was a hushed voice to her, Evie was describing the ceremony for Markie. ". . . an' Annie is wearing her mama's wedding veil which is very old an' fine threaded as a cobweb." She made a mental note to tell Jack to be careful with that dress. "Her wedding dress has lace around the collar and down the sleeves and a lace band around her waist. She is wearing her beautiful hair loose an' it comes down clear past her butt."

"Is she carrying the handkerchief?"

"She sure is! An' she's holdin' the dried flower bouquet that the twins made."

"Good! What about Jack?"

"Oh, Markie!" She sniffed. "Your brother is so manly looking! He has on store-bought pants and a boiled shirt with his new buckskin overshirt with the beaded belt. His face has been shaved red and his hair's slicked worse'n I've ever seen it."

"Does he look happy?"

"If I wanted I could count every tooth in his head."

Markie covered her mouth and giggled. "What about Abel?"

That threw her. "Abel who? Oh, *Abel!*"

"Yeah, you know."

"Oh, yeah." Evie stretched her neck and could see Abel O'Neal standing in the back of the room. "He does look . . . sorta sad, yet he was the first person to greet Annie when she came in. I saw them hug hard and kiss each other on the cheek. I hope for Annie's sake that he's all right about this."

"Oh, yeah, he's fine. You know he doesn't really love her with that kinda love."

"He doesn't?"

"Nuh-uh."

"Who does he love?"

"Nobody . . . yet."

In a way Markie understood how Abel felt because she felt pretty bad herself! About losing Jack.

Maw must've said something to him because he came looking for her a few days ago and found her down at the creek fishing. She already had four big bass, two perch and four yellow cat, but Maw'd said she was making fish cakes for the wedding and she did not want to stint anybody. So that's how Jack had snuck up and caught her sniffing and then of course, he had to know why. "Cause you're leaving," she said. "An' 'cause nothin' will ever be the same again."

He replied that he was only moving three miles away but he said he supposed the other part was true. Nothing would ever be the same again because now there'd be Annie. (He couldn't even say her name without sounding all gooey.)

Markie said she didn't see why he couldn't stay at home and he said there wasn't room and besides, he and Annie wanted to be alone and she'd understand some day.

It had been Markie's experience that if she knew a grown-up long enough the grown-up would one day say those words to her. They all did. Sooner or later. *You'll understand some day.*

What she would like some grown-up to say to her—just once—is: *I'm gonna tell you this so you can understand it right now! To-day!*

Anyway, then Jack said nobody would ever take her place in his heart, that deep inside his chest there was a locked door with a sign on it that said "Goober" and that she was the only one who would ever be allowed in that special place. No matter how long either of them lived.

Boy she'd felt a lot better after that. Especially since that was also when she realized it was up to her to cheer up Abel O'Neal. And she knew just how to do it.

Goldie told her that Abel O'Neal was going to build his own place—a house just a bit beyond the old mission ruins. Emma'd complained to Goldie about being all alone. Far from it! She still had the two Williford girls and Jane Yellow Cat and then she had just taken in that little orphan boy, Enrique Garza, and if that wasn't enough, she was going to marry Sheriff Goodman!

Markie thought the Sheriff would probably want to continue to live at the jail, but even if he didn't it would still be way too crowded for Abel. He needed peace and quiet to study, although why he needed any more studying, she did not know. He was already as smart as a person could be and live.

Markie was going to surprise him and give him his puppy today so he'd have something to love that was all his own. She'd been about to tell him earlier but he'd been busy talking to Goldie. It sounded crazy, but she thought she overheard Abel say that he wished somebody'd shoot him.

"Dearly beloved . . ."

Markie heard her maw sniffing and felt for her hand. "Don't be sad, Maw. I'm here."

The ceremony was being performed by one of Sweet Home's newest settlers, the Reverend Hollis Rogers. He would take some getting used to after the circuit preacher who came by Sweet Home every six months or so and married anybody who had two dollars. When Annie and Jack came to stand before him, Jack'd bent his head and kissed her lightly on the lips and the reverend had a hissy. "Here! Here! That's supposed to happen at the end of the ceremony. Not at the beginning."

Unexpectedly, the reverend gave a short sermon about the sanctity of married life before he began, and when he was finished he gave them another look of admonition. Annie wondered why, and finally decided it was because he'd been about to tell them to join hands but they had already done so.

He led them through their promises to love, honor and obey each other and at last concluded with . . . "Annie and Jack are now husband and wife. Those whom God hath joined together let no man put asunder."

The reverend tried looking down his long nose at Jack—no easy feat since he was about two feet shorter. "*Now* you may kiss the bride!"

Jack did and soundly enough to raise catcalls from the rangers and the color on several ladies' cheeks.

While Annie hid her blazing face in his chest, Jack held up his hand and called for silence. "Listen up, you all. Before we let loose and tear into this great food, Abel O'Neal's got something important to say."

Abel stood and cleared his throat. Annie looked at him and again she was sure he must be ill! He looked terrible. His skin was a sort of ugly greenish hue and his eyes were like two glowing coals. This too, she was sure, was all her fault and weltered in guilt until Jack whispered. "Abel was drunk as a lord last night!"

"Really? Abel?" He was speaking.

"I'm sure everyone here knows about Hap Pettijohn's death a few weeks back. Well, before he died he came to me about preparing his Last Will and Testament. Having no living kin he was concerned about his freight yard, wagons and mules. He was also concerned about the families of the rangers who have been killed in the line of duty. Anyway, the long and short of it is this . . . he gave the freight line to the Dares with one condition: That they put one quarter of its annual earnings with Mr. Cooper, who is to hold the money until a deceased ranger's family needs some of it. Jack Dare and myself will dole out some of the money to them. Whatever it takes to help them get back on their feet."

There was a loud snort from Jesse McIninch, who had started on the panther piss hours ago. He'd started crying about poor ol' Hap having no kin, forgetting entirely that he had none either.

Abel had to raise his voice a little, "I almost think Hap had a premonition that his time was near, because before he came to me he already had it all worked out in his head. The freight line was the sum total of his life's work and he wanted it to benefit the men who have risked so much for this community. I'm sure you are as affected as I was by Hap Pettijohn's generosity and boundless kindness."

There was loud applause, a buzz of approving conversation

and even louder snorting from Jesse. Abel sat then he stood. "Thank you. That's, er, all."

Annie said, "Jack?"

"Hmm?"

He had fitted her under his arm and was moving his thumb up and down her ribs. It was driving her insane. "When are we leaving?"

"As soon as possible. Why?"

"I want to talk to Abel first."

"All right. Maw already told me that we can't go until we look at our presents."

She smiled. "I'll be right ba- . . . eek!"

The screech was because when she turned to go, he grabbed her arm and pulled her around the side of the porch. "A proper kiss first, Mrs. Dare."

She cut her eyes right then left. "Jack! Here?"

He nodded. "Here and now."

About five minutes later, Annie was seen walking around the side of the building, smoothing her bodice with one hand and her hair with the other and feeling like she'd just lived through a tornado.

For presents, Annie and Jack received a butter bowl, a churn paddle and a coffee mill. Dishes and tinder boxes. A pepper grinder and a timepiece for the mantel. Deerskins for the floor and buffalo skins for the walls. Several useful crocheted items, a cast-iron kettle, a three-legged *calderón,* a lamp, wicks and candles, plenty of soap, three piglets to grow and two cured hams for now, a dozen chickens and a billy goat to keep things tidy.

All practical and much-appreciated gifts, but the one that was especially favored by them both was a woven mat that Markie had made for their bedroom floor.

Chapter 32

Soon the night began to extend its mantle. Several men, including most of the rangers, had gone to help find Emil Schumacher's child but there were still plenty of revelers left; many who looked like they might make a night of it.

Jack took Annie's hand and casually led her beyond the flares. A short time later their wagon was splashing across the creek.

Annie leaned into Jack who drove with one hand holding the reins and his arm around her shoulder. Every so often he would drop a kiss on her hair or on her forehead or on her nose. She wasn't aware of anything but those kisses, until he stopped the wagon.

They were above his special spot, the place where their cabin had been built. Neither spoke but just sat and looked down at their land. Their thoughts were remarkably similar. Here is where our children will be born, and most likely here is where I will die. But, God willing, not for a long, long time.

Rising from the chimney was a spiral of wood smoke that was blue-gray against the sky. Through one window came a pinpoint of light that flickered through the trees.

"Someone left a candle burning."

"Me." He squeezed her. "I didn't want you to come into a dark home."

"And a fire in the hearth?"

"Cause I didn't want you to be cold."

She looked away then back. "Is there any chance of that tonight?"

"No, ma'am, I can guarantee you that there is not."

"Oh, Jack . . ." She wrapped her arms around his waist. He gathered her in and tucked her head under his chin. Annie felt loved and safe, at peace with herself and the world.

"Abel all right?"

"Yes. He forgave me earlier—that was so important to me—and he said that he too had been afraid that we would lose our friendship. Oh, that made me feel so much better."

"Abel O'Neal's a good man, an' he'll get better with age. He can't hold his likker worth a damn, but he'll do well in Tejas. Mark my words."

"I hope you're right. He deserves everything that life has to offer. In particular, he deserves the unlimited love of a wonderful girl."

Then she added, "Jack, I saw you talking to Blue and Goldie earlier. Is anything wrong?"

"Blue'd heard that Riley Mott is alive an' talkin' trouble. We're gonna keep an extra eye on Markie for a while. That's all."

Mott and the other man who'd kidnapped them from the school had left as soon as they dropped them at the Crow's Nest. She'd overheard them say they were going to get Mott sewed up and that had been the last they'd seen of them. Recalling how much pain Mott was in, she could almost understand why he would seek revenge. Apparently Markie had done terrible damage to him. "I'm worried about Markie."

"Don't be, darlin'. Blue knows somebody who knows Mott an' he's gonna keep us posted."

"Do you know who the other man was?"

"Nuh-uh."

Annie had seen them so briefly, the one not at all, and the only thing she recalled about Mott was the reddish mustache he wore past his chin. The next thing she knew she and Markie had been blindfolded (Later, Markie got a good laugh out of that!) and tied onto a horse.

"Don't think about it now, darlin'."

"I'm not. I'm sure you Dares can protect your women."

"That why you married me?"

"It was a selling point . . ." She sat up suddenly. "What was that?"

"That bark?"

"Yes."

"A fox."

"Really?" She settled back. "Suppose it is the same one who loves fried chicken?"

"Not fried. Jus' plain chicken. Well, maybe with a little salt an' pepper."

"Did you make that up about the fox raised by human beings?"

"Yeah."

She looked up at him. "Did you?"

"Sure."

"Jack Dare, you devil"

"I'da done worse'n lie to get you."

"And now you've got me."

"Yep." He kissed her and she settled back against him.

He seemed in no hurry to leave. That surprised her a little. No. Actually it surprised her a lot. "Jack?"

"Mm?"

"I was, ah, wondering why we don't go home?"

"Ah. What you mean is, how come I've tried to get your clothes off you for days an' now that I can, why ain't I in a bigger hurry?" When she didn't answer, he jiggled her a little. "Well . . ."

"Yes," she whispered and felt her cheeks burn.

"Because I want to remember this night. The moon an' these stars. How the cabin looks through the trees. Your face. Your hair. Everything. I'm in no hurry." He tilted her chin up with his finger. "Nothin' we do will be rushed tonight."

When the kisses ended, she said, "But Jack . . ."

"Hmm?"

"I've seen enough moon and stars. I want . . ."

"Yes?"

"I want you to kiss me like you did before."

"Before?" She looked down but he made her meet his gaze. "When before?"

"When you climbed in my bedr- . . . eek!"

A casual observer might have watched the way that wagon took the hill and thought the poor people within it were being pursued by wild Indians . . . unless he waited long enough to hear the ringing cry that knocked small branches from the trees.

"YEE HAA!"

ABOUT THE AUTHOR:

Wi-nem-ah is a native of San Angelo, Texas. Her Indian heritage is Cherokee.

ROMANCE FROM JO BEVERLY